HEART OF A
HIGHLAND
WARRIOR

ALSO BY ANITA CLENNEY

HEART OF A
HIGHLAND
WARRIOR

ANITA CLENNEY

Montlake
Romance

Text copyright © 2014 Anita Clenney

Published by Montlake Romance, Seattle

www.apub.com

ISBN-13: 9781477818275
ISBN-10: 1477818278

Cover design by Anne Cain

Library of Congress Control Number: 2013919707

Printed in the United States of America

This book is dedicated to The Honorable Susan E. Cox; Jeffrey V. Mehalic, Esquire; Adam M. Salzman, Esquire; and Peter B. Morin, Esquire. Thank you.

CHARACTER INDEX

19TH CENTURY CHARACTERS

Faelan Connor – Legendary warrior from 19th century who wakes up 150 years later in a time vault

Tavis Connor – 19th century warrior who follows his brother Faelan to the 21st century

McGowan (Aiden Connor) – Father of Faelan and Tavis

Ian Connor – Brother of Faelan and Tavis

Bessie – Ian's wife

Alana Connor – Sister of Faelan and Tavis

Liam Connor – Brother of Faelan and Tavis who was killed young

Marna – girl who likes Tavis

Isabel and Frederick – Bree's great-great grandparents who knew the Connors in the 19th century

Quinn Douglass – Warrior and Keeper of the Book

21ST CENTURY CHARACTERS

Anna MacKinley – Warrior

Bree Connor – Faelan's wife and Shay's half-sister

Shay Logan – Cody's fiancée and Bree's half-sister

Cody MacBain – Warrior and Shay's fiancé

Marcas MacBain – Warrior and Cody's brother

Lachlan MacBain – Warrior and Cody's brother

Ewan MacBain – Retired warrior and father of Cody, Marcas, and Lachlan

Laura MacBain – Mother of Cody, Marcas, and Lachlan

Jamie – Warrior and Shay's ex-fiancé

Samantha Skye – FBI agent who likes Jamie

Ronan Connor – Warrior and Declan's twin

Declan Connor – Warrior and Ronan's twin

Edward – Bree and Shay's father

Layla – Bree's mother who died at 25

Nina – Shay's aunt who raised her

Matilda – Nina's cousin

Angus – Deceased warrior and Anna's friend

Niall – Warrior

Shane – Warrior

Duncan – Warrior who's in love with Sorcha

Sorcha – Warrior who flirts with Duncan

Tomas – Warrior and clan medic

Brodie – Warrior

Sean Connor – Warrior and Keeper of the Book

Coira – Sean's wife and clan nurse

Old Elmer – mysterious hermit

VILLAINS

Voltar – Ancient demon

Tristol – Ancient demon

Druan – Deceased ancient demon

Malek – Deceased ancient demon

Bart – Dungeon guard

Lance – Dungeon guard

The Dark One – Creator of demons and vampires

PROLOGUE

HIS ARSE WAS NUMB FROM THE STONE PEW. HE'D BEEN SITTING here most of the night, staring out the window at his brother's grave, thinking about what had to be done. About who would make the sacrifice and who would be left to go home and tell their mother. He had won, but it hadn't been easy.

A shadow fell across the floor as his younger brother joined him on the pew. They sat side by side in silence, looking at the graveyard. "There must be another way," his brother said.

"There's not, and you know it."

"Think what you're doing. You don't know what you'll wake to. By then, the world might be naught but ashes."

His gaze dropped to his hands spread across his kilt, and he remembered the blood, the torn flesh. "I have to take that chance."

"Then I'll go."

"No. I gave my word." He nudged his brother with his elbow, trying for a smile though he felt dry as leather inside. "You need to stay. You might be barmy at times, but you're a thinker, a puzzle solver, and this trouble won't be easy to sort out. Besides, I know what you're hiding under that pretty hair. A mate mark."

The teasing fell flat, and a surprised look crossed his brother's face. He touched his neck. "How did you know?"

"I'm not an idiot. You've been letting your hair loose. You've never liked it down." And he'd peeked while his brother was sleeping to make sure he was right. "For Bessie, I'd guess."

"I can't do anything about it for three years."

"But she's your mate. That's a rare thing to find before your duty is up. I don't have a mate and don't intend to find one. It has to be me. Do you have the book?"

His brother nodded and patted a satchel hanging over his shoulder.

"We should hurry, before they get back." The husband and wife knew some of the secrets, but not all.

The brothers rose and approached the front of the chapel. The youngest held the oil lantern as the elder one opened the secret catch in the wall. The door hadn't been used in some time. It groaned and grated as the opening was revealed. Musty air covered him like a shroud as he walked down the rough steps to the suffocating darkness of his tomb. The cellar was smaller than the chapel above it. Only a portion of the area here had been dug out and the floor laid with stones. The box waited for him in the corner. It looked beautiful in the dim light. But they were all beautiful, despite what they were made to contain. He'd never given them much thought until this moment. They simply served a purpose. He swallowed and walked toward it, heartbeat drumming in his ears.

His brother touched his shoulder. "Let's find another way. There has to be another way."

"There is no other."

He took the satchel from his brother and put it inside the box. Hands gripping the edge, he pulled in a shallow breath. It was hard to breathe now.

"This isn't right."

He didn't turn to look at his brother. He didn't want him to see his fear. "It will work," he whispered. "It must." He steadied himself and climbed in as his brother held the lantern high. The wood was cold and hard under his head. He shifted and pulled a dirk from his boot. Just in case.

His brother was crying. Silent tears streamed down his face.

"Do it," he said, fighting back his own tears.

"I can't." His brother's voice broke on a sob.

He reached for his brother's hand and gripped it hard, feeling the calluses and scars from their childhood. "Do it now. Do it for him." He pulled his fingers away.

The lid started to lower, and he heard a ragged cry from outside as darkness swallowed him. His throat tightened until he couldn't breathe, and finally, one tear slid—

CHAPTER ONE

B REE STARED AT THE ROTTING COFFIN, WONDERING WHO WAS inside. On the other side of the open grave, the big white cat stared at Bree, its hypnotic green eyes so similar to Bree's as Ronan frequently reminded her.

"It could be someone local," she said to the cat. "But why dig up some old farmer's grave? Maybe it's a soldier from the Civil War." Sometimes the bodies had to be buried wherever they lay. But this wasn't the first grave near her house that had been disturbed. Her favorite grave, the unmarked one in the graveyard behind her house, had also been dug up. She'd thought Druan might have opened it in his search for the missing key to Faelan's time vault. But Druan was dead now, and this hole was fresh.

Could have been a Civil War buff looking to add to his collection. Or her collection. Not all Civil War buffs were male. Bree was proof of that. The Civil War was her area of expertise. She'd spent untold hours taking part in reenactments and searching fields for buried treasure with her father. He wasn't her real father, but an uncle who'd pretended to be her father. She still had a hard time with that. They'd been so close, like two peas in a pod, her mother said. The mother who wasn't really her mother but her aunt.

Bree rubbed her belly and wondered how she'd explain all the craziness to her little girl or little boy when the time came. How would they tell the child that her—or his—father was over a century old? That one set of grandparents were even older, one of them perhaps a vampire hunter, and the other set was really a great-uncle and great-aunt who had pretended to be Bree's real parents in order to protect her? She still had so much to learn about her real parents, Edward and Layla.

The best part was that Bree had gotten a sister out of the craziness. Shay. They had different mothers, but Edward was also Shay's father. Bree had always wanted a sister, so much so that sometimes she'd pretended Emmy the panda was her sister.

A glint of metal along the bottom of the coffin caught Bree's eye, pulling her from her musings. "There's something under the coffin," she said, partly to herself, partly to the cat as she peered into the hole. "I wonder if I have time to check it out before Faelan and Ronan get back from Albany." They were at the castle meeting with the other warriors. Jamie had something urgent he needed to discuss. She thought the cat rolled its eyes, but it was probably her imagination. "Faelan will kill me if he catches me even messing with a grave in my *condition*. That's what I get for marrying a Highland warrior from the nineteenth century."

He still didn't get the whole women's lib thing. Modernizing him was turning out to be a slow process. She smiled, picturing his handsome scowl. Not that she wanted him totally modernized. His chivalrous, protective nature was a pain in the butt sometimes—actually, a lot of the time—but he was just so hot when he went all he-man on her.

The cat continued to watch her, not answering—not that she expected it to. But this cat wasn't quite normal. He had shown up at Shay's house in Virginia. No one knew where he'd come from, but he appeared intent on hanging around. He'd sort of adopted himself into the clan.

Why shouldn't she check it out? She was an expert. This is what she did. She looked around to make sure Faelan hadn't arrived, then started climbing down into the hole. "Hiss if you see my husband coming," she said to the cat, who moved closer to the edge of the hole, watching her with what appeared to be a scowl.

"Don't scowl at me. You're the one who led me here." It took some delicate maneuvering to get down. In the past, she would have jumped, or shimmied down like a kid, but she had to worry about jolts and jarring the baby inside her. She noticed the lid of the coffin was slightly ajar, as if someone had already tried to open it. Or get out. Everyone had heard stories about people being accidentally buried alive. They had been only stories to her until she'd seen a coffin in England with bloody claw marks inside the lid.

Shuddering just a little, but not enough to make her leave, she knelt on top of the coffin since there wasn't enough space to reach the other side. Leaning, she grabbed for the shiny object. She heard a crack, and the lid shifted. "Drat." She tried to see inside, but it was too dark. Stretching again, she dug until she'd freed the object. "Oh my." It was a dagger. Still kneeling on the coffin, she cradled the dagger in her hands. It was covered in dirt. She used her shirt to wipe it clean, and her breath caught as the metal emerged. It was stunning. Old. Seventeenth or eighteenth century.

"What the hell are you doing?"

Blast. Bree looked up at Ronan, who was glaring at her. "I found a dagger."

"I don't care if you found the pope buried down there. Are you insane? Do you know what your husband is going to do to you if he sees you there?"

"Where is he?"

"Right behind me."

"Thanks for the warning," she muttered to the cat, and then she saw it was gone. She looked up at Ronan. "Help me climb out before Faelan gets here."

"I don't want to be here when he finds you. I'll get blamed for another one of your fiascos."

"Don't you dare leave me in here."

"You got yourself in." He looked at the mud on her shirt. "Good God. Did you fall in?"

"No. Come on, help me. Getting out of here isn't going to be as easy as it was getting in."

With a scathing sigh, Ronan bent down and reached for her. Bree stuck the dagger into her waistband and took his hands. Ronan pulled her slowly out of the grave but didn't let go even when she was on solid ground. He looked like he wanted to shake her, but his hands on her shoulders felt more like a caress. "You're driving me crazy." A look too similar to longing crossed his face, and even though she was madly in love with Faelan, she couldn't deny the tingle she felt. Ronan was gorgeous, not to mention sexy as hell. He left a trail of broken hearts behind him, or so the other warriors said. Ronan begged to differ, but Bree was certain the trail was there whether or not he had anything to do with it. Women turned to mush whenever Ronan was around. He must be giving off mega-pheromones or something if even she wasn't immune.

"I turn my back for a bloody minute, and you've got your damned hands all over my wife."

Ronan rolled his eyes as Bree turned and looked at her husband, who was stomping toward them. His hair was loose, the way Bree liked it, and he was wearing his kilt. God, he was a sight.

"I was making sure she didn't fall into this hole," Ronan said.

"Hole? Damnation. We haven't been back from Scotland a full

day, and she's already found a bloody hole." Faelan's jaw went slack. "That's a grave. What's it doing here?"

"Don't ask me," Bree said. "I didn't put it there. I just found it. It could be a soldier from the Civil War."

A look of guilt crossed Faelan's face.

"Hell no," Ronan said. "Don't even go there."

Bree wished she hadn't mentioned the war. Faelan had been sent by Michael the Archangel to stop the ancient demon Druan from his part in stirring up the war, but something had gone wrong, and Faelan was the one locked in the time vault instead of Druan. Needless to say, Faelan hadn't stopped the war. He'd slept through it and the century and a half that followed. Though the clan had stressed that it must have happened that way for a reason, Faelan still felt responsible for the failure.

"I don't know why you keep doing this to yourself," Ronan said. "For the last time, you couldn't have stopped the whole bloody war. Nobody could have. It must have been some kind of test. To teach you a lesson, you thick-headed bastard."

Ronan was one to talk about guilt. He still believed he was responsible for his brother Cam being captured and killed by vampires.

Faelan made a grunting sound that might have been agreement or a curse. Then he turned to Bree. "You're not thinking about climbing down there and opening it, are you?"

Guilt trip averted. "Me?" she exclaimed, glancing at Ronan, who looked like Joan of Arc with muscles and a sex change. Faelan did tend to blame Ronan for Bree's mishaps whenever he was around.

"You're a magnet for holes and graves," her doting husband said.

True, she found more than her share. Perhaps she should stop looking for them. Graves, not holes. She liked graves. The holes just seemed to find her.

Faelan gave Ronan a disgruntled look and moved closer, looking into the hole. "You shouldn't even be out here," he said to Bree. "I'm going to find some way to keep you from wandering."

"Good luck," Ronan muttered.

"I was just going outside for some fresh air," Bree said, "and I saw the cat acting strange."

"He's always acting strange," Faelan said.

He did come and go as he pleased, often tagging along with Shay or Bree when he wasn't stuck with Matilda, who believed the cat warded off vampires. She was convinced it had killed the vampire that had gotten inside the secret passage of the clan's castle in Scotland. The warriors thought she was insane until they saw the pile of dust. That left them with three possible explanations. None of which were logical. Either the cat killed the vampire, or Matilda's bottle of water, which she had thrown at the vampire, had killed it. She believed the water was holy since it had been clutched to her breast in terror as she prayed. The last possibility was that the vampire had committed suicide to get away from Matilda. Bree's money was on the cat.

"It was walking with . . . purpose," she said. "So I followed it."

"Probably looking for a mouse," Faelan said.

Bree looked at the coffin. "It led me to this grave. It was here a minute ago. I think it left when you showed up."

"Smart cat," Ronan muttered.

"This is the second grave opened near the house," Bree said. "I think it must be a Civil . . . someone looking for treasure."

Faelan shook his head. "In the same spot where my time vault was buried?"

"The same spot?" Ronan looked at the open field, bordered by trees. "You're right. I didn't notice before."

Neither had Bree. Faelan had shown them roughly where he had encountered Druan and the other ancient demons—Malek, Voltar, and Tristol—before Druan trapped Faelan in the time vault.

"Aye." Faelan crossed his arms over his chest and gathered his face into a spectacular frown. "Too much of a coincidence for me."

"Bloody odd," Ronan agreed.

"Maybe someone thought it was senseless to waste a perfectly good hole," Bree said. The Civil War had started not long after Faelan's time vault was buried. It was possible that a soldier had been buried there after the time vault was moved to the crypt.

Faelan squatted, kilt dangling between his knees. "The grave wasn't open when we left for Virginia to help Cody. So who dug it up?"

"Maybe it was the cat," Ronan said, rolling his eyes.

Bree shook her head. "No, the cat wasn't here then. It was in Virginia."

"Are you serious?" Ronan asked, and then said to Faelan, "I think your wife's losing it."

Of course he was joking. But still . . . "Cats can dig," she said lamely. Especially big, mysterious cats with hypnotic green eyes.

Faelan scoffed. "If that cat's digging up graves, it's time to find him a new home."

"Maybe Anna found the grave," Bree said.

"How would she have known this grave was here?" Faelan asked.

"Maybe she discovered something in Angus's notes," Bree said. "He was sent here to look for Faelan's time vault key. He could have made some note about this spot."

"Anna hadn't found his notes when I talked to her a couple of days ago," Ronan said.

"She could have found them later. I'm surprised she hasn't come back," Bree said. "She left all her stuff."

"At your house?" Ronan asked.

Bree nodded. "Her clothes and her boots. Even her purse."

"She left her boots?" A frown started along his forehead. "She always wears boots."

"Maybe she brought another pair," Bree suggested. A demon hunter would need more than one pair of boots. Certainly one as good as Anna. "Although I don't know why she'd leave her purse."

"Can't see any female doing that," Faelan said.

"Her wallet's still inside?" Ronan asked.

"I didn't check."

"We should."

"You're worried about her?" It suddenly occurred to Bree what a great couple Ronan and Anna would make. They were both gorgeous, and despite Ronan's reputation, Bree had never seen him with anyone. The same went for Anna. She didn't even flirt, unlike Sorcha, who tormented Duncan with her blatant come-ons to any hot guy who happened to be around, which was often, since all the warriors were hot for the most part. Beauty was part of a warrior's armor. Demons were distracted by beauty like women were distracted by diamonds. In some way, Bree supposed it made sense. Distract the demon with your looks, and then catch him—or her—off guard and bam him with your warrior powers. Strength, speed, strong senses.

"Why would she leave her boots and her purse? You're giving me that look," Ronan said.

"What look?"

"The one that makes me feel like you're inside my head."

"Just wondering if you miss Anna."

"Miss her?" Ronan asked.

"She's beautiful," Bree said. "Not married."

"She is a beauty," Ronan agreed, and Faelan nodded in agreement.

Bree frowned at him. She didn't need Faelan noticing how beautiful Anna was.

"Are you playing matchmaker?" Ronan asked.

"Me?"

"Yeah. Don't tell me you're one of those women who feels it's her duty to marry off everyone around her."

"No. It's just that Anna's beautiful and you're . . . handsome." That drew a scowl from Faelan.

"I respect Anna. I don't have a thing for her," Ronan said, but he looked uncomfortable.

"Maybe she's not your destined mate, but I don't think that stops you from . . . playing," Bree said.

Something suspiciously similar to guilt quickly crossed his face. Was she on to something? Or was he just thinking of his reputation as a player?

"Anna doesn't play."

Then why did he look guilty? "Why not?"

"Bad history. She won't talk about it."

"How do you know then?" Faelan asked, giving Ronan an interested stare.

Ronan's cheeks darkened. Bree had never seen him blush. "She mentioned it . . . once."

Bree would like to know the circumstances of the *once*, but from what she could tell, Ronan didn't kiss and tell. The other warriors were happy to spread the gossip for him. "She doesn't date or anything?"

"Not that I've seen. She says she'll be a warrior forever."

Faelan looked puzzled. "I can't believe a woman would never want a husband and a family. I suppose looks like hers usually means an easy road or a hard one."

"How do you mean?" Bree asked.

"Beauty can open doors, but it can also bring unwanted attention. Make things damned awkward," he said.

Bree tilted her head and gave him a smile. "Are you speaking from experience, my beautiful man?"

Ronan laughed and punched Faelan on the arm. "You mean Agnes?"

"Angus?" Bree frowned. "What's Angus got to do with it?"

"Not Angus," Ronan said. "Agnes."

"Who's Agnes?" Bree asked.

Now Faelan was the one who looked uncomfortable.

Ronan smiled. "He didn't tell you about sweet Agnes, one of his loves?"

"You told Ronan and didn't tell me?" Bree knew they were close, but she was his wife.

"She wasn't a love," Faelan said, tossing Ronan a hateful look. "Just an irritating lass who thought she was in love with me."

"Why tell Ronan and not me?"

"I was telling him about the first demon I killed, and Agnes was there. The stupid girl had gotten lost, and when Tavis and I went to find her, we were attacked by a demon."

"You told me about the demon," Bree said, "but you didn't mention a girl." Faelan had been just sixteen, he'd told her, much too young to kill a full demon. The whole clan had been stunned. Then Kieran, one of the best trainers, offered to train him early. That was the beginning of the legend that would become the Mighty Faelan.

Bree suspected the legend had started earlier, after his little brother Liam was killed by a demon in front of Faelan and another brother, Tavis. She knew Faelan well enough that she was almost certain he hadn't been the same since the day Liam died because he was still haunted by the incident, still haunted by the demon. Bree also knew enough about human nature to know that the responsibility he felt for the clan, for her, for the world, was in some way an effort to make up for not saving Liam.

That was one reason she wasn't harder on him when he became too protective. She would think about the seven-year-old boy who believed it was his fault that his baby brother died. That made her want to wrap her arms around him and take the weight from his shoulders for a while. Then there were times when she wasn't so understanding. When she just wanted to scream at him to wake up and realize he couldn't change the past, that he couldn't protect her and the world every waking minute just because he believed he hadn't saved Liam or stopped the Civil War. Her sweet, sweet, chauvinistic, chivalrous alpha man. How would she ever make him forget all the pain he'd suffered?

"I wish I'd never told anybody about the bloody lass," Faelan muttered. "Can we figure out who this poor blighter is that's been dumped in a hole without even a marker?" He jumped down inside the grave.

"Should we call the police?" Bree asked.

"Not until we have a look," Faelan said, examining the wooden coffin. "First I want to know who used the place where my time vault was buried."

"I'll come down and help you open it," Bree said.

"No, you won't," Faelan said. "Don't even think about coming down here." A good solid glare showed her he was serious. "Ronan, keep her up there."

Ronan grinned and whispered, "If we hurry, we can sneak away before he climbs out of the hole."

"And I'll chop you up into little pieces," Faelan's muffled voice said.

"You need to get over yourself," Ronan said. "Move over. I'm coming down." He jumped down beside Faelan and studied the grave. "It's not every day you see a wooden coffin. Well, I guess you did, since you're so old."

Bree moved closer to the hole. Half her foot was over the edge. "The wood is rotten. It's certainly old."

"It can't be older than Faelan," Ronan said, examining the lid. "Not if this is the hole his time vault was buried in. Let's open the coffin and find out who's inside."

"Looks like someone already tried to open it," Faelan said. The lid creaked as they pushed it aside. Both of them went still, hunched over the coffin.

"Who's in there?" Bree asked. Faelan and Ronan's shoulders were blocking her view.

"He's wearing a kilt," Faelan said, his voice hushed.

"A kilt?" Bree moved around until she could see. The body was just a skeleton, with bits of shrunken flesh and scraps of clothing attached to some of the bones. The shirt had been light colored at one time, and the kilt primarily red. "I wasn't expecting a kilt." She looked at Faelan's kilt and light shirt and felt a chill. So much for the farmer or soldier theory. "Can you tell from the kilt how old he might be?"

"You're the historian," Faelan said.

She studied history. He'd lived it. "Oh, this might help. I found something underneath the coffin."

Faelan glared up at her. "Under the coffin? Did you climb inside this grave?"

Ronan grunted and shook his head.

Bree lifted one shoulder. "Sort of."

"Sort of!" Faelan said. "How do you sort of climb into a grave? You're pregnant, carrying my bairn, and you climbed into a grave!"

"Good grief. It's not even that deep. I've been in much worse places than this."

"We know," both men said at the same time.

This was one of those times she wanted to hit Faelan. And Ronan too. Instead, she pulled the dagger from her waistband and held it up. "Magnificent, isn't it?"

Ronan took the dagger from her. He hadn't examined it before. He'd been too busy pulling her out of the grave. "Looks old."

"I figure it's eighteenth century," she said. "Maybe seventeenth."

"Eighteenth," Faelan said, his voice just above a whisper.

"That's pretty impressive," Bree said. Then she saw he was staring at the dagger, his face ashen. "Are you OK?"

"You look like you've seen a ghost," Ronan said.

"I've seen this dagger before." Faelan reached for it with trembling hands. "It was my brother's."

Bree's eyes widened. "Your brother's?"

"It belonged to Tavis. I gave it to him for his birthday." Faelan looked back at the bones in the coffin. "I think you've found my brother's grave."

CHAPTER TWO

WE'LL GIVE HIM A REAL BURIAL," RONAN SAID TO FAELAN. Several of the warriors had met at the Albany castle to discuss the grave. The elders were in another part of the castle meeting about the same thing. The entire clan was disturbed by the discovery of the grave, but Faelan was taking it particularly hard. He'd already lost Tavis once. Lost his whole family. Now he had to deal with his brother's death all over again. That must suck. Ronan could sympathize. It had taken him a long time to get over Cam's death, if he had. He couldn't imagine having to face it all over again.

"Shouldn't we check DNA?" Cody asked. "Sam might be able to pull some strings and get it done quicker."

Cody's friend Samantha Skye was with the FBI. She sometimes helped the clan cover up activities that couldn't be explained by normal means. She complained that she risked losing her job, but they all knew she loved the danger and excitement. And she had the hots for Jamie, Shay's ex-fiancé, which made Cody happy since he was still jealous of the warrior who had almost married Shay. He watched his bride-to-be like the crown jewels in a den of thieves. Especially when Jamie and Ronan were around.

"It has to be Tavis," Faelan said. "It's his dagger, and the kilt was the right color. We know he was here. He helped dig up my time vault and move it."

"Why does everyone think he was buried at sea?" Shay asked.

Ronan felt Declan move behind him. He didn't even have to see his twin to know he was there. "Probably a cover story," Declan said. "They wouldn't want his grave connected to Faelan's hiding place."

Faelan nodded, and his hand found Bree's. "We'll have the funeral and put Tavis to rest."

Bree leaned closer and put her other hand on his chest. Her eyes rolled back in her head, and she started sliding off the couch.

Ronan shot forward, but Faelan had already caught her before she hit the floor. "Bree! What's wrong? Is it the bairn?" Faelan held her close, his face pale. "Get Tomas. Someone get Tomas."

"He's not here," Marcas said. "I'll find Coira."

Shay knelt beside her sister. "Her pulse is strong. I think she's had one of her visions. Bree, can you hear me?"

"She did get that distant look on her face." Faelan's voice was hopeful. He was terrified of losing the baby. And Bree. Like he'd lost everyone from his life before. Ronan was doing everything he could to see that Bree and the baby remained safe.

"These spells affect her more now that she's pregnant," Sorcha said, her tone edgy. "It can't be healthy for the baby."

She wasn't even flirting with Lachlan, who sat next to her. Of course Duncan wasn't here to witness her show.

"What do you want me to bloody do about it?" Faelan asked, scowling.

Ronan shook his head at Sorcha. "You're good with a sword, Sorcha, but you don't have crap for tact."

Brodie scoffed. "Sometimes I wish I lived back in Faelan's day, when we didn't have to deal with female warriors."

"I can fix it so you don't have to deal with a female anything," Sorcha sneered.

"Back off, Sorcha," Ronan said. "Go yell at Duncan."

"That's her problem," Brodie muttered. "Duncan's not here, so we're taking the brunt of her bitchiness. I wish they'd just jump in the sack and get it over with so the rest of us could live in peace."

Sorcha's face turned red. She clonked Brodie on the shoulder and left.

"Now what's this?" Coira asked, entering the room as Sorcha swept out. "Marcas said Bree fainted."

"We think she had a vision," Shay said.

"Or it's the bairn," Faelan added, stroking Bree's cheek.

Before Coira could reach her, Bree gasped and bolted upright. "Anna." She tried to stand, but Faelan held her still.

"Don't stand up," he said. "You might fall."

"He's right," Coira said. "You need to sit still." She checked Bree's pulse.

"I'm not going to fall. I just had a vision. Anna's in trouble."

"Do you know where she is?" Ronan asked. He'd been the last to talk to her.

Bree put one hand protectively over her stomach, something she did unconsciously these days. "I think she's in a castle."

"Scotland?" Shay asked.

"She didn't mention going to Scotland when I talked to her," Ronan said. "She'd just gotten back from there." The clan had two castles. The Connor castle in Scotland, the clan seat, and this one near Albany, New York, which Druan had used. They were still trying to find out how the demon had a castle that was identical to the clan's.

"Jamie called Scotland earlier," Declan said. "She wasn't there."

Cody's arm slipped around Shay's shoulder. "Where is Jamie?"

"Had something to do," Declan said. "He'll be back."

"Huh," Cody replied.

Shane stood several feet away, quietly observing as usual. "We should check the secret passages here and in Scotland. I'll take a look at these. Niall can help."

"Me? You know I hate those damned passages," Niall said. "They're made for dwarves."

"I thought it was fairies," Shane said. "Stop complaining and come on."

"I can't imagine Anna trapped inside," Ronan said, "but stranger things have happened."

"Like vampires," Brodie muttered.

Shane and Niall walked to the fireplace and disappeared through the secret door.

"I'll call Scotland and have someone check the passages there," Cody said.

"What about the jet? Has Anna taken it anywhere?" Brodie asked.

"I don't think so," Lachlan said. "I talked to the pilot this morning. I'm going to cover one of his shifts next month."

Bree groaned and held her head. Faelan held her closer. "What is it now, love?"

"It's you." She clutched his arm, her green eyes wide.

"Me?"

"You're probably crushing her," Ronan said.

Faelan relaxed his hold, and Bree turned worried eyes toward Faelan. "You're in danger too."

"Who's he in danger from now?" Ronan asked. "Druan is dead." He was the demon Faelan had been assigned to destroy.

"Not Druan. It's another demon." Bree frowned. "I think."

"You're not sure?" Ronan still didn't understand how Bree's

visions worked, but he knew enough not to discount them. She'd been right about too many things.

"He's powerful. He must be a demon," Bree said.

"Maybe this is what Jamie was talking about," Shay said.

Jamie was afraid something was brewing. He'd just destroyed a demon who had attempted to assassinate the President of the United States.

"Two of the ancient demons that make up the League are dead. Druan and Malek," Ronan said. Shay and Cody had destroyed Malek together, each giving him a killing blow at exactly the same moment, something that had never happened before as far as Ronan knew. But Shay and Bree weren't normal. They'd done things no warriors had ever done, like moving as fast as vampires. The clan believed it was something genetic they'd inherited from Edward, their father, since they had different mothers.

Shay had let go of Bree's hand but stayed close to her sister. Cody stood behind her. After she'd almost died, he never let his bride-to-be far from his sight. He was as bad over Shay as Faelan was over Bree.

"Maybe it's a vampire," Brodie said. He hated vampires almost as much as Ronan did.

"Voltar and Tristol are still out there," Ronan said. Both were bad news, really bad news. Voltar was a hate machine. He hated women, warriors, humans, even halflings—anything that wasn't pure demon. And Voltar was behind some of the worst atrocities humans had ever seen.

"I don't know," Bree said, "but we need to protect Faelan and Anna. She's in terrible danger. I sensed trouble before, but then I found the grave and I thought that must be it. I'm going to look for her. If I drive around, maybe I can pick up some sense of where she's—"

"You will not." Faelan put on his fierce, nineteenth-century warrior face. "We'll look for her. You will stay put."

"Faelan is right," Coira said. "I want you to rest. No activity for at least a day."

Faelan nodded. "That's just what she needs. Rest."

"You'd better put a lock on her door if you don't want her sneaking off," Ronan said. "Better yet, tie her up. And keep her away from Shay, or they'll be off trying to save Anna by themselves." This got him a frown from the sisters and worried looks from Faelan and Cody. Ronan envied both men and felt sorry for them too. The sisters were a handful, in more ways than one. Beautiful and reckless as hell. "I'll start looking for Anna. But I think we need to call a Seeker."

Two days earlier . . .

Anna let Bree's phone ring five times, and then she picked it up. "Hello."

It was Ronan. "Anna. What the hell? Where have you been?"

"Scotland. New York. Looking for Angus's notebook." Sitting beside his grave. Regretting that she hadn't been with him.

"You could have called and let us know you're still alive. We've got ancient demons on the loose, and you just up and vanish."

"I'm sorry. I should have called." But the grief had caught her off guard. It had hurt when she first found out Angus was dead. But the real pain had hit when she sat in his room and looked at all his things. Saw all the research he would never finish. All the puzzles he'd never solve. And when she stood in the infirmary where he'd whispered the last words to her that he would ever say. *I love you.* She cleared her throat. "I haven't replaced my phone."

"I know you needed to be alone, but you have to check in. We were worried." Ronan's voice softened. She'd heard it even softer once. That wouldn't be repeated. Not that it wasn't good. Relationships didn't work for her. She was just damaged goods. According to him, so was he.

"Time got away from me."

"I know it's been tough since you were so close. If you need a shoulder to cry on—hell. I guess you'd better find someone else," he said sheepishly. They were trying to forget their mishap, but it hadn't been long enough to erase the awkwardness. "Did you find his notebook?"

"Not yet. I'll keep looking. That notebook was like his right arm. Whatever he found out he'll have written down. How's everyone?"

"Alive. But Shay almost died. She did die, but we revived her."

"My God. What happened?"

"Malek happened. He was her stalker. You've missed a lot."

"Malek was stalking Shay? Why?"

"It's a long story, but he's dead now."

"Who destroyed him?"

"Cody and Shay."

"Both of them?"

"Yep."

"They were both assigned?"

"Shay was. It's a long story involving an unborn baby."

"An unborn baby?"

"You can ask Shay about it when you get back," Ronan said.

"You can't just drop a bomb like that and not explain."

"Yes I can. Maybe it'll keep you from running off again. There's still trouble. Voltar and Tristol are still out there, and those damned vampires. We captured the blond. He had the Book of Battles."

"We got the book back?"

"We did. Sean has it."

"I can't believe it. That's great. I wish Angus could have known. He spent so much time looking for it."

"I'm sorry about Angus, but his death wasn't your fault, Anna."

"I should have been with him."

"You were assigned a demon. You had to go. The job comes first."

Anna sighed. This was true. But if she had finished sooner he might be alive.

"Did you check the time vault?" Ronan asked.

"Not yet. I just got to Bree's. Still no idea who brought it?"

"I think Angus must have done it," Ronan said. "Who else could have brought the time vault? We know he was here looking for Faelan's key."

"Angus was too smart to try to take Druan down alone. He knew ancient demons have to be assigned."

"Maybe it was for one of the other demons," Ronan said. "The key is probably with his notes."

"Maybe he hid them in the cellar. That would be just like Angus. I'll check it out tomorrow."

"Faelan and Bree should be home in a day or so. And get ready for another wedding."

"Who now?" Anna asked.

"Cody and Shay."

"I guess I have missed a lot." After Ronan rang off, Anna hung up the phone and stared out the window at the crumbling chapel where the mysterious time vault was hidden. So Malek was dead, and the clan's Book of Battles was back where it belonged. That was great news. Then why wasn't she more relieved?

Feeling the need for fresh air, she grabbed a flashlight and walked outside. A front had moved in, breaking the lingering grip of fall, but it wasn't the November chill that made her skin tight. She'd been trained to withstand the cold. Something else was troubling her, and she wasn't sure what. But it was linked to the chapel.

In the moonlight it had a haunted, almost beautiful look. The old church had seen more than its share of life and death over the years. Beauty. Evil. Demons. Battles. Time vaults. Not many chapels could boast that kind of activity.

Before she knew it, she was heading in that direction. She passed the graveyard where Faelan had waited for Bree to wake him from his tomb. It was like a fairy tale . . . except fairy tales weren't real. Demons and monsters were. One of them had killed her best friend. Her fingers closed around her talisman, feeling the warm hum against her skin.

She entered the doorway and turned off her flashlight, letting the smell and feel of the place sink in. A sense of sadness struck her, of anguish and loss. Was she sensing Angus? Ronan was probably right. He must have summoned the time vault in the cellar. Moving slowly, she made her way toward the front of the chapel, her hands trailing over pieces of pews that had fallen prey to time. One still stood, its surface worn smooth from worshippers who'd already rotted in their graves. Stretching out her hand, she touched the cold stone and felt an overwhelming rush of sadness. She lowered her body onto the pew, trying to figure out what she was sensing. The stone was warm, as if someone had recently sat there. She jumped up and looked around, but she was alone. Troubled, she hurried to the front of the chapel.

The hidden doorway to the cellar was still blocked. Faelan had restacked the stones, covering the secret entrance. There were a few scattered stones where the wall had crumbled. It was a wonder Bree hadn't been killed when it fell, but Anna was beginning to think nothing could kill Bree. She'd survived things no human should live through.

Since she was here, she might as well check the time vault and the cellar. Both would make ideal hiding places for Angus's notebook and the time vault key. It took Anna a few minutes to remove the stones. The sensible thing would be to wait for daylight and come back when she was properly dressed and wearing boots, but she felt compelled to continue.

She dusted off her hands and re-clipped her hair that had fallen loose. Using her flashlight, she found her way down the steps to the cellar. It was bare except for the time vault. The floor and walls were stone, so unless Angus had hidden the notebook under a loose stone or inside the time vault itself, nothing was hidden here. She approached the time vault and put her hands on the lid. Her battle marks began to tingle low on her back. She was starting to get a little freaked, but she couldn't leave without checking. She lifted the lid and looked inside. It was empty.

The time vault felt warm under her hands, and the air grew too thick to breathe. Beside her, shadows shifted, gathering into a form. She lowered the lid and stepped back, then reached for the dagger she kept hidden inside her boot, forgetting that she wore only a nightgown and flip-flops. She grabbed her talisman instead and braced for battle as the apparition shaped into a man wearing a kilt. His head was bent, his hair covering his face. Sorrow rolled off him like thick mist. She could almost taste his pain.

It must be done. There's no other way.

A face began to form out of the mist.

"Angus?" she whispered. But she knew it wasn't him. It didn't feel like him. The apparition vanished—if it had even been there— leaving only shadows and darkness. Unnerved, she hurried from the cellar without even stopping to hide the entrance. She would do it tomorrow. She stepped outside the chapel and pulled in a breath of night air. Exhaustion, stress, and guilt. That's all it was. Angus was gone, and he wasn't coming back. Another whisper caught her ear, but this one was different. Real. She crept around the side of the old church and saw two figures near the edge of the woods. One was taller than the other.

"It was just a grave," the shorter figure said. He was holding a shovel. "No time vault. I can keep looking, but the prisoner must be him. The brother is in Scotland."

"I have to get him out of there before it's too late," the taller man said. There was something familiar about him, but Anna couldn't see well enough to ID him. Both voices faded as they moved farther away.

Anna crept closer.

"Wait until he leaves, then we'll attack," the taller man said. They turned and disappeared into the woods.

Attack? They must be demons. Or vampires. Were they planning to attack the clan? She had to warn them. There was no time to go back to the house to get dressed. She hurried after them, moving past the archaeological dig where Angus had pretended to be one of Druan's archaeologists as they searched for Faelan's key.

A car started up ahead. They were going to get away. Anna turned and ran full speed back toward the house. She hurried around front to her rental and yanked the door open, thankful she'd left the keys in the ignition. She kept the headlights off as she raced up Bree's long driveway to the road. Beams from an oncoming car broke through the fog. Anna stayed out of sight, waiting for the car to pass. It had to be the men. There wasn't much traffic on this road in the middle of the night. A dark car drove past. A man was driving. He looked slim. She waited until the taillights disappeared and then pulled out behind him. Far enough back so that she didn't draw his attention, but close enough to keep the car in sight. It continued for a few miles, passing the road that led to the Albany castle. Why hadn't she replaced her bloody phone? She couldn't even call for backup.

Several miles later, the car slowed and turned down a small road. When it moved out of sight, Anna shut off her lights and followed. She had no idea where this road led. It looked private. She'd best travel on foot. She looked down at her thin nightgown, frustrated that she'd gotten caught unprepared—not something that usually happened to her. She should have taken a minute to grab her clothes and boots.

She pulled a spare dagger from under her seat and opened the door. She moved quickly, keeping hidden in the trees that lined the road as she followed the skinny man's headlights. She caught up as the car entered a large gate in the middle of an imposing iron fence. As soon as the vehicle entered, Anna ducked low and ran. She couldn't climb the fence with the dagger in her hand, and she didn't want to toss it over until she knew what she might face on the other side.

Holding it in her mouth was a poor option. She had a scar on the inside of her lip from when she'd tried it while scaling a castle wall. Lifting her gown, she tucked the dagger inside the waistband of her panties. They sagged but didn't fall off. She climbed the fence carefully, one iron bar at a time. She didn't want to slice open her hip or her panties. She dropped to the other side and surveyed the place. Nothing but trees. After such an impressive gate, she'd expected some sort of estate, or at least a decent house. She looked around for the car, but it had disappeared.

She removed her dagger and ran toward the trees. Her shoulder slammed into something hard. The trees wavered, and she glimpsed an enormous structure as the force of the impact knocked her flat on her back.

She sat up and caught her breath. Her feet were missing.

She pulled one leg back, and her foot reappeared. The place was cloaked, just like the Albany castle. She stretched out her finger, and it vanished. Cautiously, she put her head through the invisible veil and saw a huge stone fortress. The Albany castle and the Connor castle could both fit inside this place. It had several levels, with wings and towers. A paved drive led up to the fortress, with two gargoyles on either side. Stone, wolf-like creatures lined the inside of the fence. She'd slammed into one of them, which explained why her shoulder ached.

Anna scrambled behind the nearest creature and waited to see if anyone had spotted her. Other than a soft amber glow at several windows, the fortress was dark. Who lived here? Demons? Vampires? Definitely someone who dabbled in spells. Was it the same person who'd cloaked the Albany castle? The clan hadn't figured out who was responsible for that bit of ingenuity. She focused her senses, listening, smelling, and watching for movement. Demons stank to high heaven if they were in their natural form. If not, they could be anyone. She touched her talisman, reassured by its warmth. But deep in her bones she knew something was wrong.

A soft rumble sounded beside her. Like breathing. She whirled, one hand on her talisman, the other gripping the dagger. The stone wolf was the only thing there, its teeth bared in a snarl. Anna's adrenaline surged even though the creature wasn't real. She stepped away, anxious to get away from those stone teeth. A movement along the side of the fortress caught her eye. The skinny man was creeping around the corner, as if he didn't want to be seen any more than she did. Leaving the wolf behind her, she ran after the skinny man, keeping close to the shadows of the fortress as she moved past the long windows toward the back.

A pale blond head appeared at one window, and Anna ducked behind a tree. The person was gone when she looked back, but an icy prickle crawled over her skin. The vampire Ronan was hunting had pale blond hair, but he said they'd captured the creature. There must be others. If this fortress belonged to vampires, she was up the creek. Her talisman was useless against the creatures. The only sure way to kill them was to pierce their hearts or take their heads. She had her dagger, but vampires moved like the wind, making them a hard target.

Too late to turn back now. As soon as she had the thought, something flashed across the yard toward her, and she started running. The shape slammed in to her, sending her headlong into a tree. She lay there, dazed, but a hiss jump-started her adrenaline. A glint caught her eye. Her dagger. She'd dropped it when she was hit. She grabbed it and leapt to her feet, slicing at what she hoped was a vampire neck. It wasn't. The thing, whatever it was—she still couldn't see it clearly—picked her up and threw her against the side of the fortress. Something cracked. She hoped it was the stone wall and not one of her bones. Rolling to her side, she gritted her teeth against the pain and jumped up. She heard a howling sound, and her attacker stopped. She could see now that it was a man, short, dark, with spiky hair. He was looking toward the front of the fortress, toward the sound.

Gripping her dagger, she launched herself at him. He turned at the last second, but he was too late. Anna drove her dagger through his heart. A little more to the left than she would have liked, but it did the trick. With a startled gasp, he turned to dust before her eyes.

A vampire. A bloody vampire. The howling continued, closer now. They must have guard dogs, and nasty ones from the sound of it. She hurried toward the back of the fortress, in the direction the skinny man had gone. Away from the dogs. There was a small offset entrance around the corner. The door was ajar, as if someone had forgotten to close it all the way. There was no time to make sure she wasn't leaping from the frying pan to the fire. She had only one second to sniff for danger. She smelled sweat. Fear. The skinny man, she hoped. Better him than a pack of guard dogs.

Quietly but quickly, she closed the door and listened. Nothing on this side. Outside, the howls grew louder, more ferocious. The noise would draw any other creatures here. She had no idea if she was dealing with only vampires or if there were demons here too, but she had no choice except to keep going and try to find the way up to the first floor and back out. With a place this size, there could be dozens, or even hundreds, of vampires or demons. She couldn't take them on alone. And Ronan would want to be in on this fight. He hated vampires after what had happened to Cam.

Anna did a quick check around her. There was a faint glow like she'd seen in the windows outside. A set of descending stairs led to the nicest dungeon she'd ever seen. And she'd seen more than she wanted. Demons loved castles and fortresses. She didn't know much about vampires yet. The clan still had a lot to learn about their new enemy. This dungeon had a wide, arched corridor with suits of armor and statues lining the walls. Amber sconces provided the glow, giving the illusion of warmth when it was really cold.

The deeper she went, the more the place resembled a dungeon. There were several doors with small, barred windows. She came to another corridor and saw two cells on her right. One had heavy shackles attached to the wall above a stone bench and another set of shackles bolted to the floor. A low cry sounded from the opposite direction. An angry, helpless sound like an animal that knew it was dying. It was even more disturbing than the howling outside. She pressed herself against the wall and moved closer to the sound. A door rattled, and she heard a dull slap, like a fist on flesh, followed by a groan.

"Not holding up so well today, are you?" a man said.

She couldn't see if this was the skinny man, but it didn't sound like his voice.

Several more slaps were followed by groans. Anna moved close enough to peer inside the room. The first thing she saw was a pile of clothing on the floor, and then she saw the naked man. He was chained to a wall by his wrists. His ankles were shackled to the floor, and his back was facing her. He was young and muscular with dark hair almost touching the angry red slashes that streaked across his back. He snarled, and the muscles in his forearms bulged as he yanked at his chains.

"One more," his captor jeered. He was a big man, more fat than muscle, bald, and held a bullwhip with knots tied at the end. She couldn't tell if he was a vampire, demon, halfling, or human. He didn't smell like a demon, but if he was in human form, he wouldn't. He might just be a nasty minion. He pulled his arm back and flicked his wrist. The whip snaked through the air and landed on the prisoner's back, the knotted end digging into his ribs. The prisoner's body jerked. He cried out, and his body went slack.

Bile rose in Anna's throat. Was he dead? Her fingers tightened on her dagger, but it wouldn't be wise to intervene now. She didn't know who he was or what this place was. But it was bad.

The prisoner knew he wasn't dead. He hurt too much to be dead. That was the only thing he knew about himself. That, and that he was a killer. He knew this because he was certain exactly how he'd kill the fat guard holding the whip if he could get loose from these chains and rid of the cloudiness in his head. A door slammed deeper in the dungeon, and he heard a roar. He'd heard it before. What in hell was this place? Maybe this was hell. Then he smelled it. Through the agony and darkness slipping over him, a light fragrance wafted on the air. He didn't know how, but he knew that smell.

The guard loosened the chain attached to the prisoner's shackles, and he fell to his knees. A cup was shoved to his mouth. "Drink."

He wanted to refuse, but he was thirsty. He opened cracked lips and drained the cup. His body was shaking so half the contents ran down his chin.

"If you want to use the toilet, do it now." The guard removed the shackles from his hands but left the long chain securing his feet to the floor. Still holding the whip, the guard forced him to his feet, then shoved him toward the strange pot in the corner. The prisoner stumbled into place and started to lift his kilt, and then realized he was naked. He took aim, as best as he could with shaking hands. Bloody hands. A memory pulled loose from the emptiness of his mind. A man lying on the forest floor with deep slashes running the length of his chest. The prisoner could almost smell the blood. The man moved, his eyes widening with recognition. Pleading. Pleading for what? Mercy?

The prisoner looked at his bloody hands again. Had he killed the man in the forest?

"You gonna piss or not?"

Through swollen eyelids he saw the guard leering. He always watched when he was naked or exposed. Bloody pervert. The prisoner managed a few drops, but it hurt too much to stand. He pushed the lever, this time too near collapsing to marvel at the water swirling as the pot emptied.

The guard forced him back to the wall and shackled his wrists, bumping the prisoner's swollen finger. It was a clean break. It should heal in a few days if they would stop beating him. "Don't cause trouble and I'll give you double food rations tomorrow." The guard's voice was sharper than usual, his smirk replaced with a worried frown. "Make me look bad in front of the master, and as soon as he's gone again, you'll starve. I'll tell him you're failing his experiments."

The prisoner slumped against the wall, wincing when his back grazed the hard stone. But exhaustion pulled at him stronger than pain. The burning in his body gave way to goose-flesh from the cold. With no windows, the only way he could guess the time of day was by mealtimes. It must be evening. The fragrance was still there. Did the guard not notice? The scent pulled at him, but he couldn't place it. At the least, it took his attention off his raw back.

He cradled his head between the wall and his raised arm as he'd done for the last, what . . . fortnight? Longer? He'd lost track of time. As soon as he closed his eyes, the dreams would likely return. Maybe this time they'd tell him who he was.

Anna hid behind a statue and waited until the guard left the room. He was alone. The man he'd tortured was still inside. Alive? Dead? He'd closed the door, so she couldn't see. The guard had to be eliminated. She didn't know exactly who or what he was, but he was evil. He reeked of darkness and greed.

Her talisman wouldn't work if he was a vampire. So she stepped out from behind the statue, raised her dagger, and let it fly. The guard turned at that moment, and the blade caught him in the shoulder instead of the heart. He let out a terrible roar, and Anna started toward him to finish him off.

"Stop," a man ordered behind her, and a gun dug into the back of her skull.

"Stupid bitch!" the bald guard yelled. "Who the hell is she? No one's supposed to be down here."

"I got her." The man moved around to her side, keeping the gun at her head. It was the skinny man she had followed. Neither of them appeared to have fangs. Maybe they weren't vampires.

The guard yanked out Anna's dagger and pressed his hand against the wound. "Shoot her if she moves."

"Who are you?" the skinny man asked.

"And how the hell did you get here?" The fat guard nursed his wound. "Are you one of the new ones? You're supposed to stay upstairs."

"I followed him," Anna said, motioning with her thumb at the skinny guy.

The guard frowned. "Lance? Where were you?"

His hand shook, but he covered it by changing positions. "Just went out to run an errand." His voice sounded as shaky as the gun. He was lying to the guard.

"He was talking to someone, a tall man," Anna said. "Very secretive. When he left, I followed—" The gun smashed into her temple, and everything went black.

Anna woke to shouts and the sounds of running. She lay on a stone floor. It was dark here. No sconces. She had no idea how she'd gotten here or how long she'd been unconscious. She didn't feel any pain except for the violent headache from where the skinny guard had hit her.

"I think he went this way," someone called.

She stood and tried to adjust her vision, but it made her head hurt worse.

"How did he get loose?" the fat guard yelled.

"I don't know, but the master will flay us if he escapes."

"There won't be anything left of us to flay if this monster gets hold of us."

Monster? Was he talking about the man he'd tortured? He hadn't looked capable of escaping, much less hurting anyone. Anna listened to the sounds of the hunt, doors clanging and the guards shouting as she tried to get her bearings. She felt a warm breath on her neck and froze. She wasn't alone. Whoever or whatever was behind her was close. Instinctively, Anna eased her hand toward her talisman. It wasn't there. She lowered her hands, quickly but quietly checking to see if it could have fallen and caught on her gown. It was gone. A sick knot settled in her stomach. The guards must have taken her talisman and her dagger. She'd never lost her talisman, never even taken it off. A warrior was only half a warrior without her talisman.

"Who are you?" she said, keeping her voice calm.

No answer. Another warm breath. Closer? Her heart was pounding in her ears. If this was a vampire, she was screwed. Fists clenched, she slowly turned. The only think she could make out was a tall shape. Broad. Male. Definitely a male scent. There was something wild about the smell. Not quite human. The guards were yelling, coming closer. The shape let out a roar, and Anna threw a hard kick at his midsection. It didn't connect. The darkness had swallowed him. She spun, straining to see him. Nothing. She heard breathing several feet away. Without her weapons, she wasn't as effective, but she still had her senses, strength, and speed. She rushed toward the sound, and as she swung at his head, she saw another shadow dart past. There were two of them? She could see one of them now, and she struck. An arm reached out and grabbed her wrist, blocking her blow. She pulled free and went for him again. He ducked, but he wasn't nearly as fast as before. Or he was a different one. One what?

She aimed a kick at his chest, and he let out a groan. Then arms grabbed her, locked around her, and she smelled blood. She heard sniffing. Was he crying? She hadn't hurt him that bad. She'd just gotten started. The arms weren't pinning her now. He seemed to be holding on to her to keep from falling . . .

Over his labored breaths, she heard the guards coming.

"We need to check this section. He can't have gone far."

She stepped back, and the shape slid away with a thud. Anna moved to the corner of the cell, away from the voices and whoever she had fought. Where was the second man?

"What happened to the lights?" the fat guard asked.

"I don't know. They were on earlier when I brought his food."

"Turn them on."

"I'm getting them now."

The lights came on, the dim glow almost a shock after the pitch-black darkness. She was in a cell, and a man lay on the floor. Dark hair covered his face, and he wore a white shirt and a kilt. Or the shirt had been white at one time. Now it was smeared with blood. Like his hands. He couldn't be the one who'd stood behind her. He'd moved too fast, like a vampire. This looked like the man she'd seen in the torture room. At least he was dressed now.

The guards caught sight of the man and cursed. "How did he get here? I left him in the torture room," the fat guard said, confirming Anna's suspicion.

"I didn't bring him here." The skinny guard was defensive.

"I didn't either . . . holy hell. It must have been the hybrid."

"Why would he do that? And how did he get the door open? I've got the key."

"What is he? A ghost—dammit. What's she doing here?" The fat guard had caught sight of Anna. "What the hell's going on?"

"I did put her here," the skinny guard said. "I had to lock her up quick, and I only had this cell key. The hybrid must have brought him later."

The fat guard cursed. "We don't have time to move them both. We have to find that damned hybrid. Put one of them in the next cell."

"She's conscious," the skinny guard said. "I'll move her."

"I'm surprised she's alive, as hard as you hit her. And just as she was starting to talk. I think you are hiding something, Lance."

"She was getting ready to attack. I saw her muscles tense." Lance, the skinny guard, opened the cell and pointed his gun at her. "Get out here."

Anna walked to the cell door. Lance's eyes were filled with hatred. He was hiding something from the other guard, and she'd outed him. As soon as he found the right moment, she knew she'd be dead. "What are you?" she asked. "Vampire? Demon?"

Fear and hatred flashed in his eyes, and he opened the door to the adjoining cell. "Get inside."

As Anna entered, she glanced back at the man lying on the floor in the other cell.

Lance slammed the door. "What are we going to do with her, Bart?"

"We'll have to deal with her in the morning," the fat guard said. "Let's find the hybrid."

"I don't know why they don't just destroy him since we have the new specimen."

"The master wants to make sure this one works out first," Bart said. "Let's go deal with this mess."

"You gonna leave him unchained?" Lance asked, nodding toward the other cell.

"He's no threat in that condition," Bart said. "And I drugged him earlier. I'll chain him in the morning."

She'd beaten up a tortured, drugged man. Hell, what a night. She waited until the footsteps faded and then walked to the bars between their cells. The dungeon was still relatively dark, even with the sconce, and she couldn't see the man clearly. She could only assume he was alive. "Hey," she whispered. "Can you hear me?"

His fingers twitched, and he tried to move but collapsed to the floor again. His hair still covered part of his face, and he wore a beard. From what she could see, his eye and cheek were swollen and streaked with blood. Like Angus's.

"Who are you?" she asked. "What are you doing here?"

He rolled slightly, and his hair fell back from his face.

Anna's breath caught. "Faelan."

CHAPTER THREE

Anna pressed closer to the bars. It couldn't be Faelan, could it? She'd just talked to Ronan. He said Faelan and Bree should be home soon. Unless they had been captured in the last few hours. Could he be Duncan? He and Faelan looked enough like to be brothers. No, this man had a beard. Faelan and Duncan had both been clean-shaven in Virginia. But that was a few days ago.

She studied him a minute longer, the length of his hair, the shape of his head. Definitely not Duncan. But she couldn't be sure this wasn't Faelan. Whoever he was, he needed help.

"Can you move closer?" Anna asked. All warriors had basic medical training. She didn't know what she could do with these bars between them, but she had to try.

He must have heard her because he started sliding closer. It was slow, and she cringed as he groaned in pain.

"What's your name?" she asked.

His eyes opened, and Anna saw a flare of recognition before they closed again. Was it him? Good God. The clan must not know, or this place would be surrounded by warriors. And Bree would fight the Dark One himself to free Faelan. Anna reached through the bars and touched his hand. A jolt ran up her arm. Blimey. What was that? She'd touched Faelan dozens of times sparring with him. He'd beaten her every time, but he'd never shocked her.

She checked his hand. No wedding ring, but he did have a broken finger. There wasn't a talisman at his neck, but the guards could have taken his too. She needed to see his chest. A warrior's battle marks were as good as fingerprints, and she knew most of the warriors' marks from sparring with them, since males usually sparred shirtless.

She shook his arm gently, and he hissed. She yanked her arm back. Maybe he wasn't human. But he looked so much like Faelan. Demons could shift into human forms, but she'd never known a demon that could shift into a known identity. Even if that were the case, a demon would never be able to maintain his human shell if he were this injured.

"Can you roll over? I need to see your chest." Hopefully he'd think she was checking his injuries.

He grunted and tried to move. It took a minute, but he managed to roll onto his side. She pulled his shirt aside and looked at the tattoos on his chest. Battle marks. Her heart sank. If the Mighty Faelan was trapped in here, what did that say for the rest of the clan? But something was different about these marks. She looked closer. It was difficult to see in the dim lighting, but she was certain these weren't Faelan's marks. Then who was he?

"I need to check your injuries." She'd probably inflicted a couple of them. She put her arm through the bars and checked his pulse. Strong. Alternating bars, she checked him over. There was a knot on his head and a couple of cuts on his neck that had already dried. She already knew his back was a mess. There were cuts on both calves and a small pool of blood at the edge of his kilt, making her wonder what else they might have done to him after she was captured.

She eased his kilt up until she found the source of the blood, a cut on the front of his thigh. Warriors healed quickly and were immune to most diseases, but they weren't immortal. If they were injured badly enough, they could die. Like Angus. And she wasn't positive this man was a warrior. She looked around the cell to see if there was anything she could use to clean his wounds. The floors and walls were lovely, but the cells were bare except for a toilet in one corner, a sink with a cup and paper towels, and a stone bench with a folded blanket.

"I'll be right back," she said, unsure whether he could even hear her. She filled the cup with water and grabbed the roll of paper towels. She worked on the cut on his thigh first, cleaning off the worst of the blood. He was shivering when she finished, from pain or from the cold. She didn't clean his back since his shirt was stuck to his wounds. She would do that later, after they'd escaped. There had to be a way out of this place.

He shivered again, and Anna worried that he was going into shock. She got the blanket and stuffed it through the bars, spreading it over his body as best she could. Then she checked his pulse again. Still strong.

She spent several minutes checking the cell for some way out, but the bars were secure, and she didn't have anything to pick the lock. There wasn't even anything she could use as a weapon. If the bastards got close enough, she'd strangle them with her bra.

The man moaned, and Anna went back to him. Squatting next to the bars, she slipped her hand through and touched his face. Still cold, but no fever. That was good.

He seemed unsettled. He tried to raise himself to one arm. "Piss."

"What?"

"Piss." The man fumbled with his kilt and lifted the front.

Anna's eyebrows rose. Was he going to do it right here on the floor? "Wait! You have a toilet." Damn. He couldn't walk to the toilet. He'd been drugged. Grabbing the cup still sitting on the floor, she tilted it just in time. She looked away, trying to give him privacy. His hand was unsteady, and she was afraid he'd end up soaking the floor. Anna cursed under her breath and reached through the bars. She put her other hand over his, guiding his aim.

What a bloody freakin' day. She'd gotten captured by God knew what kind of creatures, there was a monster hybrid on the loose, and now she was helping a man she didn't know piss in a cup. When he was finished, he groaned and fell back, not moving. She lowered his kilt and emptied the cup in the toilet. When she returned, she straightened his blanket and sat on the floor next to the bars, afraid to leave him alone.

After ten minutes with her teeth chattering and her head drooping, she lay down, trying to draw what little heat she could from his body.

A smell woke him. Something tugged at his memory. Hugging a woman? No. Fighting . . . He opened his eyes. He was lying on the floor. A blanket had been thrown over him, and a woman lay inches away in the next cell, her back to him. She wore a short gown that left most of her legs bare. His eyebrows rose, and he winced at the movement. His face felt bruised and swollen. She must be a whore. What was she doing here? He pulled in her scent again, and he smelled something else. Blood. What had they done to her? Had the guard ravished her?

If that bastard had hurt a woman, whore or no, he'd wrap his hands around that thick throat and squeeze until there was no bloody life left in the man. When he could move. Damnation, he felt like he'd been trampled by horses. He looked at the floor and saw the bloodstain, there and on his kilt. It was his blood, not hers. His body hurt from head to toe, but he was warmer than he'd been for a fortnight. The blanket must have been her doing. Memories shot through his head. A woman's voice whispering to him. Soft hands checking for wounds, holding his hand while he pissed. Bollocks. And he smelled worse than a sweaty horse. He hadn't bathed in days.

"Well, now, isn't this cozy?" The guard stood outside the cell. His arm was bandaged.

The prisoner didn't recall attacking him. He didn't think he'd been capable in his condition. Had the woman done this? Not likely. What could a woman do against a guard? He heard an indrawn breath, and the woman jumped up, her back to him. All he managed to do was roll over. Since he didn't have a sporran, he dropped his hand over his groin, but the guard had already seen his reaction to the woman.

"Nature blessed you, warrior, so you might manage it through the bars. We could use some entertainment."

An unholy light lit the guard's eyes, sending dread to the prisoner's heart. He struggled to his feet, longing for his dirk. He would drive the blade up under his ribs, directly into his heart. The guard would be dead before he hit the floor. He must be a killer, else how would he know that?

The guard opened the woman's cell and stepped inside. "Time to start talking. Who are you?"

She didn't answer.

"Did you come for him?" He nodded toward the prisoner. "Strange clothing for a rescue. You couldn't have come for the other one. He's been here over two years. No one knows about him."

"Do you know her?" the guard asked him.

"No." He didn't know anyone. Or did he know her? Was that why he'd felt the beginning of a memory?

The guard advanced on her, but she didn't back up. Her body tensed, balancing. She was prepared to fight. Another rush of dread filled him. The guard would kill her.

"Answer me," the guard demanded, clenching his fists. "Who are you? How did you get in?"

"You'll need more than your fists to get me to talk," she said.

Was she insane? The prisoner moved closer to the bars separating the cells. His body was still weak, but anger and fear gave him strength.

"I can make you talk." The guard pulled out his pistol. "Lance, come here."

Lance arrived, and the guard handed him the pistol. "If she struggles, shoot her." The guard grabbed the woman's arm. "Tell me who you are."

"No."

The guard slapped her.

The prisoner's fingers pressed into the bars. He heard a growl and realized it came from his own throat. Then a startling thing happened. The woman punched the guard in the face and then kicked him in the chest. He fell backward, smashing into Lance. The gun flew from his hands. Damnation. Lasses didn't fight like that. Maybe his dream of fighting with her wasn't a dream.

"Bitch!" The guard jumped up and grabbed the pistol, pointing the weapon at her head.

"Just shoot her," Lance said. "The master will be here soon. We don't need trouble."

"No. Get on the floor." The woman's face was still hidden, but her anger was apparent in her stiff movements. "Now."

She sat down, awkwardly, because of her short gown. The guard pointed his pistol at her chest and shoved her back onto the floor. She tried to sit up, but the guard straddled her. He ripped the top of the woman's gown, baring part of her breasts. Not overly large, but plenty. He sneered as he unfastened his belt. "Somebody needs to teach you a lesson. Human women are only good for one thing."

A cry of rage rolled up the prisoner's throat. "Get off her."

"Sedate the prisoner," the guard ordered Lance. "Then leave."

In one swift motion, the woman lifted her legs, baring a backside covered in a tiny white cloth and the most bizarre shoes on her feet, and wrapped her legs around the guard's chest, yanking him backward. At the same time, she swung her arm toward the pistol. It fired into the ceiling. She ducked, and the guard scrambled to his feet.

The prisoner growled and pulled against the bars. He felt the wounds on his back open with the effort. He wasn't aware that Lance had entered the cell until something sharp jabbed him in the arm. He turned and swung at Lance, throwing him against the cell door. The prisoner started toward him, but Lance scrambled out of reach. The prisoner's legs went weak as a new lamb's. His mind blurred as Lance shoved him onto the bench. As the shackles closed around his wrists, he saw the woman's face for the first time.

But it wasn't the first time. He'd seen those turquoise eyes before.

⁂

Anna jumped up and lunged at the guard again, striking him in the groin. It wasn't a direct hit, but he groaned and staggered back. Still, he held on to the gun. She expected him to shoot her, but a roar echoed down the corridor.

The guard cursed, holding his crotch with one hand and the gun with the other. "I thought you sedated him."

"I did."

"He's out of control. We'll have to give him more." The guard hobbled to the door.

"He's not the only one out of control," Lance said, looking at Anna. "We need to kill her."

"Not until I get what I want."

Anna backed against the wall, anger and fear making her blood pound. She didn't know if he meant answers or rape. She didn't mind a fight, but rape . . . the thought made her sick. Her mother had been raped. It had ruined her life.

The guard slammed the door and started to lock it. "The lock's broken. The bullet must have hit it. We'll have to move her."

"Not if we kill her," Lance said. "We have too much to worry about with these other two."

Did that mean there were only three of them being held here? The prisoner, the hybrid, and her?

"No. The master will want to know who she is. She must be a warrior. She had one of those necklaces."

She touched her bare neck. Warriors didn't lose their talismans. It just wasn't done. What a bloody mess she'd gotten into.

"Put her in with Faelan for now. I'll deal with her later. Move," he ordered her. He stayed several feet away, aiming the gun at her head as Lance unlocked the other cell and shoved her inside. "We're not finished. You'll pay for this." The guard gave her a dark look, and the two left.

Anna turned to the prisoner. He sat on the stone bench, his arms shackled to the wall above him, his bare feet shackled to an iron ring in the floor. Dried blood smeared his kilt and shirt. He was unconscious, head cradled between his upraised arms and his chest. Who was he? The guards thought he was Faelan, and he did resemble him, but they were wrong.

She touched his arm, and he yanked at his chains and opened his eyes. Anna leaned back. She had no doubt he could be dangerous. His dark gaze locked on her, and something zinged along her nerves. "What's your name?" she asked.

He looked disoriented, but his gaze was steady. "Faelan."

He couldn't be. He didn't have Faelan's battle marks. "What's your last name?"

"Last?"

"Faelan what?"

He frowned and shook his head. "I don't remember."

Amnesia? They had beaten him so badly it was no surprise. "Where do you live?"

He closed his eyes for a moment. "I don't know."

"How do you know your name is Faelan?"

"That's what they call me."

"Hold on, I'm going to try to free you." Anna tested the shackles and chains. They were strong. She needed something to pick the lock. Her hair clip. It had a sharp edge. She touched her head, but the clip was gone. It must have fallen out when she fought the guard. She hurried to the bars and scanned the floor of the next cell. The clip was lying in a corner. She lay on the floor and stretched out her arm. Too far. Blimey. She reached around behind her and unhooked her bra. She shrugged one shoulder free, then the other, and wiggled out of it.

The prisoner watched, his brows drawn together. If he hadn't looked so broken, his astonishment would have been comical.

"I'm sure it isn't the first time you've seen a bra." Holding one end of the bra, she knelt and tried to snag the clip through the bars. It was sort of like fishing. It took several tries to retrieve the clip. When she got it, she scooped it up and hurried back to the man. She stuck the pointed end in the lock. She wasn't as good at picking locks as Ronan, but she wasn't bad. Her efforts paid off, and she heard a click as the shackle released. She opened it, and the prisoner's arm dropped. His wrist was raw from where he'd pulled at the chains. The second shackle proved harder. Anna glanced at his face, only inches from hers. She felt a jolt of something, but decided it was sympathy or shock.

His eyes moved over her face. He frowned and shook his head.

"I'm Anna. Anna MacKinley."

"Anna?" He said the name stiffly, but there was no doubt he was a Scot. And a warrior. Why hadn't she seen him before? There were some smaller clans who kept to themselves. Perhaps he belonged to one of them. But it didn't answer the question of what he was doing here and why the guards called him Faelan. A thought was forming in her head, but it was so outlandish, she didn't give it credit.

"Do you remember how you got here?" she asked.

"No. They've taken my memories with their damned potions and needles."

"An amnesia drug?"

"I don't know. I woke once, and they were taking my blood. And I think they branded me."

"Branded?"

"There are marks on my chest."

Strange that he would refer to them as brands and not tattoos. Maybe they weren't battle marks. Lots of guys had tattoos on their chests. But he didn't remember who he was, so it was possible he didn't remember that he was a warrior. "Can I see them again?"

He looked slightly taken aback. "Aye." He pulled his shirt aside.

They both jumped when she touched his skin. Her fingers ran over the marks, confirming what she'd seen before. "I don't know who you are, but you're not Faelan."

CHAPTER FOUR

THE WOMAN STARED AT HIM WITH THE MOST STARTLING BLUE-green eyes. They reminded him of water he'd seen in Greece. Greece? He dug through the fog in his head, grasping at the small thread of recognition. Was he from Greece? But the memory moved past like a wispy cloud on a windy day.

He looked away from her breast jiggling a hand's length from his face as she worked on the shackle. "How do you know I'm not Faelan?" He was oddly distressed by her words. He had felt a connection to the name. The only connection he had in the midst of this darkness. Until her. She was bonny. Perhaps the most beautiful woman he'd ever seen, and that made him nervous, but he didn't know why.

"I know Faelan," she said.

"You know him?" That was a bloody odd thing, for her to know someone by the name his captors were calling him. "And you're familiar with his chest?"

"Of course." At his questioning look, her dark brows drew into a delicate arch.

"How do you know him?" he asked, hoping the words didn't sound as impolite to her ears as his.

"He's a friend."

Friend. That could mean anything. "Why would they call me Faelan if I'm not him? Is it a common name?"

She continued to work on the shackle. "No. Uncommon, in fact."

Yet she knew a man named Faelan, the very name they called him. Very odd indeed.

"Well, we know you're Scottish." She nodded to his kilt.

"Do you want me to try?" he asked, looking at the shackle.

"I think I can get it. We need to get out of here. We'll have to set a trap and attack him. Maybe one of us can play dead, then we'll attack him when he comes to check. I wish I had my dagger."

Damnation. What kind of woman carried a dagger? The shackle clicked open. He removed it while the woman, Anna, started working on his feet. The shackles there opened easier. When he was free, he stood, wincing.

"Are you all right?" Anna asked, looking him over. "They've beaten the crap out of you." She looked oddly guilty when she said it.

He frowned at her rude speech. Obviously a whore, which made him wonder again if she was telling the truth about this Faelan. More likely he had used her services. She was the bonniest thing he'd ever laid eyes on. He didn't visit whores himself, but he'd be sore tempted with this one. How could he know he didn't visit whores when he didn't recall his own name? He touched his face and winced.

"Aye. If feeling like you've been run down by a team of horses is all right." He noticed a streak of blood on her thigh, and his stomach knotted. "Did the guard *hurt* you?" Lasses like her were often ill treated, but whore or not, it made his blood boil.

She followed his gaze to her thigh and then wiped the blood with the edge of her gown. "It's his blood, so it doesn't matter."

Cheeky wench.

"Do you know how long you've been here?" she asked.

"I've lost count. A fortnight or longer."

She seemed puzzled by that. "Fortnight? What do they want with you?"

"They're testing me."

"For what?" Anna asked, smoothing down her gown.

"I don't know."

"Is your leg still bleeding?"

He lifted the edge of his kilt. Dried blood still crusted the cut on his thigh, but it had closed up overnight. "Thank you for tending me."

She glanced away. "No problem. We have to get you out of here and back to your family."

Family. Several faces rushed through his head so fast he didn't have a chance to recognize them. It was damned frustrating.

The woman, Anna, walked to the cell bars. He glanced at her bare legs, wondering why a whore would feel so familiar to him. Perhaps he had glimpsed her briefly when she was put into his cell.

She grabbed one of the iron bars and tested it, then went around the cell testing them all, as he'd done when he awoke in here. "They're strong," he said. "I've checked them all."

"We have to find some way out of here."

She was serious. Was she barmy? Women didn't break out of dungeons and fight guards. "I've tried to escape. Then they started giving me potions to keep me under control, and one of them keeps a pistol aimed at me. If they got it close enough, and I wasn't half asleep from their bloody potions, I'd disarm them and kill them both."

She turned and looked at him. "I think I know what you . . ." Her mouth closed, and she shook her head slightly. He wondered what she had been going to say, but she bent to inspect the lock, which bared her legs almost to her arse, and that's all he could think about. The polite thing to do would be to look away, but he couldn't make himself. She must turn a good profit. "How did you get here?"

"I followed the skinny guard, Lance."

"How do you know Lance?" Had he used her services?

"I saw him talking to someone outside my friend's house."

He glanced at her indecent gown and wondered if her friend was a whore too.

"I wanted to know why he was there." She continued prowling the room, an odd action for a woman, but she moved with grace and power that tightened his loins. What the hell was wrong with him, thinking about how bonny she looked when they were both trapped in a dungeon, and he still didn't know how he'd gotten here, or why? They just dragged him away and beat the hell out of him, waited for him to heal, and did it all over again. He would have tried to escape—he was certain he could kill the guards—but every time they opened the door, they either had that bloody pistol or slipped him a potion that made him helpless as a bairn.

What now? Even if he could escape, he couldn't leave a woman here. Not even a whore. Not after the things they'd done to him.

The guard appeared at the door holding a plate. "Stand back." He set the plate down and held the pistol on them as he unlocked the door. He slid the plate inside. "Eat," he said, leering at her. "You'll need your strength." He tossed in a basket with towels. "And take a bath, both of you."

The woman's eyes met his. He saw a flicker of alarm underneath that bravado. The guard expected them to bathe, without privacy. They both ate their food, and he tried not to think about it. It didn't work. There wasn't a lot of her that wasn't uncovered, but he was unusually curious what the rest looked like.

"Don't they believe in cooking?" she asked, taking a small bite of the rare steak.

He shrugged. "They prefer it bloody."

"I'm not surprised," she said. "I wish I had a bowl of cereal."

What was cereal? A roar echoed somewhere in the dungeon before he could ask.

"That must be the hybrid," she said. "What is he?"

"I don't know."

"If they're calling him a hybrid, he must be a mix of two different species."

She seemed troubled by the thought, as he was. He found it just as troubling that she wasn't hysterical at the thought of something as alarming as hybrids. "I've heard him, but I haven't seen him." He took a bite of his meat, wiping his mouth on the back of his hand.

"I think he saw you. The guards said they didn't move you from the torture room. They thought he carried you back here. Do you remember anything?"

"Someone carried me, I think."

"Maybe the hybrid felt sorry for you? They're probably doing the same thing to him that they're doing to you—" She broke off.

Were they trying to turn him into a hybrid? He looked at Anna's legs stretched in front of her. Long, firm, and very bare. What would they do with her?

"Could I have a drink of your water?" she asked.

Her cup was in the other cell near the pot. His face warmed, remembering how she'd used hers. He handed his over. "I'm sorry you had to . . ." He wasn't sure how to phrase it, but she knew what he meant. She didn't look at him but focused instead on his cup.

"It's OK." A slight smile touched her lips. "I've faced a few embarrassing situations before."

"Aye?" He kept forgetting what she was, or what he suspected she was. She looked like a whore, but although she acted damned strange, she didn't have the manner of a whore.

She handed his cup back. "They keep talking about their master. Do you know who he is?"

"I don't know his name, but I've seen him. I feel I ought to know him." He'd dreamed of him, dreams that felt real, like memories trying to surface.

"What does he look like?"

"Black hair, long. Pale, bonny face." Speaking of bonny . . . "Is there someone looking for you?" he asked. "Do you have a husband?" He didn't want to just come out and ask if she was a whore.

"I'm not married." Her voice was firm, almost as if he'd insulted her.

Aye, a whore then. A woman with her beauty couldn't have escaped male attention for long. "What about family?" Everyone had family. The thought made his chest tight. He must have a family. Were they searching for him?

"None." Her voice sounded flat. Bitter.

"They're dead?"

"My mother is. I don't have a father."

Everyone had a father. "What about brothers, sisters?" He saw faces in his mind, but the vision vanished as fast as it had come.

"No. I have cousins and friends," she said, her voice warming. "They're all I need."

What kind of friends allowed a woman to sell her body? "Are they looking for you, do you think?"

"I don't know if they've realized I'm missing." She sounded worried. "I've got to get out of here. I think someone's going to attack them. I have to warn them."

"What makes you think that?"

"Something I overheard from the man Lance was talking to."

This made very little sense. What was her connection to this place and to Lance? It was apparent that he didn't want her here, and the fat guard, Bart, hadn't expected her.

After they ate, he waited as long as he could. "They don't offer much in the way of privacy. I need to use that fancy pot."

She stared at him until he felt uncomfortable. Perhaps it was an insult to mention it after she'd had to help him piss into a cup, but bodily functions didn't consider circumstances.

"Fancy pot?" She looked at the pot, her expression puzzled.

"Sorry to mention it, but . . ."

"Don't worry about it. I'll . . . just be over there." She stood and walked to the front of the cell, turning her back to him.

When he was finished, he turned to her. "If you need to use it, I'll watch for the guard."

She shook her head and then uttered a soft thank-you. "What did you call it? A fancy pot?"

"Aye. It's . . . strange."

She looked even more puzzled. "Interesting," she said quietly.

It was that. He wished he'd had one at home. Another flash . . . a big house. A castle? But the image quickly faded. He didn't know if he was remembering this place—it must be some sort of castle— or someplace else. "We're not going anywhere tonight," he said. "Might as well clean up a bit. I'm sure I don't smell too good. They haven't let me bathe for a while." He'd been chained most of the time.

She glanced at the sink. "I probably don't smell like flowers either."

She smelled like heaven. "I'll hold the blanket if you want to bathe first," he said, inspecting the basket. He pulled out cloths and a bar of soap. "Look here. There's another wee brush so you can clean your teeth."

She gave him an odd look again. "You go first. You need to clean your wounds."

It was awkward, but she held the blanket up for him. He tried to remove his shirt, but it was stuck to the cuts on his back. He could rip it off, but they would start bleeding again. He cursed softly as the shirt pulled at the dried blood and raw skin.

"Is something wrong?" she asked.

"Aye. My shirt's stuck to my back. I don't want to reopen the wounds. Do you think you could help me?"

She lowered the blanket and put it on the bench. "I'll have to wet the shirt to loosen it from your cuts."

She ran the water until it was warm. A delightful thing, he thought, having warm water right out of a pipe. Even more delightful, her hands on his back as she put the wet cloth over the wounds, soaking his shirt. It stung, but her touch took his mind off the pain.

"I think it's working." She gently lifted the shirt away from his back in the places where it had been stuck. "You should be able to take it off now."

He stretched, feeling the shirt freely move. "Aye. That does it."

"Do you need help?" She glanced at the floor. "The wounds on your back need to be cleaned. I don't think you can reach them."

He swallowed and nodded. "That would be helpful." Among other things. He turned his back and shrugged slowly out of his shirt, tossing it onto the bench next to the blanket.

"My God. What have they done to you?" She gently bathed one of the wounds. "What do they want? Usually a person is tortured to get information. Secrets."

What would she know about torture? "If they wanted me to tell them secrets, they shouldn't have stolen my memories. I don't know anything to tell them." Not even his name. Apparently it wasn't Faelan as he'd been told.

It took several minutes. Long, aching, sweet minutes with his body feeling the closest thing to pleasure he'd felt in many a fortnight.

"There. That's as good as I can do without a first aid kit."

A what? He didn't ask. He was busy trying to calm his body enough to turn. It wasn't working. He reached for the blanket and held it in front of him. "Thank you."

"You should finish up. You have more wounds to clean."

He'd like for her to clean them all. Blimey, he'd let her wash every part of him. She took the blanket from him and put it back in place, and he resumed bathing. He removed his kilt and cleaned his face and the cuts on his body. When he'd gotten off most of the blood, he soaped up, washing his chest, belly, arms, and oxters before moving below the waist. He ran the cloth over his groin, thinking what it'd feel like if it was her hand. He didn't stay there too long for fear that he'd embarrass himself.

The sound of the washcloth moving over his skin made Anna tingle in places she didn't want to tingle. She turned her face, and a movement caught her eye. There was a small hole in the blanket. She'd seen lots of naked men. On the battlefield, forest or city, privacy was compromised. But this man . . . holy cow. He was like a beautiful painting that had been vandalized. Perfectly muscled hips and thighs and a sleek broad back, marred with bruises and cuts.

He turned slightly, and her breath caught. He was rubbing the soapy cloth over his groin. She quickly raised her gaze to the symbols arcing across his chest. Though they were marred by a couple of bruises—his chest seemed to have fared better than the rest of him—she was almost sure they were battle marks.

Battle marks had a kind of a presence about them, as if they were alive. And these made her hands tremble with the urge to touch them. She did look away then, keeping her eyes closed so she wasn't tempted to find the hole again.

"That's better," he said, nudging the blanket down. His clothes were still dirty, but his skin was clean, and the swelling in his face was going down. He healed quickly. "I'll hold it for you, if you'd like?"

She balked at the thought of undressing so near a strange man, especially one this hot, but after moving stones in the chapel and fighting the guard, she needed to clean up. It would take more than water to erase the feel of the guard straddling her. Watching his blood drain from his body might help.

After the prisoner raised the blanket high enough to block his face, she stripped off her dirty gown and panties and laid them beside her bra. She could hear him breathing on the other side of the blanket. Using the second washcloth and the bar of soap, she washed her face first, the warm water making her long for a bathtub. She washed her body next, hurrying as the man's breath grew ragged. Holding the blanket at face level must be a strain with his body still weak. Or perhaps he'd also found the hole.

She sped through her routine, pleased to find basic toiletries— toothbrush, toothpaste, hairbrush, and deodorant. What kind of place was this? Beat a man with a whip, then give him toothpaste and deodorant.

"I'm finished," she said, and he dropped the blanket, his eyes glittering as he stared at her. He draped the blanket over his arm. "Do you want to sit?"

The stone bench was the only place to sit besides the floor, so they both sat on the bench, side by side. Anna shivered, and he handed her the blanket. "You take it. I'm not cold."

He was lying. When his arm brushed hers, she could feel the chill of his skin. This place was like a freezer. How could it be so much colder here than it had been at Faelan and Bree's? It felt more like January than early November. Was that part of his torture? Freeze him half to death?

"Thank you." She wrapped it around her, leaving an edge free for him. "If we sit closer, we can share it."

He nodded and scooted next to her. She could still smell the blood on his kilt and shirt, but his body smelled clean, male. It gave her the strangest sensation, sitting in near darkness with a man she didn't know, who she suspected was a warrior, though he didn't know it. Could he be Austin, the warrior from Canada who'd been attacked by vampires on the way to meet Angus? This place had vampires. Austin could have followed them here after the attack. But he didn't sound Canadian. He sounded like a Scot. And while tattoos were popular, and it wasn't uncommon to see a man in a kilt—less so in America—there were too many signs that he was a warrior. His appearance, his manner, the way he moved. And those marks. If they weren't battle marks, why did she feel like they were whispering to her?

They sat side by side, wrapped in the blanket. His body was warm next to hers, making her sleepy. Unnaturally so. Had the guard put something in her food? She tried to imagine how it would have been for him, here alone, beaten, no memories, no answers, and no one to talk to except his tormentors. He must be strong, mentally as well as physically. "I don't how you've survived being here."

"I don't have a choice. I can't let them kill me. So I sit here night after night waiting to remember something, waiting for them to make a mistake so I can escape."

"I'm sorry. I promise, we'll find a way out of here."

He gave her a puzzled glance. "You must have had a hard life," he said.

His words surprised her. There was no way he could know about her past. She didn't talk about it. "Why do you say that?"

"I've never seen a woman so . . ." He seemed to be searching for the word. "Strong," he finally said, but Anna didn't think that was his first choice.

"Thank you," she said, not sure it was a compliment. All warriors were strong, but she didn't tell him that. She couldn't tell him who she was until she was sure who he was. Clan secrets had to be kept. "You're strong too. You would have to be to survive the torture. The tattoos on your chest, you don't recall getting them?"

He touched his chest. "No. It's an odd thing what being alone does to you, having no idea who you are. Sometimes . . ." He paused and gave her a sheepish grin that made her body feel weightless. "Sometimes I feel like the marks are talking to me. Barmy, aye?"

If the marks were what she thought, it wasn't barmy at all. Her battle marks had kept her sane many times. Another cry sounded from outside. The hybrid? "What is this place?" she said, shuddering.

"The guards don't talk much, other than taunting me."

"Lance is sneaky. I couldn't see the man he was talking to just before I followed him, but he doesn't want the fat guard to know about it."

"Did you recognize the man he was talking to?"

"No. But he was huge." Not many men were that size. Maybe he wasn't a man. Could he have been the master? But why would Lance be sneaking around? Anna squirmed trying to get more comfortable. The bench was hard.

"Are you still cold?"

"I'm fine." He must not have believed her, or he was still cold himself. He shifted, somehow making their bodies fit together even tighter. She did start to feel warmer.

"Does Lance know you followed him?" He stifled a yawn.

"He does. I told the fat guard, Bart. Lance wasn't happy. He wanted him to kill me. I wonder what he's hiding that's so important."

The prisoner turned and stared at her, which put them almost nose to nose. Or nose to shoulder. He was a lot taller than she was. "He must be trying to silence you. One of us will have to stay awake in case he comes back. Why don't you get some sleep? I'll keep watch."

"You need rest more than I do. You're injured." But she was so tired she couldn't keep her eyes open. "I think we've been drugged."

"I suspect you're right. I feel unusually sleepy. The guards have been on edge. Their master is coming soon. You sleep first. I'll rest in a bit."

She tried to stay awake, but her eyelids were too heavy. She woke in the night, warm. His arm was around her shoulders, and she was slumped against him. He'd tucked the blanket around her and was holding it in place. She straightened, scanning the cell to see if they were alone. They were. His arm tightened around her, and he leaned his head against hers. There was something so comforting about the position that she ignored her numb butt.

"Are you all right?"

"Just stiff."

He shifted. "Aye, I can't feel my arse. Wish I couldn't feel my back."

Leaning against the wall couldn't be doing his wounds any good.

"We could stretch out on the floor," he said.

But that would be even more intimate. They were in a prison dungeon. Did it matter? They both rose slowly. "I wish there was a bed."

In the darkness, she saw him glance at her breasts. "Aye. The floor's not much for sleeping. I'd rather have the ground and soft leaves."

It would be an improvement over stone. They chose a spot near the corner of the cell. He spread the blanket, and she lay down near the edge. Without words, he lay next to her on his side, close, but not touching. He pulled the remaining half of the blanket over them.

"Are you warm enough?" he asked.

"Yes."

"Your chattering teeth tell a different story."

"Guess they don't want to pay the heat bill." She'd never been this bothered by cold. It must be the drug.

"I can move closer, if that's all right."

She would have let him lie on top of her to get rid of this chill. Or maybe it was the drug. She wouldn't have minded letting him do more than just get rid of the chill. That wasn't like her. "Thank you," she said, and he shifted closer. She turned on her side, and he tucked the blanket tighter around them. She could feel him brush against her, but not pressing. "There must be someone wondering where you are." Maybe a wife who might be upset that his body was tucked against hers. If she loved him, she'd be more upset at what they'd done to him than who he was sharing his body warmth with.

"I would hope."

He sounded so lost, Anna's heart broke a little for him. With no memory of who he was, he was completely alone. "It must be terrible not to remember your name or where you came from. Where your family is." Not that she had a family now. Her only family was her friends. Did they even know she was missing? Were they in danger? Lance's buddy could have already attacked them. If something happened to them, she would be as alone as the prisoner.

"Aye," he said softly. "It is that."

She wanted to help him. All she could do was share her body heat. "When we get out, I'll help you find them." And she was determined to get them out.

"That's very kind of you."

She lay there feeling his heart beat against her back and the movement of his chest as he breathed. And she was glad she wasn't alone.

After a moment, his voice brushed her ear. "I've no memories of my own. Perhaps you could share something of yours with me? Tell me about when you were a child."

She never talked about her childhood. But somehow here in the dungeon with this stranger who had no memories, it seemed safe. Whatever she had, good or bad, it was more than he had.

"I lived with my mother. I never knew my . . . father." Her mother hadn't either. "My mother was a powerful woman at one time. Very strong." Strong enough to make tough decisions. "And kind. But something terrible happened, and it destroyed her." For years she'd believed her mother had died at the hands of a demon when she'd really killed herself. The clan hadn't told Anna. That made her angry, but she understood in a way. She had just started her duty. Knowing the truth would have destroyed her. She would never have known if Angus hadn't found her mother's death certificate. "I miss her." There were times when she'd felt her mother's love. When they'd almost felt normal.

"I'm sorry it was bad. Didn't your mother tell you anything about your father?"

"No. She never spoke of him." And Anna learned not to ask.

"Do you live nearby?" he asked.

"No. I have a flat in London, and I spend a lot of time in Scotland."

"Scotland?" He sounded the word as if testing it.

She suspected he knew Scotland well. "I travel a lot for work."

"What do you do?" he asked, and she thought she heard a note of suspicion in his voice.

"Um, it's hard to explain." As much as she wanted to open up to him, she couldn't say much until she was sure he was a warrior.

"Why do you have to work?"

Odd question. "Everyone has to work if they want to eat." Her job just wasn't typical. Not many humans got their orders from an angel. "My friends help me." She thought of the others—Ronan, Sorcha and Duncan, Faelan, and now Bree, Shay, Cody . . . Angus. They were her family now. And she'd abandoned them to stew in her grief over Angus. Angus would be pissed if he knew. Maybe he did know. Maybe he was watching her now. Watching them. Maybe she was loopy with drugs. She definitely wasn't herself. She almost felt drunk. She snuggled closer to the warmth at her back, wishing the prisoner would hold her even tighter. *God, what did they give me?* she thought, as the weight of her lids pulled her under.

CHAPTER FIVE

A GROAN WOKE ANNA. A STRONG ARM, BRUISED AND LACED with cuts, was wrapped around her waist. Her instinct was to fight, but she felt a warm breath caress her ear and the body at her back, and she remembered where she was and who held her.

"No," he whispered. "They'll forget." His arm tensed, and his breath came faster, harsher. "No!"

Anna strained against his arm, and he tightened his grip, making it hard to breathe. She broke his hold and rolled over, putting her hand on his face to calm him. His arm came out, catching her in a blow that knocked her against the wall.

Winded, Anna crawled back to him. "Wake up." He continued tossing, throwing the blanket aside. He smacked his head on the floor, and she wondered if some of his injuries had come from fighting his dreams. Ducking to avoid another blow, she dove between his fists and grabbed him. If he didn't stop, he would reopen all the wounds on his back. He grunted and tried to swing again, but she kept her arms tight around him, avoiding the injured areas. It wouldn't help for long. He was as strong as a bull. "Wake up!"

His eyes opened, but they were vacant. There was a damp trail at one corner. She released his arms and leaned back. "Are you OK?"

He didn't speak. He covered his face, and Anna could hear his labored breathing. He lowered his hands, and the look in his eyes was so lost, she couldn't help but touch his face. He pressed his cheek against her palm.

When his hand touched her side and moved over her back, winding in her hair, she didn't resist. Not when he gently pulled her face to his or softly touched her cheek. His breath was warm as his mouth met hers. She felt the rough edge of a healed cut at the top of his lip. He tilted her head and kissed her. Neither hard nor soft. Just desperate. Like a man lost at sea, clinging to the only spot of dry land. Sensations curled in her belly, spreading outward until she was wrapped in the taste and feel of him. His warm tongue, his beard tickling her chin, his hands tangled in her hair and bare legs against hers. He rolled, putting her underneath him, cradling her head.

She was afraid of hurting him, but she needed to touch him. Gently, she held onto his shoulders, feeling the power and strength in the muscle and bone. He had no restraints. He was touching every part of her that he could reach. Part of her brain was sending off alarm bells, but her desire was too strong. She wanted his skin against hers. Him inside her. She moved her hips against his and he settled deeper between her thighs. His kilt had lifted, and all that separated them was the thin cloth of her panties.

A moment of clarity dulled her passion. What was she doing? The drug must be lowering her inhibitions. She didn't react this way. She knew the dangers involved with sex. She put her hands on his chest. "Stop."

He leaned back and looked at her. His eyes were glazed and he was breathing hard. "Stop?"

"This is too fast. I'm sorry."

"Forgive me." He started to roll off her.

"Don't move or I'll shoot." The guard stood outside the cell with his gun pointed at them. "Don't stop now. It's just getting good."

"Bastard," the prisoner muttered, shifting his weight off Anna. "What do you want?"

The guard looked at Anna. "I'd like some of that."

"Over my dead body," Anna said. Or his.

"I've never tried it that way, but I've heard there's some appeal," the guard said.

A low growl came from the prisoner's throat. Anna knew the guard was as good as dead. The only question was when, and who would get to him first, the prisoner or her.

"Don't touch her." The prisoner's voice was hard.

The guard sneered. "Or what? What will you do?"

"I'll drive my dirk straight through your bloody heart."

"But you don't have a dirk, do you?"

"Then I'll do it with my bare hands. I'll tear your chest open with my fingers and rip out your heart."

Hatred seethed from his eyes. "You're not so special. I don't know why he bothers with you. This experiment will fail, just like the other one. And you," he said, glaring at Anna. "I'd kill you now if you weren't worth more to me alive. If you don't want me, then you can do him. I'd just as soon watch anyway."

Anna's throat dried. "No," she croaked.

"Your choice. Him or me."

"No." The prisoner's body was tight with anger. "I'll tell the master what you've done."

There was a flash of fear in the guard's eyes, but he just laughed. "What'll he care? That's what you're here for anyway. Feeding and breeding. That's why I like working here. I get to watch the breeding."

Breeding? Anna met the prisoner's shocked gaze. They were going to breed him.

"Get on with it," the guard said. "This is better than what you'll be bred to later."

"No," the prisoner said again.

The guard aimed the gun at Anna. "Do it or I'll kill her. Then I'll kill you. I'll tell the master the hybrid killed you both. He's killed plenty of others. The master will believe it. Now pick up where you left off. Show her what women are good for."

The prisoner looked at Anna, his face hard. "We're in a mess here."

Anna nodded.

"If I could just get to him without that bloody pistol," he whispered, but they both knew it was impossible. "We can pretend. With what we're wearing, we might fool him. I don't know what else to do."

They had no choice. "What if you act like you're having . . . trouble. If you go slow, maybe he'll get frustrated and come in here himself. We can grab the gun and kill him." Her stomach heaved at the thought, but if it got him within it would be worth it. If they didn't kill him now, he wouldn't stop at one show, and he might want the next turn.

"All right."

"Stop your whispering and get on with it," the guard ordered.

The prisoner squared his shoulders and turned to the guard. "I've been wanting to do this anyway." He whispered to her, "I'm going to kiss you. Pretend to struggle." He took a breath and lowered his head. His lips were stiff against hers.

She pushed at his chest, and it wasn't just an act. She was working hard to stave off a full-blown panic. *Pretend you're sparring with him.*

"That's it," the guard said. "Take her clothes off."

The prisoner lifted his head, putting an inch between their mouths. "No," he called out. "I like it better this way."

"How are you going to do it with her panties on?" the guard asked.

"Panties?" The prisoner stilled. His fingers brushed the side of her hip where the elastic of her panties was. "These?"

He didn't know what panties were? Her crazy theory might not be so crazy after all. "Yes."

He tensed as he slid his hand underneath her gown. "I'm sorry."

"Do it." Anna felt the last of her strength draining. If they didn't get this over quickly, she was going to panic and start struggling for real. That could get them both killed. "Hurry," she whispered. "Let's get this over." She managed to pretend she was struggling while helping him get the panties off.

"Bollocks." He looked shaken. He moved his arm behind her neck, the other supporting his weight. He let his leg slide between hers and pressed his lips to hers. Anna wiggled back and forth as if struggling.

"Lift your kilt," the guard ordered.

"I'm going to kill him," the prisoner whispered as he lifted the front of his kilt.

Anna looked up at him as he lowered himself between her legs, and she knew from the deadly look in his eyes, this man was a warrior. A very old warrior if she was right.

They were flesh to flesh now, but with their bodies so close and his kilt covering his backside and her thighs, the guard couldn't see what they weren't doing. She gasped for effect. "Grunt or something," she whispered.

The prisoner grunted and pretended to thrust as she continued to struggle underneath him. She felt him growing hard against her. If they weren't careful, they'd be doing more than pretending.

"Raise your kilt," the guard said. "You're covering the goods."

The prisoner cursed. He lifted his kilt and pressed closer.

"What are you waiting for, warrior?" the guard growled.

"It's not easy with an audience. Maybe you want to come in and try."

Anna's whole body tensed, though she knew this was part of their plan to trap the guard.

"I'll get Lance to hold the gun," the guard said. "Maybe he'll want a turn too."

Anna dug her fingers into the prisoner's arms. She knew her nails were digging into his skin, but she was afraid to let go. Afraid the guard and Lance would come and take his place. Their plan hadn't worked. "No," Anna whispered. "You have to do it."

"What?"

"Do it," she choked out. "Or he will." That would be worse than death.

"I don't think I can," he said.

"You have to. I don't want him, and I don't want us to die." She couldn't let him die without him even knowing who he was. She knew who she was. Knew her path in life. He might have a family out there searching for him. Grieving. "We were about to do it before the guard came. Just pretend he's not there."

His jaw clenched, and he slipped his hand between her legs. He touched her softly, but still she tensed. "I'm sorry," he whispered.

A harsh breath left him as he gently opened her, and she felt a millisecond of something entirely unexpected as his warm flesh brushed against hers. His eyes widened, and she saw him swallow. "I'm so sorry." Then a nudge for entry, and he slipped just inside.

Anna closed her eyes, trying to block it out. It wasn't the physical discomfort. He was being gentle. It was her mind that felt violated.

The prisoner stilled, but his heart and his cock still throbbed. He was afraid for her, but his body was responding in spite of the danger. He had one quick thought that he should be glad his body cooperated, because if it hadn't, the guard would have done it himself, and he wouldn't have been gentle about it. If she was a whore, she was likely used to it, but he wasn't going to let anyone treat her rough.

The prisoner pushed farther inside. His cock should be limp as a piece of rope. But it wasn't. He didn't look at her. He couldn't, so he looked at her hair instead. "God forgive me," he uttered as he began moving inside her.

He tried to be gentle, but she was upset. Her eyes were closed, and her hands were on his waist, but it wasn't an embrace. Instinctively, she was trying to push him away.

He slowed down, trying to block the pleasure surging through his loins, but he was already worked up from before, and he hadn't been with a woman in too long. And never one so bonny. He didn't allow himself to get close to beautiful women. They were dangerous. But his cock didn't know that. He felt the tension rising. He had to stop before it was too late. Would the guard notice? The last stroke was too much. Pleasure erupted inside him, and he quickly pulled out, spilling his seed onto her thigh.

He lay quietly between her legs, horrified at what he'd done. Would the guard want a turn the minute he moved off her? If he came in without Lance, that'd be just fine. He would kill the bastard and get it over with. She lay silent beneath him, her eyes wide with fear. He knew that she waited for the guard as well.

"Not yet," she pled when he started to move off her. Her hands gripped his shirt. In the dead silence between them, he heard the guard chuckling, then the sound of footsteps as he moved away. A trickle of sweat ran down the prisoner's temple. He looked back to be sure the guard had left them.

"I'm sorry," he muttered yet again. He moved off her and dropped his kilt, then gently pulled her gown lower. He grabbed the cloth she'd washed with before and awkwardly cleaned off her leg.

She rose to her feet and tugged at her gown, though it

wouldn't go lower. Her hands were shaking as she reached for her undergarment.

The prisoner put the cloth under his kilt and cleaned himself off, turning his back to give her a moment's privacy to get decent. He heard her at the sink. When the water stopped running, he faced her. "Are you all right?"

She stood with her arms wrapped around her shoulders, her eyes on the floor. "It wasn't your fault. You had to do it."

But he didn't have to enjoy it. He felt like an utter bastard, not knowing whether to comfort her or leave her alone. He reached out for her, and she flinched. "Lass, look at me."

She met his gaze, but her lovely eyes were flat. "I'm fine. Sex is better than death." She retreated to the bench and sat on the far edge, tugging her gown so hard the prisoner thought it might tear. She stared at the floor, her face tight.

He stood helplessly in the middle of the floor. He went to her again, softly touching her. This time she didn't flinch. He rubbed her arm awkwardly, his own eyes stinging with shame. He'd spent himself in pleasure while she was in pain. He was no better than the guard.

"I . . . I shouldn't have . . ." He swallowed. "I've not been with a woman for so long . . ." But that was no bloody excuse.

"It's over. Neither one of us had a choice." Her eyes were cold and calm now. This was the woman who was brave enough to fight the guard. "He'll pay. I'm going to rip his balls off."

"No. I'll rip them off. One at a time. We have to find a way out of here." The guard wouldn't be satisfied now. He would want more.

Footsteps sounded on the stairs, and they heard the frantic voice of the guard.

"Master, I didn't expect you back this soon."

The master appeared around the corner, his long black hair and face bonny as a lass's.

The prisoner heard Anna gasp. "Tristol!"

CHAPTER SIX

ANNA JUMPED TO HER FEET, ADRENALINE FLOODING HER BODY as she stared at the ancient demon. Every warrior knew Tristol's name and his face—although he looked a little different than the pictures, more human—but Anna had never seen him in person. Where most demons were hideous, Tristol was beautiful.

He was rarely spotted. Faelan had been the last known warrior to see him, along with the other three demons who comprised the mysterious League of Demons. That was back in 1860 when Druan locked Faelan in the time vault. What was Tristol doing here? The prisoner had also moved, placing his body between her and Tristol.

This must be Tristol's fortress. Did he know that vampires were sneaking around the place? Or had he invited them? It was beginning to look as if the demons and vampires were working together.

Tristol moved closer, his movements so smooth she hardly saw him step. "Who brought her?" he asked the guard, his voice deadly quiet.

The guard shrank back. "She sneaked in, master."

"Sneaked in? The place is cloaked."

"I know, master. That's why I didn't kill her. I figured you would want to know how she got here. I think she's a warrior. She wears one of those necklaces."

Tristol walked closer to the cell. He was tall, stunning, his body graceful but full of power. His eyes were dark as sin. A curl of something dark and sweet rolled through Anna, numbing her shock and fear. She wanted to move closer, to feel his presence. She grabbed the prisoner's hand and felt him flinch when she touched the broken finger. She softened her grip.

Tristol's gaze hadn't left Anna. "That's because she is a warrior. The most powerful female warrior in the clan. Hello, Anna."

"You know me?" Anna was surprised. Rumor had it that Tristol was the Dark One's favorite demon. What would he know about her?

"Of course I know you. May I ask how you breeched my fortress?"

Anna stepped beside the prisoner. She could feel the tension in his body. She held tight to his hand as she fought Tristol's pull. "I followed one of the guards here."

"It was Lance, master," the guard said from behind Tristol.

"He wasn't supposed to leave," Tristol said.

"I told him that," the guard said nervously, "but he had some errands. If you know the truth of it, I don't trust him."

Tristol glanced at the guard. "Did you kill him?"

The guard shuffled nervously. "No. I thought you'd want to question him too."

"I do. Tell me, Anna, where you saw my guard."

"Let us out and I'll tell you."

Tristol laughed, his perfect white teeth glistening.

Anna felt the pull again. It was bizarre to have a demon affect her this way. She hated demons. She was born to hunt and kill them.

"I can't do that," Tristol said.

The prisoner was staring at Tristol, muscles tensed. "What do you want with us?" he asked.

The ancient demon studied the pair. His gaze moved from their faces to their linked hands. "I need your help."

"Our help? That's why you've been torturing me."

"Torture?" Tristol turned on the guard. "I told you to test him, not torture."

The guard backed up. "He's exaggerating, master."

"Does this look like an exaggeration?" Anna asked, glancing at the prisoner, whose bruised face and bloodstained clothing gave testament to his treatment. "You should see his back."

"That's because he tried to escape," the guard said.

"Liar," the prisoner said.

Tristol was very still. So still it made Anna afraid. The guard was shaking in his boots. Tristol turned toward him, whispered something, and left.

The guard stood in front of the prisoner's cell, his manner docile. "Time for another trip."

The prisoner's body tensed. "Move back and be quiet," he whispered to Anna, and then he stepped away from her, toward the door.

"Not you," the guard said. "Her. Let's go."

"No," the prisoner whispered. He gripped Anna's hand so hard it hurt. "No!"

The guard opened the cell and took out his gun. "Now."

The prisoner kept his body between Anna and the door. "No. Take me."

The guard pointed his gun at Anna. "Get out of the way, or I'll shoot her. You think she'd be just as pretty missing a finger or a toe? Maybe an ear."

Anna pulled her hand free and touched the prisoner's arm. "Please." If he didn't stop, they would hurt him again. She was afraid he couldn't withstand another beating. "I'm coming." *You fat toad.* She went to the door and slipped out. The guard locked it as the prisoner rattled the bars.

"Take me!" he roared. "You bloody bastard."

"Not this time," the guard said.

The minute Anna stepped outside, she turned on the guard. She spun and kicked him in the crotch. He doubled over, and Anna lunged for his gun, but the guard quickly recovered and jumped out of reach, pointing the weapon at her head.

"Stop," the prisoner pleaded.

Anna took her eyes off the angry guard and looked at the prisoner. His eyes were desperate. "Don't fight him. He'll make it worse. I beg you."

She clenched her jaw and let the guard march her toward the torture room. She glanced back and saw the prisoner pulling against the bars.

Tristol watched from the shadows as the warrior tried to bend the cell bars. His muscles bulged, and one of the bars gave. Magnificent. Tristol smiled. This was what he wanted to harness. Even brutalized—and the guard would pay for taking it too far—the warrior was powerful and fiercely loyal. He would fight to the death for Anna. Both were characteristics Tristol hoped to breed into his vampires.

And Anna was a surprise. A pleasant one. She had a body and face that would bring human males to their knees. Tristol wasn't usually attracted to human females, but this was the closest he'd gotten to Anna, and he had to admit that she was one of the most stunning of any species that he'd seen. Even imprisoned, with her gown torn and dirty, she exuded beauty, power, and grace. But that beauty was wrapped in fury now. If not for the gun, the guard would already be dead instead of nursing sore balls.

Both warriors would have to be moved. Tristol didn't trust the bars or his guards now. It was obvious that Bart was lying. He would pay for abusing the experiments. Lance would pay too. It was time to take charge of this experiment. The outcome was too important to let anything stand in the way, even the Dark One's frequent summons, which were interfering with Tristol's plans.

The breeding plan had been twofold. Feed his vampires some of Faelan's blood to strengthen them and then breed the warrior with his most powerful female vampire. If the outcome was successful, he would gather more warriors. He hadn't planned to use female warriors yet, since they couldn't produce as many children as quickly. But since Anna was already here, why waste the opportunity? He would breed her with one of his male vampires. There was no one quite like Anna. No one with her pedigree, though she didn't realize it. He had only discovered it himself recently. If he could combine her strength and prowess with that of his strongest male vampire, the results could have great potential.

A roar sounded down the corridor, and Tristol had a brilliant idea. His hybrid had some vampire blood, but was still mostly human. Tristol hadn't been able to determine his ability to reproduce since the hybrid killed all the female vampires as soon as they were brought to him. There was more warrior blood in him than vampire blood. Perhaps he would recognize Anna as a fellow warrior and not kill her. With Anna's genetics and the hybrid's, a child born to them could prove to have extraordinary abilities. If the plan succeeded, then he would give her to his best male vampire. Or keep her for himself.

He hadn't created his own offspring because a child could become a weak link. Most ancient demons avoided procreating for the same reason. The other demons would use the child against the father. Especially in his case. All demons were bitterly jealous of his position. But two of the League were gone. After Voltar was destroyed, Tristol would have greater freedom to pursue his goals.

In a black mist, he moved to the cell where the warrior was still struggling to break free. "Calm yourself," he said to the warrior. He didn't want him injuring himself to get to Anna.

The warrior had no choice but to stop moving, but his face was still filled with rage. Along with the swelling, he made a frightening sight.

"Sleep. You will need your rest."

The warrior tried to fight it, but his eyelids started to droop, and he leaned against the wall.

"Sleep," Tristol said again, and when the warrior slumped to the floor, he went to catch up with the guard and Anna.

Anna wanted to rip the guard into pieces. She was considering giving it another go when Tristol appeared in front of them. She stopped in surprise. Where had he come from? Again, she felt the compelling pull and had to force herself to stand still.

"Change of plans. Put her back there," he said, nodding deeper into the dungeon.

"But he's—"

"Yes. Exactly."

The guard's look of surprise didn't bode well with Anna. When she glanced back at Tristol, he was gone, as if he'd simply vanished. She wasn't aware of any demons with that ability.

"Let's go then," the guard said.

"Where are you taking me?"

"To see him." He gave her a cruel smile.

Him? Surely he didn't mean the hybrid. "Are you taking me to the hybrid?"

"You know about him?"

"I heard you talking. What is he?"

"You'll see." He sneered at her. "And he'll probably be the last thing you see. The other women didn't last ten minutes with him. And they were special." The guard sniffed Anna. "You smell good. Really good. Maybe he'll like you."

"Get your nose away from me or I'll break it."

"Let's see if you talk that tough after he's finished with you."

The hybrid must be part of the breeding plan. God no.

Anna considered her options. The guard was out of reach. If she attacked him, he'd probably shoot her. Even if he didn't, if she managed to kill him, Tristol would come after her. He was probably watching now. She'd never seen anyone move with such stealth. She couldn't attack Tristol without being assigned. That would be instant death. And Tristol would take out his anger on the prisoner.

The only thing she could do was wait for a better opportunity. Where? In a locked cell? Piss-poor options. Better than dying now and leaving the prisoner alone in this hellhole.

The guard forced her down the long, dark corridor. They paused at a doorway blocked by iron bars. The guard pushed a lever, and the bars lifted.

Lance appeared behind them. "What are you doing here?"

The guard paused, repositioning the gun at Anna's head. "Taking her to *him*."

Lance seemed surprised. "He's going to breed her?"

Anna's throat tightened. The other man she'd felt in the cell when she woke up must have been the hybrid. He hadn't killed her then, or done anything worse. Maybe he wouldn't this time.

"She'll probably be killed like the others," the guard said. "Why are you here? The master is looking for you."

"Tristol's servant had a question for you. I can take this one if you want to go."

The guard looked hesitantly at Anna. "Hell, she'll die anyway," he muttered. He handed Lance the gun and hurried away.

Lance's helpful expression faded the minute the guard left. "Just you and me now," he said, pressing the gun to her head. She felt a sting in her arm.

"What was in that needle?" she asked, rubbing the spot. Had he drugged her or poisoned her?

"Something to keep you from fighting back. When he's finished with you, you won't be talking to anyone." Lance laughed and steered her several more yards toward a thick iron door. "Step back."

Anna debated whether she could take him. He wasn't as strong as the fat guard, but he had the gun, and the drug was already kicking in.

He unlocked the door and shoved her inside. "Good riddance," he said, slamming the door.

She pressed herself close to the door and reached for her talisman, forgetting it was gone. She searched the shadows of the dark room. There wasn't even a sconce here. Slowly she made out shapes in the dark. A sink, like the one in her cell, and a toilet, a bench. This one even had a bed. And someone was in it. A sound came from the bed, something between a growl and a cry.

She stayed near the door, fists clenched, ready for an attack. But her legs were already wobbling from the drugs Lance had given her. This would probably be her last fight. Images raced through her mind. People she loved. The people she considered her family—Angus, Ronan, Faelan, Duncan, even irritating Brodie with his pranks. And the women. She'd never been close to women, only Sorcha, until Bree and Shay. Then there were the people she hated—like her father. You didn't have to know someone to hate them. And lastly, the prisoner. She couldn't leave him alone with these monsters. He was powerful, but he was hurt.

The figure on the bed sat up. The next minute he had her by the throat. Nothing could move that fast except a vampire. He—she could tell by his size and smell he was a male—stood close, sniffing her. A burst of adrenaline cut through the fog of the drug. Lifting her arms between his, she jabbed him under the chin and shoved his chest. She didn't have any weapons to pierce his heart or remove his head, so she went for his groin, hoping vampires had balls to go with their fangs. But he was too quick and jerked back. She glimpsed dark hair and white teeth, but no fangs.

She only saw his face for a moment. In the time it took her to blink, he flipped her over and lifted her gown. Not again. But he'd stopped. His hands were running over her battle marks. Then he leaned over her, close as a lover, and put his head next to hers. He sniffed her. Anna stayed still and tried to think how to get out of this. She would die before she let him rape her. The prisoner was different. She felt something for him. He'd been kind . . . and gentle.

Slowly the hybrid rose, pulling her with him. He sniffed her again as his fingers dragged along her skin, brushing her hair off her cheek. She heard a short, hard exhale, the sound loaded with shock. "I know you," he whispered.

And she knew his voice. But he was supposed to be dead.

CHAPTER SEVEN

THE DYING MAN PULLED IN ANOTHER SHALLOW, WET BREATH. *"You have to protect it. Swear you'll protect it."*

"I swear," the prisoner said, watching the man's life fade from his eyes.

The prisoner woke with a start. He was in the cell, not in a forest with a bleeding, dying man. Anna! He jumped to his feet and stumbled to the cell door. He was dizzy, his legs weak. Bloody potions. He put his foot against one bar and wedged his back against the wall, pushing with all his strength. His legs shook too badly to do much good. Curse the bastards. Curse them all. His eyes blurred as the guard appeared, carrying the woman. She wasn't moving. Was she dead?

"I'm surprised you can stand after I drugged you." The guard bent down and laid her on the floor outside the cell.

"What have you done to her?" The prisoner knelt and put his arm through the bar he'd bent. Her hand was still warm.

"You've bent the bars," the guard grumbled. "You'll have to be moved. Stay back."

"What are you doing?"

"If you want her in there with you, then move away from the door."

He stood and moved out of the way. The guard unlocked the door and dumped Anna inside. The prisoner couldn't attack with his legs weak as twine and Anna injured. He knelt and put his ear to her breast. Her heartbeat was strong. She was just unconscious. What had they done to her? He checked her over. No cuts or bruises anywhere that could be seen. Did he dare look elsewhere? He settled instead for running his hands over her. No blood, but she moaned and started to shiver.

Gently, he picked her up and carried her to the corner where his blanket lay. Cradling her head, he laid her down on the blanket and sank to the floor beside her. When he was situated, he lifted her onto his lap, holding her against his chest, and covered them both with the blanket. She shivered against him, but in minutes, he felt her skin growing warmer.

They hadn't beaten her, but the guard might have assaulted her. At least she was alive.

Her eyes opened, wide with alarm, and her body tensed.

"It's all right," he said, loosening his hold.

"You," she mumbled, and sank back against him. He pulled her closer. Her body was limp. The guard must have given her a potion too.

From somewhere in the dungeon, the other prisoner roared, but this time it sounded different. Lonely. They had to find a way out before the guard took her again. But his eyelids were drooping.

Tristol watched the young male drag the screaming woman through the veil that cloaked the fortress. The boy knew they weren't allowed to feed here unless the human was one of theirs. If the fortress was discovered by humans, he would have to move it again. If the underworld found it, there would be hell to pay. He was too close to accomplishing his goal to worry about moving.

He needed four things now. His breeding plan, the Book of Battles, the emerald, and the death of Voltar. Tristol would prefer the warriors kill Voltar so he didn't have to hide it from the Dark One, but if the warriors failed he would do it himself. Everything was falling into place. He would not allow a reckless youth to ruin his plans now.

He shifted into a black mist and rushed at the pair. The young male vampire turned at the last second, his eyes wide with horror as Tristol materialized in front of him. His face went even paler than it had been.

"You know the rules." Tristol searched his memory for the man's name. "Philip, you were told never to bring anyone here. We have humans on site for the job. If you need to feed otherwise, you must do it discreetly outside of this place."

"I'm sorry, master. It won't happen again."

"No. It won't." Tristol knocked Philip out before draining his blood, and then he turned to the human, who had fainted. When he was finished with both, he left them there and continued to the house. Philip's parents would not be happy. He was their only son. It was unfortunate, for vampires were too few, but secrecy was crucial. His plan could not be compromised now. Tristol's personal servant, Joseph, met him at the door. He trusted his servant more than anyone.

"There are two bodies near the veil," Tristol said. "Dispose of them."

"Yes, master." He handed Tristol a cloth to wipe his mouth.

"Move Faelan and Anna to the secret tower tonight. No one is to know they're there."

"Shouldn't the guards do that?"

"They won't be here long. They've been abusing Faelan."

"Move the hybrid as well?"

"No. Leave him there for now. Has Joquard returned?"

"Not yet."

What was taking him so long? He should have found the Book of Battles by now. Tristol wanted it returned to him and hidden away where other demons couldn't find it. They all wanted the book so they could learn the name of the warrior assigned to destroy them and kill the warrior before he, or she, reached maturity. All but Tristol. His name wasn't in the book, and he had to be careful that the other demons didn't ask why.

"I have to leave again."

"So soon?" Joseph asked.

"The Dark One has summoned me. He's talking of restructuring things. He's becoming tiresome."

"Careful how you speak of him," Joseph said. "The Dark One rules the underworld."

For now, Tristol thought. After his breeding plan proved successful, and after the emerald was found and Voltar was dead, Tristol would give the Dark One the Book of Battles as a gift to persuade him to welcome his vampire children back into the fold. And in time, they would take over the world and the underworld. Tristol would rule it all. "Have you seen Lance?"

"No, master."

"Have him killed when you find him." Tristol walked through the large room, which was lit by sconces he'd liberated from one of England's lustier kings. He'd liberated more than the king's possessions, some of his best lords and ladies too. Even one of his wives. Royalty, peasants, it made no difference. The offspring between humans and vampires refused to thrive any more than the offspring of pure-bred vampires. The army he'd worked so hard to rebuild was headed for extinction, again, if he didn't find a way to strengthen them and improve breeding. His hope now rested in his enemy. Warriors. They were human, but stronger, faster, better. If this plan was successful, he would create an empire of warrior vampires.

The vampires who had been lounging about the room stood as Tristol walked in. He gave them a brief nod and continued upstairs to his private rooms, where no one was allowed except his servant. He opened the door to his suite and stepped inside. The furnishings were lavish, with antiques and trophies that had begun to lose their appeal.

He opened his closet, which was the size of a small house, and stripped off his clothes. He reached for a black robe and slipped it on as he approached the secret door to the dungeon. The lever was hidden behind a long mirror he'd taken from yet another king. It was a hobby of his, stealing from royalty. When the door to the passageway opened, he shifted into a mist and streaked through the crooks and turns until he reached the dungeon.

He found Bart in the corridor. The guard lowered his head in deference to Tristol and moved aside. A cry of rage sounded behind the thick iron doors at the far end of the dungeon. "Was the mating successful this time?"

Bart hesitated only a second. "He didn't kill her, so I assume so, master."

"Did you drug both of them as I asked?"

"Yes, master. As soon as they fell asleep."

"Good." Tristol moved so fast the guard had no time for fear. He was dead before his body dropped. Tristol grabbed the key and moved to the Mighty Faelan's cell. The warrior sat against the wall, holding Anna in his arms. Protective, even though he was unconscious. What would it be like to have someone care enough to want to protect him at risk to their own life? The closest thing he had was Joseph. The others feared him, admired him, lusted after him. But they didn't love him. The only ones who had truly loved him had died more than a thousand years ago.

CHAPTER EIGHT

Lance slipped through the forest. The wolves wouldn't start prowling the grounds until midnight. He hurried to his car, hoping this would be his last time inside the veil. He drove quickly, parking in the appointed dark alley. He checked his watch. Where was he? He turned as a dark shape materialized from the shadows, huge even in human form. He looked like a giant biker with his faded leather pants, wild brown hair, and rugged face. "Master, you're here."

"Is everything ready?"

"Yes. Tristol left the fortress. You have two days."

Voltar folded his massive arms over his chest. "Lead me to the warrior."

"Tonight? The wolves will start moving soon." And he didn't want to be there. He'd heard Tristol order Joseph to have him killed. But he was just as afraid of the demon standing in front of him.

"Then we'd best hurry. I want my warrior, and I want that hybrid dead."

Lance didn't mention the woman. He didn't want Voltar to know she'd followed him. And by now she should be dead.

The prisoner felt unusually comfortable. He couldn't recall ever feeling a bed so soft. He must be dreaming. He heard a soft cry and turned to find Anna lying beside him. They weren't in the dungeon. They were in a bed. A big bed. He sat up and discovered he was naked. Anna's hand was knotted in the covers, her cheeks wet with tears. Had he ravished her again? His stomach knotted. He lifted the edge of the sheet and saw her bare shoulder. She was naked as well. Where the devil were their clothes? The last thing he remembered was holding her after the guard threw her back in the cell. He must have given them another sleeping potion. Damn the things.

He wanted to touch her, but he was afraid he'd frighten her. He still felt shame at the memory of what he'd done. Knowing he'd probably saved her from death, or worse, didn't soothe his guilt. He'd taken pleasure from the act. What kind of depraved soul was he?

Was that why she cried? Reliving what he'd done or what had happened after they'd taken her away? She wasn't the crying sort. He'd known brave women—his mother was brave—but this one acted with boldness and strength he'd never seen in a woman. His mother? He got a glimpse of a fair-haired woman, but it vanished like a wisp of smoke.

Anna let out a small sob. He moved a bit closer and stroked her cheek. She turned toward his hand, and his heart flipped a few times before stilling in his chest.

"Don't," she whimpered.

What had they done to her? Or was it him she dreamed of? He must be the reason for at least some of her tears, and he reckoned that made it his duty to soothe her. He bunched the covers between them, creating a wall of sorts, and then held her closer, stroking her back through the bedding. He would get her out of this place and back to her family. To her friends that she'd told him about. To safety. That would be his mission from here on out. To right the wrong he'd done to her. *How can you undo something like that, you bloody bastard?*

He didn't realize he'd spoken aloud, but Anna jerked awake and bolted from the bed.

The prisoner's jaw dropped. Anna looked down and gasped, then put her hands over her female parts. Damnation. Before he could drag his eyes away, she jumped back underneath the covers as quickly as she'd left them. "I'm naked."

"Aye." And the sight would forever be burned into his mind.

She looked at his bare chest. "You too?"

"Someone took our clothes."

"And moved us," Anna said, looking around the room. "Where are we?"

"I don't know. The last thing I remember is the guard bringing you back to the cell. You were unconscious. Are you hurt?"

She frowned. "I don't think so."

"What did they do to you?"

The two delicate lines deepened in her forehead. "I don't know. I remember the guard opening a door. It was dark inside. I saw someone . . . I remember a roar." Her eyes grew wide, the color startlingly beautiful. "The hybrid. I think the hybrid was there."

A cold hand squeezed the prisoner's guts. The hybrid. The one they'd referred to as a monster. In a place with a breeding plan? What had they done to her? She hadn't been tortured. That quick glance at her body had told him she was uninjured. On the outside anyway, but some injuries didn't easily show. "You don't recall anything?"

She shook her head.

He recalled how bravely she'd fought against the guard. Something must have happened. Why take her away and do nothing to her? Had she blocked it? "Perhaps they've taken your memories too."

"Lance gave me a shot. The drug must have made me forget what happened. But I do remember Tristol." She looked like she wanted to jump up. "I can't believe he's here, right under our noses. I have to go back and warn the clan."

"You know him?" The odd thing was that he felt he did too.

"Every warrior knows Tristol. He's a demon. A powerful demon."

"Demon." As he repeated the word, a memory struck him so hard he felt as if he'd been kicked in the head by a horse.

The man's skin thickened, the bones lengthening, not human. Then a child screamed. He knew the child. Was it his?

He rubbed his head.

"What's wrong?" Anna asked.

"My head. What do you mean, a demon?" More flashes. *Ugly faces and sharp teeth.*

"Humans aren't the only creatures on this earth that walk upright. Demons disguise themselves as humans, but they're trying to destroy us. That's where warriors come in. They protect humans by destroying demons or locking them away. And I'm almost certain you're a warrior." Anna touched his chest, running her fingers over the marks there. They were tingling. "These tattoos on your chest. Do you remember getting them?"

His hand immediately went to his chest, and his fingers brushed against hers. "No."

"Did you have a talisman, a necklace, when you came here?"

His hand moved higher. He didn't feel anything, but he imagined something warm there. Something metal. "I think so. I'm not certain."

"You touched your neck when I mentioned a talisman. I think your brain is trying to remember."

"You think I'm a warrior?"

"Everything about you says you are. These marks on your chest. I'm sure they're battle marks. Each warrior is marked according to his weaknesses and strengths. Most males have them on their chest. Mine are on my lower back."

"Yours? You're a warrior? A lass?" In spite of his throbbing head, he gave her an indulgent smile. The trauma of this place must have gotten to her.

Anna's shoulders straightened. Her beautiful eyes were fierce. "I'm a warrior."

"You're not a . . . prostitute?"

"What?" She gaped at him.

"I thought . . . your dress, it was . . . short."

"No, I'm not a prostitute." If she spoke the truth, and he believed she did, she should have been more offended. As it was, she looked intrigued, as if she'd solved a mystery. "I'm from Clan Connor."

He struggled to catch his next breath. "Connor?"

Her eyes narrowed, making them look like slivers of jewels. "Do you know the name?"

"I don't know." But his head felt like it would split down the middle. "How could I be one of these warriors and not remember such a thing?"

"It's amazing that you're not a vegetable after all they've done to you. All the drugs and beatings. After we get out of here, I'll take you to a doctor I know. Maybe that'll help us find out who you are."

It gave him a warm feeling that she had said *us* after all she'd suffered at his hands. "I'm sorry for everything."

"If you apologize again, I'm going to hit you." She stared at him, her face fierce.

While he was trying to figure out what to possibly say, she looked around the room. "We have to figure out where we are."

"It's a sight better than that dungeon. It looks like a tower." The room was round, with stone floors covered by plush rugs that must have cost a fortune. The bed they were in was a four-poster. The comforter was a rich brocade like he'd seen once in a palace in India. India? Another memory? Tapestries and sconces hung on the walls, while ornate tables and chairs decorated the room.

"I don't care if it's the White House. I want away from this place," Anna said.

He didn't know what a white house was, but he was all for leaving too. "Got any fig leaves? I've broken out of towers before, but never naked—damnation, I think I remembered something else. A castle . . . and screams." He was so encouraged by the glimpse, he started to get up, but stopped when he saw her eyes widen. "We can't stay under the covers forever. There's got to be something in here we can wear. I'm going to see what I can find." He slipped out of bed, holding a pillow over his groin. He walked around the room, looking for anything that might be used for clothing, taking care to keep his arse turned away from her. He must have failed because in a minute she cleared her throat.

"You need another pillow," she said.

He glanced back at her and saw her quickly look away. "Or you could just close your eyes."

She snorted. Snorted?

Did all female warriors make such rude sounds? Though she looked very bonny when she did it. He was relieved she was acting more like the brave, bold woman he'd seen when she'd first arrived. Not the one who'd looked haunted and broken. He didn't particularly like bold women, but it was the lesser of two evils. "Why would they move us from the dungeon to a tower?" He opened another drawer and found it empty. "And why did they take our clothes?"

"Remember what the guard said about breeding? Tristol mentioned testing. Maybe you passed the tests."

"You think Tristol is planning to breed me to his demons? Like hell he will. I'll rip his bloody bonny head off, demon or no."

"I doubt that."

He glared at her. "You think I can't do it?" How could he protect a woman who had no confidence in him? Hell, how could he protect a woman when he didn't know his own name?

She shrugged one shoulder, a lovely shoulder. "It wasn't an insult. Tristol is a demon of old."

"What does that mean?"

"The ancient demons are incredibly powerful. They have to be assigned."

"Assigned?" The headache was coming back.

"They have to be matched to a warrior's skills and strength."

"Assigned or not, I won't sit here and let him breed me like a stallion." And what about her? Was she part of this breeding plan too? If this Tristol didn't have some use for her, he would have killed her. *I remember a roar, she'd said.* The only roar he'd heard had come from the hybrid. A male.

He saw a door and opened it, thinking it might be a closet.

"Bollocks. What's that?"

"Have you found a way out?" Anna grabbed a pillow from the bed and joined him. "It's only a bathroom."

"Bathroom?" There was a tub, but it was large enough for a small family. It had basins and a pot like the one in his cell, and another contraption enclosed in glass. It was strange looking, but he had a feeling he'd seen one before. He tried to focus on the strange room and not all the bare skin sticking out from behind the pillow next to him. He stopped and turned to the tower door. "Someone's coming."

"I don't hear anything."

A moment later, a voice ordered, "Open it!"

The prisoner grabbed a heavy vase from a table and stepped in front of Anna.

"The master will be angry," another voice said.

"I'll do it myself." The door flew open, and a man stepped in. He was dressed in black and had long blond hair, pretty as a woman's, and pale blue eyes.

Anna softly gasped and stepped beside him. The bloody woman wasn't easy to protect.

Another man rushed into the room, holding a box. Tristol's manservant. He'd seen him a few times before. "Are you a fool?" he asked the blond, without his usual quiet dignity. "Someone might have seen you. You know he has this section secured."

The stranger came closer, his movements smooth, as if he slid across an icy loch. "I'll be damned." His blue eyes moved intently over the prisoner, from the pillow covering his groin to his hair. "The resemblance is amazing. I would believe it myself, but I saw him recently, and he didn't have this." He reached out and tugged the prisoner's beard.

The prisoner reacted so quickly it surprised even him. He grabbed the pale-haired man's arm, gripping it hard.

The man hissed, revealing broken fangs.

The prisoner jumped back in alarm.

"Who are you?" the blond man asked.

The prisoner didn't answer.

"Who wants to know?" Anna asked.

The blond frowned and then looked at Anna. "So this is why no one can find you. How did she get here?" he asked the servant.

"Apparently she sneaked inside the dungeon."

The pale-haired man looked around the room. "This is as good a place as any to keep them while I unravel this mystery." He moved toward the door. "Say nothing to Tristol. I don't know who he has here, but it's not the Mighty Faelan. I'll try to find the real warrior and capture him before Tristol realizes he's been duped. Otherwise, all our lives are going to be hell."

He breezed out of the room, and the servant stared at the prisoner. His face seemed to ripple, and for a moment the prisoner thought he glimpsed a woman's face.

He turned to them, his expression blank now. "I'll be back with food."

"I'd rather have answers and some bloody clothes," the prisoner said.

"The master has new clothes for you as well." He set a box down. "I believe you'll find everything here."

"Did you see his teeth?" he asked when the servant had gone.

"Fangs. He's a vampire."

"Vampires don't exist." Not anymore. He frowned. Was that another memory?

"I wish, but I'm afraid they do."

"Are you certain?"

"I killed one on the way here. And unless I'm mistaken, this blond is the one Ronan's been following."

"Damnation."

"You say that a lot."

"What?"

"Damnation."

"My apologies. I shouldn't curse in front of a woman."

"I don't mind. I just know someone else who says that."

"This Ronan who's following the vampire?" She seemed overly familiar with too many men.

"No, not Ronan."

"Who is he?"

"A warrior. We're part of the same clan. He's obsessed with the blond vampire. He got away from Ronan when we were fighting Druan."

"Druan. I think I've heard that name before."

"I'm not surprised. Every warrior knows his name. He's powerful."

"Like Tristol."

"Yes. I have to let the clan know that Tristol is here and that he's working with vampires. Obviously he wants Faelan for his breeding plan. Bree isn't going to like that."

"Is she another warrior?"

"And then some."

He didn't understand her meaning, but they had other priorities. "Then let's get dressed. I don't feel like fighting in nothing but my skin."

Anna took her clothes into the bathroom while he shaved and dressed in the clean kilt and shirt the man had left. When she reappeared, his mouth dropped. Her dress was indecent, cut up to her thighs and down between her breasts.

"You can stop gaping," Anna said.

The prisoner averted his gaze. "Surely you don't plan to wear that."

"It's this or the sheet."

He looked at the bed, as if considering it. "How can you even climb in that garment?"

"I've climbed in worse."

"He's coming back."

The servant entered the room and set down a tray of food, better than what they'd been fed in the dungeon. Her stomach growled, but there was no time to eat. As soon as he turned to go, Anna grabbed a napkin and put it behind her back. Just before the door closed, she darted forward and stuck the folded napkin between the casing and the lock.

The prisoner looked impressed.

"The oldest trick in the world," she said. She put her ear to the door. "It's quiet."

"Wait a moment until we're certain he's gone."

"We can't wait long. He'll be back." She didn't want either of them here for whatever Tristol had planned. Flashes of a dark room and mournful cries stirred in her mind, but she couldn't sharpen the image. She wasn't sure she wanted to. "We need weapons. I wish I had my talisman."

His hand rose to his neck. "I know that word."

"Talismans are a warrior's weapon against demons, though they don't work on vampires. The only way to kill the creatures is to cut off their heads or pierce their hearts. We need a sword or something sharp."

The prisoner braced his foot against the four-poster bed and yanked, breaking off a jagged piece of the antique post. He grinned and gave it a couple of practice swings, as a warrior might with a sword. "Like this?"

"Good thinking." Anna broke off another post, and the prisoner emptied a pillowcase and put the food and bottled water inside. Armed with their crude weapons, they slowly opened the door. The structure they were in was round with stairs circling the outer perimeter. "We're definitely in a tower."

"That should make it easier to determine where we are," the prisoner said.

"I don't know. This fortress had several towers. Guess we're going down. We'll have to risk running into someone."

"Towers often have a door leading to the roof. Perhaps we can climb down and avoid getting caught."

He was remembering more about his past. She had her own theories, but she didn't want to spring them on him. Now wasn't the time. "If I remember the size of this fortress, we'd have a long drop if we fell. But it's worth a try."

They checked the small area but didn't find any other way out. "I guess we take the stairs," he said.

They crept down the narrow staircase, armed with their bed-post stakes and the pillowcase of food that the prisoner held in his other hand. "We should be nearing the bottom," Anna said after they had descended dozens of steps.

"I hear voices."

His hearing must be excellent. Hers was as well, and yet she hadn't heard anything. "We'll have to be very quiet from here on out."

"I'm not as light of foot as my brothers," he whispered. "They say I stomp like a bull—" He stopped and frowned.

"Your memory is definitely coming back." If his brothers were quieter than he was, then they were damned good.

They continued without speaking and soon came to a door. The voices were louder. "We must be on the second or third floor," Anna whispered. "I'll check." The door was unlocked. She eased it open and saw a large room filled with people. Before she could move, a woman walked by. There wasn't even time to shut the door. Anna froze, but the woman moved on without a glance. A man followed behind her, pausing briefly to sniff the air as he passed.

"They can't see us," the prisoner whispered after they were gone.

"It's cloaked," Anna whispered. "He's cloaked the tower, just like he did the fortress."

"What do you mean?"

"He puts a cloak around things, like a magic veil, so it's invisible from the outside. This entire fortress is cloaked. No one would know it's here unless they ran into it. That's how I found it. Problem is, we don't know how far the cloak extends around the tower, what its inner dimensions are, and how it works. Once we step into this room, they might see us."

"And just because they can't see us doesn't mean they can't hear us," he said. A second man approached. He slowed and sniffed, lips drawing back to reveal fangs. Anna stood still, not breathing. The vampire frowned and continued walking.

"Vampires," she whispered. "This sucks. They have a really strong sense of smell." At least that's what she'd gathered from her brief experience with the creatures. "We need to test the cloak. I'll step out and see—"

The prisoner pulled her back. "I'll do it." He scowled. First, he extended his bedpost stake out a couple of feet. No one in the room seemed to notice. "I think if we stay close to the wall we'll be all right. Follow me."

The prisoner led the way. Backs against the wall, they crept past the vampires lounging in the richly furnished room. The lighting was low, but Anna could see that some of the creatures were elegant, lean and pale, some Goth. Several couples were drinking in dark corners. Not from glasses, but with fangs sunk into throats as bodies writhed in passion.

"Bloody hell," the prisoner whispered just above his breath.

A gaunt-looking man walked by, his eyes ringed with red. He stopped and turned, looking straight at Anna through the veiled air. His nostrils flared, and he stepped closer.

Anna froze, her hand tightening on the bedpost stake. She felt the prisoner beside her, but she didn't dare move or glance at him. Anna closed her eyes and focused on the prisoner's scent and not the bloodlust in the vampire's eyes.

The vampire stepped closer. His lips pulled back, baring sharp fangs. Anna looked deep into his red-rimmed eyes as he stared blankly at her. The prisoner's fingers tightened on his stake, and he lowered the pillowcase of food to the ground. If the vampire took one more step Anna knew the prisoner would attack.

"Don't," she mouthed, feeling for his hand. Across the room, a woman glanced in their direction. Smiling, she called out to the man. He sniffed again, shook his head, and walked to the woman. She lifted her hair, and the vampire sank his teeth into her neck. Her body went stiff, either with pleasure or pain.

"We've got to get out of this room or go back to the tower," the prisoner whispered.

"I'm not going back."

He pointed to an elaborate door at one end of the room. "Let's try to reach that door. It seems to be the only one that's close to the wall." He led her past another couple. Anna looked back and didn't see the prisoner had stopped to avoid the servant. She plowed into his back causing both of them to stumble. Her stake flew out of her hand and landed at the feet of the red-eyed vampire. He raised his head, his fangs red with blood. The other occupants of the room looked at the bedpost and then lifted red-tinged eyes to Anna and the prisoner.

CHAPTER NINE

WE'RE OUTSIDE THE VEIL," ANNA SAID.
"Run," someone yelled. Anna thought it might have been
the servant. The prisoner grabbed Anna's arm as she reached down
for her stake, and they started to run through the dimly lit room.
They didn't get far. Hisses cut through the air as the vampires
rushed at them in a streak of light, circling them. Anna and the
prisoner stood together, stakes gripped in their hands as they faced
the fanged creatures standing only feet away.

Anna was sure they would have attacked immediately if they
weren't trying to figure out who they were and where they'd come
from. The vampire with red-rimmed eyes moved first. He leapt at
her, and she was pulled aside as the prisoner yanked her arm,
flinging her behind him. He swung his bedpost like a sword,
knocking the red-eyed monster to the floor. Anna attacked, driving her stake through his heart. He vanished in a pile of dust.

The others looked stunned. "You have to cut off their heads or
pierce their hearts," she yelled, taking advantage of their hesitation.

"If I had a bloody sword, it would help," the prisoner said.
Another one rushed them, and he drove his bedpost into its heart
with one powerful thrust.

Definitely a warrior. But there were too many vampires. They would never defeat them all. Someone screamed, and everyone turned. A man stood at the back of the room. He towered over them all, a giant of a man with long, brown hair, and dressed like a biker. He let out a growl, and his skin stretched and bones lengthened, until he didn't resemble man, but a monster with gray skin and yellow eyes.

"Oh my God." Anna felt her mouth drop.

"Kill them all!" the demon roared, and more demons burst into the room. Hisses filled the air as the vampires rushed at the demon and his allies.

"We have to leave. Now," Anna cried. But the prisoner stared at the demon, his face as pale as his shirt. Anna grabbed his hand and yanked. "Come on!"

He moved ahead, using his body to shield her from the fighting creatures. The room echoed with screams and roars. The vampires were fast, but the demons were stronger and appeared to be winning.

The prisoner tried to open the fancy door, but it was locked. He stepped back and threw his weight against it, and when it gave, he shoved Anna inside the dark room. She found a light switch and turned it on. Treasures and antiques filled every space.

"Damnation." The prisoner glanced around, grabbed a heavy cabinet, and dragged it in front of the door. "See if there's a door or a window."

They ran around the room, searching for an exit as screams sounded outside the door. Anna passed a shelf filled with every kind of emerald imaginable—emerald rings, emerald amulets, emerald daggers. She yanked aside a pair of heavy burgundy draperies and saw they were still at least three stories above the stone wolves guarding the front of the fortress. "We're not getting out this way unless you know how to fly—" Anna glanced over and saw a woman, wantonly dressed, holding a broken bedpost.

"This is no time to be worrying about how bonny you look." The prisoner appeared next to the woman, his handsome face—not quite as swollen now—wearing a frown.

It was only their reflection in a mirror. Anna felt a sense of weightlessness as she stared at the image. The mirror troubled her in spite of the fact that demons and vampires were fighting outside, and she and the prisoner would probably be killed by the victors.

The prisoner pulled her away. "Keep looking. There might be a secret door."

Probably. The room reeked of secrets. But where? They didn't have much time. Avoiding the mirror, she helped him search the room as screams continued outside. His kilt swirled around powerful legs as he pulled a bookshelf away from the wall.

"Here, I've found something." He pointed to a hairline crack in the stone, the size of a small door.

A crash sounded behind them. The heavy cabinet blocking the door fell to the floor. The huge demon stood in the doorway. This close, there was no mistake. It was Voltar.

All warriors knew what the demons of old looked like. Photos and information about the demons were listed in the clan's databases, even known human aliases. Anna had never expected to encounter Voltar. He was one of the most powerful demons in existence. Why was he in Tristol's fortress killing vampires? Why were vampires even here? They hadn't looked like intruders. They'd looked right at home.

The prisoner moved in front of Anna, gripping his stake.

"I've been waiting a long time for you," the demon said to the prisoner as he advanced slowly toward them. He smiled, his teeth sharp in a thickset jaw.

"Don't—" Anna warned the prisoner.

But he was already rushing at Voltar with a war cry that made the hair on Anna's arms stand. He drove the pointed end of the stick at the demon's head, but Voltar laughed and ducked clear.

"No," she yelled. "You can't fight him. He's an ancient demon." But the prisoner didn't listen. He fought harder. Turning, he swung his makeshift stake at the demon's head. This time, the demon miscalculated and didn't move quickly enough. The wood smashed into the side of his head, and the giant demon staggered.

"Oh hell." Anna raised her stake and rushed to join the fight. She kicked Voltar in the chest. He grinned, and his thick arm snaked out and grabbed her foot. Dancing for balance, she drove her stake at his chest, but it barely stuck. He growled and removed the stake while still holding her foot. The prisoner lunged at Voltar, breaking his hold on Anna. She fell to the floor, watching as the demon wrapped both massive arms around the prisoner, trapping him. The prisoner fought with his feet and forehead, butting Voltar in the chin. The demon opened his mouth wide and sank sharp teeth into the prisoner's shoulder. Then he flung him away with a swipe of his claws.

There was a scraping sound behind her and a familiar roar. A man burst out of a small door in the wall. His clothes were tattered, and his hair and eyes wild. Most of his face was covered by a beard. The hybrid.

The next sequence happened as if she watched from outside her body. The hybrid rushed at Voltar, moving as fast as a vampire. The two sprang together in a clash of claws, fists, and teeth. Anna rushed to the prisoner. He lay on the floor, his shirt drenched in blood from his shoulder and his stomach. She pressed her hands to his wound. At this rate, he would bleed out. Just feet away, Voltar and the hybrid were locked in vicious combat. The hybrid picked Voltar up and threw him across the room. Then he approached Anna. She stood and faced him, ready to fight if she must. But the hybrid didn't attack.

"Take him and go," he said, shoving something cold into her hand. "Second door on the left." Something flashed in his eyes. A memory tried to resurface in her mind. Then the hybrid bent over the prisoner. Before Anna could even move to defend him, the hybrid rose and hurried back to the demon, who had risen to his feet with a terrible roar.

Two talismans lay in her palm where the hybrid had placed them. Hers and another. It must be the prisoner's. Why would the hybrid help them? The memory tried to resurface again, but there wasn't time to sort it out. She bent down next to the prisoner and noticed blood at the corner of his mouth. Was he hemorrhaging? She put her talisman on and slipped the other talisman over his head. If it wasn't his, she would have hell to pay from the Council. Talismans were sacred. And dangerous.

"You've got to get up," she said, shaking him.

He roused, and she helped him to his feet as Voltar and the hybrid hissed and clawed at each other across the room. Panting, Anna dragged him toward the secret door. With one arm around her shoulder, the two of them scuffled through the passageway. It was black inside, and it took all Anna's vision to make out the walls. She had no idea where the passage led, but if it didn't lead somewhere fast, he would die.

Second door on the left. She dragged one hand along the wall at shoulder height, feeling for something that might indicate a door. Neither of them spoke. The prisoner's breath was shallow. It was a wonder he was alive after taking on an ancient demon. That meant death unless the demon was assigned. What about her? She'd battled him too, though not as fiercely as the prisoner. She wasn't at her best, but she didn't feel like she was dying.

After several minutes, the mustiness of the passageway changed, and she got a whiff of fresher air. She felt a bump on the wall and found the first door. She continued, praying the hybrid hadn't lied. "There's the door. Hold on." *Don't die on me.* She found the catch. The stone grated as the door opened, and they stumbled into the dark night.

"This is the side of the fortress. We have to get to the front. My car is hidden outside the veil." She needed to get him to a hospital, but they would ask questions she couldn't answer. The Albany castle had an infirmary and warriors to help, but she couldn't risk Voltar or Tristol following them to the castle. The clan hoped to keep its use secret. Then again, it was cloaked like Tristol's fortress, so he probably knew its location already. He'd probably cloaked the bloody thing himself, unless cloaking was something all the ancient demons could do. That could help explain why the ancients were so adept at avoiding capture, or even being seen.

"Car?" His voice was thick.

They moved unchallenged to the front. No one tried to stop them, but the stench of demons was strong. Had they left anyone alive? The only sound came from the other side of the fortress. Snarls and howls. The guard dogs must have something cornered. She hadn't seen them, but they sounded big and fierce. When they got within view of the gate, Anna saw the stone wolves were gone, and the growling sounds were moving this way.

"Oh my God. Run!" She hurried toward the fence, half dragging the prisoner. She glanced back and saw the massive creatures, not stone now, but flesh and blood, eyes red, long fangs snapping like hellhounds.

"They smell my blood," the prisoner said, pulling free. "Go on without me." The wolves were only a hundred yards away.

"No." She grabbed his arm and yanked. "You're not dying on me now." But she knew as injured as the prisoner was, the wolves would catch them before they cleared the fence. She needn't have worried. The iron gate stood open. They ran through and kept on running. When Anna glanced back, the fortress was gone, though the snarling continued. She expected to see them leaping at her from thin air, but the wolves didn't follow. Maybe they couldn't move past the veil.

By the time they reached the car, she was slumped under the prisoner's weight and sweating with exhaustion and fear.

"Not again," the prisoner muttered, looking at the car.

"What?"

"I've been in one of these before."

Anna heard a roar behind them, but this didn't sound like the wolves. Voltar? Tristol? Whatever it was, they needed to get out of here now. She quickly helped the prisoner inside and reclined his seat since it seemed questionable how long he could remain sitting. Then she hurried around to the other side, started the car, and threw it into gear. With one eye on the mirror, she raced away from the fortress. Even lying down, the prisoner bounced around the seat so much Anna was afraid he'd hit his head on the door and that would finish him off. Holding the steering wheel with one hand, she leaned across him and buckled his seatbelt. Her tires squealed as she hit pavement, and the prisoner fell against the door.

She grabbed his hand. "It's OK. I'm taking you somewhere safe. Try to rest." *And stop bleeding.*

His eyes closed, and his body slumped. Anna felt his pulse. Not as weak as she had expected, but he still needed a doctor. If they didn't get away from their pursuers, she was afraid they'd need an undertaker and not medical help. Bree's house was closer. She could call Tomas the medic and have him and the other warriors meet her there. She had to warn the clan that Tristol and Voltar were here. If they didn't already know. Were the demons working together or against each other? The vampires at Tristol's fortress hadn't seemed like intruders. Everything was insane. Was this how the apocalypse would go down? The world destroyed by a battle between vampires and demons. Or would the battle be humans against vampires and demons?

She glanced at the prisoner again, strong legs covered to the knee by his kilt, his shirt soaked in blood. Why were two ancient demons so desperate to get him?

She found a wad of napkins from a fast-food drive-through and pushed them against his wound. She had to keep him alive. It was up to her. Because if he was who she thought he was, then no one was looking for him.

Of all the Seekers, he had to be stuck with this one. Arrogant prick.

"Keep up," the baldheaded man said.

Most Seekers were bald for some reason Ronan had never figured out. Maybe their heads couldn't find lost things and grow hair at the same time. But not all of them were so bad-tempered. Probably overcompensating for his lack of height. He was a full head shorter than Ronan.

"I'm on your bloody heels," Ronan said, tempted to move past him and really piss him off. Seekers hated it when someone went ahead of them. They'd found Anna's car parked on a side road in the middle of nowhere. It was already dark, not the best time to search, but it was the only time this Seeker had open, else they'd have to wait another day for another Seeker to arrive. "Are you certain she's here?" Perhaps she left her car here and rode with someone else.

"She's here. Close by. Can you take it from here?" the Seeker asked. He seemed anxious to get back.

Was he kidding? This was his job. To find people. Find things. "Sure." Asshole. He'd find Anna himself, now that he had a starting point.

After the Seeker drove off, Ronan picked up Anna's tracks in the dirt. At least a woman's. They must be Anna's if the Seeker was right. The tracks were no more than a couple of days old. What was she doing in the middle of the woods? A minute later he saw the fence. He would have assumed someone wanted their privacy, but the gates were open. He sniffed the air. That wasn't good. Demons. He pulled his collapsed sword from its sheath at his belt and pushed the button to extend it. The soft metallic ring sounded loud against the quiet of night. He walked through the gate, but there was nothing here but trees. From the looks of the gate, he'd expected an estate.

He studied the ground, trying to pick up Anna's tracks again, and plowed headfirst into something hard. Still holding his sword, he staggered back. The right side of his body vanished. "What the . . ." He stepped forward and saw a large stone wolf. Several of them, all lined up like guards. Behind them stood a tall fortress. Smack in the middle of nowhere. Cloaked, just like the Albany castle. Ripples of alarm ran across his back. Two cloaked structures just miles apart? What were the chances of that?

Crouching beside the stone wolf, he studied the place to determine the best way to get inside. Anna must be here. He wasn't about to knock on the door and see if she was a guest. The fortress was tall. Lots of windows to gain entry if he couldn't find another way in. Good thing it was dark.

He heard a sound behind him, like ice cracking on his mountain lake in the spring thaw. Warm air touched his neck, and he turned. The stone wolf stared at him. But its eyes looked red. He must be imagining it. Ronan blinked, and the wolf blinked back. Its teeth were bared, and he saw its haunches turning from stone to fur. "Holy—" He jumped aside as the wolf sprang. Its shoulder bumped him, and he fell. Rolling to his feet, he lifted his sword and faced the snarling beast. It was huge, eyes level with his. No way he could outrun it.

Ronan waited until it attacked. When it was midair, he drove his sword into the beast's heart. It was moving too fast for him to get out of the way. The wolf collapsed on him, four hundred pounds, not muscle and bone and fur, but crumbling stone.

The cracking sound started again. The eyes of the next wolf turned from stone to dull red. His whole body hurt, and it took all his strength to shove the stones aside. He leapt to his feet a second before a giant paw smashed down where his head had been. Time to go.

He sprinted to the left of the castle toward a tree with several low branches. He could feel the wolf right behind him. He grabbed one of the branches and swung himself up, scrambling to a higher branch. The wolf leapt, and Ronan climbed higher until its teeth were well below his feet. Several others joined the hunt, snapping and snarling as they circled the tree. If only he had his bow. He judged the distance to the nearest balcony. Could he jump that far? Before he could test his agility, the wolves put their noses to the air and ran off. They'd scented someone else to torment. He crouched on the tree limb, pitying whatever they'd targeted. He dropped down, landing on his feet, and hurried toward the fortress. He had to find Anna. He didn't know what she was doing here, but it wasn't likely that she was here by choice. Not with that hairy welcoming party.

The front door stood open. That in itself was alarming, even if he hadn't just nearly been eaten by monster wolves. He didn't hear anything inside. Holding his sword ready, he spun and entered. There were piles of dust everywhere. Like the ones in the battle with Druan. Bloody vampires. What the hell had happened here? Anna was tough, but she couldn't have killed all these vampires alone. Maybe the wolves? A body lay near the staircase. Not human. Demon. Not Anna's work. A demon would have disappeared if a warrior killed it. His blood started to pump harder. Bree said Anna was in danger. Was he too late? The wolves . . . maybe they were after her. He rushed back to the door as he called the castle for backup. The wolves were stone again. Whatever they were chasing had gotten away, or it was too late. But Anna could still be here. Someone was. He could feel eyes watching him.

He turned back to the wide staircase leading from the first floor. It was littered with piles of dust. He followed the trail of ash to the second floor and stepped over a pile of demon guts. This place must have been fancy without all the dust and blood.

The third floor had even more ash. More than dead bodies. The vampires had lost. At the end of one room, he saw a shattered door and found a room that had clearly been the site of a battle. Furniture smashed and things toppled off shelves. Someone was partial to emeralds.

He still didn't hear anyone, but he could feel eyes watching him. The only thing he saw was a life-size portrait of a woman in a mirror. He continued his search while waiting for the others to arrive. If Anna was captive here, she might be in the dungeon.

He discovered other dead vampires and a few demons as he made his way to the dungeon. It was nicer down here than the living quarters of some castles he'd visited, and many he'd broken into, but its purpose was obvious the farther he went. He found a room filled with instruments of torture. Blood still stained the floor. He sniffed. Not Anna's. After the vampire bite he'd gotten two years ago, his sense of smell was even stronger. He healed faster, moved quicker.

Still searching, he found cells with shackles on the walls and floors, and in the deepest bowels of the dungeon there was a room that had obviously been lived in. The door was open. Inside there was an unmade bed, a toilet, and a sink. His guts tightened into knots. There was something about the room, a smell, a feel, that made him sick. He hadn't been attacked so far, so he ignored stealth and called out Anna's name.

Where was she?

The wolves. The bloody damned wolves. She must have drawn them away.

The woman looked at the desecration. Tristol would be furious. All his hard work destroyed, and by Voltar, one of the League. She'd never liked any of them. Traitorous backstabbing bastards. But Voltar was the worst. Even Tristol considered him an enemy. She should have killed Voltar long ago. She would have killed him this time, if she'd been here. But she'd only arrived in time to see him fling the hybrid aside and run from the castle.

She had failed Tristol. She had worked hard to protect him, fighting battles he didn't know existed, paving his way to glory. For centuries she had hidden in the shadows, watching and protecting from afar. But when he really needed her, she hadn't been here.

Her gaze fell on the hybrid, who was standing in the shadow of a statue. Another enemy, but Tristol deserved this one. He'd stolen everything from the hybrid. The lost look on his face stirred her heart. He stared at the handsome warrior at the bottom of the stairs, jaw clenched under his beard. As the warrior started out the door, the hybrid started forward, then stopped. His shoulders slumped, and he dropped to the floor as if his legs had been cut away. He put his head in his hands, and she heard a raw, wounded cry. The kind of cry that only came when you were alone and thought no one listened. Her own eyes grew damp. He was bloody and bruised, would probably die from his injuries if she didn't kill him on Tristol's behalf. But something stopped her. Instead, she moved back to the emerald room. Nearly everything here had been destroyed from the battle. She moved in front of the mirror and touched the markings on the side. She closed her eyes, questioning her own sanity as the whirring began.

Ronan stepped outside the fortress, disturbed in a way he couldn't explain. It wasn't just Anna. Something else was wrong. He felt like stone, like one of those wolves. And there they were, still lined up, cold and hard, as if he'd just dreamed that not an hour ago they'd been trying to rip him apart.

He quickly checked the outside of the castle, praying they hadn't gotten Anna, but he didn't find any bodies. He did find footprints. Two sets. A woman and a man. The man was barefoot and limping. Ronan saw a drop of blood. And injured. Had they gotten away?

He hurried toward the gate to check and see if her car was still there. He stepped on the other side of the veil and heard a whirring sound like a windstorm or a helicopter. But the other warriors couldn't have arrived this quickly. He looked up, but didn't see anything.

He stuck his head back through the veil to see if it was something on that side.

The fortress and the stone wolves had disappeared.

CHAPTER TEN

ANNA HID HER CAR IN THE WOODS NEAR BREE'S HOUSE IN CASE they were followed. She helped the semiconscious prisoner from the car and put his arm around her shoulder. "We'll stay in the woods until we make sure no one's watching the place." When they reached the house, the driveway was empty and the lights were off. No one was there. "Please let them be OK," she whispered. She didn't know what the clan would do about Tristol and Voltar. If warriors had been assigned to destroy them, they'd better show up soon.

She heard a loud noise like a motorcycle. Faelan had a motorcycle, but he'd promised Bree he'd stop riding it until the baby was born. It must be Voltar. His human shell had been a biker.

"He's followed us. The graveyard. He can't get to us there." Demons couldn't step on holy ground. She dragged the prisoner toward the iron fence surrounding the graves. He stopped again, staring at the graveyard. "Hurry, before he spots us. I'm going to hide you here and lead him away."

"No."

"We don't have a choice. You're going to die if I don't."

The prisoner's arm slid from her shoulders, and he slumped against a tall headstone. "Go on," he said, clinging to the stone, his body ready to collapse but his gaze fierce. "Protect yourself."

"Then we'll both hide in the crypt," she lied. The burial site that had hidden Faelan's time vault was empty now that he'd sent the time vault back. No one would think to look inside a grave. The very reason Faelan had remained unnoticed for one hundred and fifty years. After she got the prisoner inside, she would close the lid. He was weak now. By the time he got out, she would have led Voltar away.

Working quickly, she helped him inside the crypt, which sat in the middle of the graveyard. It wasn't large, about fifteen feet square with a stone burial vault near the back to hold a casket. Or a time vault, in Faelan's case.

Strangely enough, an old wooden coffin was already inside, near the door. What was Bree up to now? She was going to drive Faelan insane yet. The coffin. That might be a good hiding place. She lifted the lid and saw it wasn't empty. The skeleton occupying the coffin wore a kilt. "That won't work. Not without crushing whoever's inside. We'll hide in the burial vault." That must be where the coffin would eventually rest.

The prisoner appeared to be leaning on the coffin for support, but when she helped him stand, he seemed distressed. He looked at the coffin and then the burial vault for several seconds through hooded eyes. "You first. I'll close the lid," he said, his voice weak.

"No. You're injured worse. I'll close the lid."

"You . . ." His eyes closed, and he started to fall.

He should be dead. Anna grabbed him. "I'm not letting you die. Now climb in there." Grunting, she pushed and shoved and got the lid partially open. As gently as she could, she helped him inside. When he was lying flat, she started to pull the cover closed.

"No." The fear on his face tore her heart. He tried to sit up. "Stay here with me. He can't get in here. That's why . . ." His body swayed.

Anna understood why he felt that way. If she were him, she would too. "OK. I'll stay." Until he passed out, which shouldn't be long. Then she would lead Voltar away. "I'm going to close the lid halfway so it'll be easier to move from the inside."

After she was finished, she climbed inside the burial vault with him and lay down. It was a tight fit. She had to turn slightly toward him to make it work. She didn't close the lid all the way. She wasn't going to be here long. Besides, he had a death grip on her hand. She tried to leave a couple of times, but each time he would rouse and wouldn't let go of her hand.

"I know my name. . . ." His voice trailed off, and his eyes closed.

Anna leaned closer, trying to hear. "Tell me."

He whispered his name as a muffled roar came from outside. "Anna!"

Voltar. She pulled her hand free and climbed out of the burial vault. He was unconscious. She couldn't let Voltar find him. Her fingers found his pulse—strong—and he wasn't bleeding now. Leaning down, she kissed his cheek. "I'll come back after I call Faelan and Bree," she whispered.

She pulled the lid closed, hoping he wouldn't wake until she got back or until she had Faelan or someone come for him. Taking care to close the door quietly, she slipped from the crypt, moving silently past the headstones to the fence near the back of the graveyard.

"Anna!"

The hair on her arms stood as a huge shadow melted from behind the chapel. He couldn't come in here, but how long could she wait him out before he sent in his minions to do the work he couldn't do? She had to draw him away so he didn't realize they'd been here. The clouds were thick, blocking the moon. She climbed over the fence and ran quietly into the woods. When she was a good distance in, she cried out as if she'd fallen. She waited until she heard the trees cracking and limbs smashing in his wake, and then she started running.

"Do you think she was inside the fortress when it disappeared?" Faelan asked.

"I hope not." Though Ronan had sensed someone watching him. Anna would have let him know if she had been there. "Her car was gone."

"She must have escaped," Shay said.

But why hadn't she called?

"How could a bloody fortress just disappear?" Brodie asked.

"I don't know." Ronan rubbed his tired eyes. "But it did."

"And stone wolves coming to life." Brodie scratched his head. "What happened to the days when a warrior killed his demon and went home and had dinner? Now we've got vampires and stone wolves coming to life and ancient demons trying to kill us. I'm getting sick of this warrior stuff."

"Your duty won't be up for a while, so stop whining," Sorcha said.

Duncan glared at Sorcha. "Do you have to be such a bitch? What the hell's wrong with you?"

"You know what's wrong with me," she said to Duncan.

His jaw clenched.

"Are you still pissed about the traitor thing?" Declan asked.

Sorcha shrugged.

There were whispers, but Ronan didn't think that was her problem. Her problem was her thick head. "If you run into one of those wolves," Ronan said, "it'll give you a new appreciation for Duncan."

She snorted. "So what are we going to do? We've got a wedding, a funeral, a missing warrior, and now a vanishing fortress with monster wolves. Which do we tackle first?"

"I think we need to postpone the wedding." Shay touched Cody's shoulder. "There's too much going on."

He didn't look happy, but he nodded. He wouldn't admit it to anyone, but Ronan knew Cody would be on edge until he and Shay tied the knot. They'd been in love with each other for most of their lives, and separated most of that time because of demons and deception. Ronan didn't blame him for wanting a ring on her finger. Say what you might about marriage being just a piece of paper, but it was a hell of a lot easier to walk away without that paper.

"I don't think that's a good idea," Shane said.

Everyone looked at Shane, who usually didn't offer his opinion on matters that didn't directly concern him.

"Why?" Cody asked. "Shay's right, there's too much going on."

"The elders are planning to take Shay away." Shane's voice was controlled, like the rest of him. "They want to study her."

"Study her!" Cody boomed. He advanced on Shane. "What do you mean?"

Shane didn't move from his perch by the door. "They want to know why she can move like the vampires."

"Calm down before you explode." Ronan turned from Cody to Shane. "How do you know the elders want Shay?"

"I heard them talking. They had a secret meeting."

"You were there?" Faelan asked.

Shane almost smiled. "They didn't see me."

"When were you going to tell me this?" Cody asked.

Shane looked nonplussed. "Now."

"What's this got to do with them getting hitched?" Niall asked.

"Because they want Bree too," Shane said.

"Bree!" Faelan said, looking like he'd been hit by a rock. "They want Bree?"

Shane nodded. "But they aren't going to take her. Yet."

"Yet?" Faelan said. "Yet!"

"Because she's married," Shane said. "And pregnant." He looked at Shay. "You need to be married soon. Or pregnant."

Cody started pacing. "We'll get married now."

"Now?" Shay said. "We can't do it now. We can't throw something together this fast. We need wedding plans."

"Wedding plans," a loud voice chimed. "We're just in time, Nina. They're making wedding plans." Matilda and Nina entered the room. Nina looked frustrated as she usually did when she was with Matilda. When he'd first met her, Ronan didn't know how Nina kept her sanity around her crazy cousin. But Matilda grew on a person, kind of like a wart. And after her run-in with the vampire in the Connor castle secret passageway, she insisted on staying near the warriors. And the cat.

"We would have been here earlier, but Matilda was looking for the cat," Nina said.

"I'm sure the poor thing is traumatized after the little incident in Washington," Matilda said.

"I heard about your little incident," Cody said. "That's why Jamie sent you here in a hired car. What I'd like to know is how the cat got inside the White House?"

"You don't want to know," Nina said, easing onto a chair.

Cody groaned.

"I think it's a great idea to get married now," Matilda said. "We need a celebration to get our minds off those vampires . . . and other unpleasant things. Nina and I will plan everything. You won't have to worry about a thing."

"No!" Shay clenched her hands. "Thank you, Matilda, but it's OK. Bree, Sorcha, and I have a lot of the plans in place already. Don't we, girls?" She threw a panicked look at the women, who looked blank, then quickly nodded in agreement.

"That's right," Bree said. "We just have to speed things up. You worry about writing your book, Matilda."

"I'm stuck on chapter two. I can't focus. Has anyone seen the cat?"

"The last time I saw it was at the grave," Bree said. "Tavis's grave."

"What grave?" Nina asked.

They explained to Nina and Matilda about the grave and about Anna. Matilda didn't know all the clan's secrets, but she had seen too much to keep everything hidden. Bree reached for Faelan's hand. "We have to bury Tavis properly first. And find Anna." She looked at Cody and Shay. "Then we'll throw the biggest wedding the clan has ever seen."

"Lachlan and Marcas took some warriors back to the fortress site tonight. Maybe they'll find her," Ronan said.

"If not, we'll call in a Seeker," Declan said.

Ronan grimaced. "Not the same one."

"Did you get that short asshole?" Declan asked.

Ronan nodded. "That's the one."

"Can I interview him?" Matilda asked. "Maybe tag along and get some good material for my book."

There was a resounding no from everyone in the room.

"Well, then," Matilda said, looking almost offended.

"I thought you were writing about vampires," Shay said.

"I've decided to write my memoirs. I'm not famous, but how many people have encountered a vampire and know real live warriors?"

Cody gritted his teeth. "You can't write about warriors. Remember, we told you about the secret."

"Oh, I won't use real names," Matilda said.

Cody clenched his hands together, and Shay patted his chest.

"And I'm including a chapter on reincarnation," Matilda said.

"I didn't know you believed in reincarnation," Nina said.

"I just started. I think the cat was human once."

The day of the funeral dawned gray, which to Bree seemed an indicator that nothing was going right. The minister was running late—not that it mattered since Faelan had vanished. Anna still hadn't shown up, which was really troubling. The Seeker who was coming had gotten delayed. And Matilda had some kind of mishap that had Cody ready to scalp her and everyone around them.

Faelan had planned to reschedule the funeral, but Ronan and Bree had convinced him to continue. Whatever was happening with the vanishing fortress and Anna was big. Faelan was the oldest and strongest warrior the clan had. They needed him to be one hundred percent, not mired in grief.

"Stop pacing," Ronan growled at Bree.

He was in a foul mood too. He was worried about Anna, afraid he'd gotten there too late to save her. "If he doesn't show up soon, he's going to miss his brother's funeral." Bree plopped down on the sofa, the same one Grandma Emily had used for years. Everything in this room was just like it had been when Grandma Emily lived here. Had Layla sat here? Layla had died when Bree and her twin were babies, so she couldn't have known her mother anyway. But it hurt more knowing everyone had kept the truth from her.

"He'll show up."

Bree laid her hand over her stomach, trying to feel the tiny life growing there. "He didn't even come to bed last night." Faelan always came to bed.

Ronan dropped onto the seat beside her. "We were out late helping Lachlan and Marcas search for Anna. He probably didn't want to wake you." He cocked one eyebrow, and a slow grin started across his face. "But if he's slacking on his conjugal duties, darlin', all you have to do is ask—ouch."

Bree pulled her hand back after smacking his chest. "You're not fooling anyone. You're feeling as guilty as Faelan. You're just flirting to distract yourself."

He touched his chest and shrugged. "You'll have to stop hitting me after my nephew is born. You don't want to set a bad example."

"If you don't stop tormenting Faelan, you won't be around to be an uncle to the baby. And you know very well we don't know if we're having a boy or a girl."

"I'll take either," he said. "Or both. Twins do run in the clan. And didn't you have a twin? I'd say your chances are pretty good." Ronan put his hand on Bree's stomach, and the baby—or babies—jumped.

"Did you feel that?"

"Yeah." Ronan stared at Bree's belly and then looked away.

"You could have one of your own," Bree said softly. He must want children, at least subconsciously. He touched her belly every chance he got.

"No thanks. Yours will do just fine. I'll have my hands full keeping your ancient husband in line."

Bree looked at her watch and stood. "I'm going to find him. He probably took a walk in the woods."

Ronan stood next to her and put his hands on her shoulders. "No you don't. I'm under orders to keep you here."

"I'm worried about him."

"He probably needs to settle his head, you know. This is hard for him, thinking Tavis died at sea, now finding out he died here. And in his mind he lost him just a few days ago. Finding the grave has brought back all the guilt. God knows he's got enough guilt anyway."

"Huh," Bree said. "You're one to talk about guilt. You still believe you're responsible for Cam's death."

"That's different." A muscle ticked, just in front of Ronan's ear. "I know I got my brother killed."

Ronan's phone rang before Bree could lecture him on his guilt over Cam. He pulled it out, answered, and Bree watched his face harden.

"What is it?" she asked, clutching his arm.

Ronan hung up. "The blond vampire escaped. What could go wrong next?"

Faelan finally arrived, and the warriors gathered under a cloudy sky to pay their final respects to Tavis Connor. His brother's final resting place would be the burial vault where Bree had found Faelan. The warriors stood somberly in front of the crypt, waiting as Faelan and Sean spoke to the minister. It wouldn't be a long service, so they hadn't even put out chairs. He'd grieved for his brother once, and now he had to do it again.

"I still think he should have done the DNA test," Shay said to Bree.

"Faelan doesn't want to wait. He's certain it has to be Tavis. It's his dagger," Bree said. "The man is wearing a kilt. The coffin is the right time period."

"Sucks for Faelan," Cody said next to Shay, idly playing with her engagement ring. "Like losing his brother twice."

"Wait," Shay said. "Isn't that the minister you said had a nervous breakdown?"

Bree sighed. "Yes, but he was the only one available on short notice."

Sean and Faelan joined them, and Faelan stood beside Bree. He reached for her hand as the minister took his place in front of the group. The wood coffin rested in the shadows behind him. Faelan had insisted on burying Tavis in his original coffin, though it was rotted in places. Faelan said his brother wouldn't have wanted to be buried in a fancy box.

"We gather here today on a sad occasion," the minister began. "But one that isn't without hope."

Bree held Faelan's hand tight as the minister continued. A minute later, something thumped in the crypt. "What was that?"

"I don't know," Faelan said, looking at the crypt.

The minister looked at the coffin. He turned back to the crowd, cleared his throat, and spoke again. "This isn't the end, but the beginning. Death is not final."

There was another loud thump, and the minister jumped. Bree wasn't sure, but she thought he cursed. He swiped a hand over his thinning hair and glanced behind him into the crypt. He sped through the rest of the funeral, periodically looking back at the coffin. "Ashes to ashes, dust to dust."

"Don't mention dust," Brodie muttered. "Bloody vampires."

A crash sounded inside, followed by a roar. The minister screamed and knocked over the makeshift podium as he raced across the graveyard. The warriors moved toward the crypt with one motion, drawing their swords.

"What was that?" Niall asked.

"It's coming out of a crypt," Brodie said. "It can't be good. I hope it's not that blond vampire."

"He's in the dungeon in Scotland," Shay said.

"Not anymore," Bree said. "Ronan said he escaped."

"You watch the front, I'll take the back," Shay said. She and Bree were the only ones able to track the vampires' quick movements, where the others just saw streaks of light. And they could fight the vampires better than the warriors could, as if something was programmed inside them to battle the creatures.

A shadow darkened the door, and a figure stumbled out. He had long, dark hair and wore a kilt and a blood-soaked shirt. There were shouts of alarm as warriors hurried toward the man.

Bree turned to her husband, who looked like he'd seen a ghost. He was gripping her arm so hard it hurt. The man in the crypt let out a wild cry and rushed at the warriors. Bree was the only one close enough to hear Faelan's shocked whisper.

"Tavis. How can you be here?"

CHAPTER ELEVEN

AVIS WOKE TO DARKNESS. THE TIME VAULT. HE WAS TRAPPED. He clawed at the lid, and then remembered he wasn't inside the time vault, but a burial vault. Anna! She was gone. He shoved the lid with his hands and feet, and it fell onto the floor with a crash.

He heard a man's muffled voice outside. Voltar? He must have found them and taken Anna. Tavis bounded out of the burial vault with a roar. The sunlight was so bright he couldn't see, but he could hear the voices. Voltar and his demons. Without waiting until his vision had adjusted, he rushed toward the sounds. He heard someone closing in on him, and he fought blind, using his hearing and his sense of smell in place of sight. Strong arms wrapped around him, holding him fast. The cold blades of several swords pressed against his neck and chest.

"Stop!" someone shouted. The bodies surrounding him vanished, and someone knelt beside him and grabbed his face. "Tavis. How can it be?"

He knew the voice and the smell. He leaned back and saw a man with dark hair and a familiar face. A guttural cry rolled from his own throat as he looked on his brother's face. "Faelan."

He raised his eyes. A crowd surrounded him, including four men who'd been holding him back, but he paid them no mind, focusing instead on the face he'd feared he would never see again. Faelan. Looking just the same as the last time he'd seen him, over one hundred fifty years ago. "Brother, you're alive."

"What are you doing here?"

"I came to find you."

"But how? Who . . . ?"

"Ian. We had to make sure you were . . . safe."

"Daft fool. I should have known you wouldn't stay behind." Faelan gripped Tavis's head and grabbed him in a hug. "It's my brother," Faelan said to the men who had stepped aside. He turned to the stunned crowd. "It's Tavis."

"The one we're getting ready to bury?" a red-haired woman asked.

"He's alive. Tavis is alive." Faelan let out a whoop, picked Tavis up, and then dropped him on his feet.

"Then who's in the coffin?" someone asked.

"Quinn," Tavis muttered.

"The Keeper?" Faelan asked.

"You were right. He does look like you." A woman stepped next to Faelan. Her eyes were wide and green as emeralds. Her clothing and hair looked different, but the rest was the same.

"Isabel?" How could she be here? In this time?

"I'm Bree, Isabel's great-great-granddaughter. He knew Isabel," she said, looking at Faelan. She turned back to Tavis, her eyes filled with tears. "How did you get here?" She gave a soft gasp. "The time vault in the chapel. It's yours."

"Aye," Tavis said.

"But Ma and Da, Ian and Alana . . ." Faelan shook his head. "You gave up your whole life."

"There was no other way. We heard about Druan's virus. We killed his sorcerer, but we knew it would only slow him down."

"Druan's dead," Faelan said.

"Faelan destroyed him and his virus," said a man standing beside Faelan. He was tall, with dark eyes that were nearly as intense as Faelan's. Handsome in the way that made women swoon.

"We knew he would try to make another," Tavis said.

"He didn't just make it, he released the bloody thing," a red-haired man said. "But Faelan's talisman ate it up like snakes swallowing mice."

"How did you get out of the vault?" a pale-haired woman asked. She had the same green eyes as Isabel's great-great-granddaughter.

"We've all got a thousand questions, but he needs to come inside," Isabel's great-great-granddaughter said. "He looks like he might faint."

"I don't faint," he muttered as they helped him inside, where everyone stared at him like something on display in a museum. Faelan sat next to Tavis, his gaze so intent that if they'd been in the right century, Tavis would have knocked him off the chair for invading his space. The green-eyed woman who looked like Isabel made introductions.

"As I said, I'm Bree, your brother's wife. You can see he's a bit overwhelmed."

Faelan had found a wife? Here? Tavis guessed he'd had no choice but settle for someone besides his destined mate, if you believed things like that.

Faelan's wife—Bree—introduced everyone there: Ronan, the handsome one; Niall, who looked like a blond ox; Cody, an intense-looking man; and Shay, the pale-haired woman with green eyes. Brodie and Sorcha were the ones with red hair. "And this is

Duncan. He's a descendant of Ian's. Doesn't he look like Faelan? And you?" Bree asked.

Remarkably so.

The red-haired woman stood near Duncan. "He looks more like Tavis than the pictures I've seen of Ian," she said, peering intently at Tavis's face.

"He should see a doctor," someone else said. "He looks like he's gonna pass out." He couldn't see who spoke. He was focused on keeping the room from tilting.

"Where's Tomas?"

"I think he's at the castle. I'll call Sean."

"Don't worry," Bree said. "Faelan went through this when he woke from his time vault. Sleeping and then eating everything in the house. You'll feel better after a couple days of rest."

He started to tell them that he had been out of the time vault for many days, but he suddenly felt too weak to explain. He had to save his words for what was important. "I can't stay. I have to find Anna."

"Anna?" Faelan asked. "How do you know Anna?"

The faces blurred into one large blob of flesh. "She hid me in the crypt."

"Hid you from who?" someone asked.

"Voltar and Tristol."

His consciousness gave way to a ring of curses.

"How did he run into Anna?"

"I guess we won't know until he wakes."

"I know you want to talk to him, but he needs sleep. Remember how you were."

"Voltar and Tristol. We're up the creek."

The voices woke him, but he didn't know who was speaking. "He's waking up."

He opened his eyes. He was lying in a bed, surrounded by people all still staring at him. "Bloody hell," he said, trying to sit.

"Lie down," Faelan said. He sat next to the bed, and Isabel—Bree—stood beside him. Ronan stood at the foot of the bed. Two of him. Tavis shook his head.

"How are you feeling?" Bree asked.

"I'm seeing double."

Bree leaned closer, examining him. "Concussion, probably. He's obviously been beaten. How many fingers am I holding up?" she asked.

"Three," Tavis said.

"Now?" She held up one.

"One." Tavis looked back at the foot of the bed. "But there's two of him."

Bree looked around. "That's Ronan and Declan. Twins."

"Good. I'm not barmy." His chest was bare. Someone had undressed him and bandaged his wounds.

Declan was introduced, as well as Shane, a long-haired, slender man standing quietly in the back of the room. Tavis vaguely remembered meeting the others.

"He needs food before we start grilling him, poor man," Bree said, touching his hand. He felt a tingle run up his arm, reminding him of the shocks he'd gotten from the guard and his bloody toys.

"Shay's bringing it," Ronan said. "Cody's bringing water and bandages."

The pale-haired woman appeared at the door carrying a tray. Ronan took it from her and carried it to the bed.

Tavis sat up. "I'm not an invalid." He didn't need all this fussing over. He needed to get out of here and find Anna. "We need to look for Anna."

"You can't look for Anna without something to give you strength," Shay said.

"I'll eat later," Tavis said.

"You might as well give up now, man," Ronan said, putting the tray on Tavis's lap. "You're outmanned by those two."

A disrespectful way to speak about lasses, Tavis thought.

Brodie nodded in agreement. "You'd have a better chance stopping a steamroller."

Streamroller? Did they all speak so strange? But he'd slept for generations. Times had changed.

"But Anna's injured."

"We're searching for her," Faelan said. "You need rest. You look like a lion tried to chew a hole in your shoulder."

"Tomas is on his way," Duncan said. The one who looked enough like Faelan and Tavis to be a brother, making Tavis miss Ian all the more. His family. They were all gone. But he'd known going in that this would be the cost. They would have suffered as well. Ian carrying a burden no man should carry. Had he managed to live a good life? Marry his Bessie, have bairns?

And poor Alana, losing Da and two of her brothers close together. And Ma. He hadn't even gotten to say good-bye. She must have been sick with grief. Had Ian told her the truth? How had she managed? What would she think to see them together now? Two of her sons, living well beyond their normal years?

"Tomas is the medic." Duncan laid a small black box type thing on a table. He'd been holding it to his ear. He must have seen Tavis frowning. "This is a cell phone. You can talk to people on it."

And he was the one with the addled brain, Tavis thought, and then decided Duncan must have been jesting. Poor time for frivolity.

A man entered the room and was introduced as Tomas. He had light hair and a kind smile.

"That was fast," Ronan said. "What'd you do? Take the helicopter?"

"I was already on my way to the castle," Tomas said. He checked Tavis over, the exposed parts anyway, while everyone watched. But after days on end alone, going out of his mind with loneliness, he didn't mind the company. In fact, he wasn't sure he ever wanted to be alone again. Anna's face came to mind. She'd saved his life. *Where are you?*

Tomas gave him medicine for the pain and declared that he would heal nicely, but he needed rest and food. But he'd slept so much in the dungeon, he didn't want to waste any more time sleeping. Not with Anna still out there.

"Do you want to rest?" Faelan asked. "Or are you up to talking? We all have questions."

Tavis answered their questions, but his mind kept drifting off, wondering where Anna was, if she was hurt. He realized Faelan was speaking to him.

"What did you ask?"

"Why is Quinn buried in a coffin where my time vault was?"

"Frederick and Isabel offered us the crypt and a grave for Da and Quinn, but we couldn't tell them you were already in the crypt. So we put Quinn in the hole where your time vault had been buried."

"We found your dagger and thought it was your coffin. We were told you were buried at sea."

"That was Ian's idea, so no one would come looking for me and find you. We weren't sure who to trust."

"But the clan already knew about the crypt," Faelan said. "They just couldn't find the key. Isabel and Frederick had it."

"Ian must have decided the Council could be trusted if he told them where you were."

"Da? Where is he buried?" Faelan asked.

"In the graveyard. I'll show you."

Faelan nodded. "After you've rested."

"We know how you got inside the time vault," Brodie said. "But how did you get out?"

"A man. He said his name was Angus."

"Angus." Faelan's jaw was tight, and the others looked similarly disturbed.

"He took me to a house. He said Druan was looking for him. For me. He thought I was you. Where is he?"

"He's dead. Druan had him killed."

"I'm sorry. I don't think I properly thanked him. He was brave."

"He was," Declan said. "Anna still hasn't recovered from his death."

Anna?

"She and Angus had a thing," Brodie said.

A thing? What was a thing? Like lovers?

"How did you end up in the fortress?" Cody asked.

"Tristol must have followed Angus and me. I was still weak from the time vault, and Tristol grabbed me, bloody bastard. I woke up in the fortress."

"You must have been there since around the time Angus died," Declan said.

"I don't know. I was unconscious part of the time. Anna arrived two days ago, I think."

"How did you escape?" Shane asked.

"There was another prisoner there. He showed us a way out of the fortress and helped us escape. We were attacked outside by wolves, but the creatures didn't follow us through the veil."

"The stone wolves?" Ronan asked.

"Stone? These were real," Tavis said. "But bigger. Fierce things."

"I ran into them too," Ronan said. "They had me up a tree. Who was the other prisoner?"

"I don't know. He was strong. He held off Voltar while Anna and I escaped."

"Held off an ancient demon?" Brodie said.

"The guards called him a hybrid." Tavis didn't tell them he feared Anna had been forced to mate not just with him, but the hybrid as well.

"What kind of hybrid?" Faelan asked.

"They didn't say, but I've never seen anyone move like him. Like a streak of light."

"That's how the vampires move," Ronan said, his jaw tight.

"I don't think we could have gotten out of there without him," Tavis said. "He gave us our talismans. The guards had taken them."

"Where did the vampires come from?" Bree asked.

"They seemed to belong there," Tavis said. "Must have been there with Tristol. Voltar's demons came in and slaughtered them."

"So maybe the demons and vampires weren't working together when we saw them in the Albany castle," Ronan said. "The vampires must have been there to spy on Druan. But why? For Tristol? What does he want with vampires?"

"I didn't even know bloody vampires existed," Tavis said. They must have hidden well.

"No one did," his brother said. "We thought Michael's vampire hunters destroyed them ages ago. I guess they weren't all wiped out."

Ronan looked troubled. "I should have known."

"No way you could have known," Cody said, nudging Ronan's shoulder.

"I should have."

"Vampires killed his brother Cam two years ago," Cody explained to Tavis. "The clan thought he was taken by demons."

"Sounds like this hybrid is part vampire," Sorcha said. "Wonder what the other part is. Maybe they were going to turn you into some kind of hybrid. Did they say what they were doing?"

Tavis felt his face growing hot with anger and shame. "They were going to use me for . . . breeding."

"Breeding?" Ronan asked. "Breed you to what?"

"I don't know. They didn't get that far."

"If Tristol and Voltar thought you were Faelan," Bree said, "then they really wanted Faelan. Why?"

"The Mighty Faelan," Niall said. "The most powerful warrior the clan's known. Why not?"

"Oh my God," Bree said. "I knew Faelan was in danger."

"Don't worry yourself." Faelan patted Bree's shoulder.

"Worry." Bree's face was flushed with anger. "I'm going to kill the bastards."

Bollocks. She was just like Anna. Were all women like this now?

"You won't touch Tristol or Voltar. I forbid it." Faelan's scowl was fierce, but it didn't seem to affect his wife.

"I don't think Voltar was involved in the um . . . breeding plan. He said he'd been waiting for me, and he wanted me dead. Tristol is the one who kept calling me Faelan."

"He's not getting his hands on either of you," Bree said to her husband.

"Did he figure out that you're not Faelan?" Ronan asked.

"I don't know. A blond man—a vampire, Anna said—he came in and saw me, said I wasn't you, and ordered Tristol's servant not to tell Tristol because he'd make all their lives hell."

"A blond vampire." Ronan's voice was hard. "I think I know him."

"Aye. Anna said she thought he was the one you were after."

"He escaped," Ronan said. "We had him in Scotland."

Bree clasped her hand over her mouth. "Do you think Tristol was planning to use Anna too? She's beautiful and strong. If they're trying to breed . . ." She didn't finish.

Tavis remembered Anna underneath him on the dungeon floor, her body soft but stiff, her fear as he fought to hold back his own pleasure. "I don't know, but they took her away once. I think they . . ." He stopped. Revealing what he feared had happened to Anna felt like betraying her trust. She hadn't even told him what had happened. She likely wouldn't appreciate him talking about it.

"You think they what?" Faelan asked.

"I think they gave her to the hybrid."

"Anna?" Ronan said. "God no."

"At least she's alive," Sorcha said.

"She probably wishes she wasn't," Ronan said. "Her mother was raped. She kept the baby and then years later she killed herself."

"Anna." Bree made a soft sound of distress. "She was the baby."

"She doesn't talk about it much, but her childhood wasn't good. I think her mother tried, but she never got past the fact that Anna was the product of rape."

"No wonder she's dead set against marriage and having a family," Sorcha said. "I would be too."

Ronan ran a finger over the collapsed sword at his side. "It didn't help that Anna had a few bad experiences herself. Her mentor tried to abuse her."

"Her mentor? Poor Anna. I hope someone killed the bastard," Bree said.

Ronan shrugged. "Anna did."

"She killed her mentor?" Brodie said. "Blimey."

"I guess you'll stop teasing her now," Tomas said.

Tavis felt sick. My God, what had he done? Maybe Anna wasn't coming back because she didn't want to see him again. He heard Bree speaking over the rushing noise in his head.

"I think Tavis needs to rest," Bree said.

"I need to wash up." He'd cleaned off as best he could in the dungeon, but he needed a proper washing. And now he needed some privacy so he could decide what to do about the awful thing he'd done.

"He can use the jetted tub," Bree said. "I'll get it started."

"You'll enjoy this," Faelan said. "We have bathrooms now, fancy things, far better than a privy or a water closet. Smell better too. They have big tubs with hot water coming out holes in the sides. Works wonders on sore muscles."

"I used one at the house where Angus took me." Almost everyone left, and Faelan and Duncan helped Tavis into the bathroom. It was a sight indeed, even better than the one he'd used before. Marble everywhere. A large tub was bubbling as steam rose from the water.

"Don't stay in too long," Bree said. "You don't want to pass out and drown." This made her blush, and Tavis thought again how bonny she was. Until Anna, he hadn't been with a truly beautiful woman. Marna had been pleasant, but no beauty. And there'd only been the one time. Her coaxing had worn him down, and they'd lain together right there in the hay. That had been over a hundred and fifty years ago. No wonder he couldn't stop thinking about sex.

"I'll keep a check on him," Faelan said.

Faelan sat on the edge of the big tub as Tavis slipped into the water. "Very nice," Tavis said.

Faelan was quiet, and Tavis saw he was looking at his back. "I'll kill him for this," Faelan said. The look on his face was fierce, reminding Tavis that Faelan wasn't just his brother. He was the Mighty Faelan.

"The guard's the one who did it," Tavis said. "He's probably dead. Tristol was angry with him. If he didn't kill him, I'm sure Voltar did. I don't think he intended to leave anyone in that fortress alive." Was he after Anna now?

"Is there something between you and Anna?" Faelan asked, as if he'd read Tavis's thoughts.

"What do you mean?"

"It's been over a century, but I know you, brother. You get a strange look on your face every time her name is mentioned."

"She's a bonny woman."

"You don't like bonny women."

"I've never met one as bonny as her."

"That doesn't explain the guilt."

Tavis looked down at the bubbling water and hung his head. "I took her."

"Took her where?"

"Took her. You know. Had my way with her?"

Faelan's jaw dropped. "You raped her?"

Tavis cringed at the word. "The guard made us."

"He forced you to . . ."

Tavis nodded and rubbed his hand over his battle marks, which were tingling. "He said he'd do it if I didn't, and then he'd kill us both. I didn't want to, but she told me to. I tried to pretend, but the guard caught on. I had to do it." The shame burned his face.

"Damnation. But it wasn't rape if she told you to do it."

"But I didn't have to enjoy it." Tavis rubbed his face. "She was scared. Now I know why, after hearing Ronan's story."

"Ah, brother." Faelan put a hand on Tavis's arm.

"Now you know why I have to find her. I owe her a debt. I have to protect her."

"Anna might not want to be protected. She's strong."

"Aye. I've never seen anything like her. She fought like a man." But she wasn't a man. She was a woman, and he owed her not just a debt, he owed her his life. "But I swore to myself that I would make this right."

"We'll find her."

"What if she doesn't want to be found?"

"You think she's staying away on purpose?"

"She must hate me."

"She put you in the crypt so Voltar wouldn't get you. That doesn't sound like hate to me." Faelan ruffled Tavis's hair like he had when they were young. "I'll do anything I can to help you. I've learned a bit about the women of this time. I don't like it, but it does have some benefits. In the bedroom they're . . . sorry."

"It's good to see that you still put your foot in your mouth," Tavis said, punching Faelan's leg.

"Don't forget, you're still my little brother." Faelan lifted his hand to punch Tavis in return, but he looked at Tavis's wounds and he stopped. "When you're done, will you show me Da's grave?"

"Aye, I will."

"I want to know everything that happened. I'm going to check in with Lachlan and Marcas. Don't fall asleep and drown. Bree will kill me if you do."

Tavis scrubbed himself, and then, wearing the robe Faelan had given him, he went back to the bedroom. He looked around for his kilt and shirt, but they were gone. There were some clothes lying on a chair near the bed. A tight, black thing that reached mid-thigh. It must have been an undergarment. Was this what men wore now? Underneath those, lying on the chair, he found breeches and a shirt without buttons, like the other men had worn.

He put them on and left the room. He wanted a few moments alone before he took Faelan to the grave. He opened the door and slipped outside. After being locked in a dungeon for so many days, the daylight seemed unfamiliar. He stood for a moment trying to reacquaint himself with freedom. He was alive. Faelan was alive. He had to find Anna, and then he could grieve for what he'd lost. But as he stood there looking at the place, memories rushed at him as fresh as if they'd happened yesterday. The horror of finding Faelan's time vault. The heartbreaking task of burying him in the crypt. Finding their father and Quinn slaughtered. Another heartbreak on top of the first. Ian crying as he closed Tavis's time vault. Now here he was, what felt like a moment later, reunited with his brother, who wasn't injured but alive and well. Married to a bonny woman. His assigned demon dead.

Hell, Faelan hadn't needed him after all. Tavis had walked away from his assignment for nothing. Not for nothing. Michael might be upset with him, but Tavis had protected the Book of Battles as he'd sworn. The book. He couldn't remember where he'd hidden it. Those first hours were only a blur.

Perhaps he'd hidden it in the chapel. Leaves crunched under his feet as he walked. The air was cool. Not as cold as it was in Tristol's fortress, but crisp. It must be November. It was shocking to see how the chapel had changed. The pews were crumbling. In fact, the whole place was. He hurried up front to the secret door. It was open now, with stones scattered on the floor. It appeared to have been sealed at some time. Tavis's throat tightened as he walked down the rough steps into the darkness of the cellar. He remembered his own fear, and Ian's, his brother pleading that there must be another way.

The time vault was still there in the corner, where he'd summoned it over a century ago. He remembered it as if it had happened yesterday. If he could just remember where he'd hidden the Book of Battles. He put his hands on top of the time vault and closed his eyes. Slowly, he let the memories in.

CHAPTER TWELVE

TAVIS WOKE WITH A GASP. THE TIME VAULT LID WAS OPEN, AND Ian stood there watching him. "Bloody hell, what are you doing?" He couldn't change his mind now. They both knew there was no other way. He sat up and realized the man wasn't Ian. He was a stranger.

Tavis's chest felt heavy. He pulled in a few more desperate breaths. It had worked. That meant his family was dead. Ian was dead. His chest ached. The man didn't look dangerous, only shocked. Had the clan sent him? Where was Faelan? Tavis didn't even know what year it was. It could be five hundred years later for all he knew.

"Faelan Connor. My God. It's true."

Tavis tensed. This man thought he was Faelan. He knew about Faelan. It could be a trap. The man could be a demon or a minion. "Who are you?" he asked.

"Angus—" His introduction was interrupted by a noise over their heads. The soft sound of footsteps. The man extinguished the light. "Quiet," he whispered.

Tavis took advantage of the darkness and climbed out of the time vault, holding the satchel and his dirk close. He didn't even hear the man move, but the dark outline of his body appeared next to Tavis. He moved quietly. Like a warrior. Or like a demon pretending to be a warrior. If Angus were truly a warrior, he should have known this wasn't Faelan's time vault.

"We have to leave," Angus said, easing toward the hidden doorway. "I have get you to safety. Stay here until I make sure it's clear." He slipped up the steps and returned a moment later, motioning for Tavis to follow him. "There's no time to hide the doorway."

Tavis stepped over a pile of scattered stones that had been part of the wall when he and Ian first entered the place. He could make out shapes in the chapel, pillars and pews, some broken. He stopped by the one he'd sat on just minutes ago with Ian. Ian. Oh God. What had they done? What they'd had to do. What about Faelan? Was he alive or dead? Tavis passed a window. It was still dark outside, with a lightening on the horizon that signaled the coming dawn. He glimpsed a figure near the graveyard.

"Stop," he whispered. "There's someone outside." Tavis signaled out the window, but the figure had vanished. "He's gone."

"Come on," Angus said. "We have to get out of here."

Tavis wanted to check on Faelan's time vault, but this man thought he was Faelan. Tavis had to protect Faelan's location until he knew if Angus was friend or foe. Tavis followed him across the yard behind Frederick and Isabel's house. It looked different. Faded and in need of repair. The gravity of what he'd done hit him like an arrow in his heart. He felt weak with it.

Angus put his arm around Tavis's back and helped him through the woods. "You look like you're going to pass out. God knows what you went through inside that time vault. Here." Angus led Tavis to a . . . Tavis had no words for what it was. It was big and made of metal, with wheels, but not like a carriage or wagon. "Get in the car." Angus opened a door and pushed Tavis inside.

Tavis stared at the inside of the thing while Angus climbed in on the other side and turned a key. A rumbling noise sounded underneath them. Tavis gripped the seat. "What is this?"

"It's a vehicle. That's the engine you hear. It runs on gasoline."

"What?"

"Fuel. I'll explain later. We've got to—dammit, there's one now."

Tavis looked out the window and saw a man coming toward them. Two men. They wavered and became one again. Or were they men?

Angus moved something, and the vehicle shot forward, throwing Tavis back in the seat. "Buckle up. There." He pointed to a strap mounted on the side near the door.

Tavis fiddled with it, finally hearing a click as he managed to get the metal pieces locked. He was alarmed, though. What would this vehicle do that would require a man to be confined like this? He soon found out. The vehicle moved faster than any racehorse, tossing them one way, then the next as Angus followed a narrow trail between the trees. They came out of the woods, and the vehicle bounced onto a road like nothing Tavis had ever seen—a dark ribbon stretching as far as the eye could see. The ride wasn't bumpy now, but so smooth Tavis couldn't tell they were moving except for the trees and signs coming at them in a blur. His head felt like it was in a barrel. Angus was saying something, but his words were jumbled together. Tavis looked at him and saw he had two heads, then one, then two, again. What the hell?

Angus frowned and reached for Tavis.

When Tavis opened his eyes, Angus was pulling him out of the vehicle. They were in front of a house, not Isabel's. "Come on, we've got to get inside before Mrs. Edwards sees you. I don't want to have to explain the kilt."

Tavis's head and stomach swirled. He felt worse than he had when he and Faelan had drunk two bottles of the elderberry wine their mother had made. He let Angus drag him inside the house and up a set of stairs. The walls were fading, and he felt himself sinking to the ground.

"Blimey, but you're heavy. Hold on. Don't pass out until we get to the bed." Angus opened a door and helped Tavis across the floor. Tavis saw the bed and white quilt coming closer and closer to his face and realized he was falling.

When he woke again, the room was dark. He heard noises outside the door. A woman's voice, and a man's. It sounded familiar. Was it Angus? He felt an odd pang, something compelling him, and Tavis started to rise, but his head spun and the darkness took over again. The next time he woke, he was alone, but at least the room wasn't spinning. He eased out of bed slowly, and his feet seemed to be working. Someone, Angus he supposed, had undressed him. He stood and saw his clothes folded on a chair near the foot of the bed.

His head was clearer now, and the grief he'd held off before hit him hard. His family was dead. All of them except Faelan. And he might be dead too. A thousand years could have passed for all he knew. Faelan could've been released, destroyed Druan, and died of old age.

He could look inside the Book of Battles and see if Faelan's name was there. Did the book give dates? It was forbidden for anyone but the Keeper to look inside the book. He'd only touched it because he'd sworn to Quinn that he'd keep it safe. Where was it? He needed to hide the book before Angus got back. He'd given Tavis no reason to believe he was evil, but until he was sure, he couldn't risk the Book of Battles being discovered. Tavis flung clothes aside but couldn't find the satchel. Had Angus taken it? Perhaps he was a demon and he only wanted the book.

Tavis put on his kilt, intending to find the privy outside. Angus had told him not to leave this room, but Tavis needed to piss. Perhaps he'd left a chamber pot. Tavis looked under the bed. Nothing there. He checked the other room attached to his bedroom and found an astonishing sight. There was a small white bowl with a water tank on the back. Similar to a contraption he'd seen once in a duke's house, but this was far fancier. He made use of the bowl, then tried to figure out how to get rid of the piss. There was no way to carry the thing and dump it outside.

He lifted the cover on the lid of the tank and saw some sort of mechanism inside. Replacing it, he noticed a small, silver handle on the front of the tank. He tried to lift it, but it didn't move. He pushed, and the water in the bowl swirled with a loud gush and disappeared. Well now. That was better than freezing your arse off in a cold privy in the middle of winter.

He explored further and discovered remarkable things. There was a basin and a tub with heated water, and knobs that controlled the spray. What else had humans accomplished in this time? Sent a man to the moon? He gave a sarcastic chuckle which echoed off the walls, making him realize how alone he was. Ian had been right. Tavis had no idea what this place was like.

He might have to ask directions to Frederick Belville's place. It wouldn't do to look as if he'd emerged from a grave. He turned all the knobs and got the water running in the fancy tub. The last knob had water shooting out of the wall. He whipped off the kilt and stepped under the spray. Two bottles stood on the side of the tub. Soap, he figured. He opened one, smelled it—pleasant—and then scrubbed his head and body.

After he'd turned the water off, he found a thick cloth hanging beside the tub. This time had certainly made some improvements, but as nice as it was having warm water coming right inside the house, the world was at stake. If they wanted to continue to live and breathe and use their hot water and bottled soap, he'd better find Faelan fast. Someone had to destroy Druan. If Faelan hadn't survived, then the task would belong to Tavis. If a warrior fell, usually his talisman went to his oldest brother. But there was no time to waste. Druan could have another virus ready by now. And God knew where Voltar was.

His stomach rumbled. He needed food. All he had was a few coins in his sporran. If Angus wasn't back by the time he was dressed, he'd leave without him. He found some odd containers next to the sink. They weren't made of glass. "Antiperspirant," he read, the words strange in his mouth. After reading the writing on the outside, he decided it was to keep a man's oxters from sweating. Maybe it was a custom in this time. It took him a minute to figure how the stuff worked. He raised an arm and smeared the stuff underneath, then did the same for the other side. It felt a bit like grease, but it smelled nice. The other container said toothpaste. He found a wee brush and cleaned his teeth, pleasantly surprised at the taste.

He heard a sound in the hall. Angus? Tavis dressed quickly and left the room. There were three other doors here, and he found himself drawn to one in particular. When he touched the door, the walls started to spin. He grabbed the door. He was still weak. Perhaps he should wait for Angus. A door opened across the landing. A man stood framed in the doorway. His hair was black as midnight, his face pale, beautiful. Before Tavis could even reach for his dirk, Tristol was next to him, and Tavis was swallowed by a black mist.

Tavis straightened. He remembered most everything except what had happened to the Book of Battles and the satchel. Angus must have taken it. Tavis left the chapel and walked to the graveyard. He passed the crypt and counted off five paces from the corner, and then found the third grave. The gravestone was smooth with age. He dropped down in front of it and ran a trembling hand over the unmarked stone.

"Da." A lump formed in Tavis's throat. It seemed just yesterday they'd dug up Faelan's time vault. His father had pretended to be strong for Tavis's and Ian's sakes, but he'd aged overnight. Tavis leaned his head against the stone. "Faelan's alive, Da. He's here with me. I'm sorry I wasn't there in time to stop Voltar."

But Voltar hadn't been assigned to him yet. If he and Ian had been there, they could have both died along with Da and Quinn. The thought was Tavis's, but he could almost hear his father speaking the words.

Why was it he was never in time? Not with Liam or Faelan or his father. What bloody good was he if he couldn't save those he loved? *Anna.* The name rushed through his head like a wind, and another memory returned. Michael standing before Tavis, telling him that he had to destroy Voltar and protect the woman. Michael had shown him Anna's face. That was why he felt a connection to her. She was part of his assignment.

He'd not only failed to protect, but he'd hurt her instead. Even knowing that they both would likely have died if he hadn't, it was still a disgrace that his body had even functioned under the circumstances. What kind of a man did that? Not a protector. "What have I done, Da?"

Faelan dropped down to his haunches next to Tavis. Tavis hadn't heard him coming. But Faelan had always been the stealthiest of the brothers. Even when they were lads, he could always sneak up on them. He was bare-chested and wore the same strange trousers that the guards had worn.

"This is Da's grave?" Faelan touched the worn stone, his face somber.

"Aye."

"He was here all the time. We thought he was buried in Scotland?"

"That's what we wanted everyone to believe."

"How did he die?" he asked quietly.

"Ian and I found him in the woods." Tavis nodded toward the path behind the chapel. "Da was already dead. Quinn didn't last long. Long enough to tell me Voltar attacked them."

"Voltar? Druan told me he'd killed him."

"Probably just to torment you. Damned demons."

Faelan stared at the blank stone. "If I hadn't got myself locked in the time vault, he wouldn't have died."

"It wasn't your fault. What we do is dangerous. Sometimes we suffer losses. We'll mark his grave. Let the world know where he rests."

Tavis nodded. "We're all that's left of the family."

"No. All those warriors you met. They're all related to us through Ian."

"Ian. It took me a long while to convince him this was the right thing to do," Tavis said.

"I don't blame him for not wanting to." Faelan shook his head. "I'm not sure I would have agreed. You should have left me to fend on my own."

"I couldn't do that," Tavis said.

"You bloody fool." Faelan hit him on the shoulder, but Tavis knew it was really a hug. "I wish you hadn't come, for your sake. But for mine, I'm glad you did. I thought I'd lost everyone."

"I wondered if I'd ever see you again. I thought you might be dead. We all did. Druan's sorcerer said he thought you were alive."

"It was a smart thing you did, killing Druan's sorcerer."

"Do you know who he was? Old Donnal."

"From the apothecary shop?"

"Aye. His real name was Selwyn. He was working on Druan's virus there. And Druan had Selwyn following another demon who was there to kill a warrior. Selwyn couldn't remember the demon's name but said it started with an L. That was when Liam died."

"The demon came to kill Liam?"

"Aye. Da wasn't the reason Liam died."

"I thought he grabbed him because he was the easiest target, the youngest of Da's boys. Did you tell Da?"

"He was dead when we got back to Frederick and Isabel's. I wish I could have told him. That would have been one less guilt to carry to his grave."

"I've thought about the demon often," Faelan said. "I think I should know him, but I can't place his face."

"I can't either. I can see him, but I can't. It was a demon who helped us find the sorcerer."

"A demon? The clan still tells the story, but no one mentioned it being a demon."

"Ian wouldn't have told. We don't know who it was, and who would have believed it anyway?"

"You don't know him?"

"Neither of us could remember his face. It was like he stole our memories." Tavis frowned. "Just like in the fortress."

"I don't know how Ian did what he did."

Tavis could still see the tears running down Ian's face as the lid closed. "I near had to knock him over the head to get him to see that it had to be me. He had the mark for Bessie."

"That soon?"

"He was hiding it. I didn't have anyone, so it had to be me." Tavis thought about Marna, her plain face that looked pretty when she laughed. "I hope he was happy."

"He didn't live long," Faelan said. "He died three years after Da."

"No." Tavis's throat tightened. He'd hoped Ian lived a long life and had lots of sons and daughters. "How?"

"Druan killed him. Unless he lied about that too. But he showed me Ian's casket just before I destroyed him. He put his hand on my head, and I saw it all. Ma and Ian's son mourning."

"He had a son?"

"Three. His wife was expecting twins when Ian died. I saw their graves."

"Bloody demon. I thought Ian would live a good long life. What about Ma and Alana?"

"Ma died when she was fifty-three. Alana lived a long time, had lots of bairns," Faelan said. "But we can't focus on what we've lost now. We have to focus on keeping you alive. On the clan's safety. Are you sure it was Tristol and Voltar?"

"I'm sure. I didn't recognize Tristol at the fortress, but as soon as I saw Voltar, my memories came back."

"You shouldn't have attacked him. You could have been killed."

"Voltar's my demon. Michael assigned him to me right after Ian and I found Da dead."

"An ancient demon?" Faelan ran a hand over his face. Then he frowned. "But if Michael assigned him to you, then . . ."

"I walked away from the assignment."

"Shite."

"Family comes first. I'd sworn to myself that I would help you get rid of Druan."

"I can't believe you ignored Michael's order. And an ancient demon, no less. You can't fight him now. You're weak still."

"I'm not even sure he's still mine."

"Maybe he's been reassigned," Faelan said. "But I haven't heard, and I think news like that would travel." He frowned. "Druan was still mine, even after all that time."

"Voltar said he'd been waiting for me."

"Then he knows? Well, you're not to go near him."

"Don't start playing big brother. I'll heal," Tavis said. "You can't fight my battles."

"Like you always try to fight mine? Whenever I'm in trouble, you're right behind me. You came after me to finish Druan off for me, thinking I might be dead. Isn't that so?"

Tavis shrugged.

"You've always been watching out for me," Faelan said. "Well, you're weak, and I'm not letting you near Voltar."

Tavis grinned. "You haven't changed a bit. Other than got yourself a bonny wife." Something he would never have. He'd decided long ago that love was a dangerous thing. He didn't believe in destined mates, the way some of his clan did. Not that it didn't happen sometimes. But more often than not, love led to heartache. Just look at their mother, losing her husband and two sons. He bore the burden of choosing to leave, adding to her pain, but he'd had little choice. It'd had to be him or Ian. Ian had Bessie. Destined mate or not, Ian loved her. Tavis had nothing but his family. He'd failed them once by letting Liam die. He hadn't been about to fail Faelan too.

"Faelan," a woman's voice called softly, interrupting them.

"That's her now, hardheaded woman. She's supposed to be resting," Faelan said, but his voice was soft, like their father's had been when he spoke of their ma. "But she won't listen, no matter that she's carrying my bairn."

Tavis felt an odd jolt hit the middle of his chest. "You're having a bairn?"

CHAPTER THIRTEEN

AYE." FAELAN SMILED. "YOU'RE GOING TO BE AN UNCLE."
Tavis was glad that his brother had found happiness, after all he had lost. "I guess there was no marrying your mate, under the circumstances."

"Bree is my mate."

"You're not even from the same time."

"I think it was meant to be this way. Perhaps it was meant for you to be here too." Faelan laid a hand on Tavis's shoulder, but Tavis was lost in thought.

"How did you know she was your mate?"

"I knew as soon as I looked at her. I recognized her. Well, first I tried to cut her head off. I thought she was a demon."

"I'm surprised she married you."

Faelan got a wistful smile. "Aye, it still surprises me too. To think that I would lose everything and find a wife from the future. It's bloody strange."

"It is, in other ways too."

"How's that?"

"Does your wife know that her family was watching over your time vault?"

"What?"

"Isabel and Frederick swore someone in their family would always protect you."

"Damnation. I don't think she knows. But Bree's grandmother did ask if I was the one in the crypt . . . bloody hell. How could I know that? Bree's grandmother died before I was released from the time vault. I guess I dreamed it. I think the vault messes with your mind. I feel like I know things I couldn't know. Like Bree. I'm sure that I knew her before. But it's impossible."

Just like it was impossible that he could have known Anna. "We left letters for you explaining what happened."

"I didn't get them."

"They were in the bottom of Da's trunk in Isabel's attic. She said she'd protect them."

"I've seen the trunk. I heard something rattling inside, but there wasn't a key."

"We wanted you to know what happened, that I was coming, so you could wake me."

"I was to wake you?" His face paled. "I didn't even know. If Angus hadn't found you . . ."

He could have been locked in there forever.

"Faelan," his wife called again. "If you don't answer me, I'm coming out there. I don't care if there might be demons watching the place."

Faelan scowled. "Damnation. I'd better go before she comes out here and falls in a hole. She finds the bloody things like a midge finds dung. Here." Faelan pulled a dagger from his belt. "This is yours."

"Where'd you find it?"

"Bree found it under Quinn's coffin."

"She climbed in a grave?" Tavis asked. She must be brave. Or odd.

"She likes graves. I'm trying to keep her from being so rash and bold, but it's slow going."

"I wondered where I'd lost it. I must have dropped it when we buried Quinn. I've been using my dirk."

"I cleaned it up. It had a bit of rust. It didn't hold up as good as you. Though you look a mess now. Your Marna wouldn't think you're so bonny now. Sorry. It seems like just days since we were there. Back then."

"Aye." But it hadn't. Several lifetimes had passed. "Is there any news of Anna?" He felt awkward mentioning her now that Faelan knew what he'd done.

"No. Lachlan and Marcas are still searching the area where the fortress vanished. The Seeker should be here soon. We'll find her."

"She thought I was you at first," Tavis said.

"We always did look alike."

"She wouldn't have gotten caught if she hadn't tried to rescue you."

Faelan snorted. "All these women keep trying to rescue me. It's bloody embarrassing. No self-respecting woman would have done such a thing in our day. Women are different now. They don't listen to a bloody thing you say. It's hard as the devil to protect them."

"I know. Anna fought like a man. I thought she was a bit barmy when she said she was a warrior."

"She's one of the strongest female warriors the clan has. She's good. They all are, but I don't understand why they want to battle. Makes no sense."

"I want to help look for her. She saved my life, and I'm afraid she'll pay for it with her own."

"You need to heal a bit more first," Faelan said, playing big brother. "Are you coming in?"

Faelan nodded and clapped his shoulder. "Aye." He glanced around the woods. "Don't be long. You're still weak."

Tavis watched his brother leave the graveyard, following the same path that his brothers and father had taken when they carried him here to be buried a hundred and fifty years ago. Tavis watched as Faelan reached Bree. She wrapped her arms around Faelan and lifted her face for a kiss. He kissed her softly, touched his hand over her stomach, which wasn't even rounded yet, and took her inside. His brother had found his home here. And his mate.

Tavis thought how familiar Anna had looked to him. How familiar she'd smelled. And he wasn't sure whether he was happy or afraid. He touched the healing cut on the front of his thigh and pulled himself to his feet, supported by the headstone of his father's grave. Perhaps Faelan was right that it was intended to be. Still, Druan had torn their family apart.

He brushed his damp eyes and heard someone behind him. Female, from the pretty smell.

"Oh, I'm sorry."

He righted himself and turned. It was Faelan's wife. She wore a skirt that showed almost as much skin as Anna had. Times had certainly changed.

"I didn't mean to interrupt. Faelan said you were still out here, and I was worried. You shouldn't be alone. You've been through a lot."

"No need to apologize. Aren't you supposed to be resting?"

She waved her hand. "He went off to take a shower. He'll never know."

Tavis hid a smile. Faelan had his hands full with this one.

"I see you found something to wear," she said.

"Aye. The clothes are strange." He twitched a bit, feeling constricted.

"Faelan's still trying to get used to them. He hasn't been out of the time vault much longer than you have." She looked down at his father's grave. "This is my favorite grave."

"You have a favorite grave?"

"I love graves. I've always been drawn to this one. It's his, isn't it? Your father's."

"Aye. We couldn't put his name on the headstone, in case someone came looking for Faelan."

"You showed Faelan?"

Tavis turned back to his father's grave. "Just now."

"That's why he rushed to take a shower. He likes to think in there. How awful, having to bury your father so soon after finding Faelan."

"Aye, it wasn't easy. Ian took it hard." Tavis swallowed.

"Faelan has told me so much about his family that I feel like I already know you. He doesn't like to talk about himself though."

A smile stung the cut on Tavis's lip. "You want to know what he was like?"

Her green eyes lit, and it was just like looking at Isabel. "Yes. Please."

Tavis glanced at one of the cuts on his leg that was almost healed. "He was carefree, in the beginning, always joking around. But later he was like he is now. Trying to save everyone. Trying to save the world."

"After Liam died. He told me what happened."

"Faelan blamed himself for Liam's death. But it wasn't his fault." If anything, it was Tavis's fault. If he'd gotten there faster . . .

"It wasn't yours either," Bree said.

Tavis frowned. Had she read his mind? "If I'd gotten there quicker, Faelan and I could have kept him from falling."

Bree put her hand over his, and he felt something run up his arm and settle in his chest. It was almost uncomfortable, like a bee sting. Then she reached out and touched his chest, right on his tingling battle marks, as if she could see them through his shirt. Maybe she had tended him and knew where they were, but it was a bloody bold move on a woman's part to touch a man's battle marks. They were personal, almost like touching someone's mouth or something even more private. He didn't want to make her feel bad, so he didn't move away. The sensation in his chest grew stronger. Bree frowned and closed her eyes. His battle marks got hotter. He was about to pull away when she opened her eyes. She looked like she was in pain.

"Are you all right?" he asked her.

"Yes. Yes," she said, as if trying to convince herself.

"Did you do something to me?"

"What?"

"It felt like you were . . . reading my thoughts or something."

"Bree can do all kinds of things other people can't," a male voice said.

Tavis turned and saw Ronan approach. He had a bow slung across his back. Was there no privacy in this place?

"She has . . . powers," Ronan said.

"Are you a—?"

"A witch?" Ronan asked, grinning.

Bree scowled and smacked his thigh. Tavis was surprised to see his brother's wife touch another man so intimately. "I'm definitely not a witch. I just get these . . . feelings."

"Among other grand feats," Ronan added, standing so close his legs were almost touching Bree's.

"I was going to say Watcher," Tavis said.

"Best we can figure, she's a warrior and a Watcher."

"That never happens."

"Lots of things happen to Bree that never happen to anyone

else. Did Faelan tell you she was locked in a time vault for four days, and he used his talisman to open it? She emerged unscathed."

Tavis stared at his brother's wife. "That's not possible."

"Like I said, she's not normal."

"Stop saying that." Bree smacked Ronan's thigh again. "You make me sound like a freak."

"You're not a freak, darlin', you're special." The warrior was teasing, but there was a look in his eyes that made Tavis wonder if Faelan was certain it was his bairn that she was carrying.

"And don't you forget it," Bree said.

"Is this where the key to your time vault was hidden?" Ronan asked.

"Aye. How did you know?"

"Someone had dug the grave up," Bree said. "I figured someone was looking for something. I thought it might have been Druan looking for Faelan's key."

"I think it was Angus," Tavis said. "Ian was going to bury the key to my time vault there and leave clues so the clan would know where to find it. He didn't want my key and Faelan's kept together. Too risky. Isabel and Frederick had Faelan's."

"Did Isabel know about Faelan?" Bree asked.

"Aye. We had to make sure someone would keep the crypt safe. We couldn't let anything happen to it. Isabel and Frederick said they would make sure it stayed in the family and that someone would know to protect it."

Bree looked surprised. "Grandma knew. She was trying to tell me something before she died. I bet she was going to tell me about Faelan."

"Bree." Faelan stood at the back door.

"You should get inside before he starts yelling," Ronan said to Bree, brushing his hand over her stomach.

Was this normal behavior for this time? He wouldn't want Ronan touching Anna like that. Not that he had any rights where she was concerned.

"He's so protective sometimes I could strangle him," Bree said.

"Aye. He is that," Tavis said, smiling. It was good to know some things hadn't changed.

Bree wrapped her arms around him and hugged him, surprising him. He was just as surprised at how hard he returned the hug. Maybe she reminded him of Anna.

"Don't worry. We're going to find her."

Tavis frowned. Was she reading his mind again?

"I'm going to help them later," Ronan said. He touched Bree's stomach again, clapped Tavis on the shoulder, and took off.

"You coming in?" Bree asked.

"Soon." It was nice having people concerned about him. It was almost a bloody miracle. But he needed more time alone. When she had left, he looked at the grave again for several minutes, trying to picture his father's face as it had been in life, not the last time he'd seen it in death. "I didn't get to tell you that Liam's death wasn't your fault," Tavis said, looking at the ground where his father lay. "The demon came to kill Liam. He must have found out that Liam would be assigned to him."

Tavis heard someone else approach from outside the graveyard. Bloody hell!

"Would you like to know the demon's name?"

Tavis turned and saw Lance, the skinny guard, standing outside the graveyard fence. In spite of his weakness, Tavis leapt the fence and had his hands around Lance's throat before he could run. He could have used his talisman, but he wanted to feel the life drain from the worm's skinny body.

"Stop, please," Lance squeaked. "I want to help you."

Tavis loosened his grip. "Help me? You tortured me."

"It was the other guard," Lance said. "Tristol told us to test you, but it wasn't me who tortured you."

"You were there, helping."

"I had no choice. Voltar sent me to spy on Tristol. If I had refused, he would have killed me."

Tavis kept his hands around Lance's throat, but he stopped choking him. There was some truth to what Lance was saying. It was the fat guard who had done all the torturing. "You're working with Voltar?"

"Yes."

"Why was Voltar spying on Tristol?"

"He knew Tristol had you. He's been waiting for you for over a century. He knew you were in the time vault, but he didn't know where it was hidden."

Tavis dropped his hands but kept a close eye on Lance. "Why was he waiting for me?"

"He said you're supposed to destroy him. He read it in a book. Some old prophesy or something."

The Book of Battles. So Voltar knew Tavis was assigned to destroy him. Or had been at one time. There went the element of surprise. Did he also know Tavis had the book? If the demons got their hands on it, found out which warriors were assigned, they could destroy the clan.

"Voltar is working against Tristol?"

"Yes. They hate each other," Lance said.

"I thought the League worked together."

"When it suits them. But Voltar and Tristol want each other dead, and I'm trapped in the middle."

"Why are you telling me this?"

"I've been with Voltar for over two hundred years, but I've outlived my usefulness. If Voltar is right and you're the one who was prophesied to destroy him, then it would be in my best interest to help you achieve that."

"Why don't you kill him yourself?"

"Do you know how powerful and unstable he is? He's been the force behind some of the worst tragedies humankind has seen. Just name the major world battles, and Voltar was behind it. This century alone he's killed millions."

"This century?" While Tavis was safe in a time vault. Still, he felt a stir of memories, a battle, and a man filled with hatred, but they weren't clear.

"I forgot. You slept through it all."

"So you want me to kill Voltar for you?" Arrogant little worm. Who did he think he was?

"If you kill him, I'll disappear, never see you again. Never bother you again."

"What's to stop me from killing you and Voltar?"

"I know something else you don't . . . besides who killed Liam. I know where Anna is."

Anna had been running for what felt like hours but was probably only minutes. She knew Voltar was behind her. But he was big, and his body size slowed him down. Her legs were burning, but she couldn't stop. She had to make sure Tavis was safe.

She leaned against a tree and caught her breath. At this rate, she'd never survive. It was embarrassing, but she was injured. She'd considered circling around to her car, but her Honda rental would never outrun Voltar's badass motorcycle. She started running again, and after a few yards, she burst out of the trees.

An old camper sat forlornly in an overgrown camping space. The campground behind Bree's house had been here for a long time. According to Bree, campers had occasionally gotten lost and showed up at Bree's grandmother's house. Now they knew the lost campers were actually warriors and Seekers sent to look for the missing key to Faelan's time vault. There weren't many campers here now. Anna stretched out a burning thigh and peered in the windows of a camper that wasn't so rusty. She couldn't go on any longer without resting, so she picked the lock and went inside. If Voltar caught her, she'd blast him with her talisman and then die. At least he would be weakened. Whoever was assigned could finish Voltar off. Tavis would be safe.

He was all she'd thought about since she'd met him. His face, his bruised but magnificent body, his loneliness. It's like he'd wiggled into her brain until there was nothing but Tavis in there. She sat down on an outdated flower-print sofa and closed her eyes. Just a minute. She didn't know how far Voltar was behind her, or if she'd even been successful. She hadn't heard him for a while.

She was sitting there in a ratty old camper when Michael the Archangel appeared. Usually he came in dreams. This time she was awake. If being dead on her feet was awake. Power and energy radiated off him, so strong she had to shield her eyes. He was so glorious she would have bowed before him if she could have moved. As it was, she was frozen in awe.

"Voltar must be stopped. It is time. Tavis needs you." And just like that, Michael left, and Anna was sitting on the dingy couch with her mouth hanging open.

CHAPTER FOURTEEN

WAIT," SHE YELLED, THEN CLOSED HER MOUTH. SHE HAD questions, lots of them, but no one ordered Michael around—except one person, who was not really a person but more of an entity. So she continued sitting there as the shock faded. Had Michael just assigned her to destroy Voltar? She'd killed or suspended hundreds of demons. It was her job, her life. One she'd planned on doing until the day she died. But an ancient demon?

Voltar. Where was he? What if he'd doubled back? She jumped up and went to the door, reenergized. She ran through the woods, not so quiet this time. If Voltar was still here, she would use her talisman. She was weak, but if he was assigned to her, she might have a chance. She couldn't let him find Tavis. She had just reached the graveyard when she felt something behind her. She turned and saw something tall. Not Michael. This was dark. A black mist materialized in front of her. "What have you done?" The voice was cold, deadly, and oddly beautiful. Almost as beautiful as his face. *Tristol.*

Anna was too frightened to speak. Then a surge of adrenaline jerked her into action. She sprang from the balls of her feet with a quick lunge, leapt over the graveyard gate. She gave Tristol a forced look of defiance and felt the pull of something so strong she quickly looked away.

"Anna. Do you think a fence and some rotted bones can stop me?" She looked at him again. His eyes flashed, and he put a hand on the gate. Anna felt her heart sink. Tristol put an elegantly booted foot inside the graveyard, and he smiled, but there was anger seething underneath. Anna took a step backward. Tristol took a step forward.

What the hell? What was he? Demons couldn't step on holy ground. That was one of the things warriors had relied on since time began. And she couldn't use her talisman on an unassigned ancient demon. That would kill her. Tristol was the most powerful demon in this dimension. She had to lead him away from here, or he would find Tavis, kill him, or take him back to the fortress and torture him again. *My God,* she thought. *First Voltar, and now Tristol.*

He moved toward her so fast she could hardly see him. He stood in front of her, his face so beautiful she felt as if she were melting.

Anna looked down at the pale hand holding her talisman. A demon couldn't touch a warrior's talisman without being burned. "What are you?"

He smiled, but it wasn't a nice smile. Still, she felt as if she were melting again. "Not what you think. What have you done with my fortress?"

"Your fortress?"

"My fortress. It's gone."

"I didn't take it." Take it? What was he saying? What was she saying? No one could take a fortress. "It's cloaked. Maybe you're looking in the wrong place."

He leaned closer until only a few inches separated them. "I'm not looking in the wrong place."

"I swear. I didn't take it." *This can't be happening.* "How can someone move a fortress? Fortresses don't move."

Tristol frowned at her. "This one does."

"That's imposs—" Before she'd finished the word, Tristol grabbed her, and she was moving through the woods at warp speed.

She screamed and held on to the only thing she could. Tristol. After what seemed like seconds, they came to a sudden stop. She and Tristol were close as lovers, his arms around her waist and hers locked around him like chains. They were in the woods. She recognized the fence. The one she'd climbed to get inside the fortress. "Oh my God. How did you do that?"

Tristol grabbed her again, and they moved over the fence. Over. Without jumping. The fortress wasn't there. "You see. No fortress."

"Oh my God."

"Please stop saying that." Tristol turned to Anna, a thoughtful look on his face. "Though he would have that kind of power."

"You think God stole your fortress?" This must be a dream, and she was still in the dungeon in some drug-induced state.

"Unless you did it. Or Faelan."

"I haven't seen Faelan for days, but I can assure you I didn't do it. Neither did Tavis. He could barely move after you tortured him."

Tristol went so still it seemed as if time stopped. "Tavis?"

"Tavis, the prisoner you were torturing."

Tristol's eyes started to redden. Anna tried to step back, but Tristol grabbed her talisman again. Why wasn't it burning him?

"You mean Faelan?"

Anna swallowed, remembering what the blond vampire had said about not telling Tristol the truth, but then she thought that if she wasn't hallucinating or dreaming, she would probably be dead any minute. She was in the presence of the most powerful demon on earth. A demon who wasn't affected by her talisman. "Your vampire didn't tell you? The blond one?"

Tristol's eyes were fiery red now, making him terrifying, and yet still beautiful. "Faelan's brother is dead. He's been dead for generations."

Anna was afraid to speak or move. She'd already said too much by giving Tavis's name.

Tristol's eyes returned to normal, and he continued to study her until she felt as if all her insides had mushed together. "I had Tavis, not Faelan. And Joquard knew."

A sound came from Tristol then. Anna couldn't explain it. A simmering, tinkling, seething sound, like a million pieces of glass breaking as hot metal poured over them.

"Where is Tavis, then?" Tristol asked. His body seemed to be moving, as if he wasn't solid.

"I don't know."

"I can make you tell me."

"Maybe Voltar has him," she said, trying to deflect. "He said he'd been waiting for him for a long time."

"You saw Voltar? Where?"

"In your fortress. He was the one who killed all the vampires."

Tristol's eyes started turning red again. "My vampires are dead."

Anna did back up then. Anger and heat rose from Tristol like an oven. He made a hissing sound, and she closed her eyes, waiting to die.

"Where is he?"

Anna cracked one eye, surprised she was still alive. "Tavis?"

"No! Where is Voltar?"

"He was chasing me. I think I lost him. I don't know where he is. If I did, I would kill him."

"That's intriguing. I had other plans for you, but like you, I want Voltar removed. I have an idea." He darted at her again, and then they were flying. She passed out when they streaked past an airplane.

"How do I know you're telling the truth?" Tavis asked.

Lance flipped something through the air. Tavis's hand snaked out to catch it, his heart thudding even before he felt the metal in his hand. Anna's hairpin. "You really know where she is?"

"I do, but I'm not telling until you've helped me. It's my insurance policy."

"And the demon who killed Liam?"

"I'll tell you that after Voltar is dead. What do you say? Can we strike a bargain?"

What Tavis would like to strike was Lance's skull. "How do I know this isn't a trap laid by Voltar? Or Tristol?" And his damned breeding plan.

"That's a risk you'll have to take."

"You're an arrogant little bastard."

"An arrogant little bastard who knows where to find what you're looking for. You'll have to come alone."

A trap, likely, but what choice did he have? He had to find Anna, and he would give his arm to know who killed Liam. "I have to do something first." The least he could do was leave a message so Faelan would know Tavis had left of his own accord.

"I'll be waiting on the other side of the woods," Lance said, pointing in the direction where Tavis and Ian had found Faelan's time vault buried. "I have a car there. But hurry. Voltar is getting restless. I'm afraid he'll kill her soon."

Tavis hurried across the yard into the house. Ronan was in the kitchen standing in front of a large white box with food inside. He removed a blue cylinder and pulled the top. It hissed.

"Pepsi?" he asked, taking a large drink.

Tavis shook his head. "Have you seen Faelan?"

Ronan snorted. "He and Bree are in the bedroom. Lucky bastard."

Was he hankering after Faelan's wife? She was a bonny lass. More than bonny. There was something compelling about her.

"Aye. Have you a piece of paper and a quill?"

Ronan frowned. "There's a notepad there on the counter." He nodded toward a small square. "There's a pen beside it." Tavis picked it up and saw sheets of paper bound together like a book. A quill, different than the ones he'd seen, lay beside it.

"Looks like you're leaving someone a note," Ronan said. "You going somewhere?"

"Just writing something down." He had to go alone, or Lance wouldn't take Tavis to Anna. "I'll see you soon. I think I'll rest."

"Right."

Tavis carried the paper down the hall. He heard quiet whispers inside and a woman's laugh. He slipped the note under Faelan's door and turned to go. He would contact Faelan as soon as he found Anna. How, he didn't know. This wasn't the same place he'd left. He slipped quietly through the house and outside.

"Nice rest?"

"Bloody hell!" Tavis turned and saw Ronan on the porch.

"You're going to run out on your brother before he's even welcomed you home?"

"There's no time to wait. I have to go now."

"What's so urgent?"

Tavis gritted his teeth, his jaw still sore from the beatings.

"Anna. The guard who kept us imprisoned is waiting in the woods. He's going to lead me to her."

"Why would he do that?" Ronan asked.

"Voltar intends to kill him soon, and he'd rather I killed Voltar first."

"You can't kill Voltar. Are you crazy?"

"He's my demon. He was assigned to me."

"Hell. Does Faelan know?"

"I told him."

"Assigned or not, you're not going alone," Ronan said.

"The guard won't cooperate if there's anyone else. I have to risk it."

"You've got the hots for her, haven't you?"

Tavis didn't understand Ronan's words, but he understood the grin. "I owe her a debt."

"Go with the guard. I'll follow. I assume he's got a car."

"You can't let him see you."

"I won't. I'll hang back. Come on. We'll need water and food." They walked inside, and Ronan opened the large white box again and took out two clear bottles. "Water," he said, handing one of them to Tavis.

It felt like the bottles in the house where Angus had taken him and the ones in Faelan's bathroom.

"Plastic," Ronan said. "I don't think they had it in your time. Makes things a hell of a lot easier. And if this guard's right about Anna, she may need food and water." He picked up two strange-looking satchels from a table along the wall. He put one of the bottles of water inside. "Here, strap this on." He demonstrated by hooking one of the satchels over both shoulders. "It's like a big sporran for your back."

Ronan waited inside the house while Tavis went ahead to meet Lance. He was just out of sight of the house when a figure materialized from the trees. "Where's your car?" Tavis asked. But it wasn't

Lance. It was the quiet warrior with long hair. Shane. "Damnation. Is everyone following me?"

"I wasn't following you," Shane said. "Duncan and I were patrolling. I heard something and came to check it out."

He must have heard Lance. "I'll check it out. You can go back."

"I don't think so," Shane said.

Tavis wanted to punch a tree. "I have something to do, and I need to do it alone."

Shane shook his head. "Faclan won't be happy if I let you leave alone."

"Hell. I'm not alone. Ronan's already coming."

"Then there'll be three of us. Lead on."

There were actually four. When they got to Lance's car, Duncan was sitting on the hood, and Lance was shackled on the ground.

CHAPTER FIFTEEN

H EY," Duncan said.
"Damnation. Is the whole clan here?" Tavis asked. This was just like having Faelan and Ian sticking their noses in his business.

"Just us," Duncan said. "What's the plan? Lance says he was going to take you to Anna, and that you were going to kill Voltar. That's bloody insane since Voltar is an ancient demon, but I assume you lied to find Anna."

"I didn't lie. I was assigned to destroy Voltar before I went into the time vault."

"Hell," Duncan said.

Shane shook his head. "You're not strong enough to fight him yet."

"I have to get Anna."

"Is there something we should know?" Duncan asked.

"No."

"If there is you might want to let the clan know," Duncan said.

Shane cleared his throat. "People in glass houses and all that."

Whatever he meant made Duncan scowl. "We're going too."

"You're as stubborn as Ian," Tavis said.

"He's descended from Ian," Shane said.

Tavis frowned. "This won't work with all of us here."

Duncan reached down and took off the shackles, which had a paralyzing effect on a demon. Lance jumped back, his eyes wide.

"Lance, that's right, isn't it?" Duncan asked, and Lance nodded. "This is how it's going to happen. You can lead us all to Anna, and we'll get rid of Voltar." Duncan pulled in a breath. "Or we'll kill you now and let our Seeker find Anna."

Lance darted glances from one to the other. "How do I know you're not lying?"

"You'll just have to trust us," Tavis said. "Where is Anna?"

"She's at Voltar's penthouse."

"Penthouse?" Duncan said. "Finally, a demon without a castle or a fortress."

"Refreshing," Shane said. "Where is it?"

"New York City," Lance said.

"I hate the city," Duncan said. "We'll take the small plane."

"What about him?" Shane asked, nodding toward Lance, who looked like he might piss himself.

"We'll blindfold him," Duncan said. "Where're your keys, Lance? I'm driving."

Lance shakily handed over his keys.

"We'll leave his car at the castle and let them check it out," Duncan said. "We might find out more about his plans."

"Ronan's coming too," Shane said to Duncan. "He's following in his car."

"Good. Tell him to meet us at the castle. We'll load up on weapons." Duncan put the shackles back on Lance. Shane blindfolded the demon and shoved him in the back seat of his Ford Expedition. He and Tavis sat on either side of Lance, keeping an eye on him while Duncan drove. They passed another road, and a car pulled out behind them.

"There's Ronan," Shane said.

Duncan pulled out the strange box with lights and buttons again. A cell phone, he'd called it.

"Ronan," a voice said. It was Ronan's voice, coming over the box.

"This is Duncan. Shane and I are going with you. We're in Lance's car."

"Good. The more of us there are, the less likely Faelan is to kill us."

"If we come back with news that Voltar's dead, that'll temper his anger," Duncan said. "Tavis told you Michael assigned Voltar to him?"

"Yeah. Where are we going?" Ronan asked.

"Lance says Voltar has a penthouse in the city."

"A penthouse?"

"Yep, a penthouse," Duncan said, steering Lance's car with one hand, which was making Tavis nervous. These vehicles went too fast as is. "Call the castle and see if Lachlan's there. If he can take us, tell him to get the plane ready and loaded with weapons."

"Will do," Ronan said. "See if you can get any information out of Lance without taking the shackles off."

Shane shook Lance a few times and got him out of his stupor long enough to give them an address for Voltar. Then they stopped by the castle to pick up weapons and to meet Lachlan. The Albany castle, the clan called it now. Nigel had once lived there, and then the League of Demons had taken it. Druan had called it home until he was destroyed. Now the clan had taken it over for their own use.

The castle was still cloaked, just as it had been the last time Tavis was here. And it still felt just as bloody strange to see something so big appear out of nowhere. The exterior looked the same as it had one hundred and fifty years ago when he and Ian sneaked in and stole the Book of Battles. Though it hadn't had all these modern vehicles surrounding it. Tavis didn't go inside. They were in a hurry and didn't want the Council finding out what they were doing. They were supposed to be informed whenever a warrior battled an ancient demon.

Duncan drove around to the back to a large road with the strangest looking vehicle Tavis had seen yet. It looked like a bird. "What is that?"

"That's an airplane," Duncan said.

"What's an airplane?"

Duncan and Shane looked at each other. "You think he's like his brother?" Shane whispered.

Tavis had no idea what they were talking about, and they never explained, because a dark-haired man ran up to meet them. He had one of those faces like Ronan's, the kind that made women blush.

"Damn, he does look like Faelan. I'm Lachlan, Cody's brother. Welcome home." He showed them a compartment in the airplane that was loaded with weapons, some that Tavis had never seen. "You can use this," Lachlan said, showing him a dagger. "Push this," he demonstrated, "and it becomes a sword."

"Damnation."

"He even talks like him," Lachlan said.

"A lot different than what we had," Tavis said. But after it expanded, the sword had the same feel. "Do demons still fight with swords?"

"The ones who need weapons usually do. But some use more sophisticated equipment," Shane said. "It pays to be well armed."

"There's not a demon out there who's quicker than Shane with a sword," Duncan said. "He's fast as lightning. Cuts their heads off before they see him swing the blade."

Shane just shrugged. After a brief conversation, they took Lance—still blindfolded and shackled—to the airplane. They put him in a seat and put a strap around him. A seatbelt.

"Grab a seat," Ronan said.

Tavis sat down near a window, looking around the space in awe. The inside was much larger than a car. He felt more comfortable in this.

Duncan, Ronan, and Shane found seats while Lachlan walked to the front.

"This is isn't like the other cars I've seen," Tavis said.

"Car?" Ronan said, lifting a brow.

The others looked guilty. "We weren't sure whether to tell him or not. Sometimes fear of the unknown is the worst part."

"What the hell are you talking about?" Tavis asked.

"This isn't a car," Ronan said. "It's an airplane. It flies."

"Flies?"

Ronan moved his hand in front of him. "In the air."

"Like a balloon?" Tavis asked.

"Yeah," Duncan said, nodding his head. "Like a hot air balloon." His voice lowered. "Just a little faster."

After Tavis's stomach had settled back into place, he glanced at the others, who were watching him with curious expressions. "You could have warned me."

"Your brother hates airplanes," Duncan said. "We were afraid you'd feel the same, and we don't have time to waste convincing you. Driving by car would take too long."

After Tavis got over the shock of flying higher than a bird, he found himself enjoying the ride. While they flew—which he decided he quite liked—they educated him on all the wonders of this age, from TVs to Internet and satellites. Tavis's head was near bursting with all the knowledge he'd learned.

"I hope this weasel isn't lying about Anna," Ronan said as they neared the airport.

"Even if she's not there, we can get rid of Voltar," Tavis said.

"Your ship docked in New York City when you came for Faelan, didn't it?" Duncan asked.

"Aye."

"You're in for a surprise. New York's changed while you slept. That's it down there."

Night was falling, and the scene below him was brighter than thousands of stars on a clear winter night. "It's beautiful."

"Not from the ground," Duncan said. "Down there it's a mad-house of taxis and noise and evil. Demons love the city."

"They did back in my day too."

The airplane landed in a private terminal at JFK airport. Tavis's stomach was a little out of sorts. A large car was waiting for them. A rental, Duncan said. They quickly transferred the weapons to the car and loaded up. Again, Tavis and Shane sat with Lance, keeping a close eye on him, and Ronan and Lachlan sat in the last row of seats.

Tavis was stunned at the size of the city, the buildings and vehicles. And the number of people on the streets. "And I thought it was busy when I was here. Where do all these people live?"

"Up there," Duncan said, pointing to buildings as tall as mountains.

"How can we find Voltar in a place like this?"

"We have his address." Duncan pointed to a lighted box in the front of the car. "GPS. It'll take us straight to his penthouse."

Was there any convenience humans hadn't engineered?

"Looks like a nightclub," Ronan said as they pulled up outside the building. A line of people stood outside wearing the most out-landish dress Tavis had ever seen. Near the door, a man was letting them in one at a time. He looked like a warrior, with wide shoulders and thick arms.

"He probably wants it to look that way," Shane said.

Lachlan gave Lance a hard shake. "Is this it?"

Lance half opened his eyes, looked at the scene, nodded, and then fell back against the seat when Lachlan released him.

"He must have a place over the club," Duncan said.

"Is this normal?" Tavis asked. "The way they're dressed?" Or undressed. One girl wore nothing but black tights and some kind of skimpy material over her private parts. Her hair was dark blue.

Lachlan grinned. "This is mild compared to some places you can find. Not that I go there," he said when Ronan cocked a brow.

"So how're we gonna do this?" Ronan asked.

"We need to split up," Duncan said. "Two of us hit the back, look for a way in. Two of us go in the front. One can stay in the car and keep an eye on the door."

"I vote for Tavis watching the door," Ronan said.

"Like hell." Tavis opened the car door and got out. "I'm going in."

Doors opened quickly, and they all spilled out. "Great," Ronan said. "Let the nineteenth-century warrior who's been sleeping for a hundred and fifty years go into the nightclub. We'd better all go and make sure he doesn't behead someone."

Tavis started toward the crowd of people, flanked by Ronan, Duncan, Shane, and Lachlan. The crowd was thick, and Tavis's eyes skimmed the people, noting that they were all watching with interest. The women wore bold looks of appreciation, even invitation, looks he'd only seen on the faces of whores. The men looked wary, other than a few who looked as interested as the women. One woman asked if they were members of a rock band. Whatever that was.

"Back of the line," the big man said as they approached.

"We're expected," Ronan said.

The big man looked them over and frowned. "Names?"

Lachlan spoke up. "We're extra security."

"He didn't tell me," the man said. "Let me make a call." He reached for his little box. His cell phone.

"That's not necessary," Tavis said. "Lance is with us. He's in the car."

"Lance." The guard cursed. "Nobody ever tells me what's going on. Where is he?"

"I'll get him," Duncan said. He walked back to the car and opened the door. The car rocked around in a manner that made Tavis wonder if Duncan was bouncing Lance off the seats, and then Lance exited the car, unshackled. Duncan walked close to Lance as they approached the door. Tavis suspected Duncan was holding him up. It was surprising he could even walk after just having the shackles removed. Duncan leaned down and whispered something to Lance just before they got there, and Lance's face got pale.

"Steve," Lance said as he approached the guard. He sounded and looked like he was drunk.

"They're with you?" the man asked.

Lance's head bobbed on his neck. "Yesss," he slurred.

The man frowned and lifted a cord, and they walked inside. The room was filled with people and noise and lights. Tavis capped his hands over his years and yelled, "What's that sound?"

"Music," Ronan yelled back.

Music? That thumping noise? The crowd moved together in unison. When his own body started swaying, he realized they were dancing. If one could call it dancing. Women and men, paired in all manner of shapes and genders, were grinding their hips together. "Damnation," he said, but the noise drowned him out.

In one corner, away from the bumping and grinding bodies, was a tavern or a pub. People were sitting on stools holding drinks. Tavis was glad Duncan led them in that direction because the music was frighteningly hypnotic.

Behind the bar, a thick man with short hair was serving drinks. He looked up and nodded his head at Lance. Duncan said something to Lance, and he pointed toward the back. The man behind the bar watched as they walked to a set of steps. The music became a muffled roar as they moved farther away. Tavis turned to Lance. "Where is she?"

Lance looked frightened. "On the top floor. There's an elevator."

Lachlan reached under his coat and pulled a pistol from his belt. He walked over and pushed a button on the wall, and a metal door slid open. Holding the pistol in front of him, he looked inside and nodded. "It's OK."

They all stepped inside, but Tavis held back. The room was tiny, not large enough for all of them to stand comfortably.

"It's an elevator," Duncan said. "Like stairs, without steps."

Tavis stepped inside, and Shane pushed a button. The floor began to move. Tavis grabbed the wall, and the others grinned. He felt the little room moving, and in a moment, the doors opened. Shane, the closest to the door, looked out, checked both directions, and motioned for them to come on. This was different than the first floor with all the people and the noise. This had fancy stone floors and walls.

"Which way?" Duncan asked Lance.

"End of hall," Lance said. He was still moving like a rag doll, but he looked more frightened than ever.

"Is there another way in?" Ronan asked.

"Just the balcony, but it's a long climb," Lance said.

"So you know where he's keeping Anna?" Lachlan asked. "A bedroom, bathroom, closet?"

"I'm not sure. Don't you think you need to have your guns and swords ready in case he's here?"

"You said he wasn't here," Shane said.

"In case . . . I'm wrong." Lance looked so scared now that he was trembling. "I'll wait near the elevator. I don't want to get in the way."

"I think he's lying about Anna—" Ronan didn't finish his

sentence. The door at the end of the hall burst open, and Anna ran out. A roar of angry voices sounded behind her.

Everyone looked like statues for a moment, and then they went into action.

"What are you doing here?" she asked.

"Rescuing you," Ronan said. "What the hell are you wearing?"

"Who said I needed rescuing?"

"He did," Ronan said, nodding toward Tavis, who was very confused. Because Anna didn't look like she needed rescuing. Even though she wore the same indecent dress she'd worn when they escaped from the fortress, she looked strong and fierce. Her beautiful eyes widened when she saw him. "They found you."

"He crashed his own funeral," Ronan said. "But there's time for that later."

"Lance said Voltar had taken you," Tavis said.

"No," Anna said.

"He must have lied so I would kill Voltar. Are you all right?"

She nodded. "I see you're healing?"

"Thanks to you."

She glanced away.

"We can all stand here feeling awkward," Ronan said, "or we can get the hell out. Whatever's in there doesn't sound friendly."

"Tristol and Voltar," Anna said. "It's a long story." She glanced back at the door. "We'd better leave now. They're both pissed. And Voltar ordered more demons." She looked down the hall where Lance waited. "Is that Lance?" Anna's shoulders squared, and a fierce look transformed her face.

Lance turned and started running, though it was more like an awkward lurch, since he was still shackled.

"Stop him," Tavis called.

Anna pulled out her talisman and said, "Cover your eyes."

"No," Tavis yelled, but it was too late. The air sizzled and hummed, and Anna's talisman light flashed. Lance vanished in mid stride. "Why did you do that? We needed him to tell us what's going on with Voltar and Tristol."

"He wouldn't tell us anything. He's only looking out for himself. We'd better get out before they realize we're here." She started moving, and they all followed her. "Stairs," she said, shoving open a door. They pounded down the stairs and came face-to-face with a dozen men holding swords. Not men, demons. The stench was almost painful. Tavis reached for Anna to pull her behind him. She pulled away and kicked the closest demon in the stomach. He fell back against two of his companions.

The fighting was too close to use a talisman here, and there wasn't time for the warriors to retreat to safety. Tavis pulled his dagger out of his boot and stabbed the demon rushing at him.

"I've got the fat one," Lachlan said, dispatching the demon the moment his sword expanded.

Shane never spoke, he just swung, left, right, blade moving so fast Tavis could barely see it. He almost got scratched by a demon because he was so busy watching. In less than two minutes, the demons had been destroyed.

"We need to hurry," Anna said. "If Tristol and Voltar don't kill each other, they'll be headed this way."

"We're parked out front," Duncan said. "Where are you?"

"I don't have a car."

"How did you get here?" Ronan asked.

"With Tristol."

"Funny," Ronan said.

"Not really." Anna didn't smile.

"How'd you get here?" Duncan said, scowling.

"Seriously, Tristol brought me."

Duncan frowned, and Tavis was shocked again at how strong the resemblance was to himself and Faelan. "We're talking about the same Tristol, right? The ancient demon, hell's favorite son and all that?"

"Yes." She looked nonchalant, but her shiver gave her away.

Ronan grabbed Anna's shoulders and put his face close to hers. "Explain."

Pounding feet sounded on the stairs above them, blending with the thumping music coming from the club. "Later." She opened a door and stepped into the room where everyone was dancing. "Blend," she yelled over the music.

Tavis stared at the mass of flesh.

"That means dance your way out of here," Ronan said.

"I can't do this."

"It's like having sex standing up," Ronan said, pushing Tavis toward Anna. Ronan inserted himself between two dancing women, who laughed and started doing things to Ronan that people just didn't do in public.

Tavis looked at Anna. He had no idea how to do this. It wasn't any kind of dancing he'd known. She glanced at the door, where four men appeared, searching the crowd. They looked human, but they were big. Probably demons in disguise. Anna slid her arms around his waist and pressed her body closer to his. *Bollocks.* She started swaying her hips, and he moved with her. Ronan was right. It was kind of like having sex standing up. He could feel her skin against his, smell her hair. He started to understand the appeal of the dance.

Over Anna's head, Tavis saw the other warriors dancing their way to the entrance. Lachlan was with a woman who resembled a vampire more than some of the vampires in Tristol's fortress. Duncan was moving swiftly from one partner to the next, barely pretending to dance, and was already near the door. Shane and a woman with short blond hair were pressed together. Shane spun her, and when she circled around, he had moved several feet away near Duncan.

"Hurry," Anna whispered. "The demons are getting closer." Tavis and Anna kept moving, pretending to dance, but pushing through the crowd until they reached the other warriors.

"They haven't spotted us," Ronan said. "Slip out one at a time."

"What about Voltar and Tristol?" Tavis said. "We can't just let them go."

"If we're lucky," Anna said, "they'll kill each other."

"What have you done with my fortress?" Tristol roared. "It's gone."

"I didn't do anything with it," Voltar said. With the fortress. He'd done plenty with the inhabitants, vile creatures.

"You killed my vampires. Slaughtered them."

"They were an abomination. You are an abomination. Part vampire, part demon." Voltar spat. "You sicken me."

"You're stuck in the Dark Ages. You should have learned your lesson with that damned minion you had decades ago."

"He was brilliant," Voltar said. "One of the few humans worth a damn."

"He was an animal. He tortured and killed for no reason. You need to wake up and realize that times have changed over these hundreds of years."

"Hundreds of years for me. Far longer for you. Does the Dark One know you're two thousand years old? Or have you tricked him too?"

"We will finish this battle," Tristol said. "If you breathe a word of this to the Dark One, I'll kill the thing closest to your heart."

There was nothing close to Voltar's heart except his desire to kill Tavis. "The warrior? Kill him. I don't care."

"Not him," Tristol said. "Her."

"A woman close to my heart. I don't think so."

Tristol frowned. His face was more beautiful than any woman's. Maybe that was part of the reason Voltar had hated him for so long, even before he'd known Tristol's secret. He reminded Voltar of a woman. "You don't know," Tristol said.

"Know what?"

"That you have a daughter."

"A daughter?" Voltar laughed. "Do you think I would spawn a female? I would kill her first."

The door opened, and four of Voltar's demons came in. "Did you know the female warrior was here, Anna?" one of the demons asked. "There were several warriors with her."

Voltar turned on Tristol. "You brought warriors to my home." He pulled out a square box. It was similar to a stun gun, but this one had been altered by a sorcerer. Voltar hated sorcerers too, but they had their uses at time. He fired the stun gun at Tristol. The current hit him, and Tristol froze. Voltar waited to see if he would move, but he stood there with the same expression on his face, hands and body positioned exactly as they had been a second before. Voltar walked closer and circled his enemy. He didn't move, didn't blink or breathe. Voltar laughed. "It worked. The Dark One's pet is nothing but a statue. I don't know if you can hear me, but I'm going to kill you, and I'll rule the world." His plans to get rid of the President had been foiled by Jamie and that stupid woman and the cat, but he would try again.

CHAPTER SIXTEEN

H URRY," ANNA SAID. THEY ALL PILED IN THE CAR, AND AS IT would happen, Anna was seated next to Tavis. Neither of them had planned it. In fact, he was sure Anna would have sat somewhere else if she'd had a choice.

This was going to be awkward. "Are you all right?" he asked. Duncan drove the car onto the road so quickly that Anna was thrown against Tavis.

She quickly sat up and folded her hands in her lap. "I'm fine. Have you seen Faelan?"

"Aye. Thank you for putting me in the crypt. For leading Voltar away from me." A bloody stupid thing for her to do, but he appreciated the effort and the thought.

"You're welcome. I'm sure he was happy to see you."

"And surprised. Are you sure you're all right?"

"Of course," she said stiffly.

This wasn't the woman who'd tended his wounds and cared for him. Stuffed her blanket through the bars of the cell to keep him warm. Helped him piss in a cup. He still cringed to think of that. This woman was distant. Cold.

"Time for explanations," Ronan said. "Why didn't you call for help?"

"I didn't have a phone."

"Why didn't you get one?"

"I didn't have time. I got captured the night I talked to you."

"If you'd had a phone, you could have called us, and we would have stormed his bloody fortress," Ronan said.

"Do you want to hear what happened or not?"

"Tell us," Duncan said.

"After I left Tavis in the crypt, I tried to lure Voltar away." Anna glanced at Tavis. "He followed me, and then I lost him. Tristol showed up a few minutes later. He wanted to know what I'd done with his fortress."

"He thinks you took it?" Ronan asked.

"Not anymore. He thinks Voltar did it."

"So Tristol, hell's favorite son, brings you to Voltar's penthouse? Why?" Duncan asked.

"He hoped I'd kill Voltar for him. He doesn't like Voltar very much. I gathered that the feeling is mutual."

"I guess he doesn't know a warrior has to be assigned," Lachlan said.

"Or doesn't care," Duncan said. "Tristol must know Anna's strong. Even if she wasn't assigned to Voltar, she could do some damage. I doubt Tristol cares whether that monster kills her too."

"Tristol has some interesting abilities," Anna said. "He can walk on holy ground. He can touch a talisman and not get burned. And he can fly."

"I take it you don't mean he's a pilot," Lachlan said.

"No, like a bird. We passed an airplane."

"A demon who can fly." Ronan shook his head. "What the hell?"

"Maybe he's some kind of special demon," Duncan said. "They say he's the Dark One's favorite. Maybe he's given him some other powers."

The warriors exhausted the possibilities about Tristol's strange powers, and the conversation drifted to the best shortcut back to the airport.

"Why are you being so bloody stiff?" Tavis whispered softly to Anna. He understood that she must still be troubled over what had happened, but she'd felt enough for him to help him escape, to risk her own life to make sure Voltar didn't find him.

She turned her head and glanced at him. Barely. She licked her lips. "It's been a long day."

Tavis didn't speak much for the rest of the trip. He concentrated on the feel of Anna's leg pressed against his, though she was doing everything but clinging to the door to put some space between them. When they got to the plane, she waited until he sat, and then sat behind him. He mused over the situation as they flew back to the Albany castle. It was highly irritating to have her behaving so brusquely when they'd been so close in the dungeon. He glanced back at her in irritation and saw her watching him with stark fear on her face.

She couldn't keep her eyes off him. She was still trembling from the ride in the car. The feel of his body so close to hers reminded her of the other time when his body had been close to hers. Inside hers. But before that. Before the guard came and saw them . . . She'd never felt anything like having him kiss her and touch her. Her excuse was that it was the drug the guard had given her, but she wasn't drugged now, and she still couldn't get him out of her head.

Tavis turned and looked at her then. He held her gaze a moment, then clenched his jaw and looked away. He was hurt. And worried. She could see it in the slope of his shoulders. Wide shoulders. Beautiful shoulders. Beautiful chest. Would she ever get the image of that damned soapy washcloth out of her head? She knew he felt something for her. Probably just gratitude and lust. She always got the lust.

That was the part that frightened her. Not physically. Mentally. Sex represented control. Loss of control for her. Wielding control for him. Not him. She closed her eyes in frustration. Tavis hadn't done anything wrong. He wasn't the one who'd raped her mother and left her pregnant with a child she didn't want but was unwilling to abort. Tavis wasn't the one who'd trained her, mentored her, and when she'd begun to trust him like the father she never had, wanted her to show appreciation for his work. Appreciation with her body.

Sex sucked. Love sucked.

Didn't it? What about Ronan? That hadn't sucked. Bad timing. Wrong person. But it hadn't been bad. Just awkward. And Tavis . . . before the guard came, that had been amazing. She wasn't being fair to him. They'd shared some kind of connection in the dungeon. Maybe just because they were both prisoners trapped and scared, but she'd felt something for him that she'd never felt for a man before. The thought of exploring it made her sick to her stomach.

When they reached the castle, Faelan came charging out to meet the plane. "He looks like an angry bull," Ronan said.

Tavis knew that look too well. "Aye. I'll handle him." When he was pissed the only thing to do was to confront him head-on.

"Good," Lachlan said, shutting himself in the cockpit when Faelan started pounding on the door to the plane.

Tavis had to wait for Ronan to open it. He couldn't figure out how to get out of the confounded thing.

Faelan stood there, his hands clenched, eyes frightened. "You just leave without telling me? Go off on some bloody mission without a word? You've just come back from the dead."

"I had to do it. Lance said I had to come alone."

"Alone?" His incredulous glance swept over the others, who were looking at their feet, twiddling their thumbs. Lachlan was watching from the window in the front of the plane.

"They weren't supposed to be there," Tavis said. "They waylaid me."

Ronan jumped down and stood next to Tavis. "Lance told him he had to come alone or he wouldn't take him to Anna."

"You found Anna?"

"Aye. I didn't want him going alone, so I followed," Ronan said. "Same with Shane and Duncan."

Cody stalked up to meet them. He didn't look any happier than Faelan. "You could have told us you were going," Cody said, frowning at Lachlan, whose face vanished from the window.

"I did. I put a letter under Faelan's door. I didn't want to knock. You and Bree were . . . engaged."

"And he did leave a letter," Ronan said. "I saw him write it."

"I didn't see it." Faelan looked around and spotted Anna standing behind the others. "And where the bloody hell have you been? And what're you wearing?"

"Don't start with me, Faelan." Anna walked off the plane.

"She's in a foul mood," Ronan said. "But she's been visiting with Tristol and Voltar, so I don't blame her."

"Tristol and Voltar!" Faelan eyebrows rose, and he looked like a duplicate of Duncan, who'd moved next to him. Everyone started talking at once.

Cody held up his hand. "Hold on. Come inside and let's get the story straight. Bree needs to know Anna's OK. She's been worried sick. Everyone has."

"I'm sorry," Anna said. "There wasn't time to warn everyone."

"If you'd bothered to replace your cell phone, you could have called," Ronan said.

Anna didn't answer. They all walked toward the castle, but it was slow going with everyone along the way stopping to talk. By the time they got inside, they had an entourage. Anna had been missing for some time, and the whole clan had been worried.

The interior structure of the castle was so similar to the one Tavis had grown up in that he felt homesick. He expected to see Ian and Alana rushing out to greet him. Instead, Bree and Shay ran down the hall. "You're back. Thank God." Bree hugged Anna and suddenly jumped back as if she'd been burned.

Anna peered at her. "Are you OK?"

Bree appeared at a loss for words. She must be overcome with emotion. Tavis remembered when his mother was pregnant with Alana. How easily she'd cried.

An elderly man and woman joined them. Both were white-haired, with happy faces and warm eyes. The man stared at Tavis and then grabbed him in a hug.

The move surprised Tavis, but he hugged him back. When the old man stepped away, he looked up at Tavis, his eyes glistening. "I never thought to see such a remarkable thing in all my days."

"Sean, Tavis has no idea who you are," the woman said, smiling at him like his mother used to.

"I got a bit ahead of myself. I'm Sean Connor, and this is Coira. We're your family." He beamed, hunched his shoulders, and chuckled.

Tavis nodded to them. "Tavis Connor, and I'm very glad to meet you both."

"He's overwhelmed, Sean." The woman took Tavis by the arm. "What you need is a good meal."

Food. "Aye. I am hungry."

"Come along then," the old man said, "and let Coira feed you. You've a lot to learn. Times have changed. Even in my lifetime. I hardly recognize the world sometimes. But you'll sort it all out. Your brother did. He's become a whiz at texting."

Tavis didn't know what texting was. Perhaps a new kind of weaponry. Coira led the way to the kitchen. It was similar to the one at home, but there were more of those modern appliances like the ones he'd seen at Faelan and Bree's. Several people were in the kitchen working at large ovens. Some were baking bread, others chopping vegetables. He had a wistful moment remembering how his mother had fussed about having to feed so many warriors, even with help, when everyone knew she loved every moment of it.

Tavis ate some bread and stew and answered more questions. When he'd finished, Sean took one of Tavis's hands and one of Faelan's. "A family reunion. That's what we'll have."

"What about Voltar and Tristol?" Sorcha asked.

"They'll have to wait," Sean said. "This is a once-in-a-lifetime event. I won't let the demons ruin this moment." He stopped and paused. "Your brother Ian, he's not coming is he?"

Tavis shook his head. "God, I hope not."

"With two of you here, I was beginning to wonder if the whole family was coming."

"Ian stayed behind to take care of Ma."

Sean's lips pressed together, and he nodded. "I understand. You're a brave lad for doing what you did. And he's a brave one for staying behind. Makes me proud to be a Connor."

Warmth stirred in Tavis's chest. He'd worried that he'd arrive to find Faelan dead, Druan on a rampage, or worse, the world already destroyed. But he'd found his family. Part of his family. His eyes strayed to Anna, whose eyes were damp. She turned her head.

Two older women entered the kitchen. One of them had the reddest hair Tavis had ever seen, and her clothes looked like an artist had splattered her with paint. "Look, Nina, he looks just like Faelan," the redhead said, moving right up to him and inspecting him like he was a wax model. He wouldn't have been surprised if she pinched him. And she did, right on one of his healing cuts. "Almost like twins. Triplets if you count Duncan. All three of you look alike."

"I'm Nina, Cody and Shay's aunt. I'm so glad to meet you. It's just amazing that you're here."

"And I'm Matilda, their aunt. Or practically their aunt."

"It's a pleasure to meet you both." He tried not to stare at Matilda, but he'd never seen anything quite like her.

"Let's hope you can still say that in a week," Nina said, frowning at Matilda.

"I'm sorry we missed your funeral," Matilda said. "But we're pleased as punch that you're alive. Maybe I could interview you. I'm writing a book, and I'm interested in learning more about time vaults."

Tavis was almost certain the Council wouldn't allow any books to be written about time vaults or any other thing connected to the clan. But she was probably just barmy. He'd been warned about her on the airplane.

"Matilda, leave Tavis alone," Nina said.

"We'll talk later. Will you be here for the wedding?" Matilda asked.

"Wedding?"

"Cody and Shay's?"

"Well I reckon I'm not going anywhere."

"Good." Matilda came closer and gave him a squeeze. "I'm glad you're here," she said, looking wise in spite of her strange hair. "Faelan needs someone from his family." She looked misty-eyed and then cleared her throat. "I'm going to find the cat. I think he's upset with me."

Coira rolled her eyes. "I need to take a look at Tavis's injuries."

"Better go with her," Sean said. "We'll meet you in the library and get acquainted."

Coira took Tavis to the infirmary and checked his injuries, tsking as she bandaged. "If I could get my hands on that demon, I don't know what I'd do to him."

Tavis didn't know what he'd do to Tristol. He wasn't his demon. But he knew exactly what he'd do to Voltar when he got his chance. He regretted leaving him in the penthouse, but it would be foolishness to take on him and Tristol at the same time. They would have to die separately.

As she worked, Coira asked about his past, pulling information out of him that he didn't know he even remembered. Things from his childhood. When he had been bandaged to Coira's satisfaction, they went to the library. Tavis was introduced to other warriors he hadn't yet met, so many he couldn't recall all their names. They gave him a warm welcome and asked too many questions, but he understood that everyone was curious about him. It wasn't all pleasant. They discussed Voltar and Tristol, and a pall settled over the group when they learned that Tristol wasn't bound by some of the rules as the other demons.

After a while Tavis started missing parts of the conversation because he was trying to watch Anna. She and Ronan had their heads close together talking. He felt the sting of jealousy. Was there something between her and Ronan? They were both attractive, and he hadn't seen Ronan with anyone except Bree. Anna glanced across the room at Tavis and slipped out of the library.

Tavis followed her outside, wondering if she was meeting someone. A woman as beautiful as Anna would have many suitors.

Anna turned around, hands on her hips. "Are you following me?"

"What if I am?"

"I don't like being followed."

"I don't like being ignored."

"I'm not ignoring you."

"Yes you are. You won't even look at me."

She looked at him then, and he felt the impact of her gaze like a fist to his stomach. What was this effect she had on him? It was almost painful. He'd never felt anything like it. He'd felt attracted to women, bedded a few, and with Marna he'd felt a fondness, but this tearing, gnawing desperation was hell.

"You only did that to prove me wrong," he said.

She rolled her eyes and stepped closer to him. He could feel the heat rising off her body. How was that possible? "I just want some time alone," she said. But she didn't move away. She stared at his mouth and swallowed. The pulse at her throat ticked like a pocket watch, mesmerizing him. He wanted to put his lips against it and taste it.

"You're standing very close to me for someone who wants to be alone," he said.

She shook her head and turned to walk off. He didn't follow her this time. He needed to go somewhere and think. Sort out his head. He had to figure out what to do about Tristol and Voltar.

The feeling in Tristol's arms returned first, and it slowly worked down his body until he could take a few faltering steps. His eyes burned with anger, the heat so hot it felt like lasers. Voltar would die for this. As Tristol's muscles returned to normal, he vowed he would kill every demon attached to him. First he would find out what Voltar had used on him. It looked like a stun gun, but it must be powered by sorcery. Nothing had stopped Tristol before. He didn't think it had been but a few minutes, but this was unacceptable. He, the most powerful being on this earth, frozen like a petrified tree. Several of his vampires had been destroyed, his fortress stolen from under his nose, and his enemy was the one to tell him that he had not one, but two spies in his home.

When Tristol was able to move at normal speed, he zoomed through Voltar's penthouse searching for the demon. He wasn't there. He'd probably gone after Anna and the warriors. Tristol let the power and rage build into a ball of fury. It flew from his fingers, igniting the room. There were people downstairs in the club. They might have nothing to do with Voltar. Tristol streaked out into the hallway and hit the fire alarm, giving them opportunity to escape before he destroyed the entire building. That made him even angrier. He was growing a damned conscience. He'd spent too much time watching those do-good warriors. They were rubbing off on him. But even with his powers, he couldn't undo a fire alarm.

He streaked out of the burning building, past people running to escape. He stopped a few blocks over and watched Voltar's building go up in a blaze.

"Master."

Tristol turned. It was his lieutenant. "It's about time. Do you have the book?"

"I did, but they took it back," Joquard said.

"Is that why you've been avoiding me?" Was it possible that Joquard was involved in the breech? Tristol was finding it hard to trust anyone now.

"I haven't been avoiding you. But I have some troubling news about your prisoner."

"I already know. I got the wrong one."

Joquard looked nervous. "Shall I bring Faelan to you?"

"Not now. I have more pressing problems. Voltar and his daughter."

CHAPTER SEVENTEEN

W HAT HAVE YOU GOT THERE?" FAELAN ASKED.
Bree held up a little box. "One of Layla's puzzle boxes."

"That's the one that you hid under the floorboard when you were a girl."

She nodded. "Something's inside. I was thinking about Layla, and I remembered it."

"Did you get it opened?"

"No. I can't figure it out. I tried several times over the years."

"Want me to have a look at it?"

"Sure." Bree handed him the box. It was small, made of wood. "There isn't a lid."

Faelan rattled it. "There's something inside."

"I want to know what it is." She frowned. "Smash it."

"I could do that, but there must be a way to open it," he said.

"Don't you think I've tried? It won't open."

"You just haven't found out how."

"So you think you can find it when I couldn't? Me? I've spent my life exploring mysteries and looking for treasure."

Click.

"You didn't." Bree leaned closer. One side of the box had separated. "How did you do that?"

"I pressed on the sides."

"I tried that," Bree said.

"I pressed on three sides at once. Your wee hands weren't big enough. Here, it's yours to open."

Bree took the box but just stared at it.

"You're not going to open it?"

"Yes, but I've waited so long . . ."

"Well, open it or I will. I want to know what's inside."

She pulled the side that was loose, and a drawer slid out. "It's a key." She carefully removed a small skeleton key and held it up. "To what?"

"I think I know."

"You know? How could you know?"

"Follow me." Faelan led Bree out of the room and to the attic stairs. He stopped. The stairs were so narrow. And she wasn't the most graceful of women. There was the bairn to consider. "I think it's best that you stay here. I don't want you tumbling down—"

Bree started up the stairs. "They're just stairs, Faelan."

He took a large step so that he was right behind her and could catch her if she fell. "The view's nice here."

She glanced back and saw him looking at her arse. "There's more of it to see now."

"It's no bigger than it was. Now this," he said, sliding his arms around her when they'd reached the attic. He placed his palms over her belly. "I can't wait until I can see that my bairn's in there." He turned her in his arms and pulled her close. "Have I told you how much I love you and this little one?"

"Not for a few hours." Bree leaned in and kissed his neck, making his bones feel like dust. "But you can tell us anytime you want. We love hearing it."

"Do you think he can hear us?"

"Or her? No. I'm barely pregnant. It probably looks like a chicken embryo right now."

"Just spoil my mood," he said, kissing the tip of her nose.

Bree smiled. "But I'm sure if it's a boy he'll be every bit as magnificent as his father. 'The Mighty Faelan Junior.'"

"No you don't."

Bree laughed and reached up to turn on the light. "OK, show me what this key goes to." Faelan led her to a trunk. "This is McGowan's things. Sorry, your father's things," she said.

"Aye." They'd left the box holding his father's things inside. Two straight razors. One must have been Quinn's. There were other things inside. Someone must have kept them there over the years. Old clothing and such. He removed the items and felt for the slit in the bottom of the trunk. "See that? Try the key."

"That's a keyhole?"

"Aye. I had a trunk just like this. There's a secret compartment in the bottom. We used to hide weapons inside. Or anything else we didn't want found."

"You knew this trunk had a secret compartment and didn't tell me?" She looked betrayed.

"I wasn't sure you didn't know about it."

She gave him a skeptical look. "You were afraid I would rip the bottom of the trunk out to get it open."

"The thought did cross my mind."

"You know me better than that. I would have opened it carefully."

He grinned at her admission. She would have opened it if she'd known. She couldn't resist a puzzle. The only reason she hadn't gotten the puzzle box open was that she would have had to smash it to do so. "I didn't know what you were like then." Which wasn't long ago. He'd known her for only a short while, though it felt like forever. So much so that he had even started dreaming of her when she was young. Two nights ago he'd dreamed she was in the graveyard crying, upset over some boy. Druan had been outside the graveyard watching Bree. Barmy dreams.

Bree stuck the key inside the hole and turned it. "This is so exciting. Now what?"

"Lift the edge there."

"Here?" She lifted the corner, and the bottom of the trunk came up. "Oh my. There are letters." She reached inside and pulled out three yellowed letters tied with a blue ribbon. "This one has your name on them."

"Tavis said they'd written letters for me, for when I awoke." Faelan reached for them. These had waited for over a century.

"Do you want to open them with Tavis?" Bree's expression was so tender, but he knew she was dying to see what was inside.

"He already knows what's written there. I'd like you to read them with me."

Her face lit in a grin that made his heart leap. God, he loved this woman. Dangerous, bloody, bold crazy woman. He would die without her.

He carefully opened the first envelope and removed the letter. He unfolded it and looked at the neat writing on the page. "It's written in Ian's hand," Faelan said. "He was always one for letters."

Faelan,

If you are reading this, then someone has awoken you from your slumber. I hope whoever the clan sent to open your time vault has explained what happened. But Tavis and I wanted to leave letters so you would know, and to say our final farewells. The Seeker found your time vault buried in a field. We did not know if Druan was coming back soon, or perhaps watching the place. We found a husband and wife nearby who were kind. They allowed us to stay with them as we searched out a place to hide the time vault. They had an empty crypt and let us buy it. Da was heartbroken and slept the first night in the crypt. He didn't live to see another night. Voltar killed him and Quinn, according to Quinn, who was barely alive when we found them. Voltar wanted the Book of Battles. We are considering what do to about the problem. We fear telling the elders since we suspect there is traitor in the clan.

Tavis and I found a letter from Nigel Ellwood in Quinn's pocket. Nigel suspected that someone was selling warriors' names to a demon since several warriors had died under suspicious circumstances. Nigel was worried that the Keeper was involved, since he was the only one who would have had access to the Book of Battles. Nigel told the Council, and they appointed a secret group to look into matters. Nigel convinced them to let him find a place in America for the clan, a second clan seat so that they weren't all in one place. He had taken the book with him and hidden it in America as well. Most of the Watchers who were investigating Nigel's claims had also died mysteriously. Since Nigel did not know who to trust, he kept the book in America while he started work on the second castle. He figured the book was safest if it was believed missing, so he pretended to disappear himself. But now he was alarmed because he had spotted four ancient demons nearby. He was worried about the Book of Battles and had written to the Chief Elder asking him to send warriors to transport the book back to Scotland. He stressed in the letter the importance that the Keeper not be told.

We do not know the extent of the betrayal. Quinn had the letter and hadn't told the Council, so he was at least an accomplice to his father's betrayal.

We put Da in an unmarked grave. It is the third grave you will find after walking five paces from the corner of your crypt. We could not risk someone coming to visit his grave and finding the time vault. We will tell Ma the truth. And Tavis and I told Frederick and Isabel about you. They promised to watch over your time vault, and to ensure that someone else in their family takes the duty when they die, until someone from the clan comes to release you. They have the key. They will take care of it as well. We had already buried Quinn in the hole where your time vault was because at that time we had not yet told Frederick and Isabel that your time vault was inside the crypt.

Only Ma will know the truth about you. I love you, brother, and I write this with sorrow, knowing that I will never see you again. Not in this lifetime. I will comfort Ma and Alana and will see you on the other side.

With love,

Ian

The next letter was from Tavis.

Faelan,

This is a hard letter to write. I won't say much. Ian has said most of it in his letter, which he let me read. I am not letting him read mine, and you will see why. I have made a decision. I am coming to help you. I cannot bear the thought of you waking alone. Someone must be there to help you and to stop Druan if you are not able. Your talisman would most likely be assigned to me. Also, I promised Quinn I would protect the book, and the best way to do that is to lock it inside the time vault with me. Voltar wants the Book of Battles, and it would appear that there is a traitor in our clan who has been selling warriors' names to a demon or demons. Nigel Ellwood suspected it was the Keeper before Quinn. Quinn's father. We don't know how deeply this threat extends, whether the Council is involved or just this Keeper, but the book must be protected. This way, no one can get to it.

Ian will be furious with me, and I know it will take much convincing to get him to agree. It will be a hard thing for him to do, but I will make him see the necessity. It must be me. He has the mark for Bessie. I have no one but my family and my duty. I admit I am afraid. I do not know what to expect, what the time vault will be like. If I will even survive it. But if I do, we will be united again, and together we will stop Druan.

Sincerely,

Tavis

"Oh, Faelan." Bree leaned her head on his shoulder. "How wonderful and sad."

Faelan blinked hard. He missed Ian, missed them all. But now he had gotten one brother back.

"There's another letter," Bree said. "It's addressed to you and Tavis. It was mailed to Isabel."

"Then I'll wait to read it with him." He folded the letters and put them back in the envelopes and retied the ribbon.

"Why does he say he'll take the Book of Battles with him?" Bree asked. "We have the book."

"I don't know. Perhaps they decided it best to hide it in the chapel."

"Ian mentioned a traitor in his letter. I wonder if it's the same traitor Angus mentioned before he died."

After being attacked by Druan's demons in Scotland, Angus had managed to use the secret tunnel to get inside the castle. He'd shocked the clan when he'd burst into the dining room covered in blood. Before he'd collapsed, he had uttered the word *traitor*. The clan wasn't sure what he meant. He'd died within hours without explaining. But everyone agreed that it appeared he was looking at Sorcha when he spoke. "I hope Angus was talking about Nigel's suspicions."

"How would Angus know?"

"Anna said he was researching Nigel. He might have found Ian's journals. He loved leaving clues." If there was a new traitor, that meant the clan was being attacked from the inside as well as the outside. "Let's find Tavis. Ian might have known more about this traitor."

"If I had found these earlier, I could have opened your time vault sooner," Bree said. "See, it pays to snoop."

They found Tavis downstairs in the kitchen where everyone was eating. Tavis wasn't eating. He was watching Anna.

"He likes her," Faelan said quietly.

"It goes both ways."

"You think?" Faelan frowned. "Seems she ignores him most of the time."

"She's scared."

He looked at her. "She told you about that?"

"Told me about what?" Bree asked.

"Uh . . ." Damnation. "Nothing."

"Oh no," Bree said, grabbing Faelan's arm. "You know something I don't?"

"I . . . it's well . . . something happened when Tavis and Anna were captured in Tristol's fortress."

"What?"

"I really don't want to say . . . oh hell, it's killing me." He looked around to be sure no one was nearby. "Tavis and Anna had to . . . you know."

"What?"

"Have sex."

Bree's jaw dropped. "They had sex?"

"Shhh. Tavis said the guard there made them do it. Told them he'd rape Anna if Tavis didn't do it. Then he'd kill them both."

"Oh my God."

"Tavis didn't want to, but Anna told him she didn't want to die and she didn't want the guard doing it."

"Poor Anna."

"Poor buggers, both of them. Tavis is eaten up with guilt as if he'd raped her. I told him he did no such thing. The guard made them do it, and Anna told him to. What's wrong? You look pale?"

She was twisting her ring, and she looked worried.

"I can't believe this."

"I know it's a terrible thing."

"No. It's . . . she's pregnant."

Faelan's jaw dropped. "Pregnant. How do you—bloody hell. Are you sure?"

"I think so."

"She said? Isn't it too early to tell?"

"By normal means."

"You mean you . . . you saw it?"

"Unless I'm crazy. Which I could be."

Usually she was right about her feelings. "Tavis is going to have a bairn?" A smile crept over his face.

"Not necessarily." Bree's green eyes darkened with worry. "Remember the hybrid Tavis said she was taken to?"

CHAPTER EIGHTEEN

Tavis caught sight of Faelan and Bree whispering and watching him from across the room. How long had they been standing there, he wondered, hoping they hadn't seen him watching Anna. From the looks of pity on their faces, he figured they had.

They crossed the room, Faelan looking a bit nervous, and Bree's green Isabel eyes so full of sympathy. "Is there a demon sitting on my head?"

"What?" Bree asked.

"You're both looking at me strange."

"Sorry," Faelan said. "We found the letters you mentioned, that you and Ian left."

"Aye. We wanted to make sure you knew what happened."

"There was another letter too."

"He wrote more? That sounds like Ian," Tavis said.

"It's addressed to both of us," Faelan said. "I thought we would read it together."

"Aye." He needed something to get his mind off Anna. And Lachlan, who was watching her like he wanted to pull her off into a dark corner. "Is there something between Anna and Lachlan?"

Faelan looked over where Lachlan was leaning in to tell Anna something. "I don't think so. Bree?"

"He likes her, I think," Bree said. "She's never said anything about him. She doesn't really go out. . . ." She stopped and looked down at the floor as if she'd said something rude.

"Go out?"

"That means court," Faelan said. "Anna's not one for . . . for what they call dating. Seeing men." Faelan looked away too. He knew Tavis's secret. Tavis hoped the sympathy on his new sister's face wasn't because her husband had told her.

"Did you tell her?" he asked when they walked off to a quiet corner to read the letter after Bree said she had something to do.

"Tell her what?" Faelan's avoided Tavis's eyes.

"Shite. You told her what happened?"

"I couldn't help it. I thought she already knew. I thought Anna had told her."

"Damn it, Faelan."

"I'm sorry. She won't tell anyone. You can trust her."

"She'll think I'm a bloody rapist."

"No she won't. She understands. And she might be able to help Anna if she needs to talk about it." Faelan looked uncomfortable. "Do you really think she was mated with this hybrid?"

"Why else would they have taken her to him? But she wouldn't talk about it then, and now she's avoiding me like I have the pox."

"If we knew for sure, Bree might be able to help her with that too. Women like to talk about things that trouble them."

Faelan wasn't telling him something. Tavis didn't know why he wanted to know about the hybrid, but it wasn't just curiosity. That dug at his mind as they sat down and looked at the letter. It had been mailed to Isabel Belville.

Faelan and Tavis,

By now, I hope that you are both awake and well, and that you have stopped Druan. Many times I have regretted that it wasn't me who came to help Faelan. But Tavis, you insisted that it must be you, and you can be bloody stubborn. I am terrified when I think what you both might wake to. Will the world even exist? I don't know if you are alive or injured. No one but Ma knows the truth about you both. Frederick and Isabel know about Faelan, but not Tavis. I didn't want to share more information than necessary in the event they were compromised. I knew that if they saw to it that the graveyard remained in their family, the chapel would be safe as well.

I told the clan that Tavis was buried at sea. I was going to tell them that Faelan had also died, until I could determine if there were still traitors in our midst. However, the Seeker arrived before I did and told them about Faelan and the time vault. The clan was so horror-struck, and everyone wanted to know more. I was afraid if there was a traitor, the time vault would be discovered, and perhaps destroyed. I regret that I had to silence the Seeker to make sure he didn't tell where Faelan was hidden. Unfortunately, his death was in vain, for he had already told the Council. I regret his death every day, and I will until I face my own. I am still trying to find out where the threat comes from. I have not told the clan of my suspicions. I do not want to alert any traitors, if any still exist. I hope the threat died with Quinn, but there are troubling things.

Tavis, I have something personal I must tell you. I would put it in another letter, but I am out of paper, and I know how close you and Faelan are. He would find out anyway. Marna had a child. A son. Your son.

CHAPTER NINETEEN

MARNA'S FATHER CAME TO ME JUST AFTER SHE DELIV-
ered the bairn. I wasn't sure whether to believe her
until I saw how she grieved over your death. And when I
saw the bairn, he looked as much like you as a bairn can
resemble anyone. Marna's father was worried. She was not
doing well, and his wife, Marna's mother, was already dead.
Alas, Marna did pass, so Bessie and I took the boy and
raised him as our own. I know it will be heartbreaking to
find that you had a son you did not know. But the good news
is that you will have descendents. Your name will live on
through him.

He is a brave boy and looks just like you. I did not tell Ma
in the beginning. We did not want to tarnish your name or
Marna's. I had promised her father. But Ma guessed. He was
so much like you. Sometimes when she spoke of you she
would watch him with the saddest look on her face. Finally,
Bessie convinced me to tell her. She cried and called him her
little Tavis. I should have told her before. Bessie is with child
now, twins, the doctor says, so your lad will have brothers
or sisters. I am pleased, but I miss you and Faelan and Da.

One line was scratched out, and when Tavis looked closer he saw that it read.

It is a strange thing to think that when you read this I will be dead.

All my love to you both. I will see you again on the other side.

Ian

Tavis stared at the letter until the numbness in his chest turned to cold. It seemed only yesterday that he had given in to Marna's persistent attention, and a kiss led to a fondle that led to something more. But a child? They had been careful.

"Tavis."

He looked up and saw Faelan watching him.

"Are you all right? You look like a sick sheep."

"I feel like a sick sheep." Tavis rubbed his hands through his hair. "I have a son. Had. He's dead. My son, a son I didn't even know, is dead."

Faelan gave his knee a sympathetic squeeze. "I'm sorry. But do you realize that some of the warriors walking around here may be descended from you?" Faelan looked thoughtful. "Let's see. Ronan, Declan, Cam, and Duncan are descendants of Ian's oldest son. Your son. Some of our finest warriors came from you."

It was a fascinating thing, and surely it would mean more later, but right now all he could think was that he had a son who'd lived and died without Tavis even knowing it.

"Do you want to keep this quiet?"

Tavis shook his head. "He'd missed his son's entire life. Acknowledging him now was all he had. "No. I don't want to hide it." Tavis swallowed. "You saw his grave?"

"I did. He lived a long life."

"All the while I was sleeping in that damned time vault."

"I am sorry, Tavis. I wish you hadn't come. It's a joy to have you here, but if you'd stayed . . . you could have known him. Raised him."

"I couldn't stay."

Faelan's mouth thinned. "You always watched out for me. Come with me. I think we could both use a drink."

"You hardly ever drink," Tavis said.

"I think this is the time." He led Tavis to a room that resembled a tavern.

"You have a tavern?"

"It's just a game room with a bar. We sometimes play billiards or a game of darts. But on a rare occasion a whisky or ale hits the spot."

"Like when you've just discovered that your brother from another century isn't dead?"

"That would about do it." Faelan reached over the counter and pulled out a bottle of whisky. He poured a small measure into two glasses. They raised their glasses and took a drink.

"I know you're sad now, but things will get better. It's a hard thing to lose everyone in one blow. I still miss them, but it's not as hard as it was."

Tavis took another drink, feeling the burn in his throat. He didn't drink often himself. "You've found happiness here."

"I have. I wouldn't go back even if I could. I miss them, but I belong here. And I'm bloody glad you're here now."

He picked up a knife and threw it at the wall. It hit just outside the bull's-eye. "Remember that year we beat Wallace MacIntosh?"

"Aye. Stopped his bragging. Until the next year. What's this?" Tavis asked, pointing to a table with rows of figures attached to bars.

"Foosball. And that's air hockey. Want to have a go with the knives?"

"You won't cheat?"

"Me?"

"As I recall, I won the last challenge. A horse race. But you kept the white stone."

Faelan threw another knife. "I would've won if that branch hadn't hit me in the face."

Tavis took another drink. "But it did." They threw knives, losing track of the score as the conversation turned to home and family and duty.

Faelan took another drink. "You want to talk about guilt," he said as they discussed the atrocities their demons had been responsible for while the warriors slept. "I could've perhaps stopped the Civil War. Do you know how many people died?"

"Couldn't have been more than I'm responsible for. At least the Civil War was about an honest fight. A disagreement between brothers. Not just one evil bastard's attempt to control the world."

"Sometimes I feel as if I were there in the war," Faelan said. "I have dreams that feel more like memories, but they can't be. I can almost smell the gunpowder. And the faces, Bree showed me a book on the war, and some of the soldiers look familiar. General Grant. I would swear I've met him."

"General Grant? I know that name."

"You can't know that name. You were in the time vault and you haven't seen the books."

"That's bloody strange. It's happening to me too. Dreams of things I couldn't possibly have done. Battles I never fought." Tavis held up his glass. "And I hadn't had any of this. What do you make of it? Just me wishing I hadn't failed?"

"I passed it off as just dreams, but if it's happened to you . . ." Faelan was frowning at his drink. "And it's not just battles. I think I saw Bree when she was a lass. Perhaps I'm just recalling stories she's told me, but some of them I don't think she mentioned. And her grandmother. I think I talked to her before she died."

"You think we were really sleeping in there?" Tavis asked.

"Damnation. It makes me wonder." He took another drink. "Let's talk about something else." The talk moved to the advances of modern times. "You can't go back," Faelan said. "So you'll have to learn to live with all this. With the bloody computers and machines and women. God, the women. You've never seen the like. And when you find your mate, you'll burn for her like nothing you can imagine. Even now, I can't stay away from Bree. It's killing me now, not being with her."

"You are with her."

"I mean in bed. She's had a lot of stress. I decided she needed to take some time off from sex. And now it's all I can think about." Faelan threw a knife that missed the board altogether. "I hope Coira doesn't see that hole in the wall. I think I should have stopped after the second glass. I'm not a drinker."

"Aye, I hear you. The room's looking a little blurred to me."

"Here you are." Ronan and Lachlan entered the room. "We wondered where you'd gotten to," Ronan said.

"We're having a little competition and conversation," Faelan said.

Lachlan picked up the bottle of whisky. "And a few drinks, I'd say."

"I've heard how good Tavis was . . . is," Ronan said. "Want to put it to the test?"

Faelan had told them about him. Tavis's chest warmed. Or maybe it was the whisky. "Aye, I'll take you on."

"I'll take on the winner," Niall said, joining them, followed by Brodie, Shane, and Marcas.

"I'm second," Brodie said. "I can beat this big ape of a man anytime." He punched Niall, and Niall punched him back, sending him crashing into Marcas. "Easy there, Kong. I barely touched you."

And the game was on. They threw knives for a long while, and Tavis felt warmer and warmer inside. It was partly the whisky, but he also felt like he was home.

"So this is where the party is," Sean said, peeking in the door. "I thought we'd been invaded."

"Sean, join us," Niall said, holding up a knife.

"Ah, my knife-throwing days are over. I'd best get myself to bed. And don't you chaps get too carried away. I think you've had a wee too much already."

"One round with the knives," Ronan said. "You need to forget about these demons for a while as much as we do."

"One round it is, then." Sean played three, beating them all. But then he hadn't had any whisky.

"I think he cheated," Lachlan said after Sean had left.

"Sean doesn't cheat," Brodie said. "I'll cheat, but not Sean. Where's Shane?"

"He crashed on the pool table," Niall said.

"He doesn't drink much either," Faelan said to Tavis.

"I think I'd better get some rest myself," Tavis said. "Where do I sleep?"

"I can show you where Anna's room is," Brodie said, chuckling.

Niall thumped him on the head.

"Why'd you do that?" Brodie complained.

Niall thumped him again. "I like thumping you on the head."

"Don't let me deprive you of your enjoyment at the expense of my brain."

"We all need to turn in," Marcas said. "It's late."

"Come on," Faelan said to Tavis. "Bree and Shay got a room ready for you. I'll show you where it is." Faelan led Tavis upstairs to the second floor.

"This castle is just like home. Except the rugs are different and the stuff on the wall."

Faelan put an arm around Tavis's shoulder. "We'll go back and visit after we get rid of Voltar and Tristol."

Tavis patted Faelan's hand. "Is this brotherly love, or are you feeling as unsteady as I am?"

"Some of both," Faelan said with a laugh. "Here you go." He opened a door, and he and Tavis stepped inside. Bree and Shay were standing near the bed.

"It's plain as the nose on your face that Tavis and Anna—oh, Tavis, Faelan, we didn't hear you," Bree said, darting a quick glance at Shay.

"Obviously," Faelan said. "What are you doing up? You should be resting."

"I'm sick of resting," Bree said. "Is this room OK?"

Tavis looked around. It was large, with a comfortable bed and the usual furnishings. "Aye, it'll do fine. Thank you," he said to Bree and Shay.

They both gave him a smile, and he thought again how lucky Faelan and Cody were. Tavis's luck with bonny lasses had been poor. Almost deadly, in fact. But these two seemed to be as beautiful and kind as angels, in spite of the strange clothing and their boldness.

"Are you drunk?" Bree asked.

Faelan held up two fingers, measuring a pinch. "Just a wee bit."

"We wondered where you'd disappeared to," Shay said. "We were just coming to find you."

"Was Cody looking for us?" Faelan asked.

"No, he's with Declan doing something."

"If you need anything, I'm three doors down on the left. Bree and I keep a room here."

"The bathroom has toiletries. If you need anything else, just ask." Shay surprised Tavis by wrapping her arms around him and hugging him hard. Her arms were as strong as a man's. No woman in his time would have done such a thing unless she was family. He supposed she was.

"Thank you."

Shay stepped away. "I'm going to find Cody. We're still trying to decide what to do about this wedding. And Matilda. She's driving both of us crazy. Night everyone."

Bree stepped up to Tavis and also wrapped her arms around him, holding him tight. "Welcome home again, Tavis. I can't tell you how glad I am that you're here. I only wish your entire family were here."

So did he.

She leaned back and put both hands on his cheeks, which pressed her stomach closer to his. It was still flat, but he thought about the child growing inside, and the child he'd lost. Bree's eyes closed, and her hands traveled down his neck to his chest. Her forehead wrinkled, and she shook her head. He glanced up at Faelan, alarmed.

Faelan frowned and moved closer but didn't speak, so Tavis didn't speak either. Bree's eyes flew open, and she gasped.

"Bree?" Faelan touched her shoulder.

Bree stepped away from Tavis, but still watched him. "I'm sorry. I just get these weird . . . feelings."

"Did you just read his damned battle marks?" Faelan asked.

Bree gave a guilty start. "What?"

"You heard me. Did you?"

"Maybe."

"You read my battle marks," Tavis said, fascinated, and more than a little alarmed.

"I might have."

"Well," Faelan said, after Bree didn't speak.

"Uh . . . I'll tell you later. I'm getting tired."

Faelan gave her a disbelieving look. "I thought you didn't want to rest."

"I changed my mind."

"What is she again?" Tavis asked.

"Sometimes she's a bloody nuisance," Faelan said, but love poured from his eyes.

"I'm your sister-in-law," Bree said. "Your family. That's all that matters now."

There was a scratching at the door, and Faelan walked to the double doors leading to the balcony. "How'd you get out there?"

A large white cat walked into the room. It looked at Tavis with green eyes that were oddly like Bree's and Shay's.

"Matilda's been looking everywhere for you," Bree said to the cat as if it could hear her. Was his brother's wife a little barmy?

The cat walked over and jumped up on the foot of the bed.

Faelan watched it, his brows pulled together like he did when he was unsure about something. "Guess you've got the cat tonight."

"Strange-looking cat."

"You're telling me," Faelan said.

"He's special," Bree said.

"She thinks he can understand us."

Bree shrugged.

"I feel like it's reading my mind," Faelan said. "We can't seem to get rid of it. It's adopted us. Matilda thinks it wards off vampires. And she swears it saved the President."

"You jest?"

"I wish," Faelan said, looking suspiciously at the cat. "But there was a strange incident . . . never mind about that now. You need rest. And quiet. I know you have a lot on your mind."

"Thank you, brother. And Bree. I'm glad to be here."

He and Faelan shared a long look. Each of them knew how much he'd sacrificed. Then Bree and Faelan walked to the door. "Oh, and Anna's in the next room if you need anything," Bree said.

"Are you bloody matchmaking?" Faelan asked as the door closed.

"Me?" was Brcc's muffled reply.

"I think Ronan's right about you."

Tavis looked at the wall that joined his and Anna's room. Far different than the bars of a cell. He had no wish to go back, unless it was to kill Voltar and Tristol, but he missed the closeness he and Anna had shared. She was barely speaking to him now. He started to pull off his clothes and remembered the cat. It wasn't watching him. It had turned its back as if giving him privacy. Damned odd cat. Tavis went to the fancy bathroom and undressed, and then used the shower—a marvel of an invention—before crawling into bed. The cat was still there, paying no attention to him.

He climbed into bed naked. The underthings—underwear—Faelan called them, were too confining. The cat had again turned its back. The shcets felt cool against Tavis's skin, but his mind was spinning. Not just the drink. With the quiet, the revelation set in. He had a son. A little boy. Had Ian told him that Tavis was his father? Or had Ian let him believe he was his father? If Ian died three years after Tavis went into the time vault, the boy would have been young. Perhaps too young to be told his father was in a time vault and his mother dead. Poor Marna. She'd loved him, he believed, and though he couldn't honestly say he had returned that love, fondness yes, it made him sad to think of her sweet eyes, her quietly pleasant face.

Tavis's eyes stung with grief and regret, and his head throbbed with too much drink. The cat watched him from the bottom of the bed, but strangely enough, he wasn't bothered by its presence. Instead, it was comforting, and he fell asleep dreaming of Anna. The dream had turned decidedly erotic when a noise pulled him from sleep. He opened his eyes and saw a creature above him, leaning over his bed. He threw back the covers and grabbed the dagger underneath his pillow as he leapt from the bed. With an ungodly screech, the creature ran for the door. Tavis followed, hurrying after the intruder, who was running for the door. He followed the howls and raced down the hallway, heedless of his nakedness. One door slammed as others opened, and faces peered out at him. Faelan and Bree, Shay, Cody, Ronan, Nina, Duncan, Sorcha—had she come from Duncan's room?—and, oh God. Anna.

"There's something in my room," he said, and then realized everyone was staring at his groin, so he dropped his hands to cover those parts.

"Well now," Sorcha said, smiling.

Duncan stepped in front of her to obscure her view.

"Who was it?" Faelan asked. "Did you get a look?"

"I couldn't see well. It was leaning over my bed."

"Search the castle," Duncan said.

A loud screech sounded from one of the nearby rooms, followed by a crash.

Nina clasped a hand to her mouth. "That's Matilda's room."

"Stay back," Faelan said when Bree followed on his heels. Faelan opened the door, and they stared at the awful sight. The red-haired woman, the barmy one, not Sorcha, stood near the door, red hair sticking up and her eyes wide, black smeared underneath like a raccoon's, and she held the cat in her arms. Held, as in restrained. It was obvious from the extended claws and puffed fur that the cat was trying to get away.

"Did someone come in here?" Faelan asked.

Matilda shook her head and held on to the cat.

"Wait," Faelan said. "How did you get the cat? It was in Tavis's room."

Nina pushed through the others and faced Matilda. "Matilda, did you go to Tavis's room to get the cat?"

"I needed it," Matilda said. "I couldn't sleep. I had dreams."

"Matilda!" Nina gave her an exasperated look. "That cat can't protect you against vampires. There aren't any vampires in here anyway."

"You don't know that," Matilda said. "No one knew the one was in the castle in Scotland either. They might have followed us here."

"We have guards," Shay said.

Matilda caught sight of Tavis, still standing naked, with only his hands covering his front. Her eyes widened. "Oh my."

Tavis starting backing up toward his room and bumped into someone. He turned. It was Anna. Her beautiful eyes ran up and down his body. "Sorry." He backed away toward his door and opened it, hurrying inside. He shut the door and grimaced. Darn near everyone in the castle had seen his cock now. The door opened behind him. Anna stepped inside. Said cock surged, and his heart pounded. Had seeing his body made her decide to treat him more kindly? He knew that she was attracted to him in the dungeon.

"You're in my room," Anna said.

"What?"

"My room. You're in it."

Tavis looked at the scattered covers on the bed and saw that in fact he was in the wrong room. "Damn. I thought this was my room."

Anna flicked a glance over him again. "You can wait a moment until the crowd thins. I think they're ripping Matilda a new one. That woman needs a babysitter."

That would explain the raised voice in the hallway. Nina sounded furious. "I swear I thought she was a demon when I saw her over my bed. And the screeching. I guess that was the cat."

"She's obsessed with the cat." Anna glanced down again and grabbed a small blanket from her bed. "Here, cover up."

Tavis took the blanket and arranged it around him, and then looked awkwardly around the room.

"You can sit if you'd like." Anna walked to her balcony and looked out.

"I think I'd rather go out in the hallway naked and be scorned." She turned back to him. "Why?"

"It's a sight better than being ignored."

"I'm not ignoring you."

"Yes you are."

"Well, maybe I am. I'm not good with situations like this."

"Being cordial? Mere hospitality?"

She scowled. "You know what I mean. We . . . we . . . you know."

"Aye, I do." And he'd been thinking about it far too much. "I'm ashamed that I've added to your pain, after what happened to your mother and to you."

"You know about that?"

"Ronan told me. He was concerned about you. Can't we start over? Pretend we've just met and that I didn't do what I did?"

"You didn't do anything wrong. If anything, you saved me. I don't blame you."

"Then why the hell are you acting like I'm poxed?" He'd been driving himself barmy with guilt.

"I told you in the dungeon that it wasn't your fault. If you hadn't done it, the guard would have." Anna shuddered. "And he probably would have killed us."

"But I . . . I shouldn't have . . ."

"You're upset because you had an orgasm?"

Her words shocked him. Did all women speak so forward? "I have no excuse except that I hadn't been with a woman in a long time."

There were questions in her eyes, but she didn't ask them. "It was just your body's reaction. Bree said Faelan was insatiable when he came out of the time vault. I guess even though time stops, some emotions and functions build. It doesn't make sense, but then again, we're talking about a box that stops time. That shouldn't exist either by normal standards."

"I'd better get back to my room and try to rest. I have to meet with the Council tomorrow." He looked down at his blanket.

"Keep it. I'll get it later."

Tavis's stomach knotted as he and Faelan walked to the library. He couldn't put off meeting with the Council any longer, but he didn't know if he could trust them. Not after what he and Ian had read in Nigel's letter. One hundred and fifty years had passed since Tavis and Ian had discovered that letter—far longer since Nigel's accusations—and Tavis knew no more now than he had then. Didn't know what conclusion Ian had drawn. If the threat had passed. If others were involved. Quinn hadn't told anyone what his father had done, so at least two had been involved. Quinn's silence on the matter had been almost as atrocious as his father's deeds. Selling warriors' names to demons so they could be destroyed before they grew up. Like Liam. Nothing could be more despicable.

Anna and several of the warriors were already seated in the library. It was supposed to be an informal gathering, but the Council was seated apart, as if they were better than the others. And they had on their ceremonial robes. He'd always felt they were a little holier-than-thou, and this generation of elders looked just the same. Put them on a battlefield facing down a bunch of demons and then see what they thought about their rules.

Tavis took a seat near Faelan, one with a view of Anna, who was sitting next to Lachlan and Ronan, of course, and the Council called the meeting to order. Informal, his bloody arse. He told them everything he knew from the time they had followed Faelan to America to help him battle Druan until he and Anna had broken free from the fortress.

"You support this tale?" the Chief Elder asked Anna.

"Yes. I don't know about the part before I arrived at Tristol's fortress, but that's what happened after I got there." They asked her a few more questions, which she answered.

"So it is your opinion that Tristol owned the fortress and was operating some sort of breeding program?"

Anna looked at her own hands. "Yes."

"And Tristol was under the assumption that he had captured Faelan?"

"Yes," Anna said.

"Was anyone else part of this program?" the Elder asked.

"There was another prisoner there. They called him a hybrid." Anna stopped, took a breath, and shot Tavis a glance. "I don't know if he was involved."

"And what about yourself, Anna? Was anything said about involving you in the program?"

Anna's eyes widened. "Excuse me?"

"We understand that you spent some time with the hybrid."

Anna's mouth opened. She glanced at Tavis, her eyes glittering with anger. "I saw him."

"Can you tell us about that?"

"I just glimpsed him," Anna said, her back stiff. "He had escaped and had gotten into the cell where they were keeping me."

She wasn't going to mention the guard taking her to the hybrid. And how the hell had they found out? Had Faelan told? Tavis hadn't told him not to mention it. Dammit.

They asked her more about the hybrid. When she had answered their questions, the Chief Elder stared at her, his heavy-lidded gaze quite pointed. "Do you have anything else to add?"

Anna kept her chin up, but she wasn't breathing. Tavis could see that her shoulders weren't moving. "No. Nothing."

Tavis wanted to help her, to take the attention off her, and in his enthusiasm he blurted out something he'd spent over a century trying to hide. "I hope to return the Book of Battles to the Keeper within a day or so." Bloody hell. Why did he say that? He didn't know if the Council could be trusted yet.

Everyone looked at him much as they had when he'd chased Matilda out into the hallway naked. He glanced down to make sure some of his strange clothing hadn't come undone, but everything looked in order, similar to the other men's.

"What do you mean?" the Chief Elder asked.

It was too late to come up with a lie now. "I'm ashamed to admit that I don't remember where I hid it."

"You're the one who hid it?" Faelan asked. "We wondered how it had gotten in the chapel."

"The chapel?" Had he hidden it in the chapel? "My memory is still cloudy on some things."

"Well, it was a long time ago," Bree said.

"You're doing well if you can remember where you put something over a century ago," Brodie said. "Sometimes I forget where I put things a few hours before."

"It was just a fortnight ago, or thereabouts," Tavis said.

Everyone there looked confused, the Council, the warriors, even Anna. They all looked at him as if he were a simpleton. Faelan frowned. "What are you talking about, Tavis? Bree's grandmother had the Book of Battles when Bree was a lass."

Tavis shook his head. "That's impossible."

"I don't understand," Faelan said.

"I had the Book of Battles with me in the time vault."

CHAPTER TWENTY

AN UPROAR ENSUED.
"Then what book do we have?" Ronan asked.

"This doesn't make sense," Cody said.

The Chief Elder banged on the table to quiet everyone. "Are you telling us that the book we have isn't real?"

"If you've had it that long, it can't be," Tavis said. "I took the book with me in the time vault. I promised Quinn that I would protect it. Quinn Douglass, the Keeper."

"That's Sorcha's great-great-grandfather," Duncan said, looking at the outspoken woman, who looked surprised.

"He said it had been stolen many decades before," Tavis said.

"Stolen by whom?" the Elder asked. "Did he know?"

"He didn't say, except that he'd made a terrible mistake and thought he could fix it."

"You think Quinn Douglass was involved in this theft?" the Elder asked. "If the book had been stolen decades before, he would have been very young."

"We think he was protecting his father, the Keeper during that time. As he lay dying, Quinn admitted that he came to America with us to steal the book back. We thought he came with us to look into Nigel Ellwood's disappearance. He was a Watcher who disappeared."

"Yes," the Elder said. "We all know of Nigel's mysterious disappearance."

"Nigel believed there was a traitor in the clan. After one of our Watchers had had ominous dreams about Nigel, Quinn was appointed by the Council to find out what happened to Nigel and look into his accusations. After Quinn died, we found a letter on him from Nigel to the Council. He believed someone in the clan was selling warriors' names. Ian and I believed our brother's name was sold to a demon."

There was a gasp from the women, and a few of the men, and Faelan's knuckles whitened as he fisted his hands.

"Nigel suspected that the Keeper was involved. Nigel had been given permission by the Council to go to America and build a place there, a second seat for the clan, so they weren't all in one place. Nigel believed the book was in danger. He wasn't sure how deep the treachery went." Tavis cleared his throat. "Even thought that the Council might have been involved." The members of the Council looked affronted, as if it was blasphemy to utter such a thing, but Tavis continued. In for a penny. In for a pound. "So he took it with him, believing it was better for the book to be believed missing. Nigel saw ancient demons near his castle, this castle, and he wrote to Scotland asking the Council to send warriors to transport the book back to Scotland." Tavis glanced at Sorcha, who looked pale. "We believe neither Quinn nor his father told the Council."

"Oh my God. What happened to Nigel and the book?" Shay asked.

"One of the Watchers from my time said that Nigel was never seen again. Quinn knew where the book was, so Ian and I stole it back."

"Where was it?" Ronan asked.

"Right here, in this castle. Hidden in a secret compartment. Both the compartment and the castle were cloaked." He looked at Anna. "Like Tristol's fortress where Anna and I were prisoners."

"So the demons have had our clan's Book of Battles all these years it was missing?" Niall looked horrified. "Bloody hell."

The Council turned as one and frowned at Niall. It would seem cursing was still frowned upon.

"My apologies," Niall said.

"We believed one of the demons, or perhaps all of them, stole the castle and the book since it was cloaked," Tavis continued. "We figured it must be sorcery. The interesting thing is that when Ian and I arrived, we expected a battle, but all the demons were dead. Similar to how all the vampires were dead in Tristol's fortress."

"Sounds like a turf war," Declan said.

"I've heard nothing of this," Sean said, his bright eyes clouded with alarm. He was the Keeper now.

"This is disturbing," the Chief Elder said. "Very disturbing. We've never known what happened to Nigel Ellwood. It has come to our attention that Bree Connor is a descendant." The Elder's eyes fell on Bree. Faelan made a disagreeable sound and put his arm around his wife as if defying the Council to show any interest. Tavis had heard some of the warriors talking about the Council's interest in Bree and Shay because of their unusual abilities.

"If all this is true, then where did the book we have come from?" Duncan asked.

"We believe Frederick, my ancestor, found it hidden in the chapel," Bree said.

"Does this mean there are two books?" Brodie asked.

"I've never heard such a thing," Sean said. "I can't believe there were two books. We need to see the one Tavis had."

All eyes turned to him. "I don't remember where I put it. Everything is kind of muddled from then. I know I had it when I came out of the vault. I can't remember seeing it after that. Angus could have stolen it."

Anna immediately jumped to Angus's defense. "Angus wouldn't steal it. He had spent months searching for the book."

"Maybe he hid it," Faelan suggested.

"That's possible," Tavis said.

"But where?" Shay asked.

"I don't know. We were in a house of some kind. It was white, I think. There was a woman there." Tavis frowned, trying to remember.

Bree sat forward on her seat. "Mrs. Edwards's bed-and-breakfast. Angus was there. He had a notebook with him."

"That's where Tristol captured me," Tavis said.

"Remember that dream I had about you?" Bree said to Faelan. "The one where the dark-haired man snatched you? It must have been Tristol taking Tavis. He looks like you. I saw a dark-haired man in the hallway, and he gave me the creeps."

"What did he look like?" Tavis asked.

"He was gorgeous, tall, long dark hair."

"Sounds like him," Tavis said. Faelan had been there in the room next to his. What a bloody damned coincidence.

"If we'd known," Bree said, "we could have saved you so much pain."

"I'll go to the bed-and-breakfast and look for the book," Anna said.

"I'll go," Tavis said.

"I don't need help—"

"I'm coming." Tavis frowned at her.

Fire flashed in her eyes, but she didn't say anything more.

"I should let you know," Tavis said to the Council, "Michael assigned Voltar to me."

That got everyone's attention. They all started talking.

Anna stood up. "You can't be assigned to Voltar. I am."

CHAPTER TWENTY-ONE

That caused another ripple of shock. "You?" Tavis said. "That's impossible."

"Why? Because I'm a woman?"

"No, because he's mine."

"But Michael came to me," Anna said. "He told me Voltar had to be stopped."

"When?"

"Several hours ago. When did he come to you?"

"Before I went into the time vault."

"Before you went into the time vault?" The Chief Elder looked at the rest of the Council, who were talking among themselves in quiet whispers. "Do you mean to say you ignored Michael's order?"

Tavis grimaced. "I had a vow to keep."

"But this is the archangel," the Chief Elder said. "What could be more important than an order from him?"

"My brother. I swore that I would come to help Faelan and protect the book. I keep my vows. And I don't know if he meant for me to destroy him then or now."

"Voltar has committed horrendous crimes against humanity."

The Chief Elder frowned at Tavis. "He's responsible for millions of deaths."

And he might have been stopped if Tavis hadn't disobeyed his order.

"Don't do it," Faelan said quietly. "Don't let your mind go there. We've too much to deal with right now."

Tavis nodded dumbly.

"I think he's been reassigned to me," Anna said.

"No. You can't fight him," Tavis said.

"Excuse me?"

"I won't let you get hurt."

"Tavis Connor, you can't tell me what I can and can't do. That isn't how things are done in this day and age. And besides, it isn't your place."

Tavis heard a chuckle and looked around to see several grins.

"Why don't you just throw her over your shoulder," Brodie said.

"Because I'll stab him in the back," Anna said, those beautiful eyes flashing fire.

The Chief Elder banged on the table. "The Council and I will discuss Voltar's assignment with the Watchers." After a few minutes, the Elder officially dismissed the unofficial meeting, and Tavis started to leave.

"When are we going to the bed-and-breakfast?" Anna asked, her expression not far off from hostile.

"How about now?"

She looked him up and down and nodded. "I'll be in the car."

The drive was awkward and quiet. After a few minutes, Tavis had had enough. "This is bloody nonsense."

"What?"

"You going after Voltar."

"He's mine."

"I think he's mine. I don't want you to fight him. I'm afraid you'll get hurt. And I owe it to you to protect you."

"No you don't."

"I do."

"Is this a misguided attempt to ease your guilt?"

Tavis felt like she'd slapped him in the face. "What the hell's wrong with you? I took advantage of you. I'm trying to make it right."

"You can't make it right," she yelled. She closed her eyes, and then opened them again, which was a relief since she was driving. "There's nothing to make right. I told you already. You saved me. You don't owe me anything."

"Then why are you still treating me like a bastard?"

"I'm not."

"You are. You're acting like an ass. Where's the woman I met in the dungeon? The woman who bathed my wounds and kept me warm. Hell, you helped me piss in a cup."

"I just . . . it's not you. It's me."

"I don't like this you," Tavis said.

Anna sighed. "I don't either. I don't know what's wrong with me."

"I think I do. You're frightened."

"What would I be frightened of?"

"The same thing I am. This thing between us."

She looked up then. "What do you mean?"

"It's overwhelming. I've never felt this way about anyone."

Her eyes were wide. She swallowed. "That scares you?"

"It scares the hell out of me."

"So what do we do about it?" she asked.

"Stop ignoring me, that would be a start."

"I'll work on it." She glanced at him with the beginnings of a smile. "Let's call a truce." She stuck out her hand.

A truce sounded good. He took her hand, and they sealed the pact. "You're not really intending to fight Voltar are you?"

That led to another heated discussion which lasted until she approached a white house with black shutters. "Forget about Voltar for now," she said. "Let's find the book. We have a truce. Remember?"

They parked, and by the time Tavis figured out how to get the damned door open, Anna was standing in front of the car waiting for him.

"Do any of these bloody car doors open the same?"

"I forgot you hadn't been in this car before. You'll get used to it. Before long you'll be driving."

"I doubt that."

"Bree said Faelan thought the same thing. Now he's hooked on driving. Bree's working on getting you an ID. Legal papers that prove your identity," she explained. She stopped before she knocked on the door. "What are we going to say? That we think something is hidden here? Do you even remember which room it is?"

"No. Could we say we're thinking of getting a room soon and wanted to see each one? I'll see if anything looks familiar."

"I came here once," Anna said. "I was retracing Angus's steps, and Bree had seen him here. But she didn't have any rooms."

An elderly woman answered the door. She had white hair and a dress with lots of little flowers. He didn't remember seeing her, but Angus had said he'd sneaked him in. "You don't have to knock," she said, and then her gaze fell on Tavis. "Faelan. You're back. How lovely to see you and . . ." She frowned at Anna.

"I'm not Faelan," Tavis said. "I'm his brother."

"Well then, come inside. Do you need a room? I have one room left."

"Just one," Anna said.

She looked at the two of them. "Did you need two?"

"Yes, but I suppose one will do," Anna said. "I mean we are getting married."

She frowned, but her wallet won out over her morals. "I suppose that would be fine. I get a lot of nice comments about this room. It's cozy. You'll see." Mrs. Edwards took them upstairs to the room. "Your brother stayed in the room at the end. What a lovely couple. Now what do you think about this room?"

It had a big bed. That was all Tavis cared about. He didn't care about covers and furniture. He just pictured himself and Anna in the bed.

"Very nice." Anna raised her eyebrows at Tavis.

He shook his head.

"We'll take this one," Anna said.

Tavis gave her a surprised look. Had she misunderstood? "We will?"

"It's perfect."

"Right. Perfect."

"Good. Come with me, and we'll get the paperwork all sorted out." After they had finished, they went upstairs to the room.

"What are you doing?" Tavis asked. "This isn't the right room."

"We have to check the other rooms. We can't wait until they're vacant."

"What are we going to do, sneak inside?"

"Of course. We'll wait for the guests to step out, and if they don't . . ."

Women warriors. How had the clan to come to this? "We can narrow it down a bit. It isn't this room or the one where Faelan stayed. And it wasn't on the other end," Tavis said. "It must be the one across from us or beside us."

They slipped into the hall and listened at each door. All the rooms were occupied. They went back to their room to wait. Anna sat on a chair near the window. Tavis took a chair across from her.

Anna checked her watch. "They'll have to go out to dinner sometime. Are you listening?"

"What?" He couldn't stop looking at the bed, imaging him and Anna there, sheets twisted, bodies slick with sweat. Blimey, it was hot in here. He shifted in his seat and wiped his forehead.

"I know what's bothering you. I can help if you'd like."

Surge! He shifted again, wishing he had on his kilt and not Faelan's jeans. He cleared his throat. "What did you have in mind?"

"I'm a good listener. It can't be easy coming back to the place where an ancient demon kidnapped you—" Anna frowned at him. "That's not what's bothering you, is it?"

"No."

"You were thinking about sex, weren't you?"

He looked at the bed again and considered lying. "Aye."

She started laughing. He'd never heard her laugh, and he was stunned. The lust he'd felt changed to something so strong, it felt like a hand crushing his heart.

"I shouldn't laugh. I should be offended, but Bree said the effects of the time vault are very strong. Hunger in every way."

Tavis was still trying to find his voice. "You have a beautiful laugh."

"Weren't we just talking about sex?"

"Aye. We can talk about it some more if you'd like."

"Or you could take a cold shower while we wait."

"Or we could eat."

"I bet you're hungry."

"I could eat my boots if I had some salt."

"Then let's go to dinner. Do you like Mexican?"

"I've never eaten one." He grinned, and when she smiled in return, it took his breath.

"Pizza. Let's have pizza."

They walked a few blocks, and he tried to observe the other people without staring. He wasn't always successful, and he decided that there were some strange people in this time. But pizza was a blessed thing. Or maybe it was just his raging appetite.

"Do you want another slice?"

He nodded and took one. "Good," he mumbled.

She rolled her beautiful eyes. "I never would have guessed."

"You have a good appetite for a woman."

"You think I'm eating too much?"

"Not at all. I like watching you eat."

"Are we back to the sex again?"

A woman at a table near them looked over at them. He grinned. "I think we'd better change the subject."

"How about clothes?"

"Clothes?"

"You'll need some. I don't imagine you'll want to wear your brother's all the time."

"That's a good idea. I don't have any way to pay until I find my sporran. I had a few coins with me."

"They wouldn't work now anyway. Don't worry. I have money. You'll get some too. I don't know how it was done back then, but the clan pays warriors. It's not like we can have regular day jobs. We do have buffers. They're not warriors, but they help us, provide services, help keep our secrets."

"We had people like that, but not many, and we didn't call them buffers. Strange name."

"It's just a nickname because they're buffers between us and the rest of the world. Officially they're called coordinators now."

Tavis leaned back and rubbed his stomach.

"Ate too much?"

"Aye."

"You'll be happy we have these fancy toilets later."

He grinned. It was very strange but appealing to have a woman speak so bluntly. And it was pure heaven to have her not ignore him. "I reckon I might at that."

They went to several stores after they ate, and she showed him racks and racks of clothing. Some were so bizarre he couldn't imagine anyone wearing them if he hadn't spotted a few on the way here. He let Anna tell him what he needed, since it was all too much for him to comprehend. He'd traveled the world and seen different cultures, but some of the clothing he'd seen in this time defied description.

"I think people are a bit barmy now," he said after they'd returned to their room with their bags. "Why would that girl we passed on the street want her entire arm tattooed?"

"Lots of people have tattoos. We do."

"But ours mean something," Tavis said. "They're not human marks. You said yours are on your back?"

"Most female warriors get them there."

"Can I see them?"

Anna looked at him and then sighed. She turned and pulled up the bottom of her shirt. In the dungeon, he hadn't seen her back. When he'd checked her for injures, he'd done it with her clothes on, not that they had covered much. He'd seen her thighs and glimpsed the juncture he'd been forced to breech, but he'd never seen her back. Her skin was beautiful, her spine was beautiful, and if her skin drew him, her battle marks took his breath. They were low on her back, just above her trousers—jeans—circles and twining lines rising from a point above her hips, opening below her waist. He couldn't help but touch the marks. She jumped, but didn't yell at him, so he didn't stop. His fingers tingled, as did his own battle marks, as if they were talking to hers. He traced the line to her waist and down again to the point. His finger continued along the line of skin just above her jeans and then around the side and to the front. She shivered, and he moved the other arm around so that he was encircling her waist. "I can't help it," he whispered, and pulled her gently against him.

She didn't answer, but she also didn't move. Her hands had been holding up her shirt. She dropped them, and he felt her hands reaching back for his hips. She pushed back against him, and he kissed her shoulder. His hands slid lower, over her stomach and to her thighs. A soft sound rolled from her throat, and he turned her in his arms. As if they'd done it many times before, her hands circled his waist, and his cradled her to him. He lowered his head, stopping just a breath from her mouth. "I'm going to kiss you. Is that all right?"

She nodded. "You smell like pizza, but I don't mind."

He let his lips brush hers, then opened his mouth to taste her better. His hand wound in her hair, holding her close.

"I like pizza," she said, pulling his bottom lip between hers.

"Me too."

They were moving toward the bed when they heard the door to the next room shut. Anna pulled away. Her eyes were shimmering with passion, her lips moist. "They've left."

Damn. "They'll probably be gone for a while," he said, kissing her neck.

She moaned and pushed him away. "We have to go."

One minute. All he needed was one minute inside her. Probably not even that. Just a little more stroking with her hips and he'd be finished. She would need more. Especially after what had happened before. Lots of tenderness and time. They stared at each other. "Should I apologize?"

"No."

"Then I won't."

They rearranged their clothing and slipped from the room. The door was locked. "I'll pick it," Anna said. "Ronan taught me a lot of things."

"I suspected as much."

She looked over her shoulder. "You don't mean what I think you mean."

"I might. Did he?"

"Did he what?"

"You know."

Her blush was telling. "Once. We were both . . . troubled."

Tavis was shocked at the anger he felt. If Ronan had been there, he would have hit him. He knew it was unreasonable, and it made him feel bad. He liked Ronan. He was family, probably a descendent. Even if he was a womanizer. What right did he have to say anything? It was Anna's life. Tavis hadn't been here. He'd been sleeping in a time vault.

"Are you finished daydreaming?" Anna asked, frowning.

"Sorry," Tavis said.

"I've almost got it. There." Anna turned the knob, and the door opened. "Be quiet. Mrs. Edwards is nosy. If she hears anything, she'll be up here in a second."

They tiptoed in, closed the door, and Anna turned on the light. The bed was unmade, covers trailing the floor. Luggage was open on the floor. But this was the room.

Tavis walked around the room. "This is it," he said, keeping his voice low. "I remember Angus bringing me here."

Anna's mouth tightened.

"I wish he had lived," Tavis said. "He saved me. Ian left a letter for Faelan telling him about my time vault, but he hadn't found it. He didn't know about the letter until I told him. If Angus hadn't found me, I could have been locked in there forever."

"And we had no idea you were there. We thought Angus had summoned a time vault for a demon." Anna touched Tavis's arm. "I'm glad Angus found you."

And Tavis thought that was one of the nicest things she'd ever said. "As am I."

"OK, do you remember putting the Book of Battles here?"

Tavis walked around the room and opened a door. "I remember this," he said, looking at the tub.

"You think you hid it in here?"

"I don't bloody know." He checked under the basin and in the closet. "What are you doing?" Anna had lifted the cover off the back of the fancy toilet.

"Sometimes people hide things in here."

"The Book of Battles?"

"It would be just like Angus to hide it there." She smiled sadly. "He loved mysteries and secret clues."

"You loved him?"

"I did, but not like that. He was my best friend. I always figured he was the closest thing I would have to a soul mate." Her gaze met Tavis's and moved away. "It's not in here," she said, replacing the cover on the toilet. "Let's go back into the bedroom."

They searched under the bed, the shelves, the walls. Anna was bent over looking on the closet floor when there was a tap on the door. They both stopped moving.

"Mrs. Canton, are you in there?"

Anna put a finger to her lips. They hardly breathed until Mrs. Edwards's footsteps walked away. "We've got to hurry."

"She's coming back." The footsteps moved closer to the door, and they heard a key inserted in the lock.

"It's them," Anna whispered. "Hide."

Where? Tavis was about the biggest thing in the room.

Anna pointed to the bed. It was a high bed, with a lot of space underneath. She scrambled toward the bed and slid underneath. Tavis joined her, hoping his feet weren't sticking out the bottom. He heard the door swing open and footsteps.

"Thank you for dinner," the woman said.

"It was my pleasure, but I've got indigestion."

He wasn't the only one. Tavis's stomach was knotting. He slowly turned his head and looked at Anna. She slipped her hand into his. His stomach rumbled softly.

"You need some Pepto, hon?"

"What?"

"I heard your stomach rumbling. I have Pepto in my purse if you need it."

"Wasn't mine. Lord, but I'm tired."

"All that walking and eating," she said. "Let's turn in early. I brought that new book you wanted."

Tavis and Anna lay quietly as the couple readied for bed. Bloody hell. This was a mess. His back was starting to ache. His wounds had mostly healed, but one or two were still sore. And his right heel was going numb. "I say we just slide out from under the bed and excuse ourselves," he whispered to Anna when the woman started opening and closing drawers.

She shook her head. "We have to find the book," she whispered back.

The couple finally retired, and Tavis's eyes crossed as he waited to see if the bedsprings would hit him in the face. It was close.

The woman giggled. "What are you doing?"

"We're at a bed-and-breakfast. I say we get our money's worth."

"I thought you were tired."

"Just a little quickie." The bed squeaked, and Tavis heard clothing being removed. Anna's hand clenched on his, and her eyes rounded as nightclothes and underthings fell to the floor. Tavis was sweating, imagining getting caught. Imagining it being him and Anna in the bed. His cock was hard, and his stomach burned with indigestion. Damned time vault.

The woman giggled again.

To hell with this. Tavis motioned for Anna to follow him, and he slowly slid out from under the bed. The room was dark, and the lovers were so preoccupied, Tavis figured they might have a chance to get out. They'd have to come back, but by God he wasn't going to lie under the bed and listen to them while he was ready to burst. He bumped his head once, but the occupants of the bed didn't notice. He stayed on the floor until Anna was beside him, and then they crawled to the door. Tavis opened it and slipped out. Anna followed, and they quietly closed the door before hurrying back to their room.

"Can you believe that?"

Anna grabbed Tavis and kissed him.

CHAPTER TWENTY-TWO

H IS SURPRISED "WHAT?" WAS DROWNED BETWEEN THEM. HE kissed her until his lips were numb. Anna leaned back and started to unbuckle his belt. "What are you doing?"

"What I've wanted to do since I saw you," she said.

Well hell. He pulled his shirt off while she fiddled with his zipper. "Careful, I almost re-circumcised myself this morning." But she was better with zippers. Her shirt was like his, so he pulled it over her head while she pushed his borrowed trousers and underwear down. He stopped to kick off his boots, and she removed the rest of her clothing.

"Bloody hell," he said when she was naked. "You're perfect."

She was looking at him, also naked now, her eyes burning a trail from his chest to his thighs. "So are you." She ran her fingertips over his battle marks, and he felt a tingle all the way through to his back. This wasn't just desire. It was something beyond. Flames licked at his body and mind like he'd fallen headfirst into a campfire. Her fingers moved lower, down his stomach. His muscles twitched in response, right along with another part which was standing at attention. She let one finger move down the line of hair that led to his groin. His eyes followed the movement. *Don't stop.*

Don't stop. She stopped. He looked down at her, but she was focused on the neediest part of him. She dropped to her knees. *Oh God.*

When he could think clearly, he gently moved her away. "I'm not going to be any good to you if you keep that up." He lifted her and stepped closer, putting one leg between hers, running his hands over her arse. What an arse it was. He nuzzled her neck and urged her back toward the bed. "Lie down. It's my turn."

She sucked in a hard breath, and he proceeded to give her as much pleasure as she'd given him. But he was stronger, or he wanted to believe he was, so when she pulled at his hair and whispered that he needed to move now, he didn't. She twisted and moaned, and before she had opened her eyes, he moved up her body and nudged the crest of her legs. "Are you ready for me now?" He didn't want to go the last step without her permission.

She grabbed his arse and threw her legs around his thighs in one move. "Now!"

"All right," he grunted, and slid into her, trying to go slow.

She bit his shoulder. "Come on."

"Bollocks." He was burning and tingling all over. He drove into her, again and again, until he couldn't hold back anymore. He let go, and every muscle, every bone, every hair on his body felt like it came apart. When it was over, they lay close together, trying to catch their breath.

Anna buried her face in his shoulder. "I think I've made a mistake."

Tavis's heart gave a dull thud. "What?"

"About sex. After what happened to my mother, I've looked at sex as a weapon."

"Only for the depraved." Like that fat guard. "It's supposed to be like this. A thing of beauty."

"It was that," she said, running her fingers over his stomach. "And more."

Tavis's heart felt nigh to bursting. He held her closer, stroking her hip. "I remember where it is."

She smiled. "I know you know where it is."

"Not that. The book. I think I know where Angus hid it. I saw him near the bookcase."

"We've got to get back in there," Anna said.

"Aye."

"We'll do it while they're asleep." Anna looked at her watch. "It's eleven. We'll wait two hours." And maybe they could repeat what they'd just done.

They didn't need two hours. It was apparent when that the couple was sleeping. They both snored. "This is in our favor," Anna said. "We could break down the door, and they would never hear us."

"We don't need to do that. There's a ledge outside our window that leads to theirs. The glass was opened a few inches when we were there."

"I didn't notice," Anna said. "Someone might see us. Our window faces the street."

"It's dark." He pulled back the curtain. "I'll climb out and go through and get the book."

"We'll climb out and go through and get the book."

"You're stubborn."

Anna shrugged. "I'm not planning on changing."

"Let's get this book," he said.

They climbed onto the ledge. Nothing ever goes exactly as planned. They didn't count on Mrs. Edwards being outside. "What's she doing at this bloody hour?" Tavis whispered, pressing his back to the wall. Anna was right beside him.

"She's doing something to that light fixture. Good grief," Anna said. "She's replacing a bulb. Hurry."

They crept along the wall slowly. They had reached the window when the light came on. Mrs. Edwards looked at it, her expression pleased. Just then the man let out a snore that rattled the window. Mrs. Edwards looked up, and Tavis was certain they would be spotted. He started thinking of possible excuses why they were standing on the ledge outside another guest's window when an owl swooped past Mrs. Edwards's head. She let out a screech, and the owl flew away. Mrs. Edwards ran inside.

"I don't believe it," Anna said. "Saved by an owl."

"That was strange." But he wasn't going to look a gift horse in the mouth. They moved along the ledge to the next window. It was still open a crack, and the man was still snoring.

"How do they sleep through that?" Anna asked.

"Be thankful they snore. Or else we'd have to knock them out and take the book."

They lifted the window and crept inside. There was enough light from the newly replaced lightbulb outside that they didn't need a flashlight—a good thing since he didn't have one. Then Anna pulled out her phone, tapped it, and a light sprang forth.

She kept it low as he searched the bookshelf. He'd seen Angus on the side near the wall. He quietly pulled books out, stopping when the man and woman ceased snoring, and resuming when they did. He found the satchel hidden behind several books and gently removed it.

"Is that it?" Anna asked.

Tavis eased the satchel open and looked inside. The Book of Battles was there.

"This is it?" Sean asked as everyone leaned closer, trying to get a look. Anna had peeked inside, but she and Tavis had both been hesitant to touch it.

"Aye. It's the one I found in the castle," Tavis said.

"How do we know which one is real?" Duncan asked. "What if this one is the fake?"

"We'll protect both," Sean said. "But I'll study the books and see if I can figure it out. But the fact remains, the book is safe. The Book of Battles has been returned to us."

"Let's hope another one doesn't turn up," Brodie said.

"God forbid," Ronan said.

"Do we tell the Council we found it?" Tavis asked. "I hadn't intended to mention it." He glanced at Anna. "I shouldn't have until we know for sure if the Council is trustworthy."

"I think we'll keep it quiet for now," Sean said. "Only those in this room will know." He looked at each of them—Anna, Tavis, Duncan, Brodie, Faelan, Bree, Cody, Shay, Ronan, Declan, Niall, and Shane. "We need to do some more investigating. And I believe I owe you a debt of gratitude."

Tavis touched his chest. "Me?"

"Faelan told me about Ian's letter, about your son. If not for you, Duncan and I, and several others, wouldn't even exist."

"You have a son? Had a son?" Anna asked.

"I just found out," Tavis said.

"You had a son and didn't know it?" Not only had he lost his family—father, mother, brothers, sister—but he'd lost a wife and child. "I didn't know you were married."

"I wasn't." Tavis shifted uncomfortably. "His mother was a lass I knew. A nice lass," he said defensively. He cleared his throat. "She loved me. I didn't know she was with child. When she died, Ian and his wife raised him."

Anna's head was spinning with the revelation. Tavis with a son. A lover.

"As I said, I owe you my thanks, and my existence," Sean said. "Duncan and I wouldn't be here if not for you."

"Can I call you grandfather?" Duncan asked, smiling. Something he didn't do often enough.

Tavis just smiled and shook his head.

Sean handed the satchel back to Tavis. "I didn't touch your journal."

"My journal?" Tavis frowned.

"There's a journal or a ledger inside. I didn't open it. I thought it belonged to you."

Tavis reached inside and took out a thin notebook. "Angus had this with him. He must have put it here."

"I saw him with a notebook when he was at the bed-and-breakfast," Bree said.

"Angus's notebook." Anna's throat tightened. "I've been looking for it."

"Anna should have it," Sean said.

Anna took the book and opened it. Angus's scrawled handwriting was easy to recognize. *Oh, Angus.*

"Does he say anything about what happened here?" Bree asked.

Angus had lived for mysteries when he was alive, and now his death had left the biggest one of all. Anna knew Bree still felt bad that she hadn't warned Angus. She had sensed danger around him but thought he was a demon, not realizing he was a warrior working undercover.

Anna flipped through the notebook, looking for recent entries that might shed some light on his death. Angus's writing wasn't always easy to follow. He wrote as he thought. Scattered when he was distracted, and when he was hot on the trail of something he could go on and on. Reading his notebook was almost like talking to him. She could feel his excitement in the words. She skimmed the pages, recounting relevant entries, such as when he'd found

Nigel Ellwood's letter—it made her sad that he hadn't told her that—right after he'd found Ian's notes about a possible traitor in the clan.

She read aloud how Angus had thought he'd found Faelan. Ian had left clues to where the time vault key had been hidden, buried in Aiden Connor's grave, and when it didn't open the time vault in the crypt, Angus decided it must be a decoy. He'd found the second time vault in the chapel cellar and freed the warrior inside, not realizing he'd freed Faelan's brother instead. Angus's handwriting grew scratchier as he wrote. He was frantic with his discovery, and terrified that Jared, the archaeologist, would find him. Angus had suspected that Jared wasn't what he pretended to be. He'd followed Jared and discovered that he was involved in the gathering of demons. He suspected it had to do with Druan's virus.

I'm going to confront Jared and make him talk. That was his last entry. The room was silent.

"I guess he found out Jared was Druan in disguise," Brodie said quietly. "That's probably how he got some of his injuries."

"And Druan sent his demons to finish him off," Ronan said.

He'd tracked them down and killed them, but they wouldn't say who'd sent them. If only she'd replaced her phone, he might still be alive. He wouldn't have told anyone else about his discoveries until he was certain what he'd found. But he had tried to call her. If she'd known, she could have come to help him before it was too late.

"Poor Angus," Sean said.

Anna quietly slipped away as the others began talking about traitors and demons. She went to her room and sat on her bed, holding the notebook to her chest. There were other scrawled entries that made no sense. *I need to tell Anna, but I don't want to trouble her.* And later, *I must tell Anna. No matter how difficult it is.* She hadn't read those aloud. They were too personal. "Tell me what? What was so important, Angus?" Was he referring to his feelings for her?

How could she have not known how he felt? No wonder he was so angry when he found Ronan in her bed. Sex might not be the big evil she'd thought, but it caused a lot of trouble.

What was she going to do about this thing between her and Tavis? She'd never felt anything like this. It was like an obsession. She thought about him constantly. She wanted to touch him all the time. She needed space to think and remember who she was. A warrior. Always a warrior. No matter how good sex with Tavis was. And how much she wanted to touch him and hold him.

She started to lay the book aside when she noticed a piece of paper stuck between two pages. It wasn't Angus's handwriting. The paper was stained and yellow with age. It was Ian's notes. The page she and Angus had found in the treasure room in Scotland. This should be given to Tavis. His brother had sacrificed and suffered to make sure Tavis was here to save Faelan. It might be one of the few things left to remind him of Ian.

CHAPTER TWENTY-THREE

Anna walked toward Tavis's door and raised her hand to knock, but stopped.

What are you doing? You can't go to his room. Not after what happened at the bed-and-breakfast. You can give him Ian's letter later. She returned to her door, stopped, chewed her lip for a moment, and then walked back. She was still waiting for the courage to knock when the door opened. Tavis had on the boxer briefs she'd bought him. That sent a thrill up her spine—not just the sight of Tavis in his underwear, but Tavis wearing something she'd chosen for him. It was so intimate.

But she didn't want intimate. No intimacy.

"Anna?"

"You open the door in your underwear? Geez." What if she had been another woman? Sorcha for instance.

He frowned. "I knew it was you. I heard you muttering. Are you all right? You look bothered."

"I found something in Angus's notebook. It was written by Ian."

"Ian?" A pained look crossed his face. "Come in."

She looked at his body. "You're not dressed."

"Sorry." He left the door opened and grabbed a pair of jeans. Jeans she'd bought him. "I think I'm getting better at this," he said, pulling them on. He grabbed a shirt, again, one she'd bought. She was definitely feeling bothered now. There was something so intimate about seeing a man she'd had sex with wearing clothes she'd bought him.

"Are you coming in?"

Even though he was dressed, she hesitated. It didn't seem to matter what he did or didn't wear, he just affected her in the strangest way. But she didn't want him to be alone when he read it. Or maybe he would rather be alone. "I thought you might want to read it in private."

"I'd rather you were with me."

Another thrill. Dammit. Tavis Connor was derailing her plans. Maybe she needed to go back to ignoring him. But she followed him inside.

Tavis took the paper and sat on a small settee next to a lamp. "It's his hand, all right." He smiled. "He was always jotting down notes."

Anna sat beside him. "Like Angus. Did he look like you?"

"No. He was thinner, lighter haired. A bit of a mischief-maker."

"He must have been a great warrior. And a great brother. It couldn't have been easy doing what he did. I don't think I could do it."

"He didn't want to. He begged me to find another way. At the time, I thought I was the one with the hard task. Now I think it was him. He was the one who had to tell Ma she'd lost two of her sons and her husband. He had live with the worry of not knowing if Faelan and I would survive the time vaults. Or even be found. He had to raise my son." He rubbed a hand over his chin. He looked different without his beard, even more handsome, though he needed to shave again. "I'm having trouble dealing with it. It doesn't seem possible, even though I have Ian's letter as proof."

"Duncan is living proof. It isn't Faelan he resembles so much. It's you." Anna put her hand over his. "I can't imagine how it feels to lose a son you didn't know. I wish I could help you."

"You have." Tavis touched her face. "You have more than you know."

Too much intimacy. She needed to get back to safer ground. "So tell me about your son's mother."

He looked almost embarrassed. "She was kind. And persistent."

"You said she loved you?"

"Aye, so she said. I tried to . . . avoid her, but it was hard." His cheeks colored. "I mean, it was difficult staying away from her, with her coming around all the time."

"What happened? If you don't mind telling me."

"She cornered me one night, and I wasn't thinking with my brain. We were careful though. I didn't even . . ." He looked embarrassed. "Even spill my seed inside her."

Anna touched his arm, and his muscles tightened. "I'm sorry you lost him, and her."

"Thank you. Do you mind if I ask you a question?"

"I won't know until you ask."

Dark eyes, lined with thick lashes, studied her, making her stomach quiver. "Are you certain you didn't love Angus?"

"Not like that. We were best friends." At least on her part, and Angus hadn't asked for anything more. She felt a pang of sadness. If he had, would it have been a different relationship?

"He must have been barmy, then." His gaze moved over her face, and her pulse beat faster.

"But he loved me."

"You mean he was in love with you?"

She nodded. "I didn't know until just before he died. It was the last thing he said to me. I love you. I've never told anyone. I feel guilty about it. Guilty about not being here to help him. Guilty for not replacing my phone. Then I would have gotten his call. Guilty for not knowing how he felt. And a little angry at him for not telling me. We told each other everything."

"Would it have made a difference?"

"I don't think so. In fact, it might have ruined what we had. And that would have been a shame."

"They said you don't want to marry or have a family. Is it because of your past?"

She shrugged. "I just want to be a warrior. That's what I am. A warrior."

"What's wrong with being a warrior and having a family too? I mean when the time comes? You don't have to be a warrior forever." She started to squirm. She was feeling overheated and uncomfortable.

"Don't run away."

"I'm not running."

"Yes you are." He touched her face, fingers stroking lightly down her cheek, then moving to her lips. "Can you feel it too?"

"Feel what?" she asked, hoping he didn't move his hand, wondering what he'd do if she kissed his fingertips.

"This . . . this feeling between us? It's eating me alive. I can't stop thinking about you. Is it just me?"

She shook her head, afraid to say the words. But she couldn't stop herself from touching his face, feeling the strong cheekbone and stubble of his jaw. Such a sexy face. She put her hand behind his head and pulled his face to hers. "No, it's not just you," she said, and kissed him.

He kissed her back. Her hands dropped to his chest, and she felt his battle marks tingling underneath her palms. She bunched her hands in his T-shirt to stop the sensation. She opened her mouth wider and felt the tip of his tongue. How could a man taste so good? She ran her hands up and down him, touching anything she could find. Skin, muscles, cotton, jeans—it was all delicious.

"I think I'm dying," someone muttered. Tavis, she thought, but their mouths and breaths were so fused she wasn't sure.

She was lying half across his lap with his hand up her shirt when the door opened.

They both jumped, and Anna fell onto the floor.

Faelan stood in the doorway, his mouth open. His look of surprise changed into a grin as Tavis and Anna both jumped to their feet. "I'm sorry," he said. "The door wasn't locked."

"You should have knocked," Tavis said.

Faelan's grin widened. "I thought you were expecting me."

Tavis glowered at him. "What's wrong with you?"

"I'm sorry, but the looks on your faces." Faelan chuckled. "It reminded me of that time Ian and I caught you in the stables with Marna—damnation. I'm sorry, Anna."

"Forget it," Anna said, straightening her shirt. "We were just . . . discussing something."

"Aye." Faelan grinned again. "That's my favorite kind of discussion."

"I'm going to knock that smile off your face if you don't stop," Tavis said.

"You're right, Tavis. I offer my sincerest apologies to you both," he said through clenched teeth and sparkling eyes. He backed toward the door. "I'll see you in the morning." He started to close the door, then popped his head back inside. "Carry on."

Tavis started toward the door, but Anna stopped him with a hand on his arm. "He's just teasing."

Tavis scowled. "Bloody rude bastard."

"I think brothers are allowed to be rude. You're lucky to have him here to tease you."

"You're right."

"It's getting late," Anna said, feeling awkward now that the moment had been interrupted. "I suppose I should be going."

He glanced at the bed and frowned. His frustration was so obvious, Anna almost grinned. "You don't have to."

"But I should." She stood. "Good night, then."

A muscle ticked in his jaw, and his gaze dropped to her lips. "Good night."

As Anna closed the door she heard him mutter, "Bloody bastard."

Tavis lay in his bed staring at the ceiling. The cat had found its way back in and was curled on the bed near his feet listening to him complain. If Faelan hadn't opened the door, Anna would probably be lying here instead of the cat. And they wouldn't be sleeping. How was a man to find sleep knowing that? He tossed and accidently kicked the cat, who gave him an annoyed look.

He was about to drift off when he heard a sound in the room. The cat's head rose, and it stared at the wall. Tavis didn't see anything, but he heard something. The cat hissed and jumped off the bed. Tavis grabbed his dagger and walked toward the wall. Something was moving behind it. This castle was like the one in Scotland. The secret passages likely opened the same. He felt for the familiar catch and pushed. The door slid open. He heard a squeal, and a blinding light struck him in the face. He caught a glimpse of red as he threw up his hand to shade his eyes.

"Tavis, thank God it's you."

"Matilda?" Tavis flipped the switch, and light flooded the room. Matilda climbed out of the doorway, hair bright as a beacon. "What are you doing in there?"

"Looking for the cat. I got lost. Is he with you?"

Tavis glanced at the bed. "I saw him earlier, but I think he's gone now."

Matilda clutched a bottle of water. There was something written on it. "I'll tell him you're looking for him if I see him," Tavis said.

"I don't think that's a good idea. Just tell me, and I'll come and get him. He's avoiding me. Can I use your door? I don't want to get lost again. There are more secret passages in this place than a haunted house."

"Sure." He took her arm to escort her and saw "*Holy*" written on her water bottle in big black letters. He bit his cheek. "What's that?" he asked, pointing to the bottle.

"It's just plain water, but I figured it might trick them."

"Them?"

"Vampires."

"You think they might get in here?"

"They did in Scotland. You never know."

"Then do you think it's wise to go into the secret passages alone?" That's where the vampire had gotten in before.

"Probably not, but I'm worried about the cat."

Tavis smiled. "If I see the cat, I'll let you know." He looked for the cat after Matilda left, but it wasn't there. He didn't know if it had overheard and was hiding or had somehow escaped, but his brother was right. That wasn't a normal cat.

Morning came too quickly. He'd slept fitfully, and his eyes felt like they'd been pasted shut. He quickly dressed and went to find Anna. She was all he could think about. This couldn't be normal. It must be the time vault. Sorcha was just leaving the kitchen when he arrived. "Do you know where Anna is?" he asked.

"In the field with Ronan. I'm headed there now."

"Ronan? What's she doing with him?" Was he trying to get close to Anna like he was Bree?

"So what's with you and Anna?" Sorcha asked.

"What do you mean?"

"Come on. Don't play dumb. It's plain for anyone to see."

"Like you and Duncan? Even a man fresh out of a time vault can feel the tension between you two."

"You're just like your brother." She stalked off toward the field, leaving Tavis to walk alone.

A small crowd had gathered near a practice ring where Ronan and Shay were sword fighting. Tavis immediately spotted Anna. She was wearing dark trousers and a very tight shirt. Tight by nineteenth-century standards. Her hair hung down her back in a long braid. She turned as he approached, and her smile faded.

"Is that how they do things in this time?" he whispered. "Kiss a man at night and ignore him the next morning."

"You make it sound like we're dating."

"I don't really understand dating."

"It's what you'd call courting," Bree said from behind him.

He whirled and saw her smiling. "Where'd you come from?"

"I'm practicing my warrior sneak," she said. "It's the only thing your pigheaded brother will let me do."

"What's wrong with Cody?" The warrior was scowling as he watched Ronan and Shay.

"He's upset," Bree said. "He didn't want Ronan to train Shay."

Tavis didn't blame him.

"I would be out there if your hardheaded brother would calm down."

Pigheaded? Hardheaded? She knew him well. Faelan could outlast anyone in a battle of wills. "He is hardheaded."

"Hardheaded? He could drive nails with his skull."

"No. He tried that once, when we were kids."

"You're joking. He tried to drive a nail . . . oh my God."

"That was in his earlier days, before he . . ."

"Before he took the weight of the world on his shoulders."

"Aye."

"You're a good brother. He told me how you would watch out for him because you thought he was too busy watching out for everyone else."

"It's what brothers do."

Ronan and Shay handed their swords to Brodie and picked up knives. Ronan moved around behind her and held her wrist.

"Good morning, everyone," Nina said, as she as Matilda joined them.

"Has anyone seen the cat?" Matilda asked.

"You didn't find him?" Tavis asked.

"No. I think he's hiding."

"Matilda, you can't keep that cat in your room."

"I take him out for walks."

"You don't walk a cat," Nina said. "What's wrong with Cody? He looks like he's going to explode."

"He does look hot and bothered," Matilda said.

Ronan stepped up beside Shay and demonstrated the proper technique for throwing a knife. Shay grinned as he let the knife go. Before it hit the target, she had raced across the ring in a blur and caught it.

"Shite. Is that what everyone told me about?"

"That's it." She smiled. "Cool, huh?"

"Handy trait to have. What does it feel like?"

"Amazing. I wish I was out there now."

Faelan walked up behind them. "Anna, your new phone is here. Try not to let a demon eat this one. Tavis, we got your ID.

You officially exist. There are papers inside that say you're not a hundred and seventy-seven years old."

"I need papers?"

"We don't want anyone thinking you're a terrorist."

"What's a terrorist?"

"Obsessed bastards. Minions, probably. You wouldn't believe the crap demons are up to now. Sorry about last night." Faelan didn't quite hide his grin.

"Don't start this again."

"I want to ask you something." Faelan pulled Tavis aside, away from the others who were watching Ronan and Shay. "I have my reasons for asking. Have you noticed anything odd about Anna? About the way you feel around her?"

"Like wanting to bed her every moment of the day?" Tavis glanced over to make sure she couldn't hear. Not that she couldn't see it in his face every time he got near her.

Faelan smiled. "Aye. Like that. I think she's your mate."

"That can't be. I don't want a mate." And particularly not one as beautiful as Anna. It would mean nothing but heartache. Men would throw themselves at her feet, and sooner or later, she would accept one of them. Then what the hell did he want from her? Why was he following her around like a sick puppy if he didn't want her?

"You couldn't choose better than Anna."

"I know she's beautiful."

"I don't mean her beauty. She's good. Strong, loyal." Faelan gave Tavis a knowing look. "Faithful."

"Hmm."

"You've got to get over this thing you have about beauty and demons."

"Yeah, you didn't almost bed one."

"Anna's no demon. You're just making excuses because you're scared."

"I'm not scared."

"You are. Most people are scared of ugly things. You're scared of beauty. But enough with the lectures for now." He patted Tavis on the shoulder and walked back to his wife. "What are you doing out here?"

"Watching Ronan train Shay and wishing you weren't stubborn as a jackass." Bree's voice was filled with longing.

"You're not training," Faelan said. "I don't care what Ronan says."

"I don't see why not. Do you think Anna's going to stop being a warrior just because she's pregnant?"

CHAPTER TWENTY-FOUR

T AVIS'S WORLD TILTED. HE MUST HAVE MISHEARD. THE SHOCK
on Anna's face, and Bree's hand clapped over her mouth, told
him he hadn't.

"I'm so sorry, Anna," Bree said.

"Why would you say that?" Anna looked frantic.

Faelan put an arm around Bree, who was shaking. "Maybe I'm
wrong," she said.

"Wrong?" Anna's eyes were wide, scared. "You mean you're
serious. You can't know that."

"I'm sorry," Bree said again.

Ronan and Shay ambled over to see what the fuss was about.
"What's going on?" Shay asked.

"Anna's pregnant," Matilda said. "I don't mean to be forward.
But who's the father?"

Anna's mouth tightened. "Oh God." She ran toward the castle,
and Tavis took off after her.

Tristol swirled away from the disturbance in a black mist. He was beyond pleased. His hybrid had impregnated Anna. This could prove very valuable. She must be protected from Voltar. Taking her away would create too many problems. Namely, everyone would be looking for her. And he had to focus on getting rid of Voltar before his plans were ruined. Anna was probably safest here, surrounded by warriors. Tavis would die before he'd let anyone hurt her.

Tristol almost wished he had mated her with Tavis. He was remarkably strong, loyal, and tough. And he wasn't out of control like the hybrid. Perhaps next time. After Voltar was destroyed.

Anna holed up in her room, pretending she wasn't there. She ignored Bree's knocking, and then Tavis's a few minutes later. After his footsteps faded, she slipped into the hall hoping she didn't meet anyone. She ran into Niall, who was eating a sandwich nearly as thick as his arm.

"Sorry," he mumbled around a full mouth. His eyes widened, and his throat worked. Anna would have walked past him, but she was afraid he was choking. He finally swallowed. "Roast beef." He held up the sandwich. His eyes dropped to her stomach. "I was hungry." Another awkward look at her stomach. "Congratulations . . . Uh, I gotta go." He hurried away.

She was still standing in the corridor staring after him when Brodie appeared. He glanced at her stomach. "Hey."

"Hi."

"How are you?" His gaze dropped to her stomach again.

"Fine."

"Good." He kept staring at her stomach.

"Stop looking at my stomach."

"OK," he said and hurried away.

Instead of slipping out for a long walk, she went to find Ronan. He was out near the stables, looking into the woods.

"What are you doing?" she asked.

He swung around and faced her. "Nothing. Did you hear a funny noise just now? A whirring sound?"

"No. But I was inside."

He glanced back toward the trees and frowned.

"I need your help," Anna said. "I need to get away."

"From?"

"Everyone." Anna crossed her arms over her stomach. She was terrified. She'd rather face Voltar than think about becoming a mother.

"You can't leave. Voltar and Tristol are out there, and my guess is that they're looking for you."

"I'll risk it. I need to be alone. And I don't want the Council to find out."

"You can't just run off," Ronan said. "The father has a right to know what's going on. I take it we're talking about Tavis."

"Who says I'm pregnant? Bree was just guessing."

"Bree doesn't just guess. How did this happen?"

"Really?"

"You're not the kind to . . ."

"Have sex?"

"Well . . ." He scratched his arm. "I thought you had issues with sex. Not that it wasn't good with us."

Better than good, but it was just wrong. Or bad timing. Both of them had been hurting and vulnerable. Neither of them belonged there. He knew it. She knew it. So they pretty much pretended it hadn't happened. "Maybe I'm discovering its lure."

"You've got the hots for Tavis . . . bad."

Anna rolled her eyes. "Will you help me or not?"

"Where do you want to go?"

"Montana."

"It'll take me a day or two to arrange it. I have to step up security."

"I'll hide until then. Thank you." Anna hugged him.

Ronan seemed surprised. After their encounter, they didn't do a lot of touching. He pulled her closer and just held her for a minute. "It'll be OK," he whispered. "The clan will help you out. You'll have so many surrogate mothers and fathers you'll be sick of them. And you'll be a great mother." His hands slipped lower, over her battle marks—which didn't tingle when he touched them—to her butt.

"What are you doing?"

"Just making sure there's no spark. Nice. Very nice. But no spark."

"Then get your hands off my ass."

What the hell was she doing? Anna had just found out she was pregnant, and here she was in Ronan's arms with his hands on her arse. He turned around and stomped toward the house, fury in every bone in his body. That's what beauty got you. Pain and betrayal.

But how could it be betrayal if she wasn't his? He didn't even know if it was his bairn. It could be the hybrid's. Bollocks. She could be carrying a half vampire inside her. Though how anyone could know she was pregnant this soon was beyond him. But everyone seemed to put stock in Bree's feelings.

He turned around and walked back. Anna was going to need help. Voltar and Tristol were out there, and she might be carrying an inhuman bairn. Tavis had sworn to protect her. In fact, he'd been ordered to protect her. He was going to protect her no matter if she wanted it or not. When he got there, his pretty thoughts shriveled to dust. Anna was racing across the field on horseback with no saddle. He hurried to the stables and grabbed the first horse he saw—a big white stallion that had been saddled and hitched to a rail. Niall was nearby in one of the stalls. Tavis pulled the reins free and climbed on his back. The stallion reared on his hind legs, and Tavis leaned in, nudging it with his heels. The stallion dropped down and headed for the open field.

"Hey," Niall yelled.

Tavis raced after Anna. She was headed for the woods. She was fast, but his horse was faster. He caught up and yelled for her to stop. She slowed her horse and turned to look at him. Tavis jumped from the horse and walked over to her. "What do you think you're doing?"

"Riding," Anna said.

"Without a saddle? Get off?"

"What?"

"Get off."

Anna frowned, but she dismounted. "What's wrong with you?"

"I know what you're doing."

"I don't know what you're talking about," she said. "But you need to chill."

"Chill? I'll not have my bairn, or someone else's, ripped out of its mother before it's born."

She looked as shocked as if he'd slapped her. Her face went as pale as the vampires in Tristol's fortress. "You think I'm trying to kill my baby? Are you insane?"

Tavis stepped back, confused. "You're not?"

"No, I'm not, you ass." The color was back in her face. Her cheeks were hot with anger. She turned and walked back to her horse.

"You weren't," he said to her back. Shite. "Anna, wait." He ran after her. "I saw you bouncing around up there without a saddle, and I thought you were trying to lose the bairn."

"What kind of monster do you think I am?"

"I don't . . . I mean, you're kind, but they said you didn't want a family."

"I don't. But I wasn't trying to lose my baby. I would never do that. Even . . ."

Even if she'd been forced.

"I thought I saw someone I recognized."

"And you couldn't talk to him later instead of racing bareback across the field with a bairn barely set up in your womb?"

Her face paled again. "I didn't think about it." She looked devastated. "How can I be a mother? I don't know how."

Tavis slid his arms around her shoulders. "You've had some harsh things to deal with, and I'm sorry for my part. But you're good, Anna. You'll make a good mother, and you'll raise a good child. It doesn't matter if you don't know who the father is." God forbid he wasn't human.

"I do know who the father is."

CHAPTER TWENTY-FIVE

Tavis stepped back. "You know? How?" She had been with him and the hybrid within hours of each other.

"I haven't had sex with anyone but you."

"But I thought . . ." Tavis's heartbeat pounded in his ears. "You mean it's mine? For certain, it's mine?"

She nodded, and a tear rolled down her cheek.

"I'm going to be a father?" He couldn't breathe. He looked at Anna's stomach, flat and lean. His bairn was in there. His throat tightened, and his eyes began to sting.

"I need to go." He climbed on the horse and rode hard for the woods. When he reached the thick trees, he stopped and dismounted. He walked to a large oak tree out of Anna's sight and sat down. He put his head in his hands and cried. For his family, for the son he'd never known, and for the child he would know. For finding Faelan again. And Anna. He felt a prickle across his shoulders. Someone was watching him. He jumped up, thinking Anna had followed him, and then swiped a thumb over his eyes so she didn't see his tears. But she didn't appear. "Who's there?"

No one answered, but a bush moved. Frowning, he started

toward it, and then he heard something behind him. He turned and saw Faelan.

"Tavis. What are you doing here?"

"Just thinking."

Faelan frowned. "You all right?"

"Aye."

"You don't look it. I saw Anna back there. She told me you'd come this way. She had the same look."

"The bairn's mine."

"She's certain?"

"She was never with the hybrid. I don't know what to do."

A smile broke across Faelan's face, and it reminded Tavis of when they were lads. "We're going to be fathers. Both of us." He grabbed Tavis in a hug, and Tavis wondered what having one child who would be more than a century younger than his sibling would do to the family tree.

When they got back to the house, everyone was searching for Matilda. "She wanted me to give her a cooking lesson, of all things," Coira said. "But she didn't show up."

"She probably forgot," Shay said. "She gets distracted easily."

"Distracted?" Nina said. "She's insane. Ask Jamie about Matilda and the Secret Service. I swear I'm going to put her in a home."

Cody walked into the room and sighed. "What's she done now?"

"We can't find her," Nina said.

"She was inside the secret passage in my room before," Tavis said. "She was looking for the cat. She was worried about him."

"I'm afraid something is wrong," Coira said. "The cat is here. She's always got that cat with her. And I didn't pay it any mind, but she's been asking a lot of questions about the time vault."

Bree frowned. "She asked me too. She wanted to know what it

was like inside. If I felt anything. And she was asking Tavis about it. You don't think . . ."

Shay closed her eyes. "Oh God."

Several of the warriors split up to search the castle and grounds, just in case she had gotten lost. Cody, Faelan, Shay, and Nina went to Bree and Faelan's house so they could check the chapel cellar. Tavis went with them since he needed to return the time vault now that they had the key.

"Make sure she's not in it first," Shay said.

"Or make sure that she is," Cody said.

Shay smacked his arm. "Cody!"

"My car isn't here," Nina said. "She shouldn't be driving."

"Matilda shouldn't be doing a lot of things she does," Cody said. "Her recklessness is going to get us all killed."

"Calm down." Shay patted his arm. "I'm sure she's just being typical Matilda."

"You're a saint to put up with her," Cody said to Nina.

"If she doesn't settle down, I'll be meeting Saint Peter ahead of schedule."

"This brings back memories," Tavis said as they entered the cellar. This time, they had battery-powered flashlights which were a damned sight better than lanterns.

Shay stepped into the dark cellar. "Tavis, you're a brave man."

"Heavens, yes," Nina agreed. "I can't imagine coming down here and climbing into a box knowing you were going to sleep for so long."

"He is brave." Faelan thumped him on the back. "He's been watching out for me for as long as I can remember."

"Someone had to," Tavis said. "It's there." He pointed his light at the time vault.

"Look at that." Shay moved closer and touched the wood. "It's beautiful. And to think they're intended to hold something so ugly. If the demons I've seen are any indication, you and Faelan are the best looking things to come out of one of these."

"It's closed," Cody said, examining the lid.

"That was a thump," Faelan said. "Quick, open it."

The vault wasn't locked, so the lid could be lifted, but it was heavy. Faelan and Tavis opened it, and Matilda popped up like a jack-in-the-box. "Oh my God," she gasped. Her hair was wild, eyes round, and she was panting.

"What the hell are you doing?" Cody yelled.

"Calm down, Cody," Shay said. "Matilda, what the hell are you doing? You could have suffocated in there."

The men helped her out. She clutched at Faelan and Tavis for support.

Cody was furious. "Dammit, Matilda."

"I wanted to see what it was like to lie inside one. Research for my book. I didn't mean for the lid to close. I had a block of wood to stop it, but it fell. It was so dark. But I felt everything. I remember every terrifying moment." She patted her face. "Do I look any younger?"

Nina stomped her foot. "You don't look any younger, Matilda! You look like something your damned cat spit up."

"The cat. He's probably worried about me," Matilda said.

"He probably knocked the block of wood out from under the lid," Cody muttered.

Nina looked exasperated. "Matilda, you have to stop exploring like this. You're driving us all crazy."

"I am?"

"Why do you think Jamie's avoiding the castle?"

"He's busy," Matilda said. "I think he still has a few loose ends to tie up from our little adventure. Her name is Sam."

"He's staying clear of you," Nina said.

"What did she do to Jamie?" Tavis asked.

"What hasn't she done to him?" Cody said. "She drugged him and carted him off in a wheelbarrow." He grinned. "That was kind of funny. This latest disaster involved an assassination attempt on the president with the cat and Matilda loose in the White House. Jamie's not speaking to Matilda at the moment."

"It was just a little adventure," Matilda said. "The Secret Service could take some lessons from you warriors."

"Secret Service! Bloody hell." Cody held up his hands. "If you don't stop these little adventures, I'll stick you in the time vault again before Tavis sends it back."

Matilda turned a scornful eye on Cody. "Cody MacBain, I'm practically your aunt. Show some respect."

Bloody woman. No wonder the cat was avoiding her.

Anna heard voices in the kitchen. She stood out of sight, trying to decide whether to go in.

"I wish I'd been there," Brodie said.

"It wasn't funny, but if you'd seen her pop out of there," Shay said. "She looked just like a jack-in-the-box with her red hair and too much makeup. I thought Cody would choke her."

"Where is she now?" Bree asked.

"Sleeping," Shay said. "She still thinks the time vault did something to her."

"I hope it took some of the sass out of her," Bree said.

"Not too much," Brodie said. "She's growing on me."

Anna stepped into the room, and everyone looked up.

"Anna." Guilt was written all over Bree's face.

Brodie was closer to the door. He walked over and patted Anna awkwardly on the arm. "How are you feeling?"

"Fine."

He looked at her stomach again. "So can we talk about the baby now?"

"Brodie!" Bree frowned at him.

"If she's pregnant, she's pregnant. We're all thinking about it. It's the elephant in the room."

"Don't you have someplace to be?" Bree asked.

Brodie shook his head. "No."

"Then find someplace," Shay said. "We need to have a little girl talk."

"That rules you out," Bree said. "Too many muscles."

"That's discrimination. You know I love babies." He frowned and patted Anna's arm again, then walked to the door. Anna wished she could go with him. She had a good idea what the girl talk would be about. She'd been avoiding Bree and Shay since Bree's shocking revelation for just that reason. They would want to help. The men were easier, for the most part. They just looked awkward and scurried away. Except for nosy Brodie.

"And don't listen," Bree called as he left. "I know you've been avoiding me, Anna, and I don't blame you. But we have to talk about it."

"I've been avoiding everyone," Anna said. "Not just you. I needed time to think."

"I'm so sorry for blurting it out like that," Bree said. "I don't know what I was thinking. I wasn't thinking."

"It's OK. Well, telling me in private would have been preferable, but you didn't mean any harm." She frowned. "But are you sure? It's just been a few days."

"As sure as I can be. That's how I knew I was pregnant."

Anna let out a heavy sigh.

"Do you want to talk about it?" Shay asked.

No. Yes. "I don't know what to think, much less what to say. I don't want a baby."

"What about . . ." Bree glanced at Shay. "The father?"

"I think Tavis is as shocked as I am," Anna said.

"It's Tavis's?" Bree's face lit.

"I figured everyone knew," Anna said.

"Anyone can see how things are between you, but Tavis told Faelan what happened in the dungeon with the other prisoner. How do you know who's the father?"

"They took me to him, but he didn't do anything." Anna kept her face blank. She'd promised not to say anything. She didn't go back on her promises.

"Then why did they take you to him?" Bree asked. "I thought it was a breeding program."

"I guess he didn't feel like playing stud." Anna felt her face warm from the lie.

"I don't mean to pry," Shay said, "but what exactly happened with Tavis? I don't mean . . . that, but the other stuff."

Anna hadn't talked to anyone about it. She saw the sympathy on their faces, and something inside her crumbled. Her eyes misted, and she started doing the whole girly thing that she hated. She spilled it all, everything except about the hybrid.

"Tavis didn't have a choice," Anna said. "The guard would have done it himself. And it wouldn't have been pleasant."

"So it was pleasant?" Bree asked.

"Not pleasant, but . . . not as bad as if the guard had done it. He would have killed me. And Tavis."

"Tavis saved you," Shay said.

"I'm surprised he could even perform," Bree said.

"He was too," Anna said. "That's what bothers him, that he enjoyed it."

"I can see why it would," Shay said.

"He couldn't help it," Anna said. "He'd been locked in that time vault and hadn't had sex in a long time."

Bree and Shay shared a smile.

"What?"

"You're defending him."

"I'm not. It's just the truth."

"How do you feel about him?" Shay asked.

"I don't know what I feel. We were close in the dungeon. We thought we would die. He was so hurt. If you could have seen what they did to him . . ."

"Do you love him?" Shay asked.

"How could I love him?"

"He's gorgeous. You connected in the dungeon. That kind of intense atmosphere can tell you more about a person in two days than you could learn about them in two months."

"I don't want to marry and have a family."

"You don't have to marry him," Bree said. "Though it's best for the child if the mother and father are together."

"Tavis and I haven't even had a chance to talk about it. He's upset. He saw me riding bareback and thought I was trying to lose the baby."

"Were you?" Shay asked.

"No." Anna's hands clenched. What if she had been subconsciously? "I thought I saw someone in the woods, and I was in a hurry to check it out."

"He knows you weren't trying to hurt the baby now?" Shay asked.

"Yes, but he found out it's his baby. He was stunned. He thought I'd been with the hybrid too. He rode off, and I haven't seen him since."

"You need to talk to him," Bree said. "I know all this is hard, given the trouble you've had with men."

"Which apparently Ronan told everyone about."

"He was just concerned," Shay said.

"Speaking of Ronan, is there anything you want to tell us?" Bree asked.

"No," Anna said.

Bree sighed. "That's the same thing he said. I'm curious about this hybrid. What was he like?"

Anna looked down at her hands and kept her voice steady. Bree had uncanny abilities, and she didn't want her picking up on something Anna had sworn not to tell. "It was dark. It was hard to tell. He was strong."

"A vampire?" Shay asked. "Or part vampire?"

"I'm not sure." That much was true. She knew part of what he was, but not all.

"Why would he help you escape if he's part vampire?" Bree asked.

"If he was a prisoner," Shay said, "then he wasn't there by choice, no matter what he was. You're lucky he was there."

"We were." But he wasn't. "Can we forget about my unpleasant past and uncertain future and talk about this wedding?"

Tavis knocked on Anna's door until she opened it. She wore a frown and some kind of little garment that exposed her long, smooth legs. He knew just how smooth they felt against his own legs. "What are you wearing?"

She tugged at the legs. "Sleeping shorts."

"I like them. Can I come in?"

"Why?"

"We need to talk. That's my bairn you're carrying. I have a right to know what your plans are."

Anna opened the door. "Come in." She glanced at the bed. "Have a seat."

He started to sit on the settee, but they might need something with a little more breathing room. They were like fire and dry kindling together, but right now they needed to settle things, not kiss. Maybe afterward, if things went well. So he sat on the chair, and they stared at each other. "What are we going to do?"

"I need some space, so I'm going to leave for a while."

"No."

"Did you just tell me no?"

Tavis cleared his throat. "I did. That's my bairn."

"It's in my uterus. If it's really there."

"You think it might not be? Someone told me Bree's never wrong about these things."

"There's always a first time. But it's my body."

"And my bairn. It's mine as much as it's yours. I'm sorry for the circumstances, but I won't lose another child. I've already lost one."

Anna's eyes were wide, her lips parted. "I understand how you feel, but I have to get away so I can think."

"You're not going."

"Tavis, you can't control me."

"No, but I . . . bloody hell, you're carrying my bairn, and I love you—"

"What?"

"I love you." What the hell was he doing? He jumped up and rubbed his sweaty palms on his jeans. He was sick of jeans. He wanted to wear a damned kilt. "I need some space myself." He hurried to the door and walked out. His forehead was sweating, and his battle marks were burning. In love. He couldn't be in love.

He went to his room, stripped off his clothes, and headed for the shower. He passed the mirror and caught sight of his naked body. His battle marks had changed.

CHAPTER TWENTY-SIX

Tavis leaned closer and studied his chest. His marks started near his collarbone and came down at an angle over his chest. Now there was a line intertwined through one of them. He tried to swallow, but his mouth felt like it was stuffed with straw. He grabbed up his jeans and put them on as he ran to the door. He stepped out and hurried to Faelan's room. He tapped softly, and a moment later Faelan answered.

"I need to talk to you."

"All right. Come in. Bree's in the kitchen."

When he stepped inside, Tavis opened his shirt. "What's this?"

Faelan studied Tavis's battle marks. "I've never seen anything like it. When did this happen?"

"I noticed them a while ago. I was about to take a shower."

"I don't know what to make of it."

"It's his mate mark," Bree said, stepping into the room.

"How do you know that?" Faelan asked.

She walked over to Tavis and touched his chest.

Faelan frowned at her. "I don't like you touching his chest."

She ignored him and ran her fingers over Tavis's marks. *"His brother's keeper will find his heart, and together they will put the past to rest."*

"That's what his marks say?" Faelan asked.

Tavis touched his chest. "No one can read battle marks."

"Bree's not normal."

"You have a way of making that sound like an insult."

"Special, you're very special. And not normal. If you'd just stop being so reckless."

"We're not here to discuss my recklessness. Tavis needs our help."

"I don't want a bloody mate mark."

"You don't want Anna?" Faelan asked.

Tavis ran a hand through his hair. "I didn't say that."

"You don't want your child?" Bree asked.

"Aye, I want my child. Damnation. I don't know what I want."

"Sleep." Bree pulled his shirt together and patted his chest. "Everything makes more sense with a good night's sleep."

He didn't go to sleep. He walked to Ronan's door and knocked.

Ronan opened the door, his eyes groggy.

"Anna's not going to Montana."

"I know. I never intended for her to go." Ronan yawned. "Is that all you wanted?"

"Aye."

"Good night." Ronan shut the door.

Anna couldn't sleep. Tavis loved her? He'd looked as surprised and sick as she felt after he blurted it out. She wanted to laugh and run away at the same time. She pulled out Angus's notebook, wishing he was here so she could talk to him. She saw another entry that confused her.

"I've decided to tell Anna as soon as I return to Scotland. Other than me, I think Walter the Watcher is the only one

who knows the truth. He won't tell. He only told me because he knows I love her. But I can't keep something this important from her. Even though it may destroy her."

Walter the Watcher was the man she and Angus had met with before Angus left for America. Walter had known her mother. What was he talking about? She searched for several more minutes before she found the answer. And when she did, the bottom dropped out of her world.

"Bree!"

She opened her eyes and saw Faelan staring at her. "What's wrong?"

He looked at her as if she'd been levitating on the bed. "I think you were dreaming."

"So." She dreamed a lot.

"This was strange."

"More than usual?"

"You were chanting."

"That's new. What was I saying?"

"Darkness inside Anna. You said it over and over."

"Darkness inside Anna? I think I was dreaming about her."

"What does that mean, darkness inside Anna?"

"I don't know. I don't remember the dream."

"She's been through hell. It's no wonder she feels dark inside."

"There is something about her. I sensed it when I first met her. Like a shadow inside her. I thought it was because she's a loner. I hope that's what it is."

Faelan leaned up on his elbow. "You'd better not be saying she's the traitor Angus was talking about. My brother's bloody in love with her, and he's suffered enough. Losing a son he didn't know he even had. Captured and tortured by a demon who thought he was me."

And now he was going to have another child, and the mother was miserable. Poor Tavis. Poor Anna.

Bree touched Faelan's chest. "I'm sure I'm just sensing all the horrible things she's been through."

"This time you have my blessing to play matchmaker. We can't let that bairn come into this world without a proper mother and father."

"We won't."

"If that doesn't work, I'll shake some sense into both of them."

"I'm glad Tavis is here."

"Me too. It's like he never left."

"And he's going to be a father too. Both of you, fathers. And Cody and Shay are getting married tomorrow. All this talk makes me want to have sex."

Faelan groaned. "Did you have to go and say it? I'm trying not to think about it."

"I don't see the harm. I'm not under doctor's orders to rest."

"You're under my orders to rest. I'm trying to take care of you. You've had a lot of stress and the shock of finding Tavis's grave. We should wait a couple more days. At least one."

"You'd make a lousy doctor," Bree said, and pulled off her gown.

With the moon shining in through the open window, Shay could see Cody standing with his hands deep in the pockets of his jeans, and for a moment, she was seventeen again, secretly in love with her best friend. Terrified that someone would find out, never dreaming he'd felt the same way. "What are you doing?" she asked.

"I saw something outside. Ah, it's just Anna."

"I feel so bad for both of them."

"Yeah, me too. They should just get married and get it over with." Cody turned and smiled at her. "Speaking of marriage, are you ready to become Mrs. Cody MacBain?"

The wedding would take place in a little chapel on the grounds of the Albany castle. "I already am. Remember our secret handfasting?"

"Aye. And I remember the way we celebrated in the hayloft. But this is for the world to see. Are you sure you don't want to back out? I betrayed you with all those secrets and lies."

"You were trying to protect me." Shay climbed out of bed and walked over to Cody. She wrapped her arms around his waist, brushing her fingers along the top of his hips. "Just try to get away from me now." She spent a few minutes proving that she had no intention of letting him go.

"I'm sorry it's rushed, but I'll be damned if I let the Council drag you away. Maybe we should have a baby, if that'll get them off our backs."

As always, the mention of a baby made her heart ache. Cody touched her stomach and leaned his forehead against hers. She knew he was thinking of the tiny grave they'd visited on the way here. They'd stood side by side gazing down on the gravestone, and both of them had cried.

"We'll wait," Cody said, his voice thick. "Give it more time." He kissed her and stepped back. "I have something for you. We all—Nina, my parents and brothers—we thought you should have these." He walked to the mantle and brought back a box. He opened it. Inside were two thin gold wedding bands. "We think they belonged to your parents."

"Did you find their bodies?" Malek had dug up her parents' graves searching for proof that Shay was alive, when the whole world had thought she was dead.

Cody shook his head. "No. Marcas is still looking. But he found these in Malek's things."

"Why do you think they belonged to my parents?"

"There's something engraved inside," Cody said. "I don't know what it means. It's in a language I don't recognize, but my father recognized the markings."

Shay rubbed her fingers over the worn gold and strange writings, and she felt something warm inside her. Another piece of the parents she hadn't known.

"You're the most beautiful bride I've ever seen." Nina stood beside Shay in front of the floor-length mirror, her eyes bright with unshed tears. "My little tomboy all grown up and getting married." She and Matilda, along with Bree and Sorcha and Cody's mother, Laura, were helping her get ready. Mostly they were reminiscing and trying not to cry.

"Thank you, Nina. I think it's just the dress," Shay said, turning to look at the side. The dress was simple but stunning. A sleeveless creation in white satin that flowed gracefully to the floor. She and Bree had found it in a little shop in Albany. Shay wished she could have worn her mother's, but everything from her parents' lives had been destroyed to protect her.

"It's not just the dress," Matilda said. "You are such a lovely girl. If I could have had a daughter, I would have wanted her to be like you. But I couldn't have kids."

"I didn't know that, Matilda. I'm sorry. You would have been a . . . fascinating mother."

"Thank you, dear. You're sweet to put up with all my untapped maternal instincts. I know I frustrated you and the boys sometimes."

"Matilda, I adore you." Even when she was driving her crazy. "Cody and his brothers adore you too."

"Maybe you could put in a good word for me with Jamie. I know he still has feelings for you even though you're marrying Cody."

Shay still cared for him too. She'd almost married him.

"Now, Matilda," Nina warned. "Let's not talk about Jamie. It's Cody's day. I always knew you two were meant for each other."

Matilda nodded. "Lachlan or Marcas would have made you a good husband too, but you and Cody were magic. Like a fairy tale." Matilda started sniffling. "We'd better get out of here, Nina, before we ruin our makeup. It took me forever to look this good."

Nina gave Shay another hug, and she and Matilda left.

"I'm going to look for Anna," Sorcha said. "I don't know where she could be."

"With everything going on, she probably just needs time alone."

"If she doesn't hurry, she's going to miss the wedding," Sorcha said.

"You do look beautiful," Laura said. She took Shay's hands. "I'm glad you'll officially be part of the family. I always hoped it would happen." Her eyes started glistening. "Oh dear. I should go before I have both of us in tears. I love you. We all do." She hugged Shay and left. Only Bree remained.

"So are you nervous?" Bree asked.

Shay thought about it a moment and then shook her head. "Excited."

"Liar."

Shay smiled. "Well, maybe nervous too."

"I was the same way."

"You had good reason, marrying a man from the nineteenth century."

"At least you're marrying someone from this century. And one hell of a man, if I might add."

"He is hot, isn't he?"

"Completely. Sorcha still drools over him."

"Not as much as she drools over Duncan," Shay said rolling her eyes. Then she sighed. "I feel guilty getting married with so much happening."

"We're in love with warriors. There's always going to be craziness."

"Does it worry you knowing you're bringing a child into this life?" Shay asked.

A shadow crossed Bree's face. "I try not to think about it. Instead, I think how lucky I am to have found Faelan. And you should think how lucky you are that you found Cody again after all these years. So, no guilt about the wedding. If Shane's right, this might keep the Council at bay for now. You don't want them dragging you off somewhere for questioning." Bree frowned. "Or testing."

"Could they really do that?"

"I don't know. The Council makes me nervous."

"Cody doesn't like them," Shay said.

"I thought he was going to walk away from his duty when they grilled him about telling you who you really were. But everyone in the room would have walked with him." Bree touched Shay's hand. "No matter what, you have people behind you. If you get married or don't. If you have a baby or don't. The warriors will always be there to protect you." Bree giggled. "Actually we're warriors. Isn't that a hoot?"

"You're starting to talk like Matilda. You've been spending too much time with her and that cat," Shay said. "You're becoming as obsessed with it as she is."

"It's a strange cat. I can't figure it out."

"You don't think it killed that vampire too, do you?" Shay asked.

Bree shrugged. "Something killed it. I doubt it was Matilda's *holy water*. OK, enough talk. We have a wedding in," she checked her watch, "ten minutes, and a hot groom who won't want to wait."

"I can't believe Anna didn't show up to help."

"She's probably with Tavis."

"I heard suspicious noises coming from Tavis's room last night," Shay said. There was a tap on the door. "Maybe that's her."

But it was Lachlan who stuck his head in. "Looking good."

"Thanks, Lach. Have you seen Anna?" Shay asked.

"No. Thought she was up here." Lach was supposed to escort Anna down the aisle.

"No."

"She'll show up. You ladies about ready?"

"Another minute and we'll be done."

Lach winked and stepped out.

"There's a walking heartbreak," Bree said. "Just like Ronan."

"He always had some girl after him when we were growing up."

Bree made a final adjustment to Shay's hair and gave her an almost hug and an air kiss.

"What kind of hug is that?"

"The kind that doesn't want to mess up your hair, makeup, and dress."

"Forget that," Shay said, and grabbed Bree in a tight hug. "I'm so glad to have a sister."

"Me too. Did you just sniffle?" Bree leaned back. "No crying. I worked too hard on this getup. OK, sister. Let's go see that gorgeous groom."

The wedding party was waiting in the chapel wing. And from Shay's quick glimpse, it was crowded for a spontaneous wedding. They'd worked miracles to pull it off. Cody's father, Ewan MacBain, had offered to give Shay away. He had been like a father to Shay. Ewan was a retired warrior. His last mission had been to sneak Shay out of Scotland when she was a baby in order to hide her from an ancient demon who was trying to kill her. Ewan had moved his entire family and started a new life to protect her. His sons had taken part in the deception. Shay had resented them all for a while, but now she understood why they'd had to do it. She wouldn't be here if they hadn't.

Ewan smiled and reached for her hand. "Are you ready to marry my hardheaded son?"

"I am. And thank you for agreeing to give me away."

"It's my honor. Before I do, I want you to know that with or without Cody, you'll always be family. But I'm glad you two finally saw the light. I knew the first time I saw Cody trotting after you on the Big Wheel that you were meant to be." He patted her hand.

It took a minute to realize the rest of the wedding party were anxiously whispering. Faelan looked pissed.

"What's going on?" Shay asked.

"We're still missing a bridesmaid," Sorcha said.

"And a brother," Faelan added. "Tavis and Anna are both missing."

"I hope they didn't elope," Shay said.

"Tavis wouldn't do that," Faelan said, but his frown deepened.

"That would be rude, eloping in the middle of your wedding," Sorcha said.

"Maybe they're having a . . . talk," Marcas said.

"More like in a closet somewhere getting it on," Lach said.

The music started. "What do we do?" Shay asked.

"Go ahead with the ceremony," Bree said.

"The numbers are screwed up without Anna," Shay said.

"No problem," Sorcha said. "Lachlan, Marcas." She held out each arm. The men each took an arm, and they started down the aisle. Sorcha gave Duncan a gloating look as she passed him. He shook his head in disgust.

Faelan and Bree went next. When it was Shay's turn, she stepped into the aisle on Ewan's arm, and her eyes moistened to see her friends and family were there. Aunt Nina and Matilda were sitting next to Laura. She smiled at Jamie. He had been afraid Cody wouldn't want him there. Cody probably didn't, but Shay did. Jamie was part of her life. But he wasn't Cody.

She looked up and saw him waiting for her. Looking gorgeous, just as Bree had said. Shay's stomach did a roller coaster flip as Cody's intense hazel eyes watched her move closer to him. His lips were slightly parted, his hair a bit too long. He'd worn his kilt, at her request, and he looked so handsome she wanted to cry.

Finally, after all the deception and betrayal, it had all turned out perfect. The wedding was a little rushed perhaps, but perfect.

Shay was still only halfway down the aisle when the back door burst open. Everyone turned. Tavis stood there with his hands covered in blood. "He's taken Anna."

CHAPTER TWENTY-SEVEN

E VERYONE ROSE, AND SEVERAL OF THE WARRIORS HURRIED toward Tavis. Shay tried to go to him, but Ewan and Cody held her back.

"Tristol," Tavis panted. "I think Tristol has her."

"You're mistaken, warrior." The voice came from the front of the chapel. It was soft, but powerful. Tristol stood at the altar, next to the minister.

Tavis let out a savage cry and ran toward Tristol with murder in his eyes. Faelan tackled him, and they both crashed into the pews, scattering people like startled doves. Tavis tried to get up, but Faelan held tight. "Don't, Tavis. He'll kill you. I can't lose you again."

Immediately, the warriors went into action. Kilts swirled and swords rang as they formed a barricade between Tristol and the rest of the chapel.

Shay was scared, but she was also angry. She and Cody had suffered hell because of demons. Now they were screwing with her wedding? She felt the lightness that came over her when she moved like a vampire. She easily broke through the line of warriors and streaked toward the demon. "How dare you interrupt my wedding!

I've waited all my life for this." She felt a wind as Bree appeared next to her, followed by a roar that could only be Faelan.

Tristol smiled, and Shay's anger dampened at the sheer beauty of the demon. What happened to ugly demons?

"My sincerest apologies, but I came to offer my help."

"Your help?" Tavis yelled, struggling to free himself. "You tried to kill me in that dungeon. You hurt Anna."

"It wasn't me," Tristol said. "My guard did it, and he's been eliminated."

Cody and Faelan stepped between Shay, Bree, and the demon. Several other warriors followed. "Get back, Shay," Cody ordered.

"I don't think you can control your women," Tristol said, looking at Shay and Bree with admiration. "I hope you both know how special they are."

"We know," Faelan said. "What are you doing on our castle grounds?"

"It was mine before it was yours."

"How can you enter a chapel?" Cody asked. "This is holy ground."

"I have my secrets," Tristol said. "Just as you do."

Tavis broke free and rushed Tristol. Faelan tried to stop him, but he was moving too fast. Tristol moved faster. One minute he was at the front of the chapel, and the next he vanished in a black mist and materialized at the back of the chapel.

There were gasps of alarm. Shay's heart skipped more than one beat when she saw Matilda's red head peeking around the corner not ten feet from where Tristol stood.

Tavis stared at the demon, his face pale. "What the hell are you? Demons can't move like that."

"Vampires can," Bree said.

Tristol smiled and opened his mouth. Two long, sharp fangs extended, and then immediately retracted. "I guess my secret is out."

"You're a bloody vampire," Tavis said. "Those were your vampires in the fortress."

"Correct." Tristol moved like a streak of light back to them, this time staying behind the line of warriors. "If we're finished with show-and-tell, I'd like to get down to business."

"Where is Anna?" Tavis growled.

"Voltar has her."

"Voltar." Tavis paled. "How do you know?"

"I saw him take her. I came to help you get her back."

"Why would you do this?" Lachlan asked.

"I have my reasons."

"I don't trust you or your reasons," Ronan said. "You're a damned vampire."

"And you would trust my reasons more if I were a demon? Think about it. Demons are your enemy. And mine."

"So what, you're saying we're on the same side?" Duncan said.

"In this we are."

"I think you need to prove yourself, more than just darting around the room," Cody said.

"I proved myself by not destroying you. I know each of you. I've been alive longer than your great-great-great-great-times-one-hundred-grandfathers. I've watched you for many years. I could have destroyed you at any time, but I didn't."

"If you're so old and powerful, why don't you kill Voltar?" Faelan asked.

"It would be best if I'm not involved in his demise. This way, you get revenge for your brother and your father."

"Our brother?" Tavis asked. "Voltar killed Ian?"

"I meant Liam."

"Voltar?" Faelan's voice trembled. "Voltar killed Liam?"

"He found out that Liam would destroy him," Tristol said. "So he destroyed Liam first."

That must be the secret Tavis's guard had planned to tell him. Tavis and Faelan were obviously stunned. "But we know what Voltar looks like," Tavis said. "We didn't recognize him."

"It was an illusion. He plays mind games."

"How did he get Liam's name?" Sean asked.

"Someone gave him the name," Tristol said. "I think there was a traitor. Voltar has been trying to infiltrate your clan for a long time. He's done quite a lot of damage. He killed Nigel Ellwood. I rescued the Book of Battles and hid it where the others couldn't find it. I knew if any of them got it they would wipe out your clan, and that wasn't my goal. So you know my secret, and I know yours. Now I'll tell you Voltar's secret. He has a daughter."

"Voltar? There are no records of him having a daughter," Sean said.

"Not many know. Voltar didn't until I told him." Tristol smiled, and Shay felt her insides turn to mush. She didn't know if it was longing or terror. "He still doesn't know who she is. I want to be the one to tell him."

"Where is his daughter?" Duncan asked.

"She's with him, but he doesn't know it."

"So you'll lead us to him and his daughter, and we'll kill them," Niall said.

"You might want to know his daughter's name before you decide whether or not to kill her."

"Why would it matter?" Duncan asked.

"I believe you know her as Anna."

⟐

Anna looked at the chapel where Cody and Shay would marry. She had sat here all night, her head and body numb. She didn't know what time it was. After reading Angus's notes, she'd rushed out without her phone. Angus must have made a mistake. Her father couldn't be a demon. An ancient demon. Walter was the one who'd told Angus. The Watcher was the only one who knew the truth.

Anna's mother had been assigned to destroy Voltar. Before she even told anyone about the assignment, she discovered that the demon had been spotted at a bar in New York City. She went in pretending to be a patron, hoping to get him alone so she could destroy or suspend him. A biker struck up a conversation with her. She didn't realize he was Voltar. No one had seen his human shell. But Voltar knew of the great female warrior.

He hated women and wanted to humiliate her before he killed her. He dragged her into the back alley and raped her, then left thinking she was dead. But she survived. And she found out she was pregnant. After the baby was born, she went after Voltar again, and this time she saw him shift from the biker into Voltar, and knew that she had given birth to a halfling. The knowledge nearly destroyed her. Walter was the only one she'd told, and he'd kept her secret, until he told Angus.

Anna remembered the looks of horror she'd sometimes glimpse on her mother's face. The looks of fear and the way she watched Anna constantly. Rape was devastating, but it shouldn't ruin a woman's entire life. Not a powerful warrior like her mother. Who was even strong enough to rape a woman as strong as her mother had been?

An ancient demon?

She wanted to believe it was a mistake, but it explained some things Anna had never understood about herself. She was stronger than other female warriors, and she had some unusual abilities. Angus had always said she did things that weren't possible for a human, even for a warrior. And there were other things. Strange dreams. Warriors sometimes had prophetic dreams, but hers were dark. And she'd always felt so compelled by beauty, though she despised it in herself. Demons were drawn to beauty. Probably because they were so ugly. And she was one of them. Half demon. She was a bloody halfling.

She smelled the sulfur before she heard his hiss. Anna grabbed her dagger and leapt to her feet, turning to face the demon. It wasn't just any demon. It was her father.

"Anna." The words whispered from Tavis's lips. "My Anna?"

"Yes. She's Voltar's daughter."

He was the one who'd raped Anna's mother. Anna, beautiful Anna was half demon. Not any demon, but the one who had killed Liam and his father. Tavis thought he might throw up. His insides crawled and hurt.

"That's the darkness I sensed in Anna," Bree said.

"They're working together?" Sorcha asked.

"No. But when he finds out she's his daughter it won't stop him from killing her."

"How do you know she's his daughter?" Tavis asked. There had to be a mistake. Demons were evil and vile, not kind and caring.

"I make it my business to know what the rest of the League is up to," Tristol said.

"So you'll lead us to Voltar and we'll kill him?" Faelan said.

"That's the gist of it," Tristol said. "We all win."

"Until you slaughter us," Tavis said. "Or lock us up in your dungeon and torture us."

"As I'm sure you're aware, my dungeon is missing," Tristol said, his eyes reddening slightly.

"I bet you have another one," Ronan said. "What's to say after Voltar is dead you don't kill the rest of us?"

"There could be a hundred vampires waiting outside to slaughter us," Niall said.

"On my honor. I came alone. And I came to help."

"Your honor?" Tavis said.

"My honor," Tristol said. "As you've seen, I can move faster than you." He looked at Shay and Bree. "Most of you, that is. The two of you are quite remarkable."

"Assuming we agree to this," Tavis said, "what do we do next?"

"We go hunting and bring Anna home."

"Be careful with her," Tavis said. "She's carrying my bairn."

Tristol frowned. "Your bairn?"

"Aye. And I'll kill anything that harms a hair on her head. Voltar's daughter or not."

CHAPTER TWENTY-EIGHT

A M I THE ONLY ONE FREAKING OUT?" BRODIE ASKED. "THIS IS
Tristol, the ancient demon, or ancient vampire, whatever the
bloody hell he is. And now we find out Anna is Voltar's daughter."

"We're all freaked out," Ronan said.

"Maybe he's lying," Brodie said. "Then again, it might explain
why she can do the things she does." He frowned. "Do you think
she can shift?"

"She's not a demon," Tavis growled. "I don't care what her
father is. She's a woman."

Brodie held up his hands. "Sorry. I didn't mean to insult her.
Anna's awesome. But you have to admit it's a shock. I've never
heard of any such thing. A warrior and a demon."

It was a shock. Tavis had never trusted beauty. He'd avoided
beautiful women for fear that they might be a demon in disguise.
Just when he'd let his guard down and let a beautiful woman steal
his heart, she turned out to be half demon. Daughter of an ancient
demon. The very one who'd killed Liam and his father. But she was
Anna. And did it really matter who her parents were? Wasn't it the
heart that made the warrior? One thing he knew: Voltar was going
to die today.

"Bring that big rifle you showed me earlier," Tavis said. He rubbed his battle marks, which were itching so badly they burned.

"The assault weapon?" Brodie asked. "Got it right here."

"Bring everything we have," Niall said. "We don't know how many demons he'll have with him."

"Do you believe Tristol is telling the truth about helping us?" Tomas asked.

"He could have killed us in the chapel if he'd wanted to," Shane said. "Ripped us all to shreds."

"And still could," Brodie said.

"What choice do we have?" Sorcha asked. "He knows where we are, says he knows each of us personally, and he isn't constrained by the whole holy ground thing. Hell, we have to let him help. Or help him. I'll gladly help get rid of Voltar."

"No one can do it except me," Tavis said. He had been tempted to sneak off and go on ahead to find Anna, but he would need help. Voltar wouldn't be alone. If Tristol wanted Voltar dead more than he wanted Anna or Tavis tortured, that was good enough for now. Later, they would settle the score. He would still make Tristol regret what he'd done to Anna. To him.

"The Council thinks you were both assigned," Sorcha said.

Another reason they needed to hurry. God knew what she might try. "I know what Michael said."

"Maybe that was before you defied him and went into the time vault," Sorcha said.

"He's not reassigned. Anna's mistaken. I'm not letting her kill him."

"She'd be killing her own father," Sorcha said. "You're still in love with her? Even knowing what she is?"

"And what if I am? Do you have anything to say about it?"

Sorcha raised a brow. "Not a thing. Other than best wishes. Invite me to the wedding and all that."

Tavis turned back to his weapons, tucking another collapsed sword onto his belt.

"Are you sure you want to wear a kilt?" Faelan asked. He lowered his voice. "We're not just fighting alongside men now. In our day it didn't matter if a kilt stayed down or not."

"I don't bloody care what my kilt shows. I'm more comfortable fighting in it, and I can't make a mistake. They've all seen it anyway."

"Whatever floats your boat."

"What's that mean?"

Faelan frowned. "It's something Ronan says. I need to check on Bree. I'm afraid she'll do something barmy."

"You don't have to go with me," Tavis said. "I know you worry about Bree and the bairn."

"I do have to go. It's my fault you're in this mess."

"I chose to come," Tavis said.

"You're my brother. I won't lose you. The others will keep an eye on Bree and Shay."

Cody walked over. He had pistols on each side of his belt, a dagger, and a worried frown. "You don't think Shay and Bree will try something stupid, do you?"

"Someone call and make sure Bree and Shay don't get any ideas about following us," Faelan said.

Brodie took out his cell phone. "I'll do it."

"They'd better stay put if they know what's good for them," Faelan said.

Brodie ended the call. "I, for one, would feel better if they tagged along. They're the ones who seem to be equipped to fight vampires."

"We're not fighting vampires," Duncan said. "We're fighting alongside a vampire, to rescue a warrior who's part demon. What's the world coming to?"

"Did you check on Bree and Shay?" Cody asked Brodie.

"Sean says they've got a bunch of babysitters. Coira, Ewan, Laura, Nina, and Matilda. I'm not sure Matilda's helping. I could hear her in the background asking if Tristol gives interviews."

"Where is Tristol?" Tavis asked.

"Outside where Anna was taken," Brodie said. "He's trying to pick up her trail, see if Voltar took her by car or on foot. I guess a vampire's sense of smell is even better than ours. And he says she smells mighty fine."

"Bastard. I'll kill him yet," Tavis said.

"Get in line," Ronan said. In addition to daggers and those fancy swords, he had a bow slung over his shoulder. "A bloody vampire on clan grounds."

"Someone needs to keep an eye on him," Tavis said. "I don't fully trust him."

"Sorcha, you take the first watch," Duncan said.

"You take it, cousin. I want to fight," she said.

"They're cousins?" Tavis whispered to Faelan.

"Not really, or so distant it doesn't count."

"You'll get to fight," Duncan said. "I'll take the second watch."

"Are you going to try to suspend him?" Ronan asked.

"I'm undecided," Tavis said. "But either way, we need to make sure Tristol doesn't see. The last thing we need him knowing is how talismans and time vaults work."

"He probably knows already," Brodie said.

They left several warriors to take the wedding guests back to the castle. Two other clans had been called for reinforcement, one from Maine and one from Pennsylvania. They were flying in and would arrive within two hours.

Tavis led the way to where Tristol waited. He put aside his hatred and focused on Anna, on what Tristol could do to help. "Did you pick up her scent?"

"Too easily. He wants you to follow."

"Where is she?" Tavis asked. "His penthouse?"

"No. It's not there anymore. It burned down. He's holding her in a cave. I'm sure he would have already killed her, but he's hoping to lure Tavis."

"Let's go then," Tavis said. "And everyone stay away from Voltar. You too, Tristol." He didn't want Tristol figuring out all their secrets.

"Be warned," Tristol said. "He's set traps. There are demons hiding in trees and underground."

"Can you point them out?" Ronan asked tightly. "I'll use my bow."

Tristol agreed, and they started off. Faelan and Cody stayed near Tavis. If he needed help with Voltar, warriors who had destroyed ancient demons were less likely to be fatally injured.

"We're close," Tristol said. "There, up in that tree. He's the lookout." He hadn't spotted them yet. A demon's eyesight wasn't usually as good as a warrior's.

"I got him. We don't want to alert Voltar with gunshots." Ronan slipped his bow off his shoulder and nocked an arrow. He lifted the bow, held the arrow against his nose, and then let go. The demon fell from the tree and hit the leaves below. "One down."

"The next one is hiding behind that outcropping of rock," Tristol said. "He's strong. I'm not sure an arrow will bring him down."

"Can't you just zoom up there and rip out his throat?" Niall asked.

"I'd rather not," Tristol said.

"But you could," Brodie said.

"I could."

Brodie stepped back from Tristol. The vampire demon smiled, and something about his expression unleashed a memory from Tavis's past. "Shite. You're the one who told Ian and me where to find Druan's sorcerer," Tavis said.

"I'd hoped you wouldn't remember," Tristol said. "But you'll realize now that I've helped your clan more than you knew."

"You're saying Tristol helped save our lives even then?" Faelan said.

Tavis was disturbed by the memory. He wanted to hate Tristol for what he'd done to him and Anna. "I'm sure it suited his purpose."

Ronan frowned at Tristol. "I remember something too."

"Doesn't look pleasant," Tristol said, studying Ronan silently. "It isn't."

"The cave is there." Tristol pointed to an area where the trees grew thicker. "He'll have lots of demons guarding her."

The warriors split up so they could approach the cave from different angles. Faelan and Tavis went with Ronan, Lachlan, and Shane. Tristol went ahead doing his mist thing.

"That's the damnedest thing I've ever seen," Lachlan said, watching the black mist vanish in the sky.

Instead of killing the demon waiting behind the rock, Ronan shot him with his bow, wounding him, so they could question him. "Where is Anna?" Tavis asked, holding a dagger to the demon's throat.

"She's with Voltar."

"Where?" Faelan asked. "What's he planning?"

"A sacrifice," the demon said.

"What kind of sacrifice?" Lachlan asked.

"He's going to sacrifice his own daughter to get me," Tavis said.

"Daughter?" The demon laughed. "Voltar doesn't have a daughter. He hates females."

"I hope you're right," Tavis said, before he drove the dagger Faelan had given him into the demon's chest.

They spaced themselves out and continued their advance. A minute later, Tavis heard a bird call. Faelan stopped. "That's

Ronan." They looked across and spotted him motioning up ahead. He held up four fingers. Tavis and Faelan worked toward Ronan. He pointed out four demons waiting on the ground near the trees. The warriors attacked as quietly as possible. Ronan took out one with his bow, and then the warriors crept up on the other three.

They were just outside the cave now. "Guess he's living in a cave until he gets another penthouse," Ronan said.

They surrounded the cave. "Where'd Tristol go?" Brodie asked. "He's the vampire. Don't they turn into bats?"

"On the count of three, we go in," Tavis said. Armed with modern weapons they hadn't had in his time, they entered the cave. It was dark and damp and ugly.

"It's not going to make *National Geographic*," Brodie said. "This is the ugliest cave I've seen."

They crept through the dark tunnels, looking for signs of where Voltar might be holding Anna. Tavis heard a deep growl, and Voltar appeared in his natural hideous form. He was flanked by eight demons, equally ugly. Each had thick gray skin and eyes that were yellow slits in a too-large head.

Tavis looked at Voltar's long arms, tipped with sharp claws, and disgust and doubt crept into his head. This was Anna's father? But he wouldn't let it take hold. Anna was pure. She was good and strong. She was beautiful. Nothing like this creature.

"Where is Anna?" he asked.

"She's close by."

"I'll trade you, me for her."

"No," Faelan said.

Tavis moved closer to Voltar. "Me for her," he repeated.

"I will take that deal. Bring Anna to me," Voltar said to his demons.

"Don't do this, Tavis," Faelan said. "We can save her. Ronan, Shane, and I will take out the others, you get Voltar."

"I have to get her to safety first."

"Bloody fool."

"You'd do the same if it were Bree," Tavis said.

Faelan grunted but didn't disagree.

"Tavis!"

"That was Anna," he said. But he couldn't see her. "Anna? Where are you?"

"Don't come here," she yelled from deeper within the cave. "It's a trap. Kill Voltar." Tavis stared at the demon, wondering whether to attack him or go after Anna. He was the only one who could destroy Voltar.

"We'll go for Anna," Shane said. "You take Voltar."

But Voltar turned and ran, surrounded by his demons. The warriors went after them, following as Voltar wove his way through the cave. Lights strapped onto the warriors' weapons lit the way. They reached a narrow section, and suddenly the walls came alive with screams as demons leapt at the warriors. In close confines, they had to resort to swords. Tavis preferred swords anyway.

Anna called out again, and Tavis ran toward her voice. Four demons held her, one on each arm, one on each leg. If she struggled, Tavis knew they would rip her apart. He was planning his attack when Tristol streaked in. The four demons dropped like flies.

There was an angry roar and Voltar rushed out of the shadows toward them. Tristol grabbed Anna, and they vanished as Voltar lunged at them.

"Anna? Where are you taking her?" Tavis yelled. With the other warriors out of the way, Tavis grabbed his talisman so he could destroy Voltar. Something slammed him from behind, and he landed hard. He looked up and saw three demons coming at him. These were powerful. They didn't need swords or fancy guns. Claws and sharp teeth would do the job.

He jumped up and drove his sword into the closest one, so hard it went to the hilt before the demon disappeared. He had just enough time to kill the second one. The third was two feet away, yellow teeth gnashing, when Tavis heard a roar and a sword tip broke through the demon's chest. It vanished, and Tavis saw Faelan, sword still extended.

"Just in time," Tavis said.

"Where's Anna?" Faelan asked.

"Tristol took her. Voltar ran after them."

"We'll hold them off. You go after Anna."

But a dozen more demons swarmed toward them, and these were even stronger than the others. Voltar had saved his best for last. Tavis was killing them as fast as he could swing his sword, as he made his way out of the cave. He was nearing exhaustion when Niall, Duncan, and the others arrived. Niall tossed one demon to the side, slamming it into the wall. When it staggered to its feet, Shane took off its head.

It was a hard fight, but finally they had killed all the demons in the cave and they took off after Voltar. Tavis ran out of the cave and almost hit Voltar. He yelled for the others to get back and cover their eyes. He reached for his talisman, but Voltar was too close. Tavis drove his sword into Voltar's thigh, pulled the weapon free, and rolled clear. He attacked again, striking at Voltar's chest, but hit his shoulder instead. He needed a deadly blow to kill a demon as powerful as Voltar. If he could get some space, he could use the talisman.

He sank his sword into Voltar's chest. It missed his heart, but the demon cried out and fell.

"Here," Faelan yelled and threw something at Tavis. Shackles. He snapped one on Voltar's wrist, but before he could get the other one on, Voltar rose up with a roar. He came after Tavis with his claws and teeth extended, his face distorted in anger. But he was moving slower. The one shackle had slowed him down. Tavis had to get the other one on or get the monster clear of the other warriors so he could use the talisman.

He was considering his options when a rock flew past his head, striking Voltar right between the eyes, just like David and Goliath. Voltar staggered, and Tavis quickly attached the shackle to the other wrist. When he glanced back, the other warriors were clapping Niall on the back.

"You got him," Faelan said.

"The other demons?" Tavis asked, stepping away from Voltar for a moment.

"All dead but one. He got away."

"We've got to find Anna."

"Where would Tristol take her?" Duncan asked. "Back to the chapel?"

"The rest of you go find her and Tristol. I still don't trust him. I'll take care of Voltar."

"I'll stay with you," Faelan said.

Brodie's eyes widened. "You'd better hurry. Your demon's getting away."

Tavis turned. Voltar was trying to run, more of a lumbering gait, a testament to the demon's power that he could still move. "Damn." They chased Voltar and caught him a hundred yards away. "You go on," Tavis said to the others. "We've got him now." And to be sure, he summoned another pair of shackles and put them on the demon. They pulled Voltar to his feet.

He looked at them with fury in his eyes, but under the paralyzing effect of the shackles, all he could do was put one foot in front of the other. He couldn't even speak.

"You killed our father," Faelan said. "And our brother when he was just a child."

"And you raped Anna's mother." He couldn't think too long on the fact that if Voltar hadn't, Anna wouldn't be here. "You'll pay," Tavis said.

"Not today." A demon stalked toward them, holding a box in his hand. He raised it, and light flashed out fast as a bullet.

Tavis felt like he'd been struck by lightning. He fell to the ground, unable to move anything but his eyes. Faelan fell beside him on the ground, suffering the same fate. He threw Tavis a frantic look as the demon went over to Voltar. He started to work at the shackles. Tavis didn't know if he could remove them or not, but either way, unless there was a miracle, he and Faelan were dead.

"Voltar!" Anna's voice boomed through the trees.

Tavis tried to signal her with his eyes. She wouldn't know that the other demon had the stun gun. It didn't matter. Anna didn't let him get close enough. She pulled out a gun with a huge barrel, raised it, and shot the demon between the eyes. He vanished into nothing, leaving only Voltar there.

Anna hurried over to Tavis and Faelan. "Are you OK?"

He couldn't answer, but enough feeling was coming back to his body that he was able to roll over and move his head.

"I love you." She dropped down beside him and kissed his lips.

Just past Anna's shoulder, Tavis saw Voltar rolling over, and he realized what he was doing. Trying to reach the stun gun. He was only a few inches away now. Tavis tried to motion with his eyes and head. He didn't know if Voltar could do any good with the thing since his hands were shackled behind his back, but he didn't want to find out.

Tavis tried more furiously. Faelan, who had also seen what Voltar was up to, was also motioning. Voltar had the stun gun in his hands. He rolled to the side so that it was pointing at Anna. She turned and looked at Voltar just as a streak of light burst forth. Tavis had some movement in his legs, so he kicked Anna, hoping to knock her clear. A black mist got there first and moved Anna aside.

"That's not nice, Voltar. Trying to kill your own daughter."

Voltar looked confused.

"You don't remember her mother," Tristol said. "She was a warrior. You raped her in the back of a little bar."

Voltar's eyes widened, and he stared at Anna.

"Your own daughter, half human, and a warrior at that. So much for your pure race." Tavis motioned for Tristol to get Anna to safety. For the second time, he grabbed her and vanished.

Voltar still had the stun gun in his hand. He didn't speak. It was clearly taking all his effort to hold the stun gun in the awkward position, but his eyes were filled with hatred. He looked at Tavis, and then turned the stun gun toward Faelan. Tavis struggled to get up. He didn't know if another hit would kill Faelan or just knock him out.

Again, he didn't get a chance to find out. A noise that sounded like a herd of elephants came trampling through the woods. Matilda burst onto the trail holding the big cat. "Attack," she said, and flung it at Voltar.

The cat leapt at Voltar and midway through the air shifted into a man wearing a long white robe as white as his hair. He landed on his feet as gracefully as a deer and knocked the stun gun from Voltar's hand.

"Oh my God!" Matilda was gaping at the man.

Tavis and Faelan were both struggling to stand.

"Tavis!" Anna rushed out of the woods. "Oh God. I thought he'd killed you. Who's he?" she asked, looking at the man.

"The cat," Matilda said.

"Old Elmer," Cody said, shaking his head. "Where's Tristol?"

"He disappeared," Anna said.

The other warriors arrived, and in the confusion, Old Elmer disappeared. Tavis and Faelan couldn't stand without help, but with Anna supporting them, Tavis summoned a time vault, and he and Anna and Faelan put Voltar inside. His eyes flashed with hatred.

"I could have destroyed you," Tavis said, "but that would have been too easy. You're going to wake again to face Judgment, and before you're destroyed for good, you'll remember that your daughter is a powerful warrior. She's carrying a child who will be a powerful warrior."

Faelan leaned over the time vault. "This is for Liam and my father, a parting gift." He stuck Voltar's stun gun between the demon's eyes and pressed the button. Voltar's eyes bulged.

"Go to hell, Voltar." Tavis slammed the lid.

CHAPTER TWENTY-NINE

I CAN'T BELIEVE HE SLEPT IN MY BED," MATILDA SAID. "I THOUGHT he was a cat. A powerful cat, but here he's a man. I feel traumatized. I can't imagine what other secrets you all have."

"I told you, Matilda, none of us knew he was a man," Nina said.

"Old Elmer," Shay said. "My God, I've known him since I was a kid." Old Elmer had lived in the woods behind her house for as long as she could remember, but he kept to himself. Every now and then he'd show up just when she was in danger and rescue her, or sneak and help Nina with projects like some kind of elf. But he didn't look like an elf, not the little pixie kind. Shay had always thought he was more like Merlin or Gandalf with his long white beard. "How is this even possible?"

"Demons can shift," Bree said.

"Old Elmer's not a demon," Shay said.

"Obviously, but if demons can shift, why not some . . . thing else," Bree said.

"But what?" Shay asked. "What is he?"

"Maybe he's a sorcerer," Matilda asked. "He looks like a sorcerer."

"No. Not Old Elmer," Nina said. "We've known him forever."

"We didn't know he could turn into a cat," Matilda said.

"We'll ask him what he is when we see him again," Nina said.

"Has anyone seen him since he attacked Voltar?" Bree asked.

"No," Shay said. "Matilda, why were you there?"

"The cat and I were just sitting up here in the room thinking about vampires, and I had this thought out of the blue. *Go into the woods.* I thought it might have been God talking to me, but with all the craziness going on, I wasn't about to go alone. So I grabbed the cat. When I saw that Voltar creature, I thought he was a vampire, so I sicced the cat on him. I guess it protects against demons too."

"Old Elmer always did have a way of showing up when someone was in trouble," Shay said.

"Like a guardian angel. Or a guardian cat." Matilda patted her hair, which was still wild after her mad dash through the woods. "I wonder if he dates."

"You look every year of your age," Faelan said, hobbling toward the infirmary.

"You don't look any better. I don't know what was in that thing, but I never want to see one again." Tavis hobbled beside him. They could walk, but not well.

"It must have been sorcery."

"I'm going to check on Anna," Tavis said.

"I'm going to find a bed."

Coira was just coming out. "How is she?" Tavis asked.

"Physically, OK," Coira said. "Mentally, not so well."

"The bairn?"

"It's too early for us to know, but assuming Bree's right, and she usually is, there's no sign of problems."

"Good. Do you think she needs more bed rest?"

"I wouldn't want to be the one to suggest it." Coira rolled her eyes. "Anna wants out of there. Come on, sit down. I need to take a look at you. This bandage needs to be changed."

"I have to see her."

Coira patted his arm. "She doesn't want company right now."

She didn't want to see him. "I don't care. I'm not waiting any longer." He went into the infirmary where Anna was resting.

She looked up when he came in.

"Are you all right?" he asked.

She nodded. "You?"

"Aye. Why did you run off from the wedding?"

"I never went. I was reading Angus's notebook and found out who my father was. That was what Angus was trying to call me about. Not that he'd found your time vault. I went for a walk to clear my head. Voltar found me. I'm sorry my father destroyed your family." Her voice was bitter.

"I don't know if you're Voltar's daughter or not, but I do know that I love you. And that's my child. If I have to take a piece of Voltar to get the two of you, I will."

Anna's mouth trembled. "But I'm part demon." Her mouth twisted with disgust. "The demon that killed your brothers and your father." She touched her stomach. "This is part demon."

Tavis leaned over the bed and put his hands over Anna's. "This is part you and part me. Part of my father is in there too. Part of my mother. Part of your mother. I won't lose you. I won't lose my bairn. Voltar's gone. I'll be damned if I let him win after he's dead."

Anna stared at Tavis for the longest time. "I need to think. Then we'll talk."

Tavis nodded. "But don't take too long."

When he went back to see her, the bed was empty. He found Coira. "She left about half an hour ago. I thought she was going to see you."

Tavis felt a rush of panic. "Did you see where she went?"

"No. I was on the phone with Tomas."

Tavis ran to her room and found her packing. "What are you doing?"

"Packing."

"Get your head out of your arse."

Her eyes widened. "What?"

"Stop feeling sorry for yourself. Look at Bree and Shay. Their whole lives were a lie. No one knows what Bree is, or Shay. They move like they're part vampire. Tristol, he's as evil as hell, but he just helped save you. He's helped us several times. There's a lot of gray in the world, not just black and white. We all have issues. We're all scarred. Get over it. You're a good warrior, you're a beautiful woman, and I love you."

"Even if I'm the daughter of a demon?"

"Even then."

"Even if that demon destroyed your family?"

"Even then. Who or what your father was doesn't matter. It's your heart that makes you human. Makes you a warrior."

"You're a bloody good man, Tavis Connor. You'll make someone a good husband."

"I'll make you a good husband."

"I don't want a husband."

"Tell Michael that."

"What?"

"He sent me to protect you."

"He did?"

"He showed me your face even before I went into the time vault."

"Why didn't you tell me?"

"I wasn't sure what to make of it myself. But he knew this was supposed to happen."

She frowned. "I think you were right about Voltar being your demon. I was supposed to help you. That's what Michael wanted me to do. He told me that you needed me."

"He was right about that. I think we were supposed to do it together. Bree said my battle marks say, *His brother's keeper will find his heart, and together they will put the past to rest.* And I did find my heart. You. And together we'll put the past to rest. I'm supposed to be here. Like Faelan is supposed to be here. You're my mate, and I want to marry you. I don't care who or what your parents are."

Anna smiled. "If you're willing to marry a demon's daughter, who am I to refuse?" She pulled up the back of her shirt.

"What are you doing?"

"Look at my battle marks."

"They're different."

"I know. Coira noticed it when she was checking me over. I have a mate mark."

"You seem excited. Why were you packing?"

"I was going to invite you to go away with me for a while. Someplace quiet. Private."

Tavis thought he might burst with happiness. He picked Anna up and swung her around. Life was good. He was in love, and he was having a bairn. "I want to go home. Will you go to Scotland with me?"

"I will."

"You did tell Ronan you weren't going to Montana?"

Anna nodded. "He said he'd never planned to actually take me. He knew we'd work it out."

"He's wiser than I thought."

They went to Scotland by jet, which was much better than by ocean. He was still amazed at the advances of civilization. It was wonderful, if a bit frightening. There was something alarming about having computers thinking like human brains.

He and Anna landed at the airport and traveled to Beauly. The land had changed, some for the better, but he missed the way it was. It couldn't go back. He couldn't go back. And he didn't want to. He belonged here with Anna.

Faelan was right. It was meant to be. There had been some suffering. He would always wonder if he could have stopped Voltar sooner and spared the world his atrocities. Just like Faelan and his guilt over the Civil War. Sean had talked to Tavis for a long time. So had Ronan, both telling him that he couldn't bear the blame for those things. That there were other factors involved, not just Tavis's part. Tavis had confided to both men about his and Faelan's dreams of battles they couldn't have fought. Sean was convinced that Michael's assignment for both Tavis and Faelan had been intended for this time, and not the past, and that perhaps they hadn't been sleeping the entire time. It didn't make sense, but Tavis hoped Sean was right. That lessened some of his guilt. They'd also talked to Anna, convincing her that it didn't matter who her father was. It still troubled her, and Tavis knew it would.

"Are you sad?" Anna asked.

"No. I'm glad. Very, very glad," he said, punctuating each "very" with a kiss.

"If you don't stop that, we'll have to pull over."

"All right then."

Anna smiled and pulled the car onto a small road that was

surrounded by fields and sheep. She smiled and ran a hand up his leg. "I'm glad you're wearing a kilt."

"Are you now?" he asked as her hand slipped underneath to his thigh.

"Aye, I am. So I can do this," she said with a wicked grin and moved her hand higher.

"Bollocks."

"I think that's about right."

"And I think if you keep doing that, we're gonna be late for the wedding." Far from fearing intimacy, Anna was thriving on it. She was almost wearing him out.

"It's a good thing I'm wearing a skirt." There was little talking for the next few minutes, just grunts and gasps. "You're killing me," he said when they'd finished.

"Should I stop?"

"No. That would kill me too. I can't live without you."

"You're just saying that because I saved your life in the dungeon."

"Ha. I would have saved you first if that damned guard hadn't tortured me. I would have wrapped those cell bars around his cursed neck."

"I know you would have, but Tristol saved you the trouble." Anna climbed back over to her side and grabbed a napkin to clean up and adjusted her skirt.

"I do owe you my life," Tavis said.

"It'll take a long time to pay me back. I'm thinking seventy or eighty years."

"I was thinking eternity," Tavis said. "And I believe you owe me your life too."

"I can live with that," Anna said, squeezing his thigh. "Actually, I think we both owe the hybrid," she said softly. "He saved us."

"What do you think happened to him?"

He woke in a bed. Not his bed. His bed was in a dungeon, in the darkened back room of a dungeon. This bed was in the sunlight. It was almost blinding. There was a comfortable mattress underneath him and a soft comforter covering him. He was naked. But clean. He could smell the soap on his skin. He didn't recall bathing. The last thing he remembered was a whirring sound. He could smell something else nice. Like flowers.

"You're awake."

He turned toward the window and saw a woman sitting there. It must be her smell that he'd caught. "Who are you?"

"I am Josephine."

"Do I know you?"

"No. But I know you."

"From Tristol's fortress?"

"Yes. I've watched you for some time."

"Do you work there?"

"Perhaps."

"Where am I?"

"Austria, for the moment. But we can go someplace else if you'd like. France, Italy. Your choice." Her voice was soft, almost magical.

"I don't have any money." He didn't have anything, not even his sanity.

"You don't need either. Just say the word."

"Scotland. I want to go to Scotland."

Tristol entered the gates of hell with apprehension. He was closer to his goal now than ever before. Even with his missing fortress and lost vampires, he would restart his breeding plan, and in the meantime, strengthen his surviving vampires by letting them feed on warrior blood. He still had Anna's child to consider, but that was only one child with two warrior parents. It would prove interesting to see if he could train that child to work for him. He felt a twinge of guilt at the thought of taking their child. Tristol recalled how his own mother had loved him, how his father had died to save him. He was letting the warriors soften him. He'd watched them so closely he felt he knew them. Respected them. They had more honor and loyalty than his kind.

He had worked too long to let sentimentality get in his way. For his race of vampires to increase in strength and size, it was crucial that he work quickly.

The Dark One was waiting. He wasn't hideous like his demonic creations. He was beautiful, as he had been created in the beginning. Lucifer. Tristol had long since suspected that his own beauty played a role in the Dark One's preference for him above other demons. He looked so much like the Dark One he could have been his son. Tristol hoped to use that to his advantage when the time came. Vampires were beautiful, or at least appealing, not ugly like demons. If he played his hand carefully, he intended to prove to the Dark One that he would be better off with vampires serving him instead of demons. And if he fell for it, then Tristol would be one step closer to his ultimate goal. Mutiny.

Tristol entered the throne room. It wasn't hot here. It was elaborate, in a dark way. Everything was made of metal and stone, with lots of obsidian and mirrors.

"Master." Tristol bowed before the Dark One.

The Dark One leaned forward, his long hair reaching to his lap. "We lost Voltar."

"I heard," Tristol said. "That's why I came."

He put a hand on Tristol's shoulder. "I'm glad you're here. Who was responsible?"

"One of the warriors. I don't know which."

"I grow weary of them. And I have lost so many of my oldest demons. Druan, Malek, and now Voltar. You are the only one who remains. I am considering sending one of the arch demons."

Tristol hid his alarm. That would destroy his plans. "They don't operate in this realm."

"It might be time to change that."

"No. Let me see what I can do."

The Dark One reached for Tristol's hand. "You are like a son to me. You bring me comfort. I don't know what I would do if I lost you."

CHAPTER THIRTY

W HEN THEY ARRIVED IN SCOTLAND, TAVIS STOOD LOOKING
at his homeplace for some time. Anna didn't rush him. She
stayed at his side, her hand in his. It was wonderful being back,
but his heart hurt knowing Ian wasn't here to annoy them with his
puzzles and pranks, and Alana wasn't here with her quick smiles.
Nor Ma and Da. He turned and saw Faelan standing nearby, and
he was thankful. He'd gotten one brother back, and he had a child.
One on the way. One buried in the ground.

Tavis went alone to his son's grave. He was buried near Ian
rather than his own wife and children, but Tavis was glad. Ian had
looked out for him in the beginning of his life. He hoped Ian would
look out for him until Tavis joined them. He wished he could have
known him. Known what kind of child he was. Taught him the
things fathers should teach their sons, how to swing a sword and
ride a horse. Teach him about respect and honor responsibility.
Ian had done that for the first part of his life. What happened to
him afterward? Did Bessie remarry? Did a stranger raise his son?
There was still so much he needed to learn.

A hand touched his shoulder. Faelan dropped down beside
him. "I asked Sean to find out as much about his life as he could.

He was a good warrior. He had two sons and a daughter. Do you realize how many warriors today are here because of you? It's a funny thing."

Tavis smiled. "Even Sean started calling me grandfather. Anna put a stop to it. She said she's not going to have someone saying she's marrying a grandfather."

"I'm glad you found Anna. You were meant to be here."

Tavis looked at the grave. "I hope you're right. I believe you are. I see that Alana named a son after you. Sweet Alana."

"I know. The worst part is, it seems like just days ago that I saw her," Faelan said.

Tavis nodded. "Instead of laughing and running, she's buried in a grave. I swear I expected Ian to come running out to meet me when I got here. God, I miss them."

"Aye. But I have you, and I'm bloody glad. Here, this belongs to you." Faelan handed Tavis the white stone. "I put it on your grave. I thought I'd never see you again in this lifetime. Perhaps our children will carry on the tradition."

"Aye, that would be grand."

"If we don't get moving, we're going to miss Cody and Shay's second attempt at a wedding."

"I hope this one proves uneventful."

Cody and Shay had decided to get married in the same chapel where not very long ago Bree and Faelan had wed. Coira and the women had worked hard to pull it all together, with Cody alongside them. He was terrified that the Council was going to come for Shay. He wouldn't let them take her, but he'd said he would prefer not to murder the Council members unless it was necessary. Anna hoped that she and Tavis would be as happy as the other couples.

"It's perfect," Shay said. "I didn't tell Cody, but I really wanted to be married in Scotland."

"You're getting your wish," Anna said.

"Ready?" Ewan asked Shay. "Let's try this again."

The music started, and Faelan and Bree went first. Marcas offered his arm to Sorcha. She was sullen. Something was troubling her. Probably the rumors about the traitor. The clan was still worried about it. Anna was planning to pick up where Angus left off and find out what really happened and who was responsible.

"Are you going to daydream all day or let me escort you down the aisle?" Lachlan asked, offering Anna his arm.

"How could I resist such an offer?" She slipped hers through and glanced at Tavis, who looked out of sorts. She gave him a conciliatory smile, and he relaxed.

"I hope there are no interruptions this time," Lachlan whispered.

"You and me too." Shay had joined Cody at the front of the chapel, and there was a moment where Anna wished it were her and Tavis. They would, in time. She'd done a full 360 to even consider marriage. Actually, she'd proposed to him.

"What's that grin about?" Lachlan asked.

"It's a secret."

"If he gets tired of you," he said with a grin, "let me know."

"He'll knock you out if you even mention it."

"Why do you think I'm telling you?" he whispered in her ear as Tavis scowled.

The wedding went off without a hitch. Shay and Cody were dazzling, and Anna was getting more excited—and nervous— thinking about her own upcoming wedding. And the baby's birth. It would be several days before her pregnancy could be confirmed by a doctor, but Anna had as much faith in Bree's feelings as she did modern medicine.

"Your turn next," Ronan said, slipping beside her at the reception. Tables had been set up outside and were loaded with food and drinks. Anna was on a food run while Tavis snagged drinks.

"Or yours. You could marry one of your many groupies," Anna said.

"You know that's a crock," Ronan said.

She smiled. She was one of the few who knew the truth about Ronan. Declan walked up next to Ronan. They could easily be mistaken for one another when they wore kilts.

Ronan smacked Declan on the chest. "Maybe Declan here's hiding a mate. How about it, brother?"

"Marriage isn't for me," Declan said.

"That's what Anna said. Now she's drooling over Tavis and having his baby."

Anna poked Ronan in the ribs. "Don't rub it in, or I'll make you pay. What's that noise?"

"Sounds like a helicopter," Declan said. Everyone looked around for the source. It seemed to be coming from the sky.

"Maybe there's a late wedding guest," Anna said.

"It's not a helicopter," Ronan said, drawing his sword. "I've heard that sound before."

Anna didn't question his actions, but drew her dagger. The air wavered, and a shadow appeared. The warriors backed up, staring in shock as the shadow formed and a fortress appeared in the middle of one of the larger fields. "It's Tristol's fortress," Anna whispered. She and the other warriors formed a line.

Tavis ran up to her. "Get back, Anna. Please."

"We talked about this. I'm a warrior."

"And you're going to be a mother."

"I can be both, for now."

Tavis growled, but he stood next to her, or rather, in front of her.

The fortress was huge, dwarfing the Connor castle, which sat nearby. The door to the fortress opened, and a man stepped out. He was smiling, until he saw the wedding party. His smile faded, and he looked stunned. He turned back to the fortress.

"No," Ronan whispered, then louder, "Stop!" He and Declan started running after the man.

"Bloody hell," Tavis said. "It's the hybrid."

Anna supposed this released her from her vow of secrecy. "His name is Cam."

ACKNOWLEDGMENTS

I HAVE SO MANY PEOPLE TO THANK FOR HELPING ME CREATE THIS story. My family, of course; my agent, Christine Witthohn; and my developmental editor, Clarence Haynes. And my editor, Kelli Martin, Goddess Jessica, and the Montlake team. You're all wonderful. Thanks for everything you do. And to my critique partner, Dana Rodgers, and my beta readers, Lori McDermit, Tamie Holman, Becca Sellers, and Fawn Johns. Thanks, ladies. You rock!

ABOUT THE AUTHOR

NEW YORK TIMES AND USA Today bestselling author Anita Clenney grew up an avid reader, devouring Nancy Drew and Hardy Boys books before moving on to mysteries and romance. After working as a secretary, a Realtor, teacher's assistant, booking agent for Aztec Fire Dancers, and a brief stint in a pickle factory (picture Lucy and Ethel—lasted half a day), she realized she'd missed the fork in the road that led to her destiny. Now she spends her days writing mysteries and paranormal romantic suspense about powerful relics, secret warriors, ancient evil, and destined love. Anita lives in suburban Virginia, outside Washington, DC, with her husband and two kids. You can learn more about her writing at www.anitaclenney.com.